DIVISIBLE MAN™

THE SIXTH PAWN

by

Howard Seaborne

ALSO BY HOWARD SEABORNE

DIVISIBLE MAN
A Novel – September 2017
DIVISIBLE MAN: THE SIXTH PAWN
A Novel – June 2018
DIVISIBLE MAN: THE SECOND GHOST
A Novel – September 2018
ANGEL FLIGHT
A Story – September 2018
DIVISIBLE MAN: THE SEVENTH STAR
A Novel – June 2019
ENGINE OUT
A Story – September 2019
WHEN IT MATTERS
A Story – October 2019
A SNOWBALL'S CHANCE
A Story – November 2019
DIVISIBLE MAN: TEN MAN CREW
A Novel – November 2019
DIVISIBLE MAN: THE THIRD LIE
A Novel – May 2020
DIVISIBLE MAN: THREE NINES FINE
A Novel – November 2020
DIVISIBLE MAN: EIGHT BALL
A Novel – September 2021
SHORT FLIGHTS
A Story Collection – June 2022
DIVISIBLE MAN: NINE LIVES LOST
A Novel – Nine 2022

PRAISE FOR HOWARD SEABORNE

"This book is a strong start to a series...Well-written and engaging, with memorable characters and an intriguing hero."

—*Kirkus Reviews*

DIVISIBLE MAN [DM1]

"Seaborne's crisp prose, playful dialogue, and mastery of technical details of flight distinguish the story...this is a striking and original start to a series, buoyed by fresh and vivid depictions of extra-human powers and a clutch of memorably drawn characters..."

—*BookLife*

DIVISIBLE MAN [DM1]

"Even more than flight, (Will's relationship with Andy)—and that crack prose—powers this thriller to a satisfying climax that sets up more to come."

—*BookLife*

DIVISIBLE MAN [DM1]

"Seaborne, a former flight instructor and charter pilot, once again gives readers a crisply written thriller. Self-powered flight is a potent fantasy, and Seaborne explores its joys and difficulties engagingly. Will's narrative voice is amusing, intelligent and humane; he draws readers in with his wit, appreciation for his wife, and his flight-drunk joy...Even more entertaining than its predecessor—a great read."

—*Kirkus Reviews*

DIVISIBLE MAN: THE SIXTH PAWN [DM2]

"Seaborne, a former flight instructor and pilot, delivers a solid, well-written tale that taps into the near-universal dream of personal flight. Will's narrative voice is engaging and crisp, clearly explaining technical matters while never losing sight of humane, emotional concerns. The environments he describes…feel absolutely real. Another intelligent and exciting superpowered thriller.”

—*Kirkus Reviews*

DIVISIBLE MAN: THE SECOND GHOST [DM3]

“As in this series’ three previous books, Seaborne…proves he’s a natural born storyteller, serving up an exciting, well-written thriller. He makes even minor moments in the story memorable with his sharp, evocative prose…Will’s smart, humane and humorous narrative voice is appealing, as is his sincere appreciation for Andy—not just for her considerable beauty, but also for her dedication and intelligence…Seaborne does a fine job making side characters and locales believable. It’s deeply gratifying to see Will deliver righteous justice to some very bad people. An intensely satisfying thriller—another winner from Seaborne.”

—*Kirkus Reviews*

DIVISIBLE MAN: THE SECOND GHOST [DM4]

“Seaborne…continues his winning streak in this series, offering another page-turner. By having Will’s knowledge of and control over his powers continue to expand while the questions over how he should best deploy his abilities grow, Seaborne keeps the concept fresh and readers guessing…Will’s enemies are becoming aware of him and perhaps developing techniques to detect him, which makes the question of how he can protect himself while doing the most good a thorny one. The conspiracy is highly dramatic yet not implausible given today’s political events, and the action sequences are excitingly cinematic…Another compelling and hugely fun adventure that delivers a thrill ride.”

—*Kirkus Reviews*

DIVISIBLE MAN: TEN MAN CREW [DM5]

“Seaborne shows himself to be a reliably splendid storyteller in this latest outing. The plot is intricate and could have been confusing in lesser hands, but the author manages it well, keeping readers oriented amid unexpected developments…His crisp writing about complex scenes and concepts is another strong suit…The fantasy of self-powered flight remains absolutely compelling…As a former charter pilot, Seaborne conveys Will’s delight not only in ‘the other thing,’ but also in airplanes and the world of flight—an engaging subculture that he ably brings to life for the reader. Will is heroic and daring, as one would expect, but he's also funny, compassionate, and affectionate... A gripping, timely, and twisty thriller."

—Kirkus Reviews
DIVISIBLE MAN: THE THIRD LIE [DM6]

"Seaborne is never less than a spellbinding storyteller, keeping his complicated but clearly explicated plot moving smoothly from one nail-biting scenario to another. As the tale goes along, seemingly disparate plot lines begin to satisfyingly connect in ways that will keep readers guessing until the explosive (in more ways than one) action-movie denouement. The author's grasp of global politics gives depth to the book's thriller elements, which are nicely balanced by thoughtful characterizations. Even minor characters come across in three dimensions, and Will himself is an endearing narrator. He's lovestruck by his gorgeous, intelligent, and strong-willed wife; has his heart and social conscience in the right place; and is boyishly thrilled by the other thing. A solid series entry that is, as usual, exciting, intricately plotted, and thoroughly entertaining."

—Kirkus Reviews
DIVISIBLE MAN: THREE NINES FINE [DM7]

Any reader of this series knows that they're in good hands with Seaborne, who's a natural storyteller. His descriptions and dialogue are crisp, and his characters deftly sketched...The book keeps readers tied into its complex and exciting thriller plot with lucid and graceful exposition, laying out clues with cleverness and subtlety...Also, although Will's abilities are powerful, they have reasonable limitations, and the protagonist is always a relatable character with plenty of humanity and humor...Another riveting, taut, and timely adventure with engaging characters and a great premise."

— Kirkus Reviews
DIVISIBLE MAN: EIGHT BALL [DM8]

THE SERIES

While each DIVISIBLE MAN ™ novel tells its own tale, many elements carry forward and the novels are best enjoyed in sequence. The short story "Angel Flight" is a bridge between the third and fourth novels and is included with the third novel, DIVISIBLE MAN - THE SECOND GHOST.

DIVISIBLE MAN ™ is available in print, digital and audio.

For a Cast of Characters, visit **HowardSeaborne.com**

For advance notice of new releases and exclusive material available only to Email Members, join the DIVISIBLE MAN ™ Email List at

HowardSeaborne.com.

Sign up today and get a FREE DOWNLOAD.

ACKNOWLEDGMENTS

This second Divisible Man novel follows in close formation with the first. While the flight crew is unchanged, it is no less important to acknowledge their roles. I've said it before; I'll say it again: Nothing leaves the ground without a host of good people contributing to the effort.

I'd like to thank my dispatcher, Stephen Parolini, for his editing expertise and the kind and often complimentary way he has of telling me something needs to be left on the ramp. Thank you to my first instructor, the late Victor Zilbert, for insisting that this machine belongs in the sky. Thanks to his business partner Arnie Freeman for a lifetime of ego refueling and friendship. Thanks to Denise Kohnke for navigation to all the best flight planning resources.

Those brave souls, the test pilots who took this thing into the air on faith, my beta readers and life-long co-pilots, Rich "Maddog" Sorensen and Robin "Polly Pureheart" Schlei, deserve special thanks for the initial airworthiness inspection.

Much gratitude goes to the ground crew at Trans World Data—to David, Carol, Claire, April and Rebecca for keeping the machine running—and to Kristie and Steve for taking over the reconnaissance so I can concentrate on flying.

I can't say enough about my sharp-eyed radar operators, Roberta and Steve Schlei, whose thorough copyediting saw through the clouds and found every needless hyphen.

And thank you, Robin, for always knowing I need to fly.

For Rich.
This trip just keeps getting better and better.

PART I

1

"I am so getting laid tonight." Pidge adjusted herself in the little black dress she had miraculously squeezed around her petite body. I doubted the structural integrity of the thing. Parts of her threatened to pop out. "Ten groomsmen, eight ushers. Fucking fish in a barrel."

"Half of them are married, Pidge," Andy warned.

"Good. Maybe they'll know what they're doing. I'm going to the bar!" She charged off toward one of eight bars on the perimeter of the wedding tent, a determined twenty-four-year-old blonde pixie in high heels.

"God help them, they don't stand a chance," I said. I looked at my wife. "What about me? Do I stand a chance?"

"Of what?" Andy fluttered her lashes at me. I made a show of examining her dress, a nearly-black, purple delight that shimmered on her curves and set off the warmth in her flowing auburn hair. Her structural integrity cried out for closer inspection.

"Of hooking up with a very hot woman tonight," I said.

"Depends." She moved closer and fidgeted with my tie. She pressed her hips against mine. "If I see one, I'll ask if she's interested."

"Oh, please, would you two get on with hating each other like a decent married couple!" Earl Jackson growled. He snagged a water glass from the round table beside us. The table seated eight. Folded place cards beside expensive-looking China displayed our names in gold script. A lavish centerpiece of sculpted white flowers dominated the table. "How long have you two been married, anyway? A week?"

Earl signs my paycheck as well as Pidge's. That and prize fighter stature topped with a permanent scowl makes him hard to ignore but I tried.

I put my hands on Andy's waist and pulled her tighter. "Has it been a week? Already?"

"Lipstick," she warned. I kissed her anyway. She kissed back. When she pulled away, she looked at Earl with green and gold-flecked eyes and said, "Three years, two months, and one day. But you're right. Hardly seems like a week." She smiled. Andy's smile and magazine model looks should carry a warning. More than a few men in the tent around us stole long glances at my wife.

"Get a room," Earl muttered. He twisted and tugged at his suit, which looked like it came off a rack in 1956. Andy threw him a loving look. A fissure appeared in his scowl. I feared if he smiled back his face might crack.

"I'm going to fix my lipstick." She gave me another sweet kiss. "Again."

"I'll stay here and count billionaires." I shamelessly watched her maneuver between the tables. Her combination of high heels, short dress, and inexplicable locomotion made me forget there were five hundred other people milling around under the gigantic tent.

Earl watched her, too. Earl Jackson loves my wife like a daughter, but also appreciates her architecture. When she slipped out of sight, he put one of his calloused claws on my shoulder. "You don't deserve her."

"Nobody does. I just try to keep up."

"So, whaddya figure? Half a million? Million?"

"What?"

He waved an arm in a semicircle. "All this. Senator Mealy-Mouth marrying off his little girl."

"I could not begin to guess. But I have to ask—how's he taking it that Sandy's marrying one of the governor's A-Team boys?"

"She would have been better off bringing home a crack addict!" Earl laughed. "Bob hates our pinhead governor. Speak of the devil."

Earl pointed at a cluster of guests. A short man held court at the center. His prominent bald spot reflected dots from the thousands of tiny white lights strung above our heads.

"If you want to count billionaires, go over by pinhead and swing a dead cat. There's half a dozen. Lester Brodling. Ira Waters. Bargo Litton, the energy guy. Couple of hedge fund guys. Fifty percent of the cash flowing into the Republican coffers in our happy 'swing state' is standing right over there eating bacon-wrapped water chestnuts."

"Your pal runs in quite the circle."

Earl snorted. "Bob? Bob may be a brainwashed elephant worshiper, but he doesn't give those kingmakers the time of day. In fact, he goes out of his way to be a pain in their collective asses. Oh, no. They're all here for the kid."

Earl might call State Senator Bob Stone names, but they had been friends since the first grade. Earl Jackson proclaims himself a life-long Democrat and keeps a framed picture of FDR on his office wall. Bob Stone waves the Republican banner, although in the last year Stone bucked his own party twice on high profile votes. Earl used it as merciless fodder for occasional Saturday morning breakfast debates with his friend at the Silver Spoon diner.

I didn't care one way or the other. Politics is the filler I mute on television while I'm waiting for the weather report. I had no stake in this extravagant wedding, either. I rode in as Andy's Plus One. She belonged to a book club with the bride, Sandra Stone, and the two had formed a friendship. I've met Sandy any number of times, but never the groom. Sandy teaches kindergarten at James Madison Elementary School in Essex. To hear Andy describe it, Sandy loves teaching as much as her adoring children love her.

Andy's invitation to the Essex County Wedding of the Century promised two free nights at the Cinnamon Hills Golf Resort, a lavish dinner, dancing, and other delights. I had no complaints. This was as close to a vacation as Andy and I expected to get for a while. We were broke.

In June, working as an air charter pilot for Earl Jackson, I crashed one of the company's Piper Navajo twin-engine airplanes. I have no memory of the event.

Three things emerged in the aftermath.

First, I became a minor celebrity. My fifteen minutes of fame came from the fact that I fell out of a disintegrating airplane at a hundred and forty miles per hour and dropped five hundred feet into a marsh. I wound up on soft earth, sitting in the pilot's seat with a broken pelvis.

Second, I spent a week in the hospital which ran up a huge bill. As a police officer, Andy enjoys health insurance through her employer, the City of Essex, but the major medical policy carries a five-thousand-dollar deductible, which wiped out our savings and put us on a payment plan. The broken pelvis still hurts, though they tell me it is healing nicely. I spent most of the last sixty days using crutches. I ditched the crutches a little over two weeks ago but don't have a lot of stamina for standing. Or sitting, for that matter. On the plus side, I can now tell when it's going to rain, and I don't have to drag myself out of bed and go running with my wife.

Third, I came away from the crash with something I can't explain.

The other thing.

I vanish. When I vanish, I defy gravity and no longer obey the physical laws governing mass and inertia. *The other thing*, I am now convinced, accounts for me surviving the in-flight breakup of an airplane. Because nobody falls that far at that speed and lives.

As of the wedding weekend two months after the crash I still had no idea what it was or how it became a part of me. I do, however, know how to control it.

Only two other people know about *the other thing.* Lane Franklin, the fourteen-year-old daughter of Essex County Air Service's office manager, learned about *the other thing* when it saved us both from a burning building. The second person who knows about *the other thing* is Sergeant Andrea Katherine Taylor Stewart of the City of Essex Police Department—my wife Andy, or Dee as I sometimes call her. She learned of it after she killed the man who put Lane in the burning building in the first place.

Andy being Andy, she had questions.

THE NIGHT I demonstrated *the other thing* to Andy she gasped at the impossibility of it. Not only because I vanished, but because I also took her in my arms and we both disappeared, then I showed her how gravity ceases to exist in the vanished state. We floated through angled sunbeams in the barn behind our rented farmhouse like a romantic pair of space station astronauts.

Afterward, we took up station on the farmhouse front porch and watched the setting summer sunshine kiss the corn tassels across the road.

"How do you know you'll come back? That you'll be visible again?" Andy demanded. "How do you know you won't get stuck that way?" Leave it to my wife to find The Worry. "Well? How do you know?"

"I don't," I said. "I just have faith that if I can turn it on in my head, I can turn it off."

"And you do that with the levers you described—the ones you imagine?"

"Yup. Push the levers up, disappear. Pull the levers back, reappear. It seems to, I don't know, *wrap* me up. You felt it, didn't you?"

"That cool sensation? Weird. Of course, what am I saying, this whole thing is weird... *Will, my God!* How is this possible?"

My wife, the cop, has a strong need to connect dots. I had a theory.

"I know you don't want to see Six Nine Tango." The wreckage of the airplane that had broken apart all around me at a hundred and forty miles per hour lay in a hangar at Essex County Airport. "But you heard Connie Walsh from the NTSB. She thinks I *hit something.* I think she's right. And I think whatever I hit—I think that's what did this to me. I think it saved me."

Andy's lower lip gained prominence, a sign of deep thought—or a signal to run for your life. I took it as the former.

I said, "You and I just floated around the barn like astronauts. I didn't want to scare you, so I kept us just above the floor. But I did some testing with this when you weren't here. I flew all over the barn, all the way up to the top, and then floated back down again. There's no way I survived that aircraft breakup and the fall—I don't care how soft the ground was —unless I *floated* down."

"The same way you got in and out of Andre's penthouse," Andy observed. She referred to the man who kidnapped Lane, the man she killed. She chased away the memory with a slug from her Corona.

"Yeah. Twenty stories up. Freaked me out."

"What did you hit?"

"Million-dollar question. Get out your science fiction catalog and pick a page. Wrinkle in time-space. Wormhole. Alien spaceship. Secret government test vehicle. Wizards flying through the RNAV 31 approach course on their brooms."

"This is insane," she said, not for the first time that evening.

We talked into the night. I flipped back and forth a few times, vanishing and reappearing, just to show her how easy it was. In retrospect, I think it scared her more than eased her mind.

Since that night, as summer slipped into fall, we talked about it often. We played with it a few more times, although Andy didn't like it when I took her along for the ride. Most of my practice sessions were conducted while she worked her patrol shift. She asked if I thought it might be radioactive and might give me cancer. She wondered if we should have a test done—at which point we both agreed we didn't want to share this with anyone. She didn't ask me to stop doing it, but I think she wanted to.

Lane often came to visit because the secret between us would have burst her open otherwise. When she visited, Andy and I took her to the barn and I let her throw her arms around me and we would vanish and fly between the rafters and beams with Andy smiling on the sidelines, tracking us by the sound of Lane giggling and laughing.

After one such session, Andy's posed another burning question.

"What are you going to do with this?"

I teased that I planned to go to Las Vegas to see how much cash I can carry out of a vault. She was not amused.

I wasn't *entirely* teasing.

During the episode that found me flying out of a burning building with Lane in my arms, I stole sixty-three thousand dollars in cash from a gang of drug dealers. I kept the money for Lane. Andy, heart and soul the professional police officer, frowned on my thievery once I summoned the courage to tell her. I reminded her the money came from the people who kidnapped and nearly killed Lane. They owed it to her. Call it reparations. Lane and her mother are not well off, so I convinced my wife we could slip the money into an education investment account for Lane, a little at a time.

Neither of us considered, even for a moment, using a dime of the money to deal with our health insurance deductible problem. I, on the other hand, wanted to go back to the hospital and have a heart-to-heart talk with a certain public relations executive who had hounded us during my stay, because of my celebrity survival status. One of the hospital's nursing assistants—later arrested for dealing drugs—swapped my pain killers with counterfeits. I figured a story like that might persuade the hospital to reduce the bill.

Andy would have none of it.

"The only reason we know any of that is because I was the investigating officer. I'm not about to use my badge to leverage freebies—not from anyone!" she declared.

Well, when you put it that way.

I could not answer her question. I had no idea what I planned to do with *the other thing.*

2

"Stewart!" I heard my name over the crowd noise and the string quartet playing in the wedding tent. Andy had not yet returned from the land of lipstick adjustment. A familiar face wove through the tables toward me.

"Jesus Christ," I said, "the people you meet when you haven't got a gun."

Dave Peterson, looking solid and tan in an expensive suit, took and shook my hand. He broadcast a smile from a wide, boyish face. An Essex County Air Service alum, Dave moved on two years ago, landing a corporate pilot job. Small air charter companies like Essex Air feed a steady stream of young pilots to the airlines and corporate flight departments. The latter had hired Dave. Before moving on to the big time, he and I did most of the flying for Earl.

"How are you, man? I heard about your fuckup!" He grinned.

"Yeah. I ruined my perfect record of one landing for every takeoff."

"Seriously, what happened?"

Most people don't ask me directly, but Dave and I flew a lot of trips and tipped a lot of after-hours beers together. Dave counted himself among the handful of people who attended the wedding when Andy and I married.

"I have no idea. Really. No clue. No memory of it."

"I heard in-flight breakup! And you wound up in a swamp? Is that really true?"

"Sitting in the pilot's seat."

"Wow. That's crazy!" He went on about it for a few minutes, interrogating me for details, for the status of the investigation, for a report on my injuries. I told him what I could, but often came back to the same blank spot in my memory. In the end, he looked at me with naked wonder. "I'm glad you're still vertical, man. Honestly."

"Not as glad as me."

He switched the conversation away from life and death—onto something genuinely serious. "I heard they pulled your ticket. What the hell for?"

"Mostly for the fun of it, I think. The NTSB people are great, but they're coming up with some blanks on this one. The FAA wants to fill in the blank with my name. And since I have this memory issue they're trying to pin 'Pilot Incapacitation' on me."

"Fuckers."

"It's not official. Temporary suspension, pending the NTSB report and review, and a medical eval. I already passed a new First-Class medical exam. The application is winding its way through Oklahoma City, I guess." I wished. Nobody had said word one to me about the progress of my application.

"Still working for Genghis Khan?"

"He hasn't fired me yet. I may be a penguin, but he's been trying to keep me busy. Wants to buy a King Air, so he has me doing a lot of legwork on that."

"A King Air! Finally!"

"What are you flying?" I jumped at a chance to change the subject.

"Falcon 20, but we just added a G-II. I'm scheduled for first officer school in December." Dave grinned.

"Gulfstream," I said, showing genuine appreciation. "The Rolls Royce of executive jets. Company must be doing all right."

"The company's opening up markets in South America, so we need longer legs. They told me to learn Spanish."

"I forgot … what do they do?"

"Prisons. Private prisons. Huge and growing industry. We're one of the largest in the U.S. and they're tapping a big market in South America. Billion-dollar industry. People can't seem to keep out of jail. Here in the U.S. the state governments want to outsource."

I gestured at the tent above us. "What got you into this shindig?"

Dave pointed at a cluster of men in suits and women in elegant wedding wear. "That's the CEO, the guy with the perfect white hair. Pearce Parks. He's got the keys to the company jet. We fly him all over. He's pals with the groom, who pals with the governor, who's around here somewhere. We had his lordship on a flight out to California just last week, although I'm not supposed to mention that. We flew into Madison yesterday. Drove up here. They took pity on us throttle jockeys and let us tag along. I'm hoping to get in a round of golf in the morning. Say, how's Andy? Is she here?"

"She is. She went to fix her face."

"That girl's face needs no fixing. You're one lucky man. She still a cop?"

"Blue to the core."

"I believe that. And Pidge? Is she still terrorizing Earl?"

"Working on killing him. She pestered him to make her his Plus One. She's here."

"No shit!"

"She's looking to get laid, but don't get your hopes up. She's got a target lock on those guys in tuxedos."

"Ah, she brushed me off a couple years ago. I don't think she likes pilots." Dave took my hand again and shook it. "Listen man, it's great to see you. I gotta get back to the entourage, but let's grab a beer after dinner and catch up!"

Dave sauntered away, leaving me to think about the great division in my world—those who fly airplanes and those who don't. And how I was among the latter these days.

3

"I saw a guy with fucking makeup on," Pidge announced as she sat down and pulled her chair up to the round table. "A dude! And it was thick! What's that shit all about?"

"Where?" I asked.

She pointed at one of the bars on the tent perimeter. The guests stood three deep attempting to refuel before the big sit-down meal. I could not pick out a dude wearing makeup.

"It's a brave new world," Earl grumbled. He waved off the waiter who offered to pour dinner wine. Earl doesn't drink.

"Bald, Caucasian, medium build, wearing a brown suit?" Andy, seated beside me, asked Pidge.

"Yeah. Who wears a brown suit to a fucking wedding?" Pidge got her nickname—Pidgeon—as a teenaged student pilot. She talks dirty and she flies. She began flying at Essex County Air Services when she was sixteen and powered her way through her ratings and licenses. On the day she earned her commercial pilot's license she walked into Earl's office and told him to hire her because she was the best pilot he would ever have on the payroll. I think he would have flatly refused, if not for the fact that what she said was true.

"I think the makeup is covering up tattoos," Andy offered.

"All over his face? Who would fucking put tattoos all over their face?"

Andy turned her head and gazed at the bar. I assumed she searched for the man with the makeup, but the look on her face said she wasn't looking as much as pondering Pidge's question.

Andy the Cop, seeing things the way cops see them.

After a moment she turned back to me and seemed to let it go. I picked up the freshly poured dinner wine and raised the glass. She followed my move.

"To free vacations," I said.

"Free vacations." We touched glasses and sipped.

The string quartet broke into a classical version of "The Girl from Ipanema," a song that always reminds me of my wife, more so in the dress she now wore. Healing pelvis or not, I planned to dance tonight. And more. The *bossa nova* beat carried my thoughts to Andy, sitting so close beside me. She caught me looking at her as she flexed minutely to the music.

"Lipstick," she warned me, reading my mind. "And I'm not going to go fix it again."

She leaned over and whispered something in my ear as a consolation, something that made me wish the dinner and dancing portion of the evening lay behind us. She stroked my thigh as she sat back in her chair.

A moment later, the string quartet stopped, and the PA system began blasting a hip hop song I'd never heard by an artist I could not possibly identify. On a stage at the center of the tent, someone picked up a microphone and announced the imminent arrival of the bridal party.

4

"Andy!"

My wife pushed back her chair and rose to embrace the bride. Sandra Stone, now Jameson, had been working her way around the room after her big entrance. A photographer trailing the bride quickly targeted the two. Behind him, an assistant with a note pad turned to a second assistant and said, "Who is that? I think that's somebody. Find out who that is."

"Oh, sweetie, you look absolutely stunning!" Andy gushed.

All brides look stunning, but Sandy Stone started from an advantage. Her light blonde hair had been spun up in a complex style accented with tiny blue flowers that caught and reflected the color of her eyes. She had sun in her skin, which set off a sweet crescent smile, framed in ruby red. I have a bias toward my wife, but seeing the two of them side by side, I had to admit that Sandy held her own. Together, they were show stopping, and the photographer snapped away, jumping from angle to angle.

"I cannot believe I made it this far," Sandy said. She flicked a bright smile at me. "Hi, Will! Your wife is gorgeous!"

"Said the beautiful bride," I smiled back at her. "All I can say, Sandy, is—holy crap!" I waved my arms. "Nice party."

She rolled her eyes. "Okay, so it's supposed to be the bride who goes berserk, right? What's the term for Groom-zilla? This is all Todd! He planned everything! I'm not even sure I picked the dress!" She laughed, an honest kindergarten teacher laugh.

"But it's beautiful. You deserve every bit of it," Andy said.

"I deserve to get out of these shoes," she said, making a face. She took Andy's hands. "I am *so* glad you came, both of you! Hi, Mr. Jackson! Don't you dare start a fight with my dad tonight!"

"Your dad and I never fight. I enlighten. He chooses not to be enlightened," Earl replied. "I promise we will behave in your honor."

Sandy leaned down and kissed Earl on his bald head. The blush that followed blended into his scowl and conjured a combination that camouflaged itself as rage. Pidge giggled.

Andy and the bride traded small talk before Sandy moved on to the next table.

"She wasn't kidding," Andy said, seating herself again beside me. "A couple weeks ago she told me she was *this close* to calling it off. It just kept getting bigger, and bigger. All Todd. Eighty percent of the guest list is Todd." Andy lowered her voice. "I was really afraid she would ask me to be in the wedding party."

"I could have helped you with that," I said. "Made you disappear."

5

"Seriously, what are you thinking of doing with it?" Andy asked one night, close to midnight, after her shift ended and we settled in on the sofa for a late snack. "*The other thing.* Assuming it stays. Assuming it belongs to you now."

"I think I did a pretty good job of busting up a drug gang," I said.

Andy frowned. When she learned of my role in rescuing Lane, while deeply grateful and a little impressed, a part of her was not happy.

"You're not trained for that," she said flatly.

"*No one* is trained for this."

"Suppose you did use it, undercover. Nothing you learn could be used to build a case for prosecution. You could not testify. It would be like planting a listening device without a court order. Not to mention you're going to want to keep it secret. Or else wind up in some government lab somewhere..." She trailed that last part off, like it had not occurred to her before.

"True, but information is information," I said quickly. "You work from anonymous sources all the time. Information doesn't have to be admissible to be effective—or preventative. I could work for the DEA. Get into cartel strongholds no one else can penetrate."

"God forbid! That's ridiculously dangerous!"

"Or be on call for the fire department if there's a high-rise fire. Just float people down to the street safely."

"This is not getting better."

"Infiltrate terrorist groups in the middle east? Dismantle rogue state nuclear programs?"

"I'm going to hit you. If you want to fight crime, how about white-collar crime? Sneak into board rooms when they meet to steal the pension plan. Catch the CEO plotting to violate SEC regulations or exposing himself to the office girls."

"Wouldn't work," I said. "It would be so boring I'd fall asleep and wouldn't be able to remember what they said. Let's revisit the Las Vegas idea. They wouldn't notice a few million missing from the counting room…"

"I would arrest you myself," she said. "Be serious, Pilot. This is a part of us now. So, I have a say."

"That's why we're having this conversation."

"Okay. Then, whatever you do with it, I need a couple promises from you." She squared herself up, facing me. "First off, no sneaking into the shower with me. I swear, I'll make you wear a bell."

"Damn. I hadn't thought of that…"

"And second," she grew serious, "I know you did some dangerous things to rescue Lane, but no more dangerous stuff. Deal?"

6

Gunfire ripped through the hubbub of dinner conversation. An automatic weapon. The rip-saw sound silenced the crowd.

"DOWN! EVERYBODY DOWN!"

A voice boomed, overly loud and distorted by the PA system that had been used for the wedding speeches and toasts. The command dominated the shocked silence suspended in the wake of the gunfire. Andy twisted, looking for the source. She reached for her handbag.

I followed Andy's searching eyes to the stage. Musical equipment and instruments stood at the ready, but the band had wandered off during the dinner hour. A man in a brown suit, his head covered with a black balaclava, held a microphone in one hand and a pistol in the other. Whoever had fired, it wasn't him.

"ON THE GROUND! COVER YOUR EYES! YOU LOOK, YOU DIE!"

The room rumbled as five hundred people squeezed out of folding chairs and found space on the ground.

Earl pulled out Pidge's chair and hustled her to the floor, then ducked down beside her. All around us heads disappeared below the table line.

Andy and I kneeled. She looked directly at me. I glanced down. She had extracted her Glock 17 handgun from her purse.

"You're outgunned! You can't!"

"I know. Too many people."

"I can." I held out my hand.

She knew what I meant. We had only seconds, time when the confusion would cover me. I reached for the pistol, but she jerked it away.

"Eyes only! Nothing else!" She gripped my arm. "Nothing else!"

I checked to be sure no one was watching. Everyone near us obediently pressed palms and fingers to their eyes. I glanced back at Andy and nodded. I made a motion as if to drop to the floor, then—

Fwooomp!

—I vanished. *The other thing* wrapped my entire body in a cool sensation. Weightlessness replaced gravity.

She blinked twice, startled by the effect.

"Get down!" I pushed her chair out of the way. She lowered herself to the floor. Head down, she gripped the pistol in her right hand and folded it out of sight in her lap. She put her left hand loosely over her eyes.

"NOW! NOW! EVERYONE DOWN!"

Another burst of automatic gunfire, painfully loud, accelerated the rumble of the wedding guests moving to comply.

Holding the back of my chair, I did the opposite. I pushed myself upright. A sea of empty tables, cluttered with glassware and plates abandoned in mid-meal, spread out around me. Five hundred people, the young, the old, the wealthy and the far wealthier all found space below the tables to lie, kneel, or bend themselves into pretzel shapes with their hands pressed over their eyes.

The few people who remained standing carried weapons.

The man on the stage paced, microphone in one hand, pistol in the other.

"This is either a robbery, and everyone goes home unhurt, or it's a mass shooting. You choose. Those of you carrying concealed weapons, know this: If anyone tries to play hero, we start shooting everybody. If anyone raises a phone or camera, we shoot everybody. If anyone looks at us, we shoot everybody. Those of you with bodyguards, we don't give a shit about you, so tell your dogs to sit!"

Caucasian. Brown suit.

Four more dressed in black patrolled the perimeter of the dance floor in the center of the tent. All four carried rifles. At least one, and probably all, had been converted to fully automatic. All four men walking the floor wore heavy vests. All four wore black full-head balaclavas showing nothing but their eyes.

As soon as I tallied up five, a sixth appeared. He jogged up the outdoor aisle the wedding party used for their grand entrance. The aisle had been laid out as a wide curve on the resort lawn, starting at the main building, arcing around a small koi pond, then sweeping into the massive tent. A natural corridor of perfectly spaced trees spread a canopy above the home stretch of the aisle. In front of each tree, a faux Greek statue stood draped with garlands of fresh flowers.

The late arriving man hurried to a span of tables set behind the head table. Piles of wrapped gifts stretched across the tables. He ignored the gifts. He jogged to the center where a tall silver urn nested in a bed of white roses. He pulled a duffle bag off his shoulder and scooped envelopes and small packages out of the urn, into the duffle bag.

It struck me as stupid. *What good are piles of checks made out to the bride and groom?*

I looked in the direction that the last man had come. Beyond a curve where the bridal aisle swung toward the resort, an embankment rose to a parking lot.

Escape route. They would have a vehicle waiting.

I rose and swung my legs to a horizontal position above my chair. Using my wrists, I pushed off the chair toward the nearest edge of the tent. My glide path avoided the tall, flowered centerpieces on each of the intervening tables. Guests huddled below me. Most froze in silence; a few sobbed. I passed over them unseen. At intervals, I grabbed chair-backs and the lips of tables to adjust my course. Reaching the edge of the tent, I grabbed a support pole and used it to accelerate.

I aimed for the first tree and screwed up. Instead of reaching the tree, my path took me to the polished Greek figure posing beside the tree, along the aisle. I worried the statue might be made of Styrofoam and I might topple it. Having no choice, I grabbed the pedestal base. My hands closed on several hundred pounds of plaster. The statue didn't budge. I stopped.

A garland of flowers linked the next statue in the line, and the next after that. I heaved myself in the direction of the second statue, brushed past it, and sailed on to the third, then the fourth where the aisle curved toward the resort. I guessed this would be the point where the thieves would break from the path, climb the embankment, and make their escape.

At the apex of the embankment, on the edge of the parking lot, I spotted the gray roof of a large crew cab pickup truck.

Bingo. Idling engine sound confirmed my suspicion.

I shifted from the statue base to the tree behind the statue and stopped, stymied. A flight path to the truck would take me uphill. But there were no trees, posts, or poles to grapple. Nothing to aim for, nothing to anchor me. Launching uphill would send me on a trajectory up and over the parking lot, with nothing to stop me from continuing to climb, higher and higher.

Once moving, unaffected by gravity, *the other thing* treats me like an astronaut in space. Without a tether, without a grip on something, I simply float. Caught on an upward trajectory, my choices would be to continue into the upper atmosphere to die of hypoxia or reappear and let gravity yank me down. Too high, and the fall would kill me. Visible, the thieves would probably kill me.

In the tent, the brown suited emcee shouted through the PA system.

"Time!"

Heavy footsteps pounded the carpeted aisle behind me, drumming the plywood laid beneath.

Calling out "Time" suggested these thieves had discipline. It gave me hope that there would be no further gunfire. Gunfire that would force Andy to break cover and shoot back.

The footsteps on the aisle behind me grew louder. I had only seconds.

I locked one arm on the tree behind the statue and turned to gather information for Andy.

One. Gun. The first thief rushed past me carrying a black AR rifle with a strap. Customized. *Gun.*

Two. Shoe. The second thief, crepe soled work boots, jeans, a wallet chain, like a biker. *Shoe.*

Three. Tree. The money guy, arms like tree branches, strong for carrying. Tattoo. Army duffel bag. Worn. No weapon. *Tree.*

Four. Door. Too fast. The fourth man, carrying his rifle, raced alongside the duffle bag man. I could not record an impression. *Door.*

Inside the tent, the man with the microphone shouted, "NOBODY

MOVES FOR THREE MINUTES!" Electronic feedback shrieked when the microphone hit to the floor.

Gunshots!

Single barking shots fired in steady succession bit into my unprotected hearing. One—two—three—four—five—six—I saw flashes in the tent.

None of the escaping thieves turned around.

Part of the plan.

Not an automatic weapon. Pistol shots.

This isn't a firefight. This is a warning.

Seven—eight—then four more in rapid succession.

Please, Andy, keep your head down!

I focused on my mission.

Five. Hive. The fifth man carried a military-style rifle. This one stopped directly below me on the other side of the statue. A hive of red hair under the edges of his mask. *Hive.*

The last man—the emcee—jogged up behind Red Hair, pistol in hand. His mask bore light smudges around the edges. Makeup.

The man Pidge had seen. He wore a brown business suit.

"Kill the first one out the door!" the sixth man ordered Red Hair before jogging up the embankment.

The fifth man took a knee and brought his weapon to bear, taking aim at the tent.

NO!

I knew who would be first out of the tent. She wouldn't have a chance. Andy would be shot just to make a point.

I didn't calculate it or think it through. I moved between the tree and the plaster Greek statue, a warrior holding a spear. I fixed my back against the tree and my feet on the warrior's back. If the pedestal had been anchored, this would have come to nothing. But the statue and pedestal together probably weighed over three hundred pounds and served as their own anchor on the grass. Eight feet up, against the tree, I prayed for enough leverage.

I shoved the statue with all the strength my legs could bring to bear. Silently, both statue and pedestal leaned over and dropped on the kneeling thief whose attention never left his optical gun sight. Bones encased in muscle and flesh snapped. He screamed. The statue compressed his crouching body. His legs twisted awkwardly. His left shoulder, crushed, took on a gruesome shape and his left arm flopped at his side. The rifle dropped to the carpet.

Halfway up the hill, the sixth man halted, turned, and aimed his weapon directly at me. I cringed, expecting a shot.

The weapon swept the space I occupied, then the aisle, then side to side. He stared at the statue wobbling on top of his man. He searched for the cause. Wild eyes followed his gunsights.

I froze my hands on the tree trunk. I held my breath.

The sixth man broke his deadly focus and raced back to his companion. Red Hair screamed and clawed at the carpeting with his right hand.

The sixth man studied the scene briefly. Then, with a gloved hand, he pressed his pistol into the outstretched hand of his comrade. He picked up the fifth man's rifle.

One handed, he aimed and fired. One shot to the head. The screaming stopped.

The big pickup truck's engine revved, calling out to these last two to hurry. The killer turned and ran, carrying the rifle, leaving the handgun.

Tires squeaked on the parking lot pavement. The engine raced. The sound faded quickly.

I HUNG FROZEN in shock for a moment, still seeing the pistol pointed directly at me, reconciling the certainty that I'd be shot with the realization that I had not been seen. I didn't think to climb higher in the tree for a look at the truck. When I began to breathe again, I eased down the side of the tree. On the back side of it, hidden from the tent, I reappeared.

Fwooomp! I stepped into view and caught sight of Andy. First out of the tent. She dashed toward me with her weapon drawn.

First out. First to be shot. I could not unsee the imagined horror.

In the tent behind her, shock wore off and people shifted to after-the-fact panic. Guests streamed out of the tent on all sides. An initial crowd rushed up the aisle behind Andy, but on finding the dead man, broke through the flower garland and crossed the lawn in the direction of the resort building.

Andy satisfied herself that the fifth man was dead. She nudged the weapon out of his reach on the off chance he resurrected himself. She hurried a few paces up the embankment, to confirm nothing was to be found in the parking lot. I noticed she had kicked off her shoes.

She returned with a scowl on her face.

"I told you not to do anything!"

"Hey!" I turned on her. "He was stationed to shoot the first person coming out. I knew that would be you. And I'm fairly sure you were outgunned. So, don't—*just—don't*!"

She met my rigid expression with her own. She could not see what I had imagined, picturing her rushing into an ambush. She could not know that even without it happening, it now existed in my head, horrible, indelible. I rolled my eyes to the sky and pulled air into my lungs to settle myself.

"Okay," she said. "Let's just deal with this."

I nodded.

"My phone is inside. I need to call the Chief," she said. She reached for me and squeezed my arm. I pressed my hand to hers.

We connected and transmitted unspoken messages.

Fresh screams came from the wedding tent.

"We need a doctor! He's been shot! Someone, call an ambulance!"

"Over here, too! Over here!"

7

Andy pulled away.

"Keep everyone away from the body," she commanded. She turned and worked her way against the fleeing crowd.

I pointed at three men hurrying toward the resort with their wives or dates.

"You, you and you. Help me," I commanded. "Stand here, here and here." I pointed. "Don't let anyone near the body."

One of the women wanted nothing to do with me. She urged her husband to keep going. He shrugged helplessly at me and followed her. The other two stepped up grimacing.

Security people hustled their important charges out of the tent, across the lawn and into the resort. My new colleagues and I waved people away from the crushed body on the aisle. A few stopped and gaped, horrified by the blood leaking onto the white carpet.

Voices in the tent cried out.

"He's been shot!"

"We need a doctor!"

I struggled to slow my heart rate.

Sirens awakened in the distance. I searched the crowd and the relative darkness in the wedding tent, trying in vain to spot Andy.

What the hell happened?

The sixth man had issued his commands, then fired a steady sequence of shots. I had taken the meter of his gunfire as a warning while he crossed the dance floor and made his exit. The shots were cadenced, measured. All for show. There was no uncontained firefight, no wild exchange. I assumed he fired his warning into the air. Had he gone mad and randomly targeted defenseless people on the floor?

Uniformed state troopers arrived. A pair of them jogged down the hill. I credited them with amazing response time, until I remembered that the governor had been somewhere in the tent.

"This is one of the perpetrators," I said to the first trooper to arrive. "These guys have been guarding the body for you." I gestured at my two companions.

"Step away from the body," he commanded. "Clear this sidewalk!"

I took the opportunity to slip away.

Large, serious men—professional security—urgently ushered their charges away from the wedding tent. One bodyguard, moving a man with white hair toward the resort building, reached out and plucked a cell phone from a bystander shooting cell phone video. The bodyguard crushed the phone with a heel, never breaking stride, never looking back, ignoring the phone owner's outcry.

I worked my way into the tent and looked for Andy.

The sun had slipped well below the trees on the far side of the lake, leaving a curtain of high, bloodstained clouds. Strung inside the tent, thousands of tiny white lights hung in vain celebration over empty tables. The wedding tent seemed to swell in size for being largely vacated. Two clusters of people remained. At the center of each cluster, someone suffered.

In the strange warping of time that surrounds any emergency, it took both forever and no time for the first ambulance to arrive. A City of Essex rescue squad parked at the top of the embankment where the thieves had boarded their getaway truck. EMTs unloaded equipment cases, descended the embankment, and hurried into the tent.

Bystanders urged and guided the EMT teams to the wounded. Someone lay prone, attended by a guest who worked with trained, bloodied hands. I took him for a doctor. He spoke to the EMTs with authority.

Blonde, beautiful and wearing twenty thousand dollars-worth of wedding dress splashed with blood, the bride knelt, cradling the wounded man's head. Bloody handprints imprinted the dress around her waist and down her thighs. She wasn't shot. No one attended to wounds on her body. Streaks of tears cut glossy paths down Sandy's face. Her new husband hovered nearby.

Andy materialized out of nowhere, issuing measured commands. She spoke to those present and into her phone. Two men in suits approached her and showed badges. She gave them urgent instructions and they hurried away in different directions.

Activity heightened when the medical team moved the wounded man onto a stretcher and rushed him out of the tent toward an ambulance. A train of shocked and worried guests, including the bridal party, hurried after it.

Officer Mike Mackiejewski appeared in his Essex PD uniform. He rushed up to Andy and she briefed him. He listened, spoke into a radio mic mounted near his shirt collar, listened for more, radioed more.

I stood a few paces from one of the bars occupying a section of the perimeter—the same bar Pidge had pointed out. I noticed the bartender, a young woman, staring, transfixed. I walked directly into her line of sight. It took a second for her to focus her eyes on my face.

"Captain Morgan, spiced, on the rocks with a dash of pineapple," I said.

The woman blinked, not comprehending. I waved a hand between us. She spoke. "Uh … I think we're closed."

"It's okay. I'm with the police. CSI. I need to test all the liquor. Let's start with Captain Morgan, spiced, on the rocks with a dash of pineapple."

She blinked at me again.

"Please."

Her hands went to work slowly, automatically. "I'm sorry. I don't—I don't know—I've never—"

"It's okay. None of us have ever. Hey!"

Startled, she looked up from the act of pouring rum over ice cubes.

"Pour one for yourself," I said.

She nodded blankly and produced another glass. Her hands did the work on autopilot. When she finished, I picked up mine and waited until she picked up hers. Her hand shook. Ice in her glass sang a tiny wind chime song.

"Relax," I said. "Take a sip."

"I can't believe this happened." She drank. "Can NOT believe this happened."

"May I ask you a question? Did you see a guy here tonight wearing makeup on his face?"

It took a moment of concentration for her to realized I had asked a question.

"Brown suit?" I prompted her. "Makeup on? On his face?"

Her face lit up. "Yes! Heavy makeup on his face! It was getting dark in here, but I totally saw it. Mostly because his skin had no sheen. You saw him, too?"

"Did he drink?"

"Water. He asked for a bottled water!"

"I don't suppose you noticed what he did with the water bottle…?"

She shook her head.

"But you did see him, you got a look at his face."

She nodded. "I was sorta fixated on his makeup."

"Did you notice anything else about him?"

She took a strong hit from the tumbler of rum. "Yes! When he asked for the bottled water, I put it on the bar, but he didn't pick it up. He just looked at it. And I thought I did something wrong you know? But he didn't say anything, and it was really, really busy, so I took another order. I think he didn't want me to see him pick it up, because he waited until I was filling the other order. I think it was because of the tattoo on his hand."

"Tattoo? Did you see it?"

"I was bending over to scoop some ice. He didn't see me looking. I saw it. Eighty-eight."

"The words?"

"The numbers. 88. On the back of his right hand."

I raised a glass to her and took a long drink. The liquid warmed my throat. The warmth spread and massaged my tight nerves.

"Was he one of them?" she asked, suddenly frightened.

"Maybe," I said. "But it's okay, he's gone now. Can you stay right here? I want you to meet someone."

. . .

ANDY INTERVIEWED THE BARTENDER. I watched the EMTs work over the second person who had been shot. I saw my wife glance out at the aisle where she had given me the assignment to watch over the dead body. Two state troopers stood near the bleeding corpse. I presume seeing them got me off the hook for abandoning my post, because Andy didn't say anything.

After assuring the woman she could finish her drink, Andy took me aside.

"I'm sorry," she said. "For snapping at you."

Her green eyes met mine. I gave her credit. Switching gears from full-on cop to something personal at this moment took a lot for her.

"Likewise," I said. "I got a little edgy, too."

The moment ended. She took my arm and pulled me farther from the nearest set of ears.

"What did you see?"

I started by describing the execution of the fifth man.

"That doesn't make sense." She shook her head. "Why leave someone who can be identified?"

"Or … why take someone with you who needs medical attention? Or whose body needs disposing of if he doesn't make it?"

"Cold."

"Killing him was cold."

"Shooting up the place doesn't make sense. They could have been in and out with no one hurt."

"Get out your phone," I said. "Record me. I'll give you what I can from when I was outside, while it's fresh. You'll have to come up with a creative way of using it because I can't be a witness."

Andy produced her cell phone and touched the screen.

"It's recording."

I closed my eyes.

One. Gun. "First guy carried a black AR-15 with a strap. There was a pin or medallion on the strap near the stock. Five eight. Hundred sixty. Black tactical pants, looked brand new." *Two. Shoe.* "Second guy, construction work boots. Crepe soles. Leather laces. Big guy. Six-foot. Two twenty, two thirty. Blue jeans with a biker chain on his wallet. Beer belly. Leather wrist bands." *Three. Tree.* "Third guy, five ten, maybe six-foot. Muscle man. Body builder. He carried a duffle bag, a military bag.

It looked well worn. Green, not tan. Black tactical clothing … um, and a tattoo! Right forearm. Emblem of some kind. Formal. A crest or a military tattoo." *Four. Door.* "Fourth guy was too fast. I could not get—wait! He carried his rifle in his left hand. Left handed." *Five. Hive.* "Number five, he's over there." I opened my eyes. "Pretty sure you can get more from him than me. And number six…"

"He did the talking, on the stage. Seemed to be in charge."

"The guy with the makeup."

"Covering a tattoo, or a face full of them."

"Andy." I touched her arm. "He gave the order to number five to cover the rear and shoot the first person to come out the door. There was no hesitation. No question. The guy went to a firing stance immediately."

"Military discipline?"

"Something like it. Although the commander obviously didn't subscribe to the doctrine of leaving no man behind. He finished number five off like it was nothing." I'd seen that kind of murder before. Too recently.

Andy switched off the recording and looked at me with naked wonder.

"What?"

"How did you do that? Heat of the moment—how did you get all that?"

"Mnemonic device. From a book. I taught myself."

She stared at me.

"I got tired of forgetting the limes when I stop for groceries."

Every now and then I get a look of unabashed admiration from my wife. Priceless.

"Can you stay with her?" She gestured at the bartender. "Until I can get someone over here?"

"Sure. What does it mean? 88?"

"I have no idea."

8

Andy didn't send anyone to speak to the bartender. Essex PD had jurisdiction over the resort and Andy was ranking officer. She quickly became the eye of the storm, issuing orders and organizing control of the crime scene. At one point she called out a command to gather all the wedding guests in the resort ballroom. I took the cue and invited the young bartender to walk to the building with me.

Putting the wedding guests in the ballroom turned it into a petri dish for rumors. One person was dead. Six people were dead. Senator Stone was dead. The bride was dead (I knew that was false). One of the robbers was dead (I knew that was true). It was a robbery. It was a mass shooting. There were two men. There were ten men. Nobody knew anything for certain. The bride, groom and the entire wedding party had been sequestered elsewhere. The governor was nowhere to be seen. And not that I rub elbows with billionaires, but the guests with the most money seemed to be long gone.

I found Earl and Pidge.

"Where the fuck did you disappear to?" Pidge asked.

"Andy shoved me to the floor. I got tangled up with the people on the other side of the table."

"This is some fucked up shit." Tough girl or not, her mascara had run.

"Bob got hit," Earl growled. "They're saying Sandy, too."

"Sandy's okay," I said. "I saw her."

"Who fucking robs a wedding? What? Did they need a Cuisinart?"

Earl shook his head at Pidge and explained. "The governor is *real* close with whatzisname, the groom. That's why His Majesty was here. The kid's been the governor's go-between with the Chinese. And there's been a lot of business with the Chinese in the last couple years. *A lot.*"

"What's that got to do with it?"

"There was a bunch of them here. They're probably all chums now, got to know each other's family and all. Got invited to the wedding."

"So?" Pidge asked.

"So, their tradition is to give the universal gift. Cash. Lots of cash. Somebody said those assholes emptied out the gift card stash. You can bet they'll burn the envelopes with checks and movie gift cards, but my guess is they coasted outta here with close to a quarter million in cash. Easy."

Earl Jackson doesn't act the part, but numerically he counts among the richest men in the county. I conceded that he knew the rare-air culture far better than I ever would.

"Fuck! I should've grabbed a couple envelopes!" Pidge exclaimed.

"I don't know where you'd put 'em," Earl rumbled back at her.

"Untraceable," I mused, thinking of the robbery.

"No fucking shit!" Pidge said.

The resort staff appeared and rolled out carts filled with chairs and tables. Something told me we were in for a long wait.

"I saw Dave Peterson," I said.

"No kidding?" Earl said. "Ungrateful little shit didn't even come over to say Hi." I happened to know Earl pulled strings to get Dave the interview for his new job, and that Earl thought the world of him. "Is he here?"

"He was planning on looking for you guys after dinner, but he was here with a bunch of his company top brass. I bet they hustled out right quick."

"Could'a at least parked their big-assed jet at Essex and bought some fuel," Earl griped.

We spent a long three hours waiting before investigators from the state Division of Criminal Investigations called us over to a table.

Looking at their credentials, I wondered if bigger guns had displaced Andy and the Essex PD.

The interview lasted only minutes. Like most of the guests—half of which had been released from the ballroom at that point—we were on the floor, didn't see anything, heard the shots, and it was all over before we knew it. That's what Pidge and Earl said.

I let them talk and nodded a lot.

9

Shortly after midnight, I keyed my way into the room Andy and I had been assigned. The room offered soothing silence compared to the tense, non-stop rumble of conversation in the ballroom. I fumbled with the lights, eventually figuring out which switches lit which fixtures.

An iced bottle of champagne, compliments of the wedding party, sat on the bureau in front of a flat screen TV. The champagne wore a coat of condensation. At least one life had been lost, a wedding destroyed, a lifetime of bad memories recorded. Yet looking at the unopened bubbly, I managed to find resentment that my plans with Andy for the night, for the weekend, had been ruined. I wasn't proud of that.

After hanging up my one and only suit, I stripped down to boxers and a t-shirt. The champagne beckoned, but I fought off the urge. If I opened it without waiting for Andy, I would drink the whole damned thing myself and wake up in the morning with the Eighth Air Force bombing the inside of my skull. I considered breaking into the minibar to see if Captain Morgan had any shipmates but imagined the same outcome and declined. Plus, even though the accommodations were generously included in the invitation, I had a feeling the minibar charges would wind up on the credit card. Tiny, expensive bottles of liquor were not in the Stewart budget.

I cracked open one of the complimentary water bottles stationed by the coffee maker, turned off the lights and stretched out on the bed.

I thought of Sandy Stone.

One hell of a way to start a marriage.

Andy knew Sandy better than I did. She told me Sandy wasn't just a silver-spoon-bred state senator's daughter, marking time until the rich husband came along. Sandy loved teaching. Despite what the bride said about her new husband running wild with the wedding plans, today had been Her Day. It should have been magical.

I wondered, not for the first time, if I hadn't cheated Andy out of Her Day, given our simple marriage ceremony. Andy's father had as much if not more money than State Senator Bob Stone, but a long-standing rift separated Andy from her father. Maybe I should have pushed Andy to reconcile with him, with her family. Maybe she harbored secret dreams of string quartets and Greek statues. All she really got out of the deal was me.

As often happened when we are apart, or the hours grow small and dark, I wondered if I was enough.

I also wondered who the hell thought putting LED lights all over a hotel room was such a great idea.

On one of those unanswered questions, I fell asleep.

10

I would find out from Andy, a little before the media got the facts straight, the good news/bad news story of what happened.

The sixth man fired twelve shots from a forty-caliber semi-automatic handgun as he exited the wedding tent. Eight of the twelve shots went through the fabric of the tent and into the sky. He fired the last four, according to witnesses who had peeked, randomly at the crowd in an act of utter cruelty.

Bob Stone, the father of the bride, took two bullets. One to the shoulder, which traveled through a lung and into his stomach. One to the side of his head, which lodged in his neck, but not before cutting a path through the lower portion of his brain. The EMTs carried him out of the tent alive. But whether he would live—or have a life—remained to be seen. The act of cradling her father's head in her lap accounted for the blood on Sandra Stone's ruined wedding gown.

Four tables away, Jason Everwood, a nineteen-year-old cousin of the bride on her father's side, got shot in the ass. The left butt cheek, to be precise, because he was kneeling on the floor beside his chair. It might have sounded like fodder for jokes, but the bullet traveled the length of his left thigh, plowing through muscle until it hit and destroyed his knee joint. Long, painful recovery lay in his future. His doctors told him the bullet microscopically missed his femoral artery. If it had touched the artery, he would have been dead in a matter of minutes.

On the opposite side of the dance floor, not far from where Andy and I had been seated, five-year-old Lisa Washington huddled on the floor in the arms of her mother when the fourth random bullet found her. The bullet hit the corner of her glasses and sheared them off her face, leaving her startled but untouched. The bullet then lodged in the plywood floor laid on the lawn beneath the circus-sized wedding tent. Lisa, a kindergarten student of Sandy Stone's, adored by her teacher, had been asked to serve as the flower girl. God grants small favors.

That no one died was pronounced a miracle by the media that swamped the story. It's a word they like to throw around. I know.

Andy and I had planned on staying the entire weekend. The Saturday wedding and reception (at which we planned to dance all night or as long as my healing bones could handle it) was to have been followed on Sunday by a day-long golf event. I don't play golf, but Andy plays with a skill honed during her days on her high school team, a team that made the state semi-finals. I offered to drive the cart for Andy. She looked forward to playing with Sandy and her new husband. Sunday night, the bride and groom planned to continue celebrating with another lawn party, this one intended for the younger, wilder demographic, with a minor celebrity rock band scheduled to play.

By dawn, the marrying families cancelled everything.

I WOKE on top of the sheets, slightly chilled, a little after four a.m. on Sunday morning. I knew without reaching across the bed that I had slept alone. I slid off the sheets and stood up. My pelvic bones sang out a familiar good-morning greeting. I stretched the pain away and slipped out a sliding glass door onto a balcony overlooking the lawn tent and lake beyond. Night shrouded the resort, holding its breath for the dawn hiding below the horizon.

High-powered lights had been set up, but I didn't hear generators. The pace of activity on the vast lawn seemed glacial compared to when I had departed. A few men and women in windbreakers moved methodically within the now taped-off scene. I looked for Andy, but could not see into the giant tent, which remained fully lit by thousands of tiny white lights. The body of the fifth man had been removed, but the Greek warrior remained on his side on the bloodstained carpet. I thought it a little ignoble, leaving him like that, after he had served so courageously.

I did not spy on the scene for long. Aside from almost nothing happening, cold air reminded me we were a little over thirty-six hours into official Fall.

I took a shower and dressed in my resort wear, black jeans and a black t-shirt, not to be confused with my everyday black jeans and black t-shirt.

I stood in earnest contemplation of an early hour prowl of the lobby for coffee when Andy clicked her way past the heavy door lock.

Hair still up, dress still alluring, high heels still working their magic, she slipped into the room like a teenaged girl returning past curfew. She turned, surprised to find me up and about.

"I was afraid I'd wake you," she said, carefully closing the door behind her, mindful of the other guests sleeping, if any were sleeping. She dropped her key, purse, and badge on the bureau, and slipped her hands around my waist. I wrapped my arms around her. The tension slid away. She rested her head on my shoulder.

"State is taking over everything," she sighed. "The chief is here. He told me to sleep a few hours and report back. You should go home."

11

I don't know if Andy slept or not. She told me to take the car and then hustled me out the door. I didn't see her again until nearly midnight Sunday. Sometimes she finishes a shift full of energy and chatter. Sometimes not. What I got from her Sunday night was that Essex PD had the lead and the jurisdiction, but the governor had assigned state DCI investigators to handle the investigation. Bob Stone was in an induced coma. And no sign of the thieves had turned up.

She disappeared from our rented farmhouse before I woke Monday morning.

On Monday night, after an eighteen-hour shift, Andy found me in a foul mood sitting in the dark on the porch. One look at the folder laying at my feet on the lounge chair told her why.

"You heard from the FAA?"

I made a face at her, nodded once, and then shook my head in disgust.

"What?"

"They want me to make an appointment with a neurologist for a full neurological exam. That son of a bitch Cyler poisoned this whole process, and now people up the line are thinking I had a seizure or stroke or goddamned heart attack! They can't pinpoint a cause for the crash so they're penciling in my name!" I wound up my right leg to give the folder a swift kick. The folder contained my collected notes and correspondence on my suspended pilot's license and FAA First Class Medical Certificate.

Andy scooped it out of harm's way.

After the crash, I was interviewed by an FAA Inspector named Joe Cyler. From the start, I had a feeling that he painted a target on me as the cause of the accident. In short order, I received a letter from the FAA Certification Branch "temporarily" suspending my pilot's license, pending review of the NTSB report. The same day, I received another letter suspending my pilot's medical certificate. I hold an Airline Transport Pilot license, which is valid only with an FAA First Class medical certification issued every six months. Either letter would have grounded me. Receiving both put me six feet under.

Andy slipped out of her vest and gun belt. She slid onto the old lounge chair beside me.

"Neurological exams are not a big deal," she offered. "I think it's just an office visit."

"They're asking for a supporting CAT scan or MRI. My choice."

"Oh."

Andy understood the implication, but I said it anyway. "Who's supposed to pay for all this?"

She took my hand. "We will. We've got room on the credit card. We'll find a way. Will, if this is what it takes, then this is what it takes."

I love her optimism, but when that optimism pops up while I'm wallowing in self-pity, it's just annoying. We needed a change of subject.

"Anything good happen?"

She shook her head.

"Did you visit the hospital?"

"No point. They moved him this morning to Madison. He's at University," she said. "He's in an induced coma, or was, when they air lifted him out this morning. It's bad. God, I can't—"

The words froze on her lips.

"Yeah," I said, "you *can* imagine." I took her hand. "Why don't we see about going down to Madison this weekend?"

"Could we? You wouldn't mind the drive?"

"State Street, love. More great restaurants than you can shake a menu at. Let's plan on it."

"That would be nice."

Her turn to change the subject.

"Want to know what 88 means?"

"Uh-oh. Somebody's going to piss off the DCI," I said. "Not to sound like a TV cop opera, but weren't you summarily dismissed from using your brain on this case?"

"No, those guys are okay," she allowed. "Although we have a difference of opinion on the direction of the investigation…"

She didn't elaborate.

"What does 88 mean?" I asked.

"The number 88 is an icon for white supremacists. Eight stands for the eighth letter of the alphabet."

I made a show of reciting the alphabet song and counting with my fingers.

"H, H," she said, cutting me off. "You know who."

"Shouldn't it be A. H.? Oh, that's right. Most of those guys can't read."

"It stands for Heil Hitler, not Adolph Hitler. You know what this means, right?"

I did but I let her tell me anyway.

"The man with the makeup is a neo-Nazi with prison tattoos. I bet he has lots of them. On his face, probably his neck. He used makeup to cover them because except for a few tramp stamps, the political wedding of the century wasn't a tattoo showcase."

"Did you share this with the state guys?"

"I did," she said.

"And?"

"It fits with the identity of the guy you beaned with the Greek god statue."

"Warrior. It was a Greek warrior. Hector. Achilles. Maybe Ajax or Diomedes." I got a look. "What? I read more than books about airplanes!"

"I continue to be impressed." She stroked my forearm.

"So, who was he?"

"Clayton Anthony Perville, late of South Carolina, and apparently a true son of the South, not to mention an alum of a string of state and federal prisons."

"A Confederate? Not a Nazi?"

"A little of both if you check out his social media. I found a few pictures of him at several different rallies. He marches under both banners." Andy stopped talking. She stared at me for a moment, then waved her hand in front of my eyes. "Hello. Are you listening?"

I was listening, but from a distance. My eyes settled on the black outside our screened in porch, and truthfully, had stopped seeing.

"Iron cross," I said. I closed my eyes. I saw him running. *One. Gun.* Black AR-15 rifle. With a strap. Customized. "Iron cross. He had an iron cross on his rifle strap." I turned to Andy. "The first guy out of the tent."

Andy gave a low, appreciative whistle. "That's some mnemonic device! What's an Iron Cross?"

"German war medal. They started giving them out in World War One. Corporal Hitler got one, I think. He reinstated it in World War Two. They gave them out by the bucket."

Andy sat back. In the dark on the porch, I could not see the expression on her face. Her posture suggested that she had adopted her own version of the thousand-yard stare.

"Not one, not two, but three Nazis…" she mused.

"Nazis," I said. "I hate those guys."

It hung in the air for a moment until she returned to me. "What?"

I laughed. "Indiana Jones. In the third movie."

"Oh." She stood up. "I have to look at something." She disappeared into the house, turning on lights as she went. The light destroyed the moody, self-pitying ambiance I cultivated on the porch, so I gave up and followed her. I found her at the dining room table, unfolding her laptop.

"What are you looking for?"

She drummed her fingers as the screen lit up. She didn't speak as much as think aloud. "The boss man had a Nazi tattoo, prison edition, on his hand and probably had a head full of them … I passed that along to DCI … They put it together with the dead man from South Carolina … another Nazi … DCI called in the FBI … Somewhere in South Carolina, they're tearing up the countryside looking for our dead man's roost, or trailer, or cabin in the woods..."

"So?"

"Because of Perville, the whole investigation has shifted to a cross-border hunt."

"So? That's good work on your part."

Her fingers started dancing over the keys. She stroked the touchpad.

"Maybe…"

A moment later, Google Maps filled the screen. I expected her to expand it to include the Carolinas. She didn't.

"Look at this," she said. "Here's Essex County. Here's the Cinnamon Hills Golf Resort."

"Scene of our sadly failed attempt at a vacation weekend," I griped, instantly wishing I hadn't. "Sorry. That was selfish."

Andy paid no attention. She studied the map.

"Remember how we found the Pan D vehicles? The ones the gang used, and then abandoned, when they kidnapped Lane?"

"Plate readers."

"Plate readers. Big brother, some people say, but an amazing resource for law enforcement." She leaned back, regarding the map, the orderly network of highways and county roads that made up Essex County. "At the wedding, you identified the getaway vehicle as a gray crew cab pickup truck. I managed to get that information into the pipeline—"

"How?" She could not have cited me as a source.

"I told them one of the guests told me they saw it, but that I didn't nail down the guest's name."

I didn't like that Andy made herself appear less than thorough just to cover for me.

"Here's the thing," she said. "They've been running plate reader data against Perville and his known associates and coming up with zip. They've been running plate reader data against crew cab pickups and coming up with nothing but legit owners. Plate reader coverage is nonexistent around the corner of the county where the resort is located—not until you get to town, or Highway 34 or the interstate—so, the running theory is that they used a pickup truck, but then ditched it somewhere and switched to something else. Or split up. We're talking about five men with guns and a big duffle bag. The point is, nothing else explains such a total blank."

"Makes sense," I said. "They were probably halfway to the Carolinas by morning, if not already there. How far is it?"

Andy shook her head. “I don’t think so.” Her fingers drummed again.

“What?”

Another shake of her head, this time as if shaking herself out of a dream. She suddenly closed her laptop and beamed up at me.

“I need to get out of this uniform,” she said. “Would you make me a honey and raisin bread sandwich?”

She abruptly stood up and headed for the stairs.

“Uh … sure.”

“Then we’ll go to bed. I’ll be going in early again tomorrow morning.”

Her French braid bounced as she took the stair steps by twos.

12

Andy didn't explain, and I didn't ask. It works that way sometimes. She'd fill me in when the pieces swirling around in her head fell into place. In the morning, I forced her to eat a breakfast of eggs and sausage, with a side of grapefruit. She rolled out of the yard before eight a.m., chasing something she could only find at her desk at the Essex Police Department.

I love my wife. I was happy to see her go.

I dressed in my usual outfit and went to the one-and-a-half car garage behind the house. Andy's car lived in the one-car side. The half-car side served to store the lawn mower and other collected yard junk. In the back, I carved out a small space for a workbench.

A bare bulb hung over the workbench. I turned it on and examined my handiwork. Four small flashlights lay in a line. Each had been modified. Instead of lights, the tips contained plastic model airplane propellers. Instead of an on/off switch, each had a slide control.

The other thing.

I control *the other thing* by imagining a set of levers, like the power levers in an airplane. Push them forward and I vanish, along with my clothing, my shoes, the junk in my pockets, and anything I shove up under my shirt—which may come in handy if Andy ever approves my plan for floating through a casino. Pull the imaginary levers back, I reappear.

The other thing not only makes me disappear, but it also removes the influence of gravity. I float. A light push in any direction sends me flying. However, once flying, I can't change direction or stop, unless I grab something. There isn't always something handy to grab.

Therein lies the mildly terrifying aspect. I fear floating out of reach of something I can grip. It's the nightmare scenario of an astronaut who slips his tether. Unlike the astronaut, I have the option of dropping out of the disappeared state. The catch is, when I drop out, gravity returns with a vengeance. From too high up, gravity can be a lethal bitch.

What's lacking is Propulsion. *The other thing* is a state of being without a means of propulsion. From a pilot's perspective, ninety percent of flying is propulsion. Without it, there is no flight.

During my first experiments with *the other thing* I went straight to the issue of propulsion. I rigged up two small electric motors, taken from radio-controlled aircraft, to fly myself around like an airplane. I wildly underestimated the power, launched myself straight up in a hay loft, and collided with the steel frame of a conveyor, nearly killing myself when the impact caused me to reappear forty feet up in the air.

"Yeah, we're not going to do that again," I said aloud in the tiny garage.

The initial motor design had been a simple on/off system. The propeller went from off to full power. I needed finesse.

The modified flashlights, which I dubbed the Mark II SCUZ, or Self-Contained Unit for Zooming, offered a solution.

After a couple weeks of shopping online, fits and starts, failures and screwups, a mix of off-the-hardware-store-shelf supplies and hobby store technology lay on the bench, ready for testing. Each had a slide which, when centered, meant Off. Move the switch forward, the propellers begin turning, slowly, producing thrust. Move the switch back, through the off position, and they reversed. Forward or reverse, the slide switch controlled the power output, from low power to full power.

I picked up each SCUZ and checked to see that the batteries were secure. I pushed the switch forward. The electric motor growled at low speed, then took on the scream of an angry wasp at high speed. At full power, I felt the little six-inch propeller generate significant thrust. I slid the control back to the off position, then into reverse thrust. At full reverse power, I felt a push back. Either way, in the vanished state with no inertia to overcome, I estimated I would have far more power than I needed.

I pulled on an old fishing vest and loaded the abundant pockets with the four power units. I planned to use only one unit at a time, but if I accelerated on an upward trajectory and the unit failed—or the batteries ran out—I wanted a backup. And three backups seemed like a better idea than one.

Loaded and ready, I moved my test flight operation to the familiar contained space of the barn. Among other advantages, the barn kept me out of the wind. In a fully vanished state, my body continued to exist with substance and form. But without gravity or inertia, my 184-pound body might as well be a dandelion fluff. One good gust and I'd be on the other side of the county.

"Attention all aircraft, this restricted area is now active," I announced after closing the barn door behind me. "Here goes nothing!"

Fwooomp! The familiar sound, which both Lane and Andy told me is entirely inside my head, signaled my disappearance. A cool sensation flowed over my entire body. The soles of my shoes immediately lost contact with the wooden barn floor. I became weightless.

"Nice and easy now."

I pulled a SCUZ (the term was growing on me) from a pocket and closed a grip on it, resting my right thumb on the slide switch.

I let myself rise a few inches, then held my hand and the unit out, pointed forward. I moved the slide switch. The SCUZ, which had vanished along with me, growled to life. I felt wind on my hand as the unseen propeller pulled air through its arc.

The barn floor shifted gently below me. The movement wouldn't have outpaced a caterpillar traversing a tree branch; nevertheless, *it worked!*

I held my hand steady and allowed myself to track forward on a line. The movement slowly accelerated. Math of some kind, beyond my training, could probably define a point at which thrust would equal the wind resistance and acceleration would cease, but for now if I did nothing to change the power setting, I would continue to accelerate.

I floated slowly toward the center of the hay mow. A giddy feeling swept through me. I knew coming into this that it would work. The failed first test had proven that much. But anticipating success didn't make this any less *incredibly cool!*

Lane is going to love this!

I angled my wrist to the right. I turned.

"Son of a bitch!" I laughed. I followed the new trajectory past a barn beam that rose vertically out of the floor. I altered the angle of my wrist again and carved a slow arc around the beam.

At this point, with no change in the power setting, I had accelerated to about twice the speed of a caterpillar crawl. I pushed the thumb switch a hair forward. The low growl became a quiet hum. My speed increased.

The floor moved faster below me. I sped up to a slow walk. I continued the arc around the beam, then straightened the line and aimed for the far wall. Halfway there, I slid the switch back to the neutral, off position. The motor stopped, but I continued gliding. The wall grew nearer. I eased the switch into reverse. The motor growled again. I slowly decelerated ... then stopped just short of the wall. I returned the switch to the off position.

"I AM A FUCKING GENIUS!" I cried out. I laughed out loud.

Using the wall to turn around, I launched again into the open airspace. I pushed the power higher, increasing the speed to a casual walk. I floated through the center of the barn, across the floor toward the far wall. Before reaching the wall, I angled my wrist, altered my trajectory, and swung in a wide, slow turn until I faced the opposite direction.

After performing a slow figure eight across the barn floor, I angled the SCUZ upward and rose in the air. The vector took me up and over the cross beams, almost to the roof, where I lowered the angle and flew myself back down to the floor. I misjudged and leveled out a little late and hit the floor with my feet. The key, I decided, is momentum management.

For the next half hour, I flew in circles and figure eights, up and down through the barn space. The combination of joy and discovery, mixed with a dream-like sensation of flight, made me whoop and laugh aloud. Caution ruled, however, and I barely used a quarter of the power available on the SCUZ. The potential power at my fingertips well exceeded the confined spaces of the barn.

After half an hour of continuous testing, the batteries, a pair of AA cells, began to run down. I noted the warning, which came in the form of needing to push the slide farther forward just to sustain the low level of power I had been testing. Skimming above the cross beams halfway between the floor and the roof, I slid the switch to the off position and fumbled the SCUZ back into my pocket. I pulled out a new one and eased it on.

Deploying the backup worked.

I flew myself to the floor beside the barn door, halted and reappeared. I stowed the SCUZ in the pocket of the fishing vest and pushed open the barn door. Outside, a clean blue sky hung over a sprawling sea of green-turning-gold corn. Distant woods showed the early touch of fall colors. A pair of turkey vultures swung in lazy soaring orbits high above the trees.

I pictured launching over the corn, setting a course for the woods and skimming the tops of the trees.

Flying.

My watch said twelve-thirty-two. I was late for work. Not for the first time, I stopped to consider that between the FAA's reluctance to let me fly for a living, and what I had just been doing … maybe I was due for a career change.

13

"Andy's on the Wife Line," Rosemary II popped her head into the pilot's office at Essex County Air Services where I spent the end of the day engaged in the critical and fulfilling task of filing charter flight manifests. I had assigned myself the job because there were no trained monkeys on duty today.

Rosemary II pointed at the blinking light on the phone. I acknowledged with a wave and picked up the phone.

"Hi."

"I need you," Andy said.

"Woman, you can't just call me and demand sex at the drop of a hat." I said it loudly, ensuring that Rosemary II heard me from down the hall.

"Cute," she said. "And, by the way, Yes, I can. However, I need you to do *the other thing* for me."

"I'll do *the other thing* if you'll do the other other thing."

"Stop it. This is serious. Can you meet me after work?"

"When and where?"

"A place called The Sports Bar, out on County VV, about five miles north of 34. Say eight-thirty?"

"Is this police business?"

"Uh-huh. On second thought, I'll pick you up at the airport at eight. We might make multiple stops."

14

"Usual disclaimer?"

"Usual disclaimer," I answered, closing the squad car door and buckling up.

"It bothers me that they simply disappeared," Andy said. "That with the massive effort put on by the highway patrol, and yes, by us locals, they didn't ping once. Nothing." She wheeled the cruiser out of the Essex County Air Services parking lot. Her headlights swept across my car. "I mean, we checked *everything*! I spent most of yesterday and today checking security camera footage where we know it brackets the highway. Nothing!"

"They had a plan. You can't catch 'em all, you know."

"Granted, but something else—it stands out to me. Three Nazis. What do you think the chances are that the remaining three are also goose-steppers?"

"Pretty good odds."

"So, try this on. What if …" Andy knows how to make a point hang in the air. After a few seconds she glanced at me. "What if they never left?"

"No run for the Carolinas?"

"No run for the Carolinas. What if they hunkered down?"

"That's harder than it sounds. You have a high-profile robbery with six—well, five armed, masked men. Some Clerk at the Super 8 Motel is likely to notice. The semi-automatic rifles might be a dead giveaway."

"Ah!" she stabbed an elegant finger in the air. "But suppose they had a place. Out of the way, off the grid, off the back roads, maybe even off-road."

"Okay, that might explain why nobody saw the pickup truck. Hmm…"

"What?"

"Well, you've got a guy from South Carolina." Even as I spoke, Andy nodded. "Prison is the great melting pot of criminal society. On a crew like this, the math alone suggests they're not all from here. Renting a place would be just as likely to draw attention, don't you think?"

"I do. I don't think they rented. I think you're right. It's a melting pot, prison lash-up crew—*and one of the crew is from around here*, and that's where they're hunkered down."

"And by extension…" I said, purposely using one of her pet expressions. She jumped to it.

"By extension, one of their number is potentially known to us. Look, you have a crew with a common bond. Heil Hitler. They probably met in prison, or various prisons—"

"Or some online Nazi dating site," I offered.

"—and via this common bond, and whatever blood oath these goons give each other when they play spin the bottle at their Hitler Youth meetings, you have trust. So, when one of them comes up with an idea for robbing a juicy target, like a big expensive wedding that's been in the papers all summer, putting together a trustworthy crew might not be all that hard."

"And the local guy puts them all up. They put on their Nazi 'jammies and make S'mores and have pillow fights until they do the crime—"

"—and instead of bolting across six states with every department in between looking for them, they're back in their hideout with the home-grown Nazi, drinking beer and comparing Nazi salutes!" Andy beamed a Eureka look at me.

"While the state police, the FBI and the Royal Canadian Mounted Police run around in circles."

We let silence in the car settle the pieces in place.

"Why do you think he fired into the crowd?" I asked.

Andy shook her head sadly. "Random violence designed to terrorize—to keep anyone from being too aggressive. Creates wounded, which creates a whole new dynamic designed to inhibit pursuit. Remember, they went into this knowing there were cops in the room, private security, and maybe even a few random concealed carries. To be honest, one guy could have snatched that urn and made a dash for the parking lot, and maybe got away with it. In all the activity, with enough of a start, that might have worked all by itself. But these guys deployed six—one to command, one to snatch, and four to make sure everyone kept their heads down. We know, then, that the tactical measure of forcing everyone to keep down was part of the planning. Which means the last bit, shooting up the crowd, was also planned. Premeditated."

"Maybe," I said. "But he had that covered when he started popping off shots at the tent. I could not see him, but even from where I was, the cadence, the steady even count of those first shots, that said it wasn't a gunfight."

"I thought the same thing," she said. "I almost came up to fire after the first shot, but then he fired the second, and the next, and I got it."

"I appreciate you not sticking your head up when four guys are standing around a room with ARs looking for targets sticking their heads up."

"The thing is, he could have let it go at that. I think everybody got it. The last four shots—that was terribly senseless and cruel. I feel so bad for Sandy, to have her father hit like that, and have her wedding ruined. And what if that little girl had been hit! Oh, my God! Sandy would never have forgiven herself."

Something gripped me, deep and low. An image of Lane Franklin chained to a wall came, unbidden. I pushed the memory away. Quickly.

"So, I understand the theory. What's the plan? I'm guessing you already tried the Essex County Nazi Directory and had no luck."

"Spent the better part of the day."

"Spill it, Sergeant Stewart. You have something cooked up."

"Ah!" The finger went up again. "You'll appreciate this. A page from the Will Stewart book. How to get people to reveal things when they think no one is looking."

15

Andy and I looked over the hood of her cruiser at The Sports Bar. Set on one corner of an intersection between a lonely county road and a road even less traveled, the bar offered no outward signs of Nazi infestation. It displayed the usual neon in the windows and the usual smattering of cars and pickups in the parking lot. Behind the bar, a weed-choked volleyball court with a torn and sagging net testified that the sports at The Sports Bar were spectator. The building had a second story. I wondered if the owner lived above the bar.

"Okay. The guy who owns this bar posted a lot of crap about how removing Confederate statues desecrates our heritage. He posted a few pictures of himself wearing a Confederate flag t-shirt. It's not terribly overt, but we have to start somewhere."

"How do you know all that?" I asked.

"More toys from Homeland. You can't believe what they have for searching social media sites."

Social media is a mystery to me, but apparently not to the U.S. government. *Another reason I don't participate.*

I blew out a sigh. "Okay, let's do this."

I had already disappeared about a mile back up the road. I unstrapped the seat belt as Andy opened her car door. She stepped out. She lingered long enough for me to grab the steering wheel and pull myself out over her seat. I unfolded my legs and took up a vertical position behind her.

"I'm going to hold your belt. Just walk normally, and don't smack me with the door." I slipped my hand around her heavy belt. She pushed her door closed, clicked to lock the cruiser, and strolled toward the bar entrance.

"This feels weird," she said.

"No mass," I told her. "The property of matter that resists acceleration."

"Thank you, Mister Science Guy."

She pulled me up a set of wooden steps, through a double-door winter entrance, and into the dimly lit bar. Once inside, I released my grip.

The bar gave no hint of anything to support our suspicions. Flat screen televisions hung from the ceiling, playing soundless scenes of a talent competition. Mirrors, glasses, bottles, and beer vendor advertising all seemed to be where they belonged. Stools nudged the bar. High-tops filled the rest of the room. A quick count tallied six patrons and one bartender, a woman. I guessed her day job to be truck driving. Maybe wrestling.

"Evening, officer!" she called out cheerfully. Maybe a little too loudly. I watched Andy finish her head count, then make a note of the door to the kitchen, the door to a back room, and a hallway leading to the Knights and Wenches rooms. Apparently, sports in The Sports Bar included jousting. "What can we do for Essex PD tonight?"

"We're looking for someone who might have been involved in a hate crime," Andy said, loudly enough that the patrons could pick up on it.

The bartender's head shook. "That's not good."

"No, ma'am, it's not good."

I took up a position near one of the high tops, halfway between Andy and the patrons, two of them at high tops, four at one end of the bar. All men.

"What kinda hate crime?" one of the men at the bar asked.

"Windows broken. Spray paint. Anti-Semitic messages. Threats. Know anybody who feels that way?"

"Can't say I do," the man said, taking a deeper interest in his beer.

Andy turned to the bartender. "How about you? Anybody come in here lately mouthing off about blacks or Jews? Maybe complaining about all those Confederate statues coming down?"

"That stuff's been on the news, but nobody in here had much to say about it," she said.

"Anybody mention anything about white power? Nazis?"

She laughed a little. "Not in here. Half the old guys who used to come in here fought the Nazis. You should'a heard 'em talk! You'd think they won the war single-handed. Not so many of them around anymore, though."

Andy produced a business card. "Here. This is important. If you hear anything, would you call me? We're not looking to jam anybody up, we just want to talk. Maybe head off some trouble."

The bartender took the card and tucked it in her shirt pocket.

"Will do."

"Appreciate it."

Andy nodded goodnight to the rest of the patrons and left. I stayed. Through a window, I watched her pull away.

"Goddamn Nazis," the beer drinker, the one who spoke up, said. "I don't know why they're allowed to parade around on TV the way they do. This is America. We spilled a lot of blood putting an end to those shitheads."

"Damn right," one of the other patrons agreed.

"My mom came from Poland," the bartender said, working her way toward the cluster at the end of the bar. "Her family was Jewish. One day they took her to a farm. She was only three. They just gave her to the family and left. That's why she lived. She remembers seeing baby chickens and crying. All her life, baby chicks made her sad. She never saw them again—her family. Mother, father, four brothers. All of them ..."

Heads bobbed in sympathy.

"Freedom of speech," someone else said. "That's why they can parade around."

"It ain't like freedom of speech would last long if they got their way," another drinker said.

"Fucking idiots," the original speaker added.

No other conversation on the subject followed. I floated to the door and waited for the bartender to step back into the kitchen. When I felt certain no one would notice the door opening and closing, I slipped out.

I reappeared outside and began walking. About a hundred yards up the road I called Andy. She picked me up a few minutes later.

"Nothing here," I said. "They think Nazis are a bunch of idiots."

"Dangerous idiots."

"All idiots are dangerous," I said. "Where to next?"

THE SECOND BAR was another bust, with a crowd embracing similar sentiments. After Andy left, the owner and bartender expressed the opinion that these play Nazis should come around on the third Thursday of the month when the VFW holds a meeting at the bar—and maybe walk out with their balls kicked up into their throats.

"You know," Andy said after picking me up. "This is nice."

"Working together?"

"Yeah."

"Tom doesn't know you're doing this, does he?"

"Oh, heavens no!"

THE THIRD BAR PAID OFF.

"Are you a cop or a stripper? Because I got a wad of singles in one pocket and a wad of somethin' else for you in the other!"

I immediately assigned the dirty, rust-eaten Ford pickup in the lot to the equally dirty loudmouth holding down a stool on the far end of the bar. He drank with a companion who slouched under a John Deere cap. I assigned the companion to the late eighties Oldsmobile. Both men looked to be on the weathered side of fifty.

The loudmouth who greeted Andy wore a work shirt with *Marty* embroidered above the pocket. I looked for tattoos and saw gone-blue faded ink running up his neck into a greasy shock of hair that hung down beneath a Goodyear ball cap.

As soon as we cleared the door, I tapped my toes on the floor and floated to the high ceiling. The tavern boasted a modest crowd for a Tuesday night. The row of Harleys parked in front belonged to a group bellied up to the bar, wearing leathers and biker boots. They were the respectable looking contingent. A pair of twenty-somethings played pool on the far end of the room, both looking like strangers to the concept of good hygiene. A heavyset man in Carhart coveralls sat in one of four booths lined up on the wall opposite the bar. He concentrated on a platter of meatloaf.

Andy ignored Marty the Loudmouth, but I noticed she positioned herself closer to him than the bikers.

Andy caught the bartender's attention and gave her speech. She added a vague reference to the would-be Nazi being a person of interest in a robbery. The bartender, bald and ruddy, kept his mouth closed and shook his head.

"Ain't no crime to hate them that's roonin' this great country," Marty the Loudmouth announced when she finished handing her card to the bartender.

"Actually," Andy said, "that's an IQ test. Do you mind my asking, sir, how many beers you've consumed this evening?"

I pushed off the frame above the door and did a slow glide to the end of the room. Touching the wall, I lowered my legs and pressed downward, away from the ceiling, until I achieved a standing position beside a high-top table. Had I been visible, I would have looked like any other patron, except bathed. The pool players had accumulated a line of longneck beers on the table. They played at a languid pace, casting one eye toward the exchange at the bar, and the other at the good-looking lady cop. The bikers watched as well, more entertained by whatever was about to happen than the dance competition on the flat screen above the bar. The meatloaf eater ignored everyone.

"Why, let me count 'em up. This here, this is … lemme see, number one!" he replied. "The first one after the one before it!"

"Cuz that's all the higher you can count!" one of the pool players said. It got a laugh from the other pool player.

"You lookin' to entrap me, officer? Maybe get me on a dee-double-you-eye? Cuz ol' Bob, here, he's my designated driver, ain't you Bob!"

Bob didn't respond.

"Well then, Bob, you be sure and pace yourself, and drive safely," Andy offered a cold smile. "I don't suppose either of you gentlemen know of anyone pretending to be a Nazi around here."

"Hey! I just realized," Marty the Loudmouth said, "it's true what they say! You can put lipstick on a pig!"

A stony silence fell on the bar. All attention shifted to the exchange. I slipped my hand around one of the unfinished beers resting on the high-top. I slid it up against my belly, lifted my shirt, and made it vanish. The bottle kissed my skin, cold and wet.

Holding the high-top for leverage, I moved closer to Marty the Loudmouth.

"Oh, I suppose you could," Andy said, "but it wouldn't make you any prettier." The cold smile stayed in place. Marty may have had four inches and sixty pounds on her, but her stance, her eyes, and the hand resting on her extendable baton said he didn't stand a chance.

I pulled the now vanished beer bottle out from under my shirt. Once vanished, it stayed vanished. I stretched and reached between loudmouth and Bob, tipping the bottle.

"I gotta tell you, I like that shade you got on. It'd look good on my —*shit*!"

He jumped back, tumbling off the stool, directly at me. I braced against the table, hooked one foot around his ankle and shoved. He went down spinning his arms.

A puddle splashed and spread out under his bar stool. He rolled upright on the floor slapping at the black, spreading stain in the crotch of his gray work pants.

"What the fuck!"

Andy said, "Bartender, I think when a patron pees himself, it might be time to cut him off. You have a good night, sir." She turned and nodded at the row of bikers, who returned broad grins. Andy strolled out the door.

Bob lent a hand and pulled his stuttering, swearing companion to his feet. Laughter breezed through the bar. I put the empty beer bottle back on the high-top and released my grip. Cool electricity tingled off my fingertips as the bottle reappeared and took its place among its brothers.

Marty the Loudmouth blustered and swore. He grabbed his beer and marched around Bob to take the dry stool on the other side.

I didn't look to see what Marty did next.

My attention pivoted to the man in the Carhart coveralls, eating meatloaf. I studied the way he leaned close to the window and followed

Andy's cruiser with his eyes. As she pulled away, he reached into his shirt pocket for his cell phone. He dialed and held it to his ear. After a moment, he lowered it, touched the screen, contemplated the phone, then dialed again. When no one answered the second call, he set the phone on the table and returned to his meatloaf.

16

"Seriously, people say that kind of shit?" I asked Andy when she pulled to the side of the road and picked me up. This time I walked almost a quarter of a mile, just to put some trees between me and the bar, because the guy eating meatloaf had a good view up and down the road.

"What?"

"Antagonize a police officer like that?"

She shrugged it off. If it had been me, my nerves would have been jangling. In my life I've been in three fights. None of them ended well—nothing like the choreographed conflicts staged nightly by action heroes on dramatic television. All three fights taught me the same lesson. Nothing is worth getting into a fight.

"It happens, usually with drunks. So?"

"I wish you would've decked him. Put him in cuffs and tossed him in the back seat here."

"Why?"

"Whaddya mean 'why?' He was aggressive, antagonistic—" Andy's smile, although she held her eyes on the road, was aimed at me.

"Rude?"

"Yeah! Really rude!" I got her point but wasn't ready to give up. "And he smelled bad! That's got to be against the law!"

"Right." My wife knows when she has won. "So? Did our beating of the bushes yield any game?"

"Yup. Guess who."

"The guy in the booth. White male, five ten, pushing one-ninety, maybe two hundred. Carhart coveralls. He had ink on his neck, just like Marty."

"Wow. You got all that?"

"He ordered the meatloaf."

"Okay, now you're just showing off. But yeah, he took a keen interest in your departure, and pulled out his phone right away. He made four calls to the same number but got no answer."

Andy sat up a little in her seat, excited. "Did you get the number?"

"No."

"Will! That was the whole point of all this! Shake the bushes, see what pops out, see if we can get someone to try to reach out to—"

She looked across the seat at me. I held up a cell phone.

"You didn't!"

"I did!"

"My God, Will! You can't steal evidence from civilians like that! I can't touch that! I can't use that!"

"It's got the number he dialed. Four times. Twice right away, two more times before I put the gleep on it." I wiggled the phone back and forth for her, like a prize. "It was kinda cool. There was a picture on the wall above his booth. Some farm horses pulling a wagon. I lifted it far enough to get it off the hook and dropped it on the table. Bam! He jumped out of his skin, and I laid both hands on the phone. It vanished. And … here I am! Bearer of the big clue that breaks the case!"

"How am I supposed to explain how we got the number? I thought you were—I don't know—going to look over his shoulder. Memorize the number. Do that magic memory trick you do."

"Really? How were you going to explain that? The Divisible Man did it?"

"The what?"

I heaved a sigh. "Remember when I told you about that whole business of blowing my chance with Mauser—when I missed his car and wound up on a roof on the other side of the street?"

Andy nodded but managed to make a face that wanted to know what this had to do with anything.

"There was this kid, looking out the window. She saw me. I mean fully visible me. And she started screaming, so I did the only thing I could think of. I disappeared. And she saw me. She saw me disappear. So, then she started screaming even more—'Mommy! Mommy! It's Divisible Man!'"

Andy laughed. It burst out of her.

"I know," I said. "'...what an extraordinary view of the world a child has.'"

Andy looked at me.

"Agatha Christie."

Andy shook her head as she put on her directional signal and made a turn. We accelerated through the night on one of Essex County's letter-designated county roads, headed for civilization.

"Give it to me," she said.

"This?" I held up the phone.

She nodded. She didn't even want to say it out loud. I handed over the phone.

"So, what's next?"

"You're going home. I'm going back to the station."

My role as Doctor Watson had come to its conclusion for the night. "We did good, right?"

She chuckled and that was all the answer I would get.

17

Andy works the three-to-eleven shift, acting as both patrol officer and patrol supervisor, thanks to her rank as Sergeant. Her next step up the ladder in law enforcement is to become a Detective and she's nearly ready for the examination. Essex PD already has a detective and budgets only for one, but that won't stop Andy from taking the exam.

She may still be a patrol sergeant, but it was a detective who came home to me that Tuesday night.

"Did you find them?" I asked before she finished closing the kitchen door.

"Nope," she said with a coy smile. "Let me get out of this uniform. Why don't you put in a pizza?"

"Okay," I said, not quite connecting the 'Nope' with her good mood.

"And do we have limes?" she asked, climbing the stairs.

We did.

Fifteen minutes later the kitchen smelled like a frozen pizza baking. Andy, hair unfurled and in her favorite boxers and t-shirt, folded her long legs under her on the sofa. We clicked icy Coronas and sipped.

"No, I didn't get a location on the phone," she answered my questioning look. She waited a moment, then broke a smile. "But I got a name! Maybe two! And a billing address!"

"Usual disclaimer," I said. "What names?"

"First, the name of the owner of the phone you stole. Benjamin Braddock. No record. He's a railroad maintenance supervisor. Can't pin any Nazi behavior on him. In any event, I'm more interested in the phone number our meatloaf lover called. Marie Paulesky," Andy said.

"So, it didn't go to a burner phone. I one hundred percent expected it to be a burner phone."

"Genuine U.S. Cellular registered account. With an address."

"Hold on a second," I said. "I hate to rain on your parade but doesn't the ordinary-ness of that make it more likely our meatloaf lover was making—I don't know—just *calls*. Like to his wife? Or girlfriend? Did we just chase a wild goose?"

Andy shook her head.

"Okay, okay," she put her hand up in a Stop gesture, "back up the truck. I never did tell you why that bar was on the list. I did a search on all the calls we had related to bars in the county. Two years ago, we had an assault complaint. Guy gets beat up. Somebody calls the cops. We respond and by the time we get there he's all about telling us he just fell down the stairs. Nobody else is around, and they don't have any stairs, but regardless he won't file a complaint. It comes to nothing. But—" she threw up an elegant finger "—I checked the transcript on the 9-1-1 call and guess what?"

"Nazis!"

Andy touched the finger to my nose.

"The girl making the 9-1-1 call said that Nazi skinheads were beating up her boyfriend."

"And she's Marie what's-her-name?"

Andy gave me an *are-you-kidding?* look. "No."

"Then how does Marie tie to Nazi robbers?"

"Geography."

"Geography! Of course, and here I thought it was Algebra."

"Geography. Do you remember the map I pulled up last night? Essex County?" I nodded. "Well, Marie Paulesky lives less than eight miles from Cinnamon Hills, and our new favorite bar is another four miles away on the same line."

I sat back. She sat back. She dipped a long, knowing nod at me.

"I looked up the address on the cell account. The property is listed under the name of Robert Stahl. I ran that name but got nothing. I did a more general run on the name Stahl and came up with an Eric Stahl. Not sure of the relationship, but guess who has a handful of arrests for assault, disorderly, etc.?"

"Like bar fight assaults?"

"Uh-huh! And guess who looks like a skinhead and has neck ink in his mug shot."

"I can't imagine."

"And guess who happens to be left-handed."

I looked at my wife. "Four. Door. Our number four thief was left-handed."

"Now, that's obviously circumstantial, and the tattoos are not definitive. I could not make it out and the recording officer didn't log a description. Tattoos are so common now. It isn't listed as Nazi symbols or numbers."

"You think this Eric Stahl could be one of the six? Hosting the hunker-down?"

Andy arched her eyebrows, and I swear the gold flecks in her green eyes sparkled. "He's the right age for it. He's twenty-eight. Marie Paulesky is twenty-six. They might be a couple. Tomorrow I plan to see what her story is. Previous addresses. Banking. Social media. I didn't have time for all that tonight, plus it was too late to make phone calls to landlords, employers, etc. I hope to see if anybody knows who she was dating."

I rubbed her thigh, smooth and creamy, thinking.

"What's next?"

"Already did it. I deployed spy satellites and tasked them to shoot reconnaissance photos of the Nazi headquarters."

"More Homeland Security magic?"

"Google," she said, grinning at her gullible husband. "If the pin dropped on the right spot, it's one very isolated hideout. Not a bad choice for a place to lie low. Oh, and guess what the Google street level view shows—never mind, I'll tell you. A gate, chains, locks, the whole deal. And what looks like posted warning signs. I could not read them, but my guess is they're not welcome signs."

"Sounds like Nazi headquarters to me."

"Here's another tiny piece. I got nothing when I tried to ping the location of the phone." She waited for me to figure it out, but I'm a little slow and she could not wait all night. "Think about it. If you want to set up your phone so us cops can't ping it for a GPS location, you must turn off your data plan, your Wi-Fi, your GPS—or else pull the battery out, which obviously nobody does, because then the phone is just a chunk of plastic in your pocket. So why am I not getting a ping on a phone for an ordinary citizen with an ordinary cell phone account?"

"The absence of evidence is evidence," I said.

"Exactly."

"You do know you're really painting a picture here," I said. "Can I assume you passed all this on to DCI and the FBI? Can you get a warrant?"

"Hmmm," she adopted a thoughtful expression. "Let's see. We have a patrol sergeant suggesting that all of law enforcement in the Midwest and Mid-Atlantic states is chasing their own tails. We have a Nazi hunt that looks a lot like a female cop taking her husband bar hopping. Oh! And we have a random name from a random number from a stolen cell phone from a guy who raised suspicion because he was eating meatloaf. Which led to a property with a No Trespassing sign. Sure. I wrote it up and e-mailed it to the director of the FBI."

"You do make a point," I said. "But you left out Divisible Man."

She chuckled. "Right. Forgot about him. I'll wake up the director right now and brief him."

She took a long pull from her Corona.

"Look, I know it's dangerous to shape evidence to fit the crime. I could easily wind up with egg on my face when it turns out Marie is just Marie, and Eric is just Eric, and he might be a skinhead ass, but an ass who has nothing to do with Cinnamon Hills. I'm going to go up there for a drive-by in the morning, although I'm sure I won't get past the gate. And it doesn't matter, because even if I had reasonable suspicion, I don't have enough for a warrant. Unless we can connect Marie Paulesky to Eric Stahl, and Eric Stahl to our Carolina Nazi, I'm not sure how we get a closer look."

I knew a way but decided to hold the suggestion until morning. The stove timer buzzed. I patted her on the thigh and bounced off the sofa to fetch dinner.

We ate pizza and she rehashed what she knew, poking at it from different angles, coming back to the same conclusion. Satisfied she could ferret out nothing further, she closed the mental file and changed her focus. She had something else on her mind. I liked to think my hand stroking her thigh triggered it. More likely, she had a charge in her veins from the evening's investigation. Either way, I didn't complain when she took my hand and led me upstairs to the bedroom.

18

"You've got to be kidding me."

My wife stood, arms folded, lower lip extended, long legs planted—the trifecta of skepticism.

"I've already tested it. It works!"

Andy took the SCUZ from my hand and turned it over in her own. She rolled her eyes and heaved a faithless sigh. "This? Will, you told me your biggest fear with *the other thing* is to wind up too high, unable to stop. That doing it outdoors scared you."

"Which is precisely why I made these."

"Okay, but let's go back to problem number one with you using *it*. Nothing dangerous. We agreed on that."

I didn't remember agreeing to anything.

"How is this dangerous?"

She held up the silly looking little unit. "Really? You're going to bet your life on flashlight batteries? And if we're right about this, and those guys are hunkered down up there, how is that *not* dangerous? They have fully automatic weapons."

"And they're going to, what? Shoot me down? Wouldn't they have to see me first?"

Her mouth opened to speak.

"I can get upwind, shut this down, and just float overhead on the breeze. Silent. I can see if there's anyone there. See if the truck is there. They won't hear me coming. They won't see me coming. I'll be out of there with nobody the wiser."

She shook her head. The gesture said, *Absolutely not.*

"I think it's more dangerous for you to go cruising by a couple times, eyeballing the place. If that's their hideout, you can bet they're watching the road. Besides, you're not likely to see anything. The driveway is at least a quarter mile through thick woods."

Andy posed to argue. A lock of hair fell across one eye, a warning flag.

"C'mon, Dee, you know I can do this."

She brushed the hair back. She turned the small device over in her hand.

"What do you call this stupid thing?"

"A SCUZ," I said proudly.

"What?"

"Self-Contained Unit for Zooming."

"Oh, you are not calling it that." She tossed it back at me and stalked away from the garage, leaving me grinning.

She called over her shoulder, "Fine. We're taking your car."

19

Despite not actually sleeping until after two a.m., Andy rose with the sun and had us on the road quickly after our brief discussion on the merits of my SCUZ. Andy drove, claiming we would get there quicker, and to that I will testify. My default speed is twelve over the limit and her lead foot puts me to shame. I confess to hoping she gets pulled over one day, just to see how she handles it, but she never does.

Essex County, like most counties in Wisconsin, is a rectangle, yet is loosely divided into thirds. The "Lakes Region," a label intended to boost real estate value for already expensive homes lining three oblong lakes, occupies the northeast corner of the county. The city of Essex anchors the southwest corner of the county. Farmland dominates the center and northwest corner. In the farthest acres of the northwest corner, a millionaire golf-lover scraped the Cinnamon Hills resort out of corn fields and a river basin. The river basin winds from west to east, fringed with a mix of marsh and state forest which extends north into the next three counties.

Google Maps dropped the pin for the Marie Paulesky address directly in the center of a thick, wooded area eight miles west of Cinnamon Hills. Viewing the satellite image of the area, Andy initially saw no sign of habitation. She had to zoom in and scroll back and forth to find a thin, winding driveway that ended in a cluster of structures. A house, a garage, a small barn, and a smaller shed. From the structures to the nearest road, I guessed the straight-line distance to be a quarter of a mile. The road carried the incongruous name of Bayview Lane and ran east to west, nowhere near a body of water.

"I have to launch on a line that will take me northeast over the house," I told Andy. "Winds at Essex County are two-twenty at five knots. Nice and light, out of the southwest. I checked winds aloft, too. Should be no factor."

My crisp pilot talk did nothing to boost her confidence in the plan. She said, "Let's do a pass on the driveway first. Who knows what has changed since those Google images were taken."

She turned onto Bayview Road forty minutes after leaving our home on the southern border of the county.

Sunshine angled down through trees riding the peak of fall color. Brilliant yellow, orange, and red splashed the wooded landscape on both sides of the road. The road scarcely spanned a lane and a half. It would be easy to monitor the scant traffic using it. I pulled on a baseball cap and slid down in the seat.

"What are you doing?"

"Woman driving with a kid," I said. "That's less threatening than two adults eyeballing the landscape."

The driveway came up quickly.

"Holy shit…" I muttered, trying hard not to gape. Andy spared a glance, but only one and drove on rigidly facing forward.

The driveway had the same gate we'd seen in the photos, but it had been reinforced. Taking a page from anti-terrorist doctrine, the owners angled black railroad ties at intervals across the driveway in front of and behind the gate. Any vehicle would have to thread its way through, very slowly. A heavy chain held the gate closed, secured with a fat padlock. Barbed wire topped the gate.

Two hand-painted signs made from four-by-eight sheets of plywood bracketed the gate.

KEEP OUT and NO ENTRY dominated the signs. I wished I had been ready with a camera because extensive writing followed on both signs. I caught a few words. Danger. Explosives. Lethal force. *Posse comitatus*. White America. Just as quickly, I reminded myself how easy it would be for the occupants to have cameras of their own.

"Okay," I said. "Even if it's not the guys we're looking for, it sure looks like a nest of vipers."

"I am less and less liking the idea of you doing this," Andy said.

"And based on what we just saw, we both know it's a far better idea than trying to sneak up there—or trying a full frontal, warrant-waving entry. I suppose you could launch a drone, but they make noise. Why wake anyone up to the fact we're looking? This is the best idea."

Her body language told me being right didn't make my argument any more palatable. "Look, I don't want to turn around and go past that again."

"Agreed."

"We'll go around. Make a big square. That will put us back where you said you want to start."

Fifteen minutes later she pulled off the county road onto a lane that accessed a corn field. Less than a hundred feet away, Bayview Road formed a junction with the county road.

"Give me your cell phone," she said.

"Why?"

She put her hand out and I obliged. "Here, you take mine. And put this on." She handed me a small Bluetooth earpiece.

I fitted the device around my right ear, inserted the ear bud, and moved the stubby microphone to aim forward along my cheek.

She dialed my phone. After a few seconds, I heard her phone ring in my ear. I touched the earpiece.

"Divisible Man Airways," I said, "If you can't see us, we've already arrived."

"Can you hear me?" Andy asked my phone.

"Perfectly." I heard her in my ear and in the car, slightly out of synch.

"Okay, we stay on the line the whole time, got it?"

"Affirmative."

"I want running commentary, but obviously not so anyone can hear you. If you need to cut off conversation, say 'Silence!'"

We stepped out of the car. I pulled the fishing vest out of the back seat and slid it on.

"Put the phone, here," she took the phone out of my hand and slid it into a pocket. "Try not to touch the screen. Those things all have fresh batteries, right?"

"All new."

"And you tested all four units?"

"All four SCUZ units are good to go!"

"I am not calling it that," she said. She looked around at the sparkling and crisp fall morning. Before the crash, a morning like this would have found us running together—or rather her running and me throwing myself down the road beside her. "One more time, Pilot. This is a flyover. Non-stop, got it? No dropping in for a closer look."

"Affirmative."

She grabbed the arm holes of the vest and pulled me into her for a rich taste of her lips. "I love you."

"Good. 'Cuz I'm kinda crazy for you."

Fwooomp! I vanished before her eyes.

"Dammit! Give me some warning when you do that!"

"Warning," I said and kissed her. She blinked in wonder.

"Yeah, that was really weird."

20

I started floating the moment I vanished. Andy let go of the vest and I drifted slowly away from the car. She put my phone to her ear.

"Can you hear me?"

"Loud and clear." I released the Velcro flap on a vest pocket and pulled out the first SCUZ. I held it out before me like anyone would hold a flashlight. I moved the slide controller forward with my thumb. The electric motor grumbled. Cool air moved across my hand.

"I can hear that," Andy warned.

"They won't. I'll stay high. When I get close, I'll drift. Silent running."

The propulsion unit pulled me forward, away from the car, over the ditch. My feet tickled the tops of tall grass, milkweeds, and cornflowers.

A flash of guilt struck me because I knew Andy stood behind me, eyes straining in a futile attempt to see me, worried and scared—and by contrast I had to grit my teeth to keep from shouting for joy.

Holy jumping Jesus! This is freaking amazing!

Flight! The intractable desire to leaving the earth for the realm of the sky, had been in my blood since I first looked up. I chased it with paper airplanes and rubber band airplanes and eventually working six days a week on a farm to pay for flying lessons. Always looking for what I called the "Peter Pan moment," when the earth falls away beneath me. I feel it every time I push the throttles forward and the wheels break their lingering kiss with the runway. It doesn't matter if it's the first flight on a crystal September morning or the sixth takeoff on an all-day charter run.

This was the Peter Pan moment in a form so pure it stole my breath. Wildflower tops moved silently past my feet. The landscape performed its magical peripheral shift, falling as I rose.

I have got *to show this to Andy!* Maybe then she would understand.

Rising with the unit angled up, I skimmed over dry corn tassels. A field spread out beneath me.

I could not help myself.

"Oh my God, Andy! You cannot believe what this is like!"

"This isn't a joy ride, Pilot. Stick to business!"

Oh yeah, I've got to take that girl for a serious ride.

"Roger that."

I had barely moved the power slide forward. Butterflies outran me. I added power and accelerated. Speed brought a whole new wave of euphoria. Blue sky above me invited me to go higher. Brown corn below me wanted me to dip down and skim my feet through the tassels. The corn field ran long and narrow beside the county road. I crossed it on a diagonal. The tree line on its eastern border approached. I angled my wrist and rose higher, higher, again feeling breathless exhilaration as everything around me fell away.

Bright, fall-colored trees slid toward me. I rose until the tops of the trees formed a plateau. For the third time in as many minutes, I clenched my teeth against a scream of pure joy.

More power. I moved faster. I felt the air accelerate against my body. I noticed a slight drift to the left as the gentle morning breeze above the trees added its influence. I corrected slightly to hold what I thought would be the best path toward the nest of Nazis.

Birds flew ahead and above me. Geese chased each other, organizing and re-organizing their V formations. A trio of turkey vultures orbited high, performing their inscrutable trick of flight without flapping their wings. Below me, among the trees, smaller birds darted. I wondered if any of them sensed my passage.

"Hey. Running commentary, please."

"It would only sound like a nature documentary," I replied. I knew better than to spill the joy I felt. That would only irritate Andy, who undoubtedly paced the road beside the car.

"I don't care. Recite poetry if you want. Just talk to me."

"Level just above the trees, speed, roughly as fast as you run. No sign of structures." I worked my pilot-to-ATC communication voice, and then threw in a little NASA. "All systems Go."

"Any sign of activity in the woods? Trails? Paramilitary crap? Gun ranges? Survivalist baloney?"

"Negative. Just trees."

I added power and picked up speed.

"I'm going a little higher for a better view ahead," I said, angling my wrist upward.

This thing really climbs!

My trajectory adjusted. I gained altitude. I leveled off thirty feet above the trees. The higher altitude diminished the sense of speed, which I estimated at fifteen knots. The drift angle dissipated, telling me that above the trees, the wind blew on a path matching my intended course, just as planned.

I moved the slide back and stopped the motor. I continued to float forward.

"I've got a gap in the trees ahead. That's our target."

"Okay."

"You're supposed to say, 'Roger.'"

"Roger."

A fourth turkey vulture joined the trio orbiting ahead. I made a note of the "traffic" as I approached the small clearing where the structures should be. The big black birds rose and fell on hidden currents, sometimes high, sometimes dropping down to my altitude. A bird strike in an airplane can be serious business. With a six-foot wingspan, having one of them collide with me fully exposed would be no fun.

"Two hundred yards to the target," I told Andy. "Still nothing but woods under me. I can see rooftops now."

I set up an angle that would put me just above the trees well before I reached the clearing, minimizing the chances I would need to use the power unit to adjust the flight path. I planned to cross the target in full stealth mode.

"How many buildings?"

Andy wanted to keep me talking.

"Can't see them all yet, but so far it looks like the same layout we saw on the satellite recon. I've got a rooftop for the house, the small barn … hold on, there's the garage. The shed is behind the barn and out of my sight line."

I dropped lower and then leveled off. The treetops flowed a few feet beneath my feet.

More of the clearing revealed itself.

"Lots of junk. Typical rural Wisconsin collection. Got a few cars, look like derelicts. The usual derelict washing machine. Not seeing other vehicles yet."

Something colorful caught my eye in the woods below. It appeared, then disappeared in the moving, unfolding gaps in the trees. Bright yellow and white. Then something else, not far from the first. Pink.

Both objects broke into the open space below me.

"Oh Christ!" I said.

"What?"

I glanced up at the vultures circling. My mouth went dry.

"What is it, Will?"

"Stand by."

I threw my wrist to the left and started a tight circle.

I looked at the forest floor below me. Yellow and white jacket with a fluffy collar and a shock of reddish hair. A girl. Grade school age. She lay face down, arms thrown forward. Pink. Another girl, smaller, a few feet away, on her back. I saw her face but could not make out features. Something was wrong with it.

"Will! Talk to me!"

I completed the orbit, never taking my eyes from the tiny bodies. There was no doubt.

"Andy," I said "There are two children. They're both dead, Andy. Jesus. In the woods, about fifty yards from the house. This is bad."

"I'm coming up there!"

"Wait!" I turned away and aimed for the house. Scanning ahead, I searched the yard as it became exposed before me. "Just wait. Let me do this."

"I'm getting in the car and going to the end of the driveway."

"I'm over the yard. Don't come up here! Wait until I can tell you what's going on here!"

She didn't answer.

I slid the power controller forward to create thrust and turned the unit with my wrist. Passing over the yard, then over the barn, I circled to the left around the perimeter of the open yard.

My heart hammered.

Children.

The turn took me to the tree line at the edge of the open space. I continued in an arc, running above the edge of the trees.

The yard lay to my left below me, lifeless. Kids' toys peppered the lawn, carelessly forgotten in the middle of play. A lawn mower slowly surrendered to high grass. A garden offered bright orange pumpkins attached to green vines. Several pickup trucks occupied weedy parking spaces, looking like they hadn't moved in years. A newer model sat on the driveway, a gunmetal gray crew cab, the same color I'd seen at the wedding.

"Andy, I've got the truck. It's here."

"Be careful!" she called out, having switched to speaker phone. I heard my car as she gunned the motor.

I didn't answer. I passed over the spot where the two patches of bright colors lay silent in the leafy forest bed. I tried not to look too closely. One glance sufficed.

Two small girls, motionless in a bed of leaves.

I clenched both my jaw and fists and tightened my orbit and descended. The yard spread out before me. I moved the slide backward in a series of pulses. The action reduced my speed. The curved trajectory took me down over the driveway, facing the house.

Blank, dark windows projected lifelessness.

I pulsed the power unit and performed a slow glide to a picture window at the front of the house. From a few feet away, I squinted into the interior. Lights off. Old furniture. Beer empties on the coffee table.

"Talk to me," Andy commanded.

"No sign of life. I'm checking windows. Let's go with silence, okay? I don't see anyone, but just to be safe. Stand by."

I pulsed my way to the corner of the house and rounded it.

The woman lay halfway out the side door, face down, black hair spread with the ends fused into a pool of nearly black dried blood. Her body blocked and held the door open. I hadn't seen her on the pass around the house. An awning over the door blocked sight of her.

She lay across the threshold. One hand clutched a jacket.

She got the kids out. Told them to run.

I maneuvered to the open screen door and gripped the edge. Thick, foul odor rose around me. Gray darkness enveloped the mudroom inside the door and the kitchen beyond. My eyes adjusted and details formed. A table. Chairs. Men seated at the chairs, slumped over their plates. Blood on the floor.

I put my hand to my face, to my nostrils. It didn't help.

Oh, you cannot be thinking of going in there!

I pulled on the screen door. Gliding forward, over the woman, I ignored the voice of common sense screaming at me. A furnace ran deep in the house. Warm air pushed past me, out the door. The open door must have chilled the house, causing the furnace to run continuously, which was not beneficial to the inert human flesh at the kitchen table.

I stopped at the kitchen doorway.

Four dead men sat around their last supper, or breakfast, or whatever it had been. The two on the side of the table facing away from me slumped over among tipped dinner ware and spilled beer bottles. Facing them, another man reclined in his chair, head tipped back, features bloated. He had a third eye, a hole in the center of his forehead beside a tattoo of a swastika. The fourth had fallen sideways, halfway off the chair, onto another chair.

Black tactical pants. A biker chain hung from the wallet of the one nearest me. I didn't need to get any closer to recognize that he was one of the thieves from Cinnamon Hills. I wasn't about to check the bloating skin for tattoos.

"Andy, it's them. They're here. Four of them. They're all dead. Jesus Christ." I pushed back and spun myself, then pulsed the unit and floated out the door, over Marie Paulesky's dead body and into the mercifully fresh air.

"I'm at the gate."

"I'll meet you there. Give me a few minutes."

"Will…" She let a long pause hang on the cellular line between us. "I know we have to call this in. But we have to figure a few things out first."

"I know. Just…I'll be there in a couple minutes."

I set the unit at a low growl and eased toward the open garage.

The mother got the children out of the house but didn't make it herself. The killer shot her in the back of the head, then stepped over her. The kids ran. They made it to the tree line, into the woods. He followed.

The open garage door exposed a dark, oil-scented space filled with both identifiable and unidentifiable junk. A boat dominated the parking space. Boxes. Disassembled machinery. Welding tanks. A workbench. The boat had what I needed.

Fwooomp! I reappeared and went to work. It took me a few minutes to free the dry, musty-smelling canvas boat cover.

Fifty yards. That's as far as they got.

The older girl must have held her sister's hand.

He shot the older girl first. She fell forward.

The baby girl took a few steps, but then turned back for her sister. That's when she was shot. Facing her killer.

Later, I wouldn't remember walking across the yard and into the woods. I wouldn't remember covering them. But I would remember thinking, *They're so small!*

The baby sister, on her back.

Birds had been at her face.

I wanted to look away, but I could not. Somebody had to look. Somebody had to know.

21

Andy waited at the gate. I eased over the tangle of barbed wire and reappeared. Andy had been pacing, but she took one look at my face and froze.

We didn't speak for a moment. I set about stowing the power unit. Words came slowly.

"Marie Paulesky. I'm betting it's her. You were right," I said, trying hard to keep a voice. Trying hard to deal in facts, not emotion. "She must have been the girlfriend. She lived here, probably with Stahl. She had two kids. I think." I suddenly realized it was possible she had more than two. "One of the six killed all four of the others, the woman, and—um, her two little—" Words jammed in my throat. "Shit! Andy, you need to find out right away if she had more kids. If she did, maybe someone got away." Even as I said it, I recognized faint hope when I saw it.

"We will. We need to work this out. We can't screw up here. And we can't—you know, have you involved."

I walked over to the gate. Stahl had used a split aluminum farm gate, but to be a tough guy, had wrapped barbed wire around the tops of both halves. It was an idiotic gesture, considering you could simply walk around the end, where the gate hinged on a post. There was no fence sealing the property perimeter. A logging chain had been looped around the center where the two halves of the gate met. A heavy padlock secured the chain.

"What are you doing?"

"Whoever did this let himself out and locked the gate behind him," I said.

"And?"

I turned to her.

"I won't do this unless you agree." I said. "Try this: Everything we said last night, when we were joking about contacting the director of the FBI. Flip it around and look at it as solid police work. You followed your theory that maybe these guys didn't head for the Carolinas. You investigated the Nazi connection. I didn't take a tour of the house, but I bet you find a swastika flag and a collection of Wehrmacht crap in there. You asked around some bars and one of the patrons remembered a bar fight, a skinhead named Stahl."

"I'll have to BS that part. I can't connect to all this through Marie Paulesky's phone number."

"Right. But you did all the legwork, found the property, drove up here to check it out. Found all this—" I pointed at the signs, which on closer inspection, contained a venomous stream of threat and hate below the KEEP OUT and NO ENTRY headlines. "You decided to stop in and ask a few questions. But you only made it into the yard when you saw the vultures circling."

"The what?"

I pointed at the sky.

"My God. That's what those are?"

"Yes." I fought off the image of the little girl's face. "You then saw the body of the woman. She's halfway out the back door. I think she tried to run."

Andy nodded.

"Then the kids. They're—um—" I needed a breath. "About fifty yards due west, in the woods. You found them. You took a boat cover from the garage to cover them. Because of the birds."

"Oh," she said, touching her fingers to her lips. "*Oh, Will.*"

We exchanged looks. I remembered what I'd seen; she imagined.

"That's when you call it in."

Andy shook off the image and considered the play. She probed for holes. Not to cover her ass, but to ensure that this was done properly, that justice was done. Had there been a threat to the living, had there been a chance of saving the children, I doubt I could have stopped her from charging up that driveway, and to hell with procedure.

"What about all this?" She gestured at the barricades.

"The gate was open when you got here," I said. "The killer left it open when he left. Are you okay with that?"

She gave a determined nod.

I turned,

Fwooomp! I vanished.

I closed a fist around the padlock. The body disappeared as if a liquid had spread around it. The semicircular shank remained visible. Where the missing body joined the visible steel shank, the metal looked faded, frayed.

I jerked the body of the lock and felt a soft tug and snap. The shank fell out of the chain loops and jingled on the ground at my feet.

Fwooomp! I reappeared and held out the padlock body for Andy to see.

She knew I'd done this before, breaking the chain that held Lane Franklin. Even so, a look of wonder crossed her face.

"Let me have that."

I handed it over. She bent and picked up the shank, then walked across the road and hurled both into the woods.

"I think we can get the car in there." I pointed at the arrangement of railroad ties, angled at intervals on the gravel driveway. "Whoever did this drove a vehicle out. He locked the gate when he left. Who knows how long it would have been before anyone went up there? My bet is we won't find the key to that padlock anywhere in the house."

Andy regarded the driveway and its barricades. "Yes, I can get a cruiser in there. You're not coming."

"Yes, I am," I said.

"No."

"Dee—"

"No," she shook her head. "Will, do you have any reason to believe anyone is alive up there?"

"No, but—"

She took my hand. "Come. Let's go home. I need to get to work so I can come back up here on duty. Like you said. Follow the leads."

I stood my ground.

"Will, please."

Nothing I said for the next thirty minutes of driving changed her mind. After setting a new world record for changing into her uniform, she left me in the dust of our driveway, feeling the ghost of her kiss on my lips.

22

I felt dumped. And angry. And depressed.

Worst of all, I got it.

Andy could not be blamed for keeping me out of the picture. She faced the daunting task of not only going back to the Stahl place and "discovering" the massacre, but then having the state investigators and FBI descend on her. She and the Essex PD had a whole new crime scene to manage. She would have enough to explain without coming up with a reason why I was standing around.

The sight of the two small girls haunted me. Puffy little jackets, probably new for school and worn proudly, now discarded in a bed of leaves.

Run. Take your sister and run! Run and don't look back.

What would a mother think and feel in that moment? Would the bullet she took have been a mercy?

I needed to shake this off.

I slid into my fishing vest.

"I need to fly," I said to the silence and the midmorning sunshine. I stood on our gravel driveway behind the house. "Fuck the FAA!"

Fwooomp! The sound in my head, a part of my life for less than sixty days, felt familiar and comforting. My feet slipped free of the gravel.

This was the very thing I had feared. Being out in the open, away from grips and pivot points, away from beams and structures.

I channeled my anger into open defiance of common sense.

Don't fly angry.

Screw that. I *was* angry. Not at Andy. I was angry at the black figure I pictured in my mind. A specter who shot a mother in the back of the head, then walked out into a yard and shot a child in the back. Then another. I was angry at the four dumb shits around that table who brought the murderer into that house, into the too-short lives of those children. One of the dead men, I felt certain, was Stahl. Did the little girls call him Daddy?

He should burn in Hell.

I extracted the propulsion unit I had used over the Stahl property and slid the lever forward. I began to move. My thumb pushed the slide for more power. The electric motor's low growl became a hum and the prop's wind over my wrist increased. I moved faster. I pointed loosely in the direction of the corn field at the back of the yard, much larger than the one I had skimmed earlier in the morning. I accelerated.

More power.

The acceleration grew to a walk. A jog. A run. Soon, even Andy could not have kept pace. The wind pressed on my skin and fluttered my unseen clothing. Faster. More power.

The corn field swept under me. I flexed my wrist downward slightly, until my feet dragged across the tops of the tassels. The friction slowed me.

More power.

The acceleration continued. I put my speed at over twenty. Now I aimed my wrist to the left, immediately changing direction. Then to the right, swinging back again. I executed a series of slalom maneuvers, back and forth. The motor hummed at less than half power. I kicked it up. I estimated my speed to be nearing thirty knots. My eyes watered.

The man wearing makeup shot up the tent, then put four bullets at random into the wedding guests. I watched him shoot a member of his crew and leave him.

It could not have been anyone but him. He killed the other four. Then a mother. Then a child trying to save her baby sister. Then—

I pushed the slide throttle to the max. The electric motor screamed. Wind tore at my clothing.

When Lane Franklin had been taken, she had been stripped and chained to a wall. A child made ready for a pedophile predator. I found her and freed her. In the process I freed something else.

Murder.

Murder in my heart. Maybe we all have it. Maybe we bury it, and the goal is to live to the end of our lives without ever letting it see daylight. I let it loose when I found Lane, but with Lane home safely, I thought I could bury it again.

I was wrong.

Racing across the corn tops, I aimed for the trees at the far side of the field. I estimated my speed between forty and fifty knots. The air resisting me felt solid. I squeezed my eyelids down to slits. They watered, and tears streaked back along the side of my head. The trees came up fast. I tilted the power unit up and zoomed past the first branches onto the plateau of treetops. The earth fell away. *Flight* flooded my soul, washing it.

Sun-painted rural Wisconsin spread out below me.

I skimmed above the trees, dipped down to follow a stream. I rode unseen above a farmer harvesting row after row of corn. I circled a lone oak tree standing in the middle of a field, where the first farmer clearing the land had taken pity on its sapling soul a hundred years ago.

I flew, and when the power unit quit, I coasted in silence as the relative wind slowly decelerated me. Then I deployed a second power unit, racing down paths in the air that existed in my eye alone.

A third unit took me home.

Minutes after coming to a stop in the farmyard, my phone rang.

"Hey," I said to Andy.

"Hey." I knew by now she had reached the Stahl property and had called it in. We shared silence now knowing each of us possessed indelible images neither of us would ever forget. "Just wanted to call."

"I'm glad you did."

I listened to her breathing. Sirens sang in the background.

"Probably be late tonight."

"I'll be here."

"Don't wait up. I mean it."

I used silence to avoid refusing her.

"They're here. Gotta go. I love you."

"I love you."

23

I spent the afternoon in the Essex County Air Services maintenance shop, keeping one step ahead of Doc, the resident airframe and powerplant mechanic. He put me to work helping with an annual inspection of a Cessna 421 Golden Eagle, a muscular twin-engine beauty built in the 1960s.

I hoped Andy would call again, but she didn't. No surprise. There hadn't been seven murders in Essex County in the last two centuries combined. Toss in the politics tied to the case and my wife carried the weight of the world on her shoulders.

"Hey!" Earl Jackson stuck his bald head and fireplug frame into the 421's cabin. I looked up from the job of removing floorboard inspection covers.

"What's up, Boss?"

"You're going to Tulsa next week," he said.

That got my attention.

"You think that's the one?" I referred to one of seven Beechcraft King Air 90s we considered as possible replacements for the Piper Navajo I had crashed.

"Could be," Earl said.

I should have been thrilled. Adding a King Air, a well-equipped turbine-engine pressurized twin to the fleet had topped my wish list for years. I should have been itching to pack a bag and go, but my first thought was whether Andy might need me.

"When?" I asked.

"Probably Monday. Also, I'm going to Madison on Friday. I want to see how Bob is doing. You and Andy should come along."

"Andy talked about going on Saturday. Let me see if she can move it to Friday." I had doubts. Andy might not see a day off for some time. Too bad. Getting a ride down and back by air with Earl would save time.

"Good." For Earl, it was a done deal. "We'll take One Nine Alpha. You're PIC." He popped back out of the cabin.

Pilot-in-command.

It wouldn't be legal. Screw the FAA.

24

"I told you not to wait up!"

Andy found me sleeping in the recliner in the living room. She stood over me in blue, badged and belted. Rather imposing.

I did what all stupid people do when awakened from a sound sleep. I pretended I hadn't been sleeping at all.

"I wanted to watch this movie," I said, trying to get my face to work.

She tipped a perturbed glance at the television.

"That's a cookware infomercial."

"And it looks delicious." I levered the recliner upright and stood up. "What time is it?"

"Four-thirty." She worked the buckle on her belt. "Let me get changed. Feel like breakfast?"

"I'd like some of what they're making." I gestured at the television. Vegetables simmered in some sort of space-age frypan. "But I'll start something. Want coffee?"

"Ugh! I'm sloshing. Coffee all night. No thanks." She headed for the stairs, shaking her hair out of the ponytail she'd worn on duty.

I rubbed my face and headed for the kitchen. Andy sloshing or not, I needed coffee.

. . .

"USUAL DISCLAIMER?"

"Usual disclaimer."

Andy breezed into the kitchen looking fresh and lively in a white sweater and jeans, her hair brushed out. I could not imagine how she moved like that after an all-nighter. She slid onto a chair at the counter-height table. "On second thought, I will take coffee. It smells a whole lot better than what came out of the Thermos on the DCI truck."

I poured and handed her a mug, then went back to rolling sausages around in a pan and stirring scrambled eggs.

She took a sip and warmed her fingers with the mug.

"It was bad," she admitted. "I'm sorry you had to see that."

"I'm sorry *you* had to see that. Were there other kids? That got out?"

Andy shook her head.

"Only the two. We confirmed it with a friend of the mother." She recounted her return to the scene with a patrol car, her approach through the gate, finding the body of Marie Paulesky in the doorway, and following the trail to the woods. "Thank you for the boat cover."

"I hope that didn't mess up the scene. I just could not leave them like that."

We didn't speak for a reverent moment.

"I told DCI that I covered them to preserve the scene from the birds. I never knew we had vultures around here. I thought they lived out west."

She went on to confirm what I saw in the house.

"It was them."

"No honor among thieves."

"Or Nazis, I guess. And we were right about Eric Stahl. He had a room full of Nazi crap. Flags. Guns. Knives. Pictures of der Fuehrer. Lots more. Sick photos from the camps."

"Any ID on the others?"

"Oh yeah. They all had ID on them. There were no cell phones, at least none we could find—which explains why mister meatloaf could not reach Marie. As soon as I can come up with a reason, I'm hauling his ass in for questioning. But they all had wallets. ID. Driver's licenses. The sixth man took all the phones but left all the ID. Stahl was the only Wisconsin native. Perville, we already knew was from South Carolina. One had a Texas DL, one had Oklahoma and one had Wyoming."

"A regular Nuremberg Rally."

"The FBI is already connecting them through prison records."

"So, which one did the dirty double-cross? My money is on the guy with the makeup."

Andy put her finger on her nose.

"Thought so. Cold blooded bastard. Why do you suppose he took the phones?"

"Ah," the elegant finger rose, "phones are spider webs. They reach out and touch others. Lots of others. You can reconstruct a lot from a phone. Who they know. Where they've been. We don't have it, but the FBI has some software and toys that would make you want to burn your cell phone and bury the ashes. That was the first thing they asked when they arrived."

I scooped breakfast onto a pair of plates and served it up.

"Wow. The feds were there! Please don't tell me they sent you out to the road to direct traffic."

Andy shook her head and gave me a look of mild wonder.

"Totally the opposite. They fell all over themselves to make nice. The DCI captain told me half a dozen times it was good work, and he put me on the phone with the Administrator in Madison. Your girl got big pats on the head, Pilot."

"She should. You solved the case for them."

"Except for the sixth man," she said, naturally refusing to accept laurels. "I'm not worried. Everybody expects to find him linked to all the others via prison records. The county coroner abdicated the case to the state. They brought a medical examiner up from Madison. He put the TOD sometime Sunday."

"The guy didn't wait long. After the job, I mean."

"Which means he has a long head start. DCI and FBI are spouting a lot of rah-rah, like they think these guys are all backwoods Nazi idiots and the last man standing is cut from the same cloth. They think it's only a matter of time before someone spots him at a BP station or Super 8. I'm not so sure."

I will bet with Andy ninety-nine out of a hundred times.

"By the way, they're pinning the shooting inside the tent on Perville. Senator Stone. That kid."

"How can they do that? It was the guy with the makeup!"

"Says who? Nobody saw the shooting. Everybody, including me, was face down—" She peered at me over the rim of her coffee mug. "—except for Divisible Man. And I can't exactly take a statement from him."

"Unreliable at best. I hear he drinks."

"Well, Perville had the gun and it matches the bullets fired at the scene."

"Perville had the gun because the other guy shoved it in Perville's hand, took Perville's rifle, and shot him with it."

"After Dimitrioclese or whoever fell on him. Again … says who? I get a strong feeling that someone *very* high on the pay scale would like to put a bow on all this. In fact, I bet we're going to see it all over the news in about …" she looked at her wristwatch "…half an hour."

"Isn't that a little hard to do when a mass murderer is on the loose and a big load of cash is still missing."

"The take from the wedding was there," she said. "The envelopes with checks and gift cards."

"What about the cash?" I asked. I reminded her of what Earl said about the Chinese guests. It prompted a sly smile. "What?"

"There's been no report of cash taken."

I sat back. We both shook our heads.

"Of course not," I said. We both knew what it meant. If cash had been in the urn, it was intended as an unreported, untraceable gift. I wondered how much Sandy Stone knew about such gifts. She grew up in a political family. She married a political operative. Kindergarten teacher or not, she could not be that naive.

"Oh!" Andy said suddenly. "We talked about going to Madison on Saturday, remember? I need to move it to Friday. They want me to meet with the people at DCI. Do you think you can swing time off with Earl?"

"Funny you should say that."

25

After breakfast, Andy announced plans to nap for two hours, then return to work.

"Tom ordered me to take the day off and check in with him tonight. But he'll be tied up at the Stahl farm all day. I want to do some poking around at the office," she said.

I suggested she nap for four hours. I reminded her that her voracious sexual appetite had us on short sleep the night before. Surprisingly, she agreed.

I don't know how she does it, but coffee didn't prevent her napping. She curled up on the bed and dropped off immediately.

I woke her at ten, giving her an extra half hour. She grumbled about it, but only as a formality. Twenty minutes later, uniformed again, she dashed out the door.

I trailed loosely behind. Earl threatened me with death if I so much as suggested taking an unpaid leave while the FAA, as he put it, pulled their heads out of each other's asses. That didn't prevent it from feeling like charity each time an Essex County Air Service paycheck direct deposited to the family checking account. My enthusiasm for reporting to the flight line without a pilot's license rapidly lost altitude as the weeks passed without word from the Feds.

September surrendered another day of clear air and high pressure, so

I spent as much of the day as possible outdoors, moving airplanes, gassing airplanes, waving the occasional visiting aircraft into parking. The air felt good, but I could not help but wish I had a couple of my power units in my pocket. The joy of that new kind of flying offered to suppress the lingering dark images I carried away from Stahl's wooded yard. I spent occasional down time sitting in the sun on the aircraft tug, thinking up new acronyms for the power units.

Before he left at five p.m., Earl reminded me that we were flying to Madison in the morning. Anticipating I would fumble the ball, he told me he also spoke to Andy, who would be tagging along for her DCI meeting.

26

Low clouds and light rain moved into Wisconsin Thursday night, dampening late September glory. I woke early to update the weather briefing and file the flight plan. I checked the convective forecast for thunderstorms and didn't see anything to sweat on the short trip to Madison. Most of the flight would be in the clouds, although I hoped we would pop out on top for some of the ride. Skimming above white clouds with blue above is my favorite kind of flying—or was. Skimming treetops may have jumped to first place.

Andy dressed while I finished my online flight planning. We had no bags to pack, since we expected to be home for dinner. I jumped into my jeans and a slightly nicer white shirt, anticipating the hospital visit. Andy looked professional in black slacks and a white sweater with a black blazer.

Earl beat us to the flight line and had the cabin-class twin-engine Piper Navajo fueled and ready. I loaded my flight kit—headset, company-owned iPad, and paper charts—and finished a walkaround while Andy and Earl sipped office coffee. Rosemary II normally opens the office at eight but came in early to make the coffee and see us off. My return to the pilot's seat, albeit illegal, brought a little dew to her eyes, although ever since I saved her daughter's life, she gets a little dewy whenever I see her. I get a lot of hugs.

"Let's kick the tires and light the fires," I said to Earl and Andy after finishing the preflight rituals.

We climbed aboard. Andy strapped in a forward-facing passenger seat in the cabin. Earl took the co-pilot's seat. I slid in the left front seat.

First time since the crash.

Nothing.

I felt nothing, other than warm familiarity with a sophisticated machine. Maybe a vague unease for having gone more than sixty days since touching the controls of this airplane's twin sister. But I got no Hollywood moment of cold sweat or self-doubt. Far from it. I was simply home again.

I ran the checklists. The engines started smoothly. Earl, playing the co-pilot, brought up the recorded airport weather broadcast, telling us we had a six-hundred-foot ceiling and two miles visibility. Comfortably scummy weather. Madison carried a thousand-foot ceiling, guaranteeing an easy breakout on the approach for landing. ATC issued the IFR clearance, which I copied on my knee board.

"Whose name did you put on the flight plan?" Earl asked through the headset intercom.

"Yours." I glanced back at Andy. She thumbed through a copy of People Magazine, oblivious to the beauty of a wing outside her window and the miracle of flight about to occur.

"Then don't fuck up, buddy."

I smiled. The smile grew as I rolled into position on Runway 13. I eased the twin throttles forward and the engines sang. Confirming the power, I released the brakes. The Navajo surged forward. Dashed centerline markings marched under the nose. Full throttle. Airspeed needle waking up.

Nose up. Wheels kiss the runway goodbye.

Peter Pan moment.

27

"I got a lot of hours in that airplane!" Dave Peterson met us at the door, pointing at where we had parked One Nine Alpha on the Wisconsin Aviation ramp at Madison.

"I thought that might be your Falcon 20 out there," I said.

"Hey, gorgeous!" Dave opened his arms for a hug from Andy.

"Oh, it's good to see you! Will said you were at the wedding. I'm so sorry we didn't get to talk."

"What a mess that was. And you've been in the thick of it, I hear." Dave let go of my wife and turned to Earl. "Hi, Boss!"

"How's life at the flight levels?" Earl shook hands with his former employee.

"Crazy. We have been on the run non-stop all week. Montana. Tennessee. Colorado Springs. Back here twice. They whistle, we fly."

Andy excused herself to visit the Ladies room.

"You just get in?" I asked.

"Yeah. We did an all-night Uber last night. That was the Tennessee and Montana trip."

"Uber?"

Dave shrugged with a roll of the eyes. "Management likes to be secretive. They tell us where to go and when to get there, then we sit up front with the door closed and the shades pulled. They tell us how many souls on board, but we don't see or talk to the warm bodies in the back. Very hush hush. The green light tells us when the cabin door is closed and it's time to go. Crazy. We call ourselves Uber drivers on those trips."

I remembered Dave mentioning that the governor had been a passenger. Accepting a ride like that, on a private corporate jet, might limber up the opposition party's tongues, especially if the corporation was connected to state policies or politics.

"What brings you to town?"

"Bob Stone," Earl said.

Dave nodded grimly. "Yeah, that's awful. I'm so sorry, Earl. I know you guys are friends."

"Damn shame," Earl said. He put out his calloused claw and shook Dave's hand again. "You ever get tired of chauffeuring corporate weenies around, give me a call. Come back and do some real flying—charter flying corporate weenies around."

Dave laughed. I read that as *Not a Chance*.

Andy rejoined us. I spotted our taxi outside.

Dave clapped me on the shoulder and leaned close, "Good luck with the feds, man."

"Thanks."

28

Earl took charge and gave the driver instructions. We squeezed into the back of the cab and let the driver have his way with us on the narrow streets of Madison. Eventually, he wheeled up in front of a glass-coated professional building.

"Goddamned aerobatic cab drivers," Earl muttered after off-loading.

"Are you sure this is the place?" I wondered. It didn't look like University Hospital to me. The sign proclaimed an array of medical entities and doctor names.

"Follow me," Earl commanded.

We fell in after him. After navigating a marble lobby, a nearly silent elevator, and a broad hallway, Earl turned us into a set of glass doors.

Neurology Associates.

I catch on, eventually. I might be a little slow, but sooner or later I know when I've been had.

"Mr. Smith for his appointment with Doctor Stephenson," Earl growled at the woman behind the counter. She took note of him and consulted her thin laptop, the only object on a spotless desktop. After a moment, she satisfied herself of something.

"Please take a seat. The doctor will be right with you." She gestured at a waiting area. I didn't see her pick up a phone or touch an intercom.

"Earl, what is this?" I demanded.

"I told him," Andy stepped in. She took my hand and led me to a short sofa. "I told him about the tests the FAA is requesting. He knows this doctor and he set this up."

"Who's Mr. Smith?"

Earl scoffed. "You ain't using your real name until the tests come back clean. In case it turns out you really are crazy. If that's the case, the test stays under the FAA's radar."

"How is that possible? With the insurance?"

"Fuck insurance. I know this guy. He's going to pound a hammer on your skull to listen to the echo, then do a quick CAT scan and MRI. One, two, three and we're outta here."

"Earl, we—"

"Doug owes me a favor. This is on the company. I need you back, buddy. My nerves can't take much more of Pidge."

I looked at Andy. She squeezed my hand.

"I don't know what to say…"

"Good," Earl rumbled. "Keep your mouth shut. Less chance he'll find out you're certifiable. They got any goddamned coffee around here?"

DOCTOR DOUGLAS STEPHENSON greeted Earl as an old friend and led us into his office. Taller than me, he towered over Earl.

"Earl and I were in Thailand together, a couple centuries ago," Stephenson said. That put him in his seventies, like Earl. The man looked a healthy fifty, with a full head of silver hair and athletic demeanor. Photos of the doctor with famous golfers lined the walls, explaining Stephenson's tan.

"We made some noise at the Big Ta-Tas Piano Bar, didn't we?" Earl grinned, then caught a look at Andy and backtracked. "Best not to revisit that, though."

"Okay, Will. Earl said you have some memory loss?" Stephenson directed us to chairs and sat down behind his desk.

"Around thirty or forty hours, it seems."

Andy dug an envelope out of her purse. "These are the notes from Doctor Morrissey, who treated Will after the accident."

Stephenson took the envelope but didn't open it.

"I spoke to Morrissey." He regarded me. "You're something of a miracle, Will."

"That's what they tell me."

"And the *Federales* think you were incapacitated? They think that caused the crash?"

"Bullshit!" Earl said. Stephenson smiled. A man familiar with Earl Jackson's opinions.

"Actually," I said, "the NTSB investigator thinks it was a midair collision, but they can't figure out what I hit."

"So, the feds want to play fill-in-the-blank with your name and your career."

"That's about the size of it."

He gave a practiced, doctorly nod of the head and smiled. "Well, alright then! Let's shine a light in your skull and prove them wrong, shall we?" He turned to Earl and Andy. "Earl, Mrs. Stewart, there's a nice coffee shop down in the lobby at the back of the building. Better than what we make here in the office. Why don't you wait for Will downstairs? I'll do the exam here, then turn him over to the girls for the scans. They'll send him down to you when he's done. I have to go, but I'll be in the office on Monday to review the scans and write a report that will make the feds look like the horse's asses they are."

We stood. Andy and Earl expressed their thanks and made their goodbyes. Earl clasped Stephenson's hand heartily.

"Appreciate it, Doug," Earl said.

"*Chan pen hni khun,*" Stephenson said.

"Bullshit," Earl growled. He slapped the doctor on the shoulder and lurched out.

29

We sat in Stephenson's office chatting amiably for a good fifteen minutes before I realized he had begun conducting the neurological exam. The doctor asked me about flying, where I started, the career path I followed. He asked about Andy, how we met, when we married, about her work. The Cinnamon Hills robbery and attack on Senator Stone still dominated the news and Stephenson seemed impressed when I bragged about Andy's role in finding the thieves. Stephenson listened and watched my eyes. I assumed he monitored my speech patterns for slips, slurs, or other signs of trouble.

I had to ask. "What was that? What you said to Earl?"

Stephenson smiled and stood up. The exam moved into a new phase. He came around the desk and sat down in front of me. He began probing and poking with long fingers, speaking as he worked my hands, my wrists.

"I was a kid, an orderly in the hospital at Udorn Air Base in Thailand, when they brought in Captain Earl Jackson after his F-4 blew up under him. The man raised holy hell. He had a hole in one thigh the size of a golf ball, but that didn't keep him down. One night he collared me—I won't say at gun point, although I would have testified to it if we had been caught—and made me help him escape."

"Sounds like Earl."

"We swiped an ambulance and drove into town. I don't mean the usual watering holes. He took me someplace way off limits. There were things going on in there, to this day, I don't know if I really saw them or not." His eyes searched a deep distance for a moment. Then he went back to squeezing my hands, arms, knees. "Anyway, I got a little too cozy with a girl who apparently belonged to someone rather nasty. Next thing I knew, I was trussed up in a back room about to have a sex change."

"Jesus!"

Stephenson bobbed his head. "Scariest moment of my life. Well, just about the time I thought about how my folks were going to take the news of my death, the door burst open and there's Earl, naked as a newborn, screaming and wearing this big feathered hat that he found somewhere. And the damned thing was on fire."

I blinked.

"Earl was a bit of an apparition, even then. But the sight of him roaring at them with his head on fire absolutely terrified those thugs and they went ass over elbows out the windows. I'm crying and whatnot on the floor, and Earl looks down at me and says, 'C'mon, kid. Let's get a beer and get this party started!'"

I had no idea what to say.

"So, to answer your question, *Chan pen hni khun* is Thai for 'I owe you.' Now, look out that window and tell me if you can read that bill-board down the street."

30

"Wow!" Andy looked up from her coffee. "That was fast."

"Nothing between his ears," Earl muttered. "Makes examination easier."

"Everything go okay?" Andy asked. I knew what she was asking. *Did* the other thing *short out the CAT scan machine or million-dollar magnetic resonance imaging equipment?*

"Far as I can tell. Nothing blew up."

She and I traded meaningful shrugs.

"Good!" Earl stood up. He clapped me on the shoulder. "If anyone can set things straight with the feds, Doug can. Top of his field."

"This was kinda sneaky of you," I said.

"Kinda? Shit, it was JFK conspiracy-level sneaky. On a short turnaround time. With your wife swearing me to silence—and she carries a gun." Earl finished his coffee and planted the mug on the table. "Let's go see how Bob's doing."

WE COULD NOT GET ANYWHERE near Senator Bob Stone. The press had been cordoned off at the lobby level. Hospital security took charge of visitation for the floor where Senator Stone remained in Intensive Care.

We were told visitors were limited to a short list. We got no farther than the first few steps off the elevator.

Earl grumbled at the hospital security officer, but the stone face of high power at a low level of bureaucracy would not budge.

"Earl, excuse me," Andy touched his arm and persuaded him to move back. She pulled her badge and a card from her purse.

"I'm Sergeant Stewart of the Essex Police Department," she said. "We're handling the investigation with DCI and the FBI. Now, you can stick to your guns and I understand that. I ask only one thing of you. Take this card to the Senator's daughter. She is a dear friend. Ask her if she wants to see me. If she says no, we will be on our way."

The security guard, perhaps aspiring to wear a law enforcement uniform one day, eyed Andy and after a moment took the card.

"Wait here."

He returned ten minutes later with Sandra Stone. Andy stepped quickly forward, past the guard, and put her arms around the bride, whose composure broke. She began to weep. Andy held her and spoke quietly into her ear. Sandy shook with deepening sobs.

"There's a lounge down the hall," the guard suggested to me.

"Right," I said. I moved forward and gestured for Andy to follow with Sandy in her arms. Earl and I found an expansive, carpeted waiting area resembling a five-star hotel lobby. In one corner, a kitchen invited visitors to refuel on fresh fruit and nutrition bars; in another, a fireplace warmed the room with eternal gas flames.

Andy helped her friend to a sofa and pointed at a box of tissues, which I retrieved. Earl and I found seats discretely nearby.

"Oh—I'm so sorry. I'm so sorry." Sandy wept. "I haven't—cried—cried all week." It came in a torrent.

I wandered over to the kitchen and checked the refrigerator. I returned with four water bottles.

Andy held her friend, repeating something soothing, something neither Earl nor I could hear.

"God!" Sandy suddenly sat up. "What is *wrong* with me!" She plucked a tissue from the box, wiped her eyes and nose, and tried to compose herself. "I am *so* sorry!"

"Sandy, stop," Andy said gently. She took her friend's hands. "You deserve a chance to feel something."

Sandy's face wrinkled up and a new set of sobs broke. These seemed less intense, cleansed a little and didn't last as long. She wiped her eyes and blew her nose again.

"Thank you," she whispered to Andy. She turned to Earl. "Thank you for coming Mr. Jackson. You've always been such a good friend to Dad."

"A good man," was all Earl could manage.

"I don't think Dad valued anyone's opinion more than yours," Sandy said, sniffling. Earl could not answer. He coughed suddenly and forced his familiar scowl back in place.

Sandy studied her hands. She drew a long breath, then released its accompanying sigh. She spoke quietly, barely audible.

"He's not coming back. He's not ever coming back. We've known. Daddy…" Large crystalline tears rolled down her cheeks. She turned to Earl. "You can go in. Please. Go ahead. You're going to want to—" she stopped, then her voice went high and thin "—to say—"

Earl stood up suddenly, his face contorting again.

"Yeah." He marched toward the hallway and his old friend.

Sandy steadied herself.

"He's been on a ventilator, almost from the start. They—ah, they confirmed there was no—no brain activity, I guess two days ago. I don't know, you lose track of time."

"I'm so sorry," Andy said.

Sandy nodded. "The announcement will be made today. After—you know—after they..." Andy moved to offer another consoling embrace when Sandy suddenly asked, "Are you staying at the Concourse?"

"I, uh—"

"We're flying back to Essex this evening," I said.

Sandy noticed me for the first time. "Will, I'm so sorry, I should have —it's nice to see you. Thank you for coming."

"I'm so sorry. About everything. Honestly."

Sandy abruptly turned to my wife. "Andy, I really need to talk to you. Not here, not now. Can we meet later? At the hotel? At the Concourse? That's where we've been staying. Todd and me."

"Sure. Anything you want. I have a meeting with the DCI people this afternoon, but we can all catch up at the hotel. My cell number is on that card." Andy pointed at Sandy's hand. The card she had given the security guard lay curled in Sandy's palm.

"They told me what you did, that you found them. Thank you for that."

Andy folded her hands over Sandy's and looked her directly in the eye. "The thieves got what they deserved. They were horrible, horrible people."

I felt proud of Andy. Someone needed to say it.

"Why don't you and Todd call us when you can. When you have a better idea of what's going on."

"No, just me. Just me. I'll call you." She looked over her shoulder at the hallway.

"Is there something wrong?" Andy probed.

Still eyeing the hallway, Sandy replied, "No one else knows this. Tomorrow the governor is going to appoint Todd to Dad's senate seat."

It might be big news, maybe huge news, in the world of politics, but it meant little to me.

Andy nodded. "I'm sure he will—"

"No, he won't. This afternoon I plan to talk to the press and announce that I intend to serve out Dad's term. It can't be Todd."

This sounded to me like trouble for a brand-new marriage. Like a decision made in a maelstrom of emotion. On top of that, absolutely nothing about Sandy's career as a kindergarten teacher conformed to a dive into politics.

"Are you sure?" Andy asked. "This is a rough time for you. And that's a big step."

"You sound like Todd. That's his answer for everything this week. I'm not his wife, I'm his china doll." She glanced over her shoulder again. Her paranoia was palpable. She leaned closer to Andy. "I need to ask you—"

"Sandy?" Todd's voice stopped her cold. She startled.

Todd Jameson stepped into the lounge. He studied the strangers sitting with his wife. For a man holding vigil for his new father-in-law, he looked remarkable. Calm. Combed. Dressed to perfection. I don't know the first thing about fashion, but I know money when people wear it. Todd Jameson's suit, shirt and tie wouldn't fit on my credit card on its best day. He projected a television anchorman presence, like someone always On.

I stood to greet the groom, but not before I caught Sandy curling Andy's business card tightly into her hand.

"Todd Jameson." He descended on me quickly, hand forward, grasping, giving an overly strong handshake that pinched the old Army Air Corps ring on my right hand. He beamed a quick political poster smile.

"Will Stewart," I said. He pumped my hand again.

"I know the name." He held the grin. "Heard about your amazing experience last summer."

"Word does get around."

"Andy, thank you for coming." He aimed his charm at my wife. She shook hands and I wondered if he tried to crush her fingers, too.

"I'm so sorry for what happened. It was a beautiful wedding," Andy said.

"I hope to make it up to my bride one day. I've been hearing your name, too. You're spoken highly of by the head of the DCI. Thank you for all you've done. I know you were on top of things at Cinnamon Hills. I'm sorry I could not thank you then."

"Don't give it another thought."

"I can thank you now, though. Your work on Wednesday, finding those—the ones who did this. You have no idea how that eases our minds. DCI filled me in. Excellent work."

"Yes," Sandy chimed in. She dabbed moisture from her eyes and adjusted herself, forcing a thin smile.

"I'm sorry to interrupt, but they kindly sent up a lunch for us, and I think my wife needs to eat. This has been a terrible week." Todd reached for Sandy's hand and helped her to her feet. Andy rose with her. Sandy turned to Andy. They hugged.

"I'll call you," Sandy said. "Later."

She walked out on her husband's arm.

Andy and I watched them go. My wife's green eyes lingered on the space they left behind. After a moment, she turned to me.

"He's a douche."

"Is that a criminal science term?"

She cocked her head to one side, thinking.

"Did you notice?" She let the question hang, trying something on in her own mind before putting it to me. Then she said, "He didn't ask how we were doing with finding the sixth man."

31

Earl marched past the visitor lounge looking like murder hunting for a victim. We caught up to him as he punched the elevator button. He didn't speak during the ride down. In the lobby, he stopped us with ground glass in his voice.

"You kids go get some lunch." We waited a moment, but there were no other instructions. Then he asked Andy, "What time is your thing?"

"They want me at the DCI office at three."

Earl ran some calculations in his head. "Okay. Meetcha at the airport at six."

He stood rooted to a spot like an old tree.

I took a tentative step toward the door. "You sure you don't want…?"

"Positive."

Andy and I traded glances and decided to evacuate the blast zone.

We sat at a cozy window seat in a State Street café. Andy studied her phone.

"They changed the meeting. Text message from Tom. He says DCI called to tell him it's been moved to the capitol. I don't know why they didn't text me."

"You mean the building with the big dome?"

Andy made a face at me. "Do you know of any other capitol buildings in Madison?"

"You never know. Could be half a dozen of them. Government runs rampant in this town."

"Right." She frowned at her phone. "He didn't say what room. I should call the DCI office."

"I'll get the check."

We had eaten a light lunch. Or as light a lunch as one can eat, given the extravagant portions. I left a third of a club sandwich on the plate. Andy left half a Caesar salad.

She caught up with me at the register.

"They said to meet in the rotunda in thirty minutes. Odd."

"Well, it stopped raining. We're a little early, but we can walk around the building with the big dome a bit. Care for a tour?"

She hooked her arm inside mine and waved the way forward. As we walked, I waited for her to bring up Sandy Stone, but she kept her thoughts to herself.

AT THE STATE CAPITOL BUILDING, we were neither early, nor did we take a tour. People stood in a line at the door, waiting for entrance through building security apparatus that looked as if it had been thrown together on short notice. By the time we cleared the metal detector, replaced our belts, phones and keys, and dealt with Andy's badge and the pistol she carried in her purse, my watch read close to three o'clock.

"That can't be it." She pointed at the center of the building. Dozens of people formed a large crowd.

"Only one way to find out."

We threaded our way toward the center of the capitol rotunda. A rank of television cameras and lights aligned with one of the stairways. People lined the second-floor railing above us.

"I think somebody got this all wrong."

"Sergeant Stewart!"

A man in a blue suit edged his way through the crowd to where we stood.

"Mike Pell. I was one of the investigators at Cinnamon Hills."

"I remember." Andy smiled. "Nice to see you again, Mike. This is my husband, Will."

"Pleasure."

"Likewise."

"We need you up here, Sergeant," he gestured back in the direction he had come.

"What's going on?" Andy asked as we wormed through the crowd.

"They didn't tell you?"

The crowd noise grew loud enough that in lieu of explanation, Pell turned and pantomimed that he would explain *up there*. He pointed at the steps facing the camera crews. We approached a yellow tape that marked the limit of public access. Beyond the tape, cameras and reporters waited. Pell turned to me and leaned close.

"I'm sorry. Authorized law enforcement only."

Andy quickly pulled me close and said, "Wait here for me."

"Not a chance."

She wheeled and followed Pell.

I undertook the dual tasks of threading back the way we had come and keeping an eye on Andy. She passed through the television crews. One or two swung their cameras at her as she followed Pell up a marble staircase toward the second floor.

At the back of the milling crowd, I found a pillar near the outer wall of the rotunda. It had space enough to pass all the way around it yet stood slightly off the main track and well out of sight of the security station. I checked for cameras and found none focused on this spot.

I walked to the pillar and hooked around it, like someone planning on reversing course. Blocked from view by the marble pillar—

Fwooomp!

I vanished. My inner organs shifted. Sudden weightlessness induced a split second of mild vertigo. I stretched out both arms, placing one palm on the pillar and the other on the wall behind it. I pushed simultaneously with both arms and rose.

Halfway up to the ceiling, I stopped. I worked my way around the pillar, then pushed on a vector that took me over the heads of the crowd, roughly following the same path I had just traveled twice. The glide took me over the tape line, over the camera crews, through the rotunda toward the marble banister edging the steps Andy had climbed with Pell.

I grabbed the banister and used it as a track to rise to the second floor. There, I stopped.

A cluster of people in business suits stood halfway down the long hallway. Andy stood out conspicuously, the only woman. She and Pell waited at the edge of the milling group.

A series of pillars ran the length of the hallway above a marble railing on the left. Offices and doors lined the right. Beyond the marble railing an atrium rose three floors, an extension of the rotunda. I worked my way forward, pillar by pillar.

The fourth pillar stood adjacent to Andy. Just as I arrived, a tall wooden door with frosted glass opened. Three men, working the Important vibe hard, stepped into the hallway. One of the three pointed Andy out to another who walked directly to her. The cluster in the hallway parted for them.

"Detective Stewart? I'm Byron Williams, Administrator of the Division of Criminal Investigation. We spoke on the telephone." He held out his hand.

"*Sergeant* Stewart, sir. Pleased to meet you," Andy said.

"I'm glad you could join us here today," Williams said. "Outstanding work on the Stone case. Tom Ceeves is fortunate to have you." Williams looked over his shoulder, down the hall. "I think we're just about ready."

I saw the questioning look on Andy's face. Williams did not.

A moment later, all heads turned. Flanked by staff, trailing security, the governor of Wisconsin walked the corridor toward Williams and my wife. Once more, the cluster of people in the hallway parted to allow passage.

"Ready, Byron?" the governor asked.

"We are."

"Is he here yet?"

"He's entering the building now. We have people meeting him and taking him to the rotunda. You can introduce him from there."

"That's good, that's good. Coming out of the crowd like that. Man of the People. I like it. Are we ready?"

"Five minutes, sir."

"Where's the AG?"

One of the governor's staff reminded him the attorney general was in

Chicago. From the staffer's expression, it was not the first time the governor had been told today.

Andy searched her surroundings. She shifted her eyes upward and stared straight at me. Smart girl. After a moment, she leaned toward Williams and touch his sleeve, speaking into his ear. She gestured at open space away from the small crowd. Without waiting for him, she moved across the corridor and stood below me. Williams followed.

"Sir, what is all this?"

"Victory lap, Detective. For a success on the Cinnamon Hills case. The governor himself wants to make the announcement. You're about to bank a lot of credit with this administration for your part in the investigation."

"Sir," she shook her head, "aren't we being premature?"

Williams looked at Andy as if he didn't understand.

"The sixth man. The man who killed all five of his comrades plus a woman and two little girls? All due respect, sir, but this is going to look like calling 'Mission Accomplished' when we're far from it. And what if, God forbid, he does something else? Kills someone else? That's going to splash back in a very bad way."

"Detective, aren't you up to speed here? On what happened last night and this morning?"

"I've been at the hospital all morning. What are you talking about?"

"We got him. The phone you found led us straight to him."

I watched Andy struggle to hold her tongue and suppress the question leaping from it.

What phone?

"Police and FBI surrounded the sixth man at his home early this morning. There were shots fired. He fought it out and then blew himself up. Another Nazi, just like the rest. Adolph Lee Nellis. No question it was him. They found the bag and some of the gift envelopes stolen from the wedding. I thought you knew." Williams gave her a pat on the shoulder. "Your good work got us there, Detective. You're about to stand in the spotlight with the governor. After that, come and see me, and you can write your own ticket."

He doled out a big smile and strolled back to join the governor.

Andy looked up. Not quite at me, but she must have sensed I was there. I pushed down to her level.

"What the fuck?" I said, voice low.

Her eyes grew wide, an expression that said, *I know!*

"He's here," someone in the cluster called out.

"Detective," Williams called to Andy. He made a *come along* gesture.

"This is *not* right," she said to the empty air where I floated.

She turned and followed the parade, trying the best she could to hang back, away from the mess about to unfold.

32

"Ladies and gentlemen, thank you all for coming out on this damp morning." The governor spoke into a microphone that had been set up on the stairway landing, a perfect stage several steps above the rotunda floor where the phalanx of television camera crews aimed their lenses up at him. Behind the cameras, the crowd pressed the yellow tape line. "We have several announcements to make and I'd like to get right to them.

"First of all, we are proud to announce that an intensive manhunt, involving hundreds of fine law enforcement officers across several states, has come to a successful conclusion. Early this morning, working on information developed by this administration's Division of Criminal Investigation—and with the help of the Federal Bureau of Investigation, the Wisconsin State Highway Patrol and numerous local law enforcement agencies—the final perpetrator in the Cinnamon Hills robbery and senseless shooting, was found, surrounded—and after refusing to surrender and opening fire on law enforcement officers and members of the FBI—was killed."

The governor paused for effect, aiming his face from camera to camera with a look that tried to say he personally stormed the killer's redoubt.

"Police and FBI agents searching the suspect's home in Grimsley,

Tennessee, report finding evidence taken from the robbery, and from the home of the suspect's former co-conspirators, who we now believe were killed by the suspect earlier this week. We will have more information on that evidence through our public information website as it develops.

"I want to take a moment to personally congratulate and point out the fine work of Detective Andrew—" he glanced down at a card in his hand "—er, Andrea Stewart of the Essex County Sheriff's Department, whose efforts led our state investigators to the scene of a multiple homicide earlier this week, which in turn led to the person responsible, the person behind last weekend's tragic robbery and horrific shooting."

The governor waved a hand in Andy's direction. Williams edged closer to her, ensuring he would be in the shot as cameras swiveled. Andy's expression remained stony.

"Detective Stewart's work is representative of the hundreds of fine police officers who put their lives on the line every day to protect us, and we salute every one of them."

Applause broke out in the crowd behind the cameras. Weak at first, but it grew when the cluster of suits behind the governor joined in. I would have given anything to drop down behind my wife, throw my arms around her and make her vanish. She stood expressionless. At best, she endured.

The governor, realizing everyone around him was clapping, joined in. Then, as it died down, he returned to the microphone.

"Although we are pleased to make this announcement, it comes this afternoon at a heavy cost. The Cinnamon Hills Robbery, as you all know, included the horrific shooting of several innocent bystanders. It is my terrible, terrible sad duty to report to you that we have just received word of the passing of a great American, a true servant of the State of Wisconsin, and a dear friend, State Senator Robert Stone, who was struck down senselessly by random gunfire during the robbery."

Absolute silence held for a moment. The governor gave it a dramatic count.

"We who serve the citizens of this state understand the duty we have, and Senator Stone above all others, would want that service to continue uninterrupted, no matter the cost, no matter the circumstances. Throughout this long week, in which we have prayed for his recovery, I have consulted with and prayed with Bob Stone's family. And as we saw this sad, terrible end coming, we all agreed that his duty lives on. Therefore, while there is much grieving still ahead of us, and much remembering, I know that Bob Stone would stand here, side by side with me, and urge us to go onward, forward. I have asked the family, and they have given their blessing to the appointment of Todd Jameson, the Senator's son-in-law, to step into the senator's shoes and fulfill the duties of his current term of office. Todd, will you please join me?"

Andy looked up. She picked out a spot where she thought I might be floating and flared her eyes in a *What the hell?* expression.

Todd Jameson emerged from the crowd, his face somber, his hands clasped before him like a minister about to cast a blessing. Spontaneous applause broke out among the suits behind the governor. It was picked up quickly by the crowd. Jameson acknowledged the applause as he crossed the floor. Cameras followed him up the steps. He shook hands with the governor. They traded words beneath mournful nods.

Theater, I thought. *Political theater.*

Todd Jameson stepped to the microphone. He thanked the governor on behalf of the family of Senator Stone. He spoke for a few minutes with a halting, emotion-cracked voice, expressing his love and admiration for his late father-in-law. He declined to take any questions.

The press conference closed quickly. A perky press secretary appeared out of nowhere to remind everyone that questions could be submitted to and would be processed through the governor's new web-based public relations portal. Ignoring that, reporters shouted questions after the departing governor and newly appointed state senator, both of whom returned the favor and ignored the questions.

I looked for a place to reappear and had settled on a route when I saw a head with perfectly trimmed and combed white hair move across the floor below me. The man jogged up the stairs and passed through a team of the governor's security. Tall and sharply dressed, he looked familiar. I tried to place him as he trotted after the departing officials. He caught up with Todd Jameson and they traded quick remarks as they walked.

Andy looked around the rotunda, her gaze high, obviously searching for me. She raised her hand and touched an elegant finger to her nose, tapping it three times.

Like I was supposed to know what that meant.

I made a guess and lined up a trajectory that would take me down to the landing beside her, to the marble banister. With the governor's security detail spread across the stairs below her, traffic on the landing ceased. The press secretary dismantled and removed the microphone, then hurried after her boss. Andy stood alone. I dropped and caught the banister, steadied myself and reached over to touch her shoulder. She jumped slightly.

"I'm here. To your right."

She watched the dissipating crowd.

"What the hell was that?" she asked through motionless lips.

"A trip down the rabbit hole?"

"We need to go back to the hospital and find Sandy. This is not what she told us."

"My bet, you're not going to find her there. Call first. I've got something I want to do. I'll catch up."

"Where are you going?"

"To eavesdrop on the Governor of the State of Wisconsin. I'll call you when I can."

"Be careful!"

I touched her shoulder again, then rotated away and shoved myself up to the second floor.

33

I chose a billiard shot. I aimed myself on a diagonal through the open atrium, toward the side opposite the tall, white-haired man pacing the hallway in front of the governor's office. From there, it would be a short shot back across the atrium to another convenient pillar.

Halfway there, I placed him. Dave Peterson's boss, the CEO of the private prison company. Parks. Of course. It connected with seeing Dave at the airport, and the Falcon 20 sitting on the ramp. The man had attended the wedding.

He paced the marble floor in the empty corridor, one hand thrust in a pocket. This presented a problem. Tall double doors stood behind Parks, closed. A simple brass plaque above the door read "Governor."

I needed a way in.

I considered knocking. Someone would answer the door, find no one there, look up and down the hall—meanwhile I would slip in over their head. Great plan, except with Parks patrolling outside the door, it wouldn't work.

Parks seemed to be waiting for an audience with the governor. They would come for him, and that might be my shot. I hung in the air just outside of the atrium railing.

With no clocks in sight, and unable to read my watch, I have no idea how long I waited. Eventually, the double doors swung open, but instead of inviting Parks in, Todd Jameson stepped out and the doors closed behind him.

Jameson grinned. "Alright." He pumped a fist. "It's done."

"All of it?" Parks demanded.

"All of it. The governor got on the phone with Litton and told him the announcement should be making news feeds. Litton said he already confirmed it, so he's putting up the hundred million."

"What about seventy-six-oh-eight?"

"With Stone gone, it moves out of committee. Clear sailing after that."

"It's about time!" Parks drew a pointed bead on Jameson with one finger. "You can't let your new wife fuck this up. I'm asking you again."

Jameson stood staring, thinking.

"C'mon, Todd! This is your moment. You're stepping across the line between the little people and the people who matter. Look, I get it, she's a babe. She's *the one that brung ya'* but we've talked about this. You know what Litton's money means. Everything changes. Imagine it."

Jameson's eyes lost focus, working to imagine it, whatever *it* was.

Parks lowered his voice. "She got you in the door. No one's going to argue that all this—it's a horrible strain for a daughter, to lose her father like that. The press is going to be all over her. A perfect excuse to get her away from all this."

"The way we talked about, Pearce," Jameson warned. "It has to be the way we talked about."

"We'll give her a chance to deal with things."

"I'll handle the funeral," Jameson said, rehearsing a mournful tone.

"She can reach out when things settle. Post some photos. Recover from the fairy tale wedding gone wrong. No one can deny her that. She needs time. And then we can make the transition."

Transition?

Transition to what? From wanting to serve out her father's term to becoming the senator's wife? In the hospital, Sandy Stone seemed set on a different path. I wondered if she knew the decision had been made for her—or if she was about to catch it on the evening news.

"Litton is writing the check," Jameson reassured himself.

"Fucking Litton is writing the check!" Parks grinned. "Told you he'd like what he saw."

34

"Where are you?"

"University Hospital," Andy said.

I stood on the capitol steps, phone to my ear. Light drizzle tickled my face.

"Did you find her?"

"No. It's all shut down here. Press is gone. Security is gone. I talked to one of the nurses. It ended hours ago, around lunchtime. She said Sandy and Todd said their goodbyes, then the doctors removed life support, and he passed almost immediately. Then Mr. and Mrs. Jameson left."

Before Jameson went to the capitol for the announcement.

"Todd came here. Do you think Sandy went to the hotel?"

"That would be my guess. I had the nurse check on something for me. I asked her to find out what they were doing with his body."

"And...?"

"Sandy signed a transport order to take him home. Back to Essex. I saw the order. He's going to Anderson Funeral." Andy and I both knew the hometown favorite funeral director, Ron Anderson. He handled the funeral for the original Rosemary two years ago. Everybody knew Ron Anderson, eventually.

"Jesus," I said, "from the wedding of the century to the funeral of the century."

"I don't know, Will. Do you think she changed her mind? Or never meant it in the first place?"

"Or was distraught?"

"No," Andy said firmly. "Just because a woman is crying—over her dying father, I might add—doesn't mean she's lost her mind."

I had the good sense to agree with her. I recounted the conversation between Parks and Jameson. "Who's Litton?"

"I'm not sure. I thought I heard the name at the wedding."

"Well, he's Daddy Warbucks. In for a hundred million on whatever Todd has cooked up."

"I want to find Sandy and talk to her. I don't see her flipping on this."

"This smells like Todd. He left here a few minutes ago. I could not follow him. I had to find a place to reappear. He's probably on his way to the hotel. But if he's there, we may not be able to talk to her. You saw how that went before."

"We'll figure something out," she said. "Let's try the hotel. Want me to pick you up?"

"It's a short walk. I'll see you there."

THE WALK TOOK LESS time than I anticipated. Andy's cab ride from University Hospital took longer. While I waited in the lobby of the Concourse Hotel, I casually asked for information about the Jamesons—whether they had checked out or not. I received a polite, *We cannot divulge guest information like that*. With an equally polite thank you, I let it go, having an ace up my sleeve.

My ace walked in ten minutes later.

"Takes forever to get a cab when it's raining," she said. "This is going to ruin my hair."

Nothing ruins Andy's hair. Women have told me they would kill for her long, naturally wavy auburn locks.

"We need super cop," I told her. "If we're going to get anything out of the hotel people."

"No worries." She drew a bead on the front desk and crossed the lobby floor, pulling her police ID and badge out of her purse as she walked.

"Hi," she said to young woman behind the counter; her name tag said Kiyra. "I'm Sergeant Andrea Stewart of the City of Essex Police Department. I need to speak to a guest, Sandra Stone, possibly listed as Sandra Jameson. It is a police matter, and it is urgent. You can call the room, but if there is no answer, I need you to take me to the room. Now."

The young woman blinked. "One moment," she said quickly. "Let me find that for you."

She rattled the keys on her keyboard, scanned her monitor, chased the information with a mouse, clicked, rattled, and found what she was looking for.

"Mr. and Mrs. Jameson checked out a little after two p.m." she said. "Two-fourteen to be precise."

It was Andy's turn to blink. "Together?"

"I wasn't on the desk, so I could not say for certain. Both keys were turned in at that time."

Andy slowly closed her ID wallet.

"Officer, if you'll wait a moment, John was on the desk at the time. Let me see if he can tell you. Wait here."

Kiyra stepped down the line to her co-worker, who was handling a check-in. She spoke to him and he looked over at Andy. He mouthed, *I'll be right with you* at Andy and then gave quick instructions to Kiyra. She took over the check-in.

"Hi, I'm John, how can I help you?" he asked smoothly, earnestly.

"John, I want to know if Mr. and Mrs. Jameson checked out together this afternoon."

"They did," he said. "She is such a lovely woman, and we all felt so bad for what she's been going through this week. I told her we were all truly sorry for her loss."

"Wait," I said. "You knew the Senator had passed? At two-fourteen, when they checked out?"

"She told me," John said. "When she said she was checking out, I asked about her father, and she told me the news."

"Did she say where she was going?"

"Home. She said she was taking her father home."

John spoke in a gentle, lilting tone. He sounded genuinely sad.

"Thank you, John."

We wandered away from the front desk. I checked my watch. Almost five o'clock.

"So," I said. "She changed her mind."

Andy said nothing.

"And Todd's taking over for Senator Stone."

Her lower lip came out, brooding.

"And your last Nazi obeyed Hitler's favorite command and fought to the death down in Tennessee."

A lock of hair slipped down over one eye.

"So, that's it. Everything wrapped up with a nice bow," I concluded.

Green eyes, flecked with gold, under long rising lashes, found me, piercing me. I've seen that look before.

"Yeah … no. I didn't think so."

35

"Will you come with me?" Andy asked.

I checked my watch. The hands pointed at eleven and one. Sleep blurred my eyes. It was either just after eleven or just before one.

After flying back to Essex and putting away the airplane, I performed my last landing of the day at home, in my recliner where I refueled with a light snack. Andy settled herself into a chair at the dining room table, with her laptop open.

Before finishing my sandwich and lowering my eyelids, I asked Andy, "Hey, what phone?"

"Excuse me?"

"The phone. They said the phone led them to the last guy."

"Oh. I talked to Pell, that guy at the capitol, before I left." She stalked back into the living room. The subject wound her up. "They found one phone." She showed me an emphatic finger.

"You told me the guy took all their phones. Spider webs."

"Well, they found one. Guess where?" I didn't guess. I waited long enough to let her impatience kick in. "It was in a rice box!"

"Maybe the guy got it wet."

Andy frowned at me. She shook her head. "Okay but think about this. They found one, just one, phone. They don't know whose phone it was, and the records on the phone show calls to only one other phone, belonging to the Tennessee Nazi."

"The sixth man."

"Really? You're part of a crew. You're from out of state. You have a phone and you only talk to one guy on the crew? When he's in Tennessee?"

"Radio discipline," I offered. "Maybe the phones were obtained only for the job and communication was strictly limited."

"Uh-huh," Andy said, not buying it. "Guess how they found it? It started ringing. DCI found it yesterday, doing a follow-up and lockdown at the scene."

She waited for me to ask the right question.

"So … who was calling?"

"Who do you think? A credit card company."

I laughed. "That's funny. A telemarketer breaks the case."

"That would be funny if it were true. But it wasn't a telemarketer. It was a customer service callback. Somebody called the customer service number, got the recording about how call volume is greater than usual, and if you leave a callback number, they'll hold your place in line, so you don't have to sit on hold—and they left the number for this phone. Conveniently, the phone rings ten minutes later—*while* the house is crawling with investigators. DCI picked up the call and got Steve from American Express."

"A Tennessee Nazi with an American Express card," I mused. "Why not?"

Andy blew out a breath. I was not her best pupil tonight.

"No. Our backwoods Nazi didn't have a credit card. Any credit cards. He had a criminal record up the wazoo and a room temperature credit rating. We checked. And the original call to the customer service line didn't come from the phone in the rice box."

"Yeah, that would have been a trick, seeing as how the guy was dead and his phone was in a box of rice."

"It came from what we think is a burner phone." She cocked her hips at me like her point had been made for her.

"I think I'm seeing the problem here." She lit up.

"I know! One phone. Set up to lead us right to the last guy. An untraceable call is made to guarantee the phone is found. Right?"

On that she turned and marched back to her laptop.

"I need to look up something."

"Dee," I said.

"What?"

"You need sleep, too."

She didn't sleep. I did. I finished the sandwich and decided to rest my eyelids for a few minutes before trying to get her to let it go for the night. Next thing I knew, she stood over me, nudging me awake.

When I could not make out the hands on my watch, I asked, "What time is it?"

"Five after eleven. Will you come with me?"

"Where?"

"I need to see Lane."

I sat up.

"Wait—what? Lane? It's after eleven."

Andy headed out of the room, then came back sliding her arms into a black leather jacket. I noticed she already had on the pancake holster she wore when out of uniform. She checked her weapon and secured it in the holster.

"I already texted her. She's expecting us."

"Us?"

"Will, she has a crush on you. How have you not noticed? C'mon."

I struggled to my feet, found my boots, and slid into them.

"An adult texting a teenaged girl after eleven at night. Isn't that a good way to get in trouble?"

"If it was you, yes. Move it, Pilot!"

36

Andy's tone took on a serious note as we pulled out of the driveway, following the headlight beams of her car.

"I hit a wall and I need Lane to do a little Photoshop magic."

"What wall?" I asked.

"I decided to spend some time looking for the sixth man."

"Well, then I can understand hitting a wall, with him being dead."

Andy paid no attention. "Do you remember, at the wedding, I told Pidge I saw him?"

"Uh-huh. A man wearing heavy makeup in a brown suit. Why? You think you can identify him?"

"I didn't …" She drew it out.

"But?"

"Okay … back at the academy, I met a retired detective. He did a visiting lecture about identifying evidence. I caught up with him in the cafeteria. We were talking—I guess I was picking his brain—and he taught me about something he called scene image memory enhancement—his trick for tapping memories of something visual."

"Hypnosis?"

"Nothing quite that fancy. He just had this trick he used when he needed to see—as he put it—*more* of something he had already seen. You look at things all the time, like a car—but did you see the color of the driver's shirt? The driver's hair? You did, but if you verbalize a description, the words end up being about the car. Red car. Mag wheels. The car gets in the way. It dominates. You know?"

"I guess."

"He said if you shut off the verbal you can see *more* of the picture—non-verbally—as an image. Like the way a baby sees things before they have words. He called it a purer, more refined form of seeing."

"Is there some science behind all this?"

"I don't know. Maybe. He told me it's just a tool, like your mnemonic device—which, by the way, you need to teach me."

I felt a tickle of pride. "What's the trick?"

"*California Girls*," Andy said. "He played *California Girls* in his head. The Beach Boys?"

"I know the song."

"Mostly the instrumental open, but sometimes even the lyrics, because they had nothing to do with what he was looking at or trying to remember. He just let the song play and visualized, non-verbally, the image, and—he said—you'd be amazed at what details your mind's eye can then see. I've tried it a few times. It kinda works."

"So, you rolled back the tape in your head, played a Beach Boys tune, and got a better look at the sixth thief?"

Andy nodded enthusiastically.

"Dee, why are you doing this? Don't they have photos of the guy? Now that they know who he is—or was?"

She reached in her pocket and handed me a folded piece of paper. I opened it while she flipped on the dome light in her car.

"Is this him? Nellis?"

"Yeah," she said. "What's wrong with that picture?"

The photo, actually two of them—portrait and profile—was the standard mug shot set. A man, late twenties or mid-thirties, weight listed at one-seventy-five, height listed as five-ten. Thin enough to be a little muscled up. Moustache drooping into a Fu Manchu, but that could have changed. Light brown receding hairline. Physically, he matched the man I had seen on the wedding aisle.

"Holy shit," I said. "When was this taken?"

"June. Bar fight arrest."

"So where are the tattoos?"

37

Lane Franklin wears the same soft milk chocolate complexion as her mother. She flashes a clone of her mother's perfect smile. She ignited the smile as she opened her front door to meet us.

"Hi, Mister Stewart!" she threw an unabashed hug around me. I squeezed her back, carefully, mindful of Andy's comment about a crush.

"Hi, Lane! Who you gonna fly for?"

"Delta Air Lines! Over twelve hundred airplanes and I plan to fly them all!"

"I believe you will."

Lane traded hugs with Andy. "What's going on?"

"Like I said, I need a little Photoshop help." Andy held up a flash drive. "Photo of a suspect."

"Cool!" Lane ushered us in.

Lane lives with her mother in a small square house on a small block in a neighborhood that sprouted in the fertile fifties when Eisenhower presided over a post-war building boom. The house belonged to a nephew of the original Rosemary, who arranged for Lane's mother to rent it when she took over the office management job at Essex County Air Services.

Rosemary II emerged from a small kitchen, wearing a duplicate of Lane's smile and a long, fluffy bathrobe.

"I am so sorry to do this at this hour," Andy apologized as they exchanged hugs.

"Nonsense! I put on fresh coffee. Take off your coats. Come in! Come in! Can I offer you something to eat? We have pie."

Andy could have called Rosemary II at three in the morning and asked her to prepare a full Thanksgiving dinner, and the woman would have asked what kind of cranberries to serve.

"Mom," Lane protested, "this is police business!"

"Police business sometimes requires investigating pie," I pointed out. "First, and most important question. What kind?"

"My special apple cinnamon, a la mode."

"Sounds like that suspect needs questioning," I said.

"That would be lovely," Andy added.

Rosemary II swept off to the kitchen. Lane held out her hand for the flash drive. Andy withheld the tiny drive. "First, I'm swearing you in as a temporary deputy."

"Essex PD doesn't have deputies." Lane is a precise, scholarly child.

"Didn't you hear the governor? Andy works for the sheriff's department now and she's a detective!" I laughed.

"Stop it. Auxiliary officer, then," Andy countered. She pressed the flash drive into Lane's hand. Lane crossed the small living room to a desk with an iMac and plugged in the drive. The iMac was big, new, and expensive—a back-to-school gift Andy and I funded using certain stolen drug money.

"There's an image on the drive called 'Sixth.' Can you make a copy of it and open it in Photoshop in a way that you can, you know, retouch it?"

Lane chased the mouse across the screen. She clicked open the Photoshop program and opened the image. Another mug shot. My first impression was of a totem or native art. Lines and letters composed tattoos across the man's forehead, cheeks, and neck. My second immediate impression sprang from the eyes, pale and cold.

The eyes chilled me. I imagined those eyes aligning the sights of a weapon on a child's puffy white and yellow jacket. No flicker of remorse as the gun fired. No glint of conscience. Something tingled at the back of my neck. I felt the black, solid shape of murder in my heart. If this man killed those children, I would happily do the same for him.

"Uuk!" Lane commented. "White supremacist?"

Andy and I, standing behind Lane, traded glances.

"Oh, don't worry. Mama teaches me all sorts of valuable things. Don't eat mushrooms in the yard. Look both ways before crossing a street. Stay away from people with Nazi tattoos and football score IQs. Basic, common sense things every child should know."

"You better!" came from the kitchen.

"Well, stay away from this one," Andy commanded, voicing my feelings.

I pointed at the screen and asked Andy, "You told me what 88 means—what does 1488 mean?" He wore it centered on his forehead at the hairline.

Lane spoke up. "Fourteen words. 'We must secure the existence of our people and a future for White Children.' I forget which of them said it. And the 88 stands for HH, which is Heil Hitler, because H is the eighth letter of the alphabet—and probably because they can't count much higher."

Andy and I gaped at her.

"What? If I'm not invited to the cool kids' party, I like to know why. Is he one of the ones you found up on that farm? The ones who robbed the wedding? It was on the news this morning!"

"I can't tell you," Andy said. "I can't share any details. And you can't speculate, Lane. Or talk to anybody about this."

"Got it." She turned and smiled up at me. "I'm good with secrets, right?"

"Right," I said. "Focus, Lane."

"Right. What do you want me to do? Age him? Give him some hair? Because he really needs some."

"I want to see if you can paint out all those tattoos. Can you do that? And show me what he'd look like with a normal face? Or if he had makeup on, covering them up."

"God didn't give him a normal face, but I'll see if Photoshop can." She paused and turned around to look at both of us. "Cool. Okay. Go away. I can't work with people looking over my shoulder."

. . .

WE ATE pie at a small kitchen table with Rosemary II. We traded small talk. We talked about Earl, and shared thoughts on how sad it was for him to lose a lifelong friend in Bob Stone. Andy shifted the conversation to Lane, and let Rosemary II brag about her daughter, her schoolwork, her recent interest in extracurriculars. Lane had joined a Philosophy Club, which came as no surprise to me.

After clearing away the pie dishes, Rosemary II checked on her daughter. Lane said she needed another hour. I felt bad that we were approaching midnight, but Rosemary II said to take as long as we needed; she was going to bed.

The rain and drizzle passed hours ago, replaced by cool, dry fall air. With few places in the small house to wait out Lane, Andy and I took a walk. A pair of strangers strolling the sidewalk of a small-town neighborhood at midnight. We garnered curious looks from a dog walker, but Andy simply waved a cheery hello and we strolled on, arm in arm.

"You think that's him?" I asked. "The sixth man?"

Andy equivocated. "I do. And I don't. He might be. And he can't be."

"That's definitive."

She acknowledged the problem with a pensive nod.

We strolled in silence before I had to ask her to spill it.

"Okay," she began, hands gesturing. "I logged in to the station server tonight. I spent the last couple hours searching national criminal databases. Feeding in search parameters. White supremacist. Nazi. Gun crimes. Male. Caucasian. Right-handed. Height and weight parameters. Tattoos. Face and hands. They're all broad sweeps, but when you put them together, you can drill down to a few hundred individuals."

"Only a few hundred," I commented. I stopped suddenly.

"What?"

"The wedding photos! It was a wedding, with cameras everywhere," I said.

Andy shook her head before I had a chance to collect my genius certificate.

"We obtained all of Sandy and Todd's wedding photos and video, but there are only two shots that show the man in the brown suit, both at a distance and with his face away from the camera. He probably kept tabs on where the official photographers were and kept an eye out for people pulling out their phones. So, there wasn't a 'wow' shot to work with."

"Oh. But you saw him. Other people had to see him."

"I did…" She hesitated. She put her hand on my arm. She closed her eyes. "That trick I told you about. I can see him. No words. I don't even want to try to use words. But I can see him." She opened her eyes. "I can give the basic cop description all day long, and if we had a sketch artist, I suppose we could get close. I decided to skip that step. Because I knew his photo had to be in the system somewhere."

We continued our stroll. The block ended. We turned the corner.

"I went to the computer. Drilled down to a couple hundred mug shots. Scanned those as fast as possible—and I mean fast on purpose—and I tagged the ones I was sure he *wasn't*. Then I dug through what was left. Around fifty."

"Yes…?"

"And there he was."

Now I stopped her. "That guy? The one you gave Lane? You really think that's him? What about the Tennessee Nazi?"

She shook her head.

"I don't think that's him," she said. "You said it yourself. Where are the tattoos? I think the rice phone was a plant."

"So, who's Lane doing the tattoo removal job on?"

"That's Garrett Foyle. White supremacist. Record for assault, robbery, murder."

"What am I not getting here? It sounds like you're undoing the biggest case in Wisconsin history—one which, I might add, you solved!"

Andy ignored my praise, as she usually does.

"Will, I went through the photos over and over, paring them down—and I kept coming back to him. Over and over. And yes, I can't be sure if I'm starting to shape my memory to his picture, but he's the only one that fits what I see when I do that trick. I play *California Girls* in my head and I can see him, at the wedding, standing by the bar, drinking a water."

"So, aside from 'they think they already got the guy' what's the problem?"

Andy brushed her hair across her right temple, an automatic gesture she used when stalling for an answer.

"I have two nagging problems with this man. First, I have been asking myself, what was he doing in the tent before the robbery? Why take that risk? Someone was sure to see him. *I saw him.* Why not just rush the place? Masks on. Guns out. Which is exactly what the other five did. I'm sure he ducked out to put on his mask. Out and back in. What sense does that make?"

I shrugged. "Reconnaissance?"

"It took them less than a minute to empty out the urn. They didn't have to reconnoiter. They and everyone else knew right where the gift cards would be."

"Okay. What's the second problem?"

Again, a frustrated shake of the head.

"He's got the perfect alibi. He's doing three consecutive life terms for murder."

38

Lane, like any other gifted child, lost herself in her work. Andy and I returned from our walk and slipped in the front door unnoticed. She hunched over the iMac screen, engrossed, the tip of her tongue peeking out at the corner of her mouth. She stroked a special tablet with a special pen, working digital magic.

We took chairs in the kitchen. Rosemary II left coffee in a carafe for us. I didn't anticipate sleep any time soon. I poured another cup. Another half hour passed.

"Oh!" Lane exclaimed, rising to the surface. "I didn't know you were here! I think I'm done. Want to see?"

My healing pelvic bones let me know I'd been sitting too long. Andy hurried to a position behind Lane. I caught up.

The man stared at us from the screen, transformed. Lane had cleaned his skin of every ink stain, yet preserved the blemishes, creases, and pure hatred simmering in the soul beneath the skin.

Andy, the bartender, and maybe Pidge had seen the sixth man. I had only seen his handiwork. Looking at the cold-blooded eyes on the screen, I didn't know if the face staring at us matched or not, but I knew the owner of that face was capable of the evil I'd seen at the wedding and later in the woods.

I looked at Andy.

She stared, motionless, her expression revealing nothing, the perfect camouflage for thoughts that spun in high gear in her mind. After a moment, she placed her hand on Lane's shoulder.

"Can you copy that to the flash drive for me? And print me a copy?"

Lane grinned. "Sure can. Did I do good?"

"You did good."

LANE PRODUCED photo paper and sized the image for a printout. Andy shot a picture of the picture with her phone, then collected the image and the flash drive, and made sure Lane didn't keep anything on her iMac.

Sitting in the car again, under the streetlight, Andy worked her phone.

"What are you doing?"

"Texting Pidge."

"Uh, it's after one thirty."

"So, if she's asleep, she'll—"

Andy's phone rang. She gave me a know-it-all look.

"Hi Pidge!"

"Girl, tell me you are off shift and ready to party!" Pidge spoke loudly through the tiny phone speaker. Bar noise rumbled in the background.

"Where are you?" Andy asked.

"Sully's! Are you coming? For real?"

"Yes. Be there in five minutes," Andy said smiling.

"Fucking awesome!" The connection ended.

"Sounds like some serious girl fun," Andy smiled at me. "I may have to leave you in the car."

"Fine with me," I said. "It's past my bedtime."

39

Sully's bar and bowling alley throbbed with loud music and twenty-somethings like Pidge, both of which made me feel old and tired at the ancient age of thirty-three. We found Pidge in a semicircular booth surrounded by a mix of young men and women in full animation over a table covered with pizza, chicken wings and conquered beer bottles.

Seeing Andy, Pidge displaced a few of her friends and scooted out the bench seat, no easy trick considering she wore the yellow version of the little black dress I'd seen at the wedding. Most of her girlfriends were similarly clad, or in tight leggings and tiny tops. Some of them bobbed and jiggled to a bass beat that could have served as a defibrillator. I caught a few of the fellows watching Pidge's movements appreciatively. And checking out my wife.

"Andy! What did you bring him for? We have all this fucking firm meat to choose from!" Pidge embraced Andy. "God, Will, I don't think I've ever seen you in a bar this late!"

"I go to bed after they serve the ice cream at the nursing home."

"Can we talk for a minute? Outside?" Andy asked.

"Lead the way!"

The music dropped to a muted bass beat outside the bar's entrance doors. A brisk night chill hung in the air. Pidge paid no attention to the cold. I wondered how much she had to drink.

"Do you remember the guy with the makeup?" Andy asked.

"Fuckin' A."

"I know you might not really remember what he looked like, or maybe didn't get a great look at him, but I want to show you a couple pictures. Just give me your feelings, okay? Gut impressions. Okay?"

"Got it!"

Andy showed Pidge a photo printout. Pidge tipped her head back and forth considering it.

"Nah, that's not him."

Andy tucked away the Nellis photo. She showed Pidge the printout of Lane's Photoshop work.

"Fucking asshole. That's him. Is that the guy they took down? Somewhere down south? I saw it on the TV tonight, but they didn't have the sound on." Pidge grinned at Andy. "Hey! I saw you on TV, too. Hanging out with the governor. Nice!"

Andy put away the photos without answering Pidge's question. She looked directly at me. "What are the chances Earl would let us use one of his airplanes tomorrow—er, today?"

"I'm not calling him at this hour."

"Fuck, we'll just steal one!" Pidge exclaimed.

"Who said anything about you?" I asked.

"Because you don't have a fucking license, dumbass. And because Andy's on the hunt and I am not fucking missing that. And because I want to be the one to tell Earl we stole one of his airplanes!" She grinned at me.

"Well, you're not flying," I told her, gesturing at the bar, thinking of the empties on the table. "Where are we going?" I asked Andy.

"Montana. Great Western Correctional," she said distantly, thinking ahead to the destination. "I need to interview a lifer."

"Lemme go throw some money on the table, and I'll be right out!" Pidge bounced through the bar doors, leaving Andy and me standing in neon light.

Andy's phone rang.

"Christ, is everybody pulling all-nighters?" I muttered. "Who is it?"

"I don't recognize the number," she said. She raised the phone to her ear. "Andrea Stewart."

I could not make out the words—a woman's voice.

"This is."

Long, urgent talking.

"Where are you now?"

"No, that's not far. Stay there, wait for me, please."

"No, just me, until we know what's going on."

"No, I know the house. Just stay there."

The call ended.

"What?"

"That was Senator Stone's chief of staff, a woman named Keller. She thinks something has happened to Sandy Stone."

Pidge reappeared, topping her tiny yellow dress with a tiny blue denim jacket. "Let's go fly!"

"Hold up," Andy said. "There may be a wrinkle. Will and I have to drive up to The Lakes and talk to someone. It might derail our plans."

"Lemme come along!"

Andy and I traded glances. "It might save time," Andy suggested, "if nothing changes and we still fly out."

"Better if she goes out to the field and gets One Nine Alpha gassed and ready. And if it's all cancelled, she can find a bar that serves breakfast."

"I know a place like that." Pidge poked me in the ribs.

"Do you mind?" Andy asked.

"Fuck, no! Call me when you know what's going on." We started for our cars. Pidge called out, "Hey! Where should I flight plan for?"

"Sioux Valley, Montana," Andy said.

"Seriously, Pidge, check the schedule. I don't want to put Rosemary II in a bind," I added.

"Yeah, yeah."

ANDY and I made the forty-five-minute drive to the Lakes Region in the northeast corner of the county in about thirty minutes. Trees tinged with fall color swept overhead on narrow country roads, looking haunted on the fringes of the headlight high beams. I searched the roadside for deer, not that it mattered. At Andy's speed, there would be no stopping.

The midnight run took us to Sunset Circle Road, which scribed a perimeter around Leander Lake, the long central finger of the three lakes comprising the Lakes Region. Homes nudging the shore of Leander Lake command some of the highest real estate dollars in Wisconsin. It wasn't uncommon to see a big, beautiful home purchased, torn down, and replaced with a bigger, more beautiful home. The rare-air money, climbing ever higher, seemed to come mostly out of Chicago and the two coasts. Few locals lived on Leander Lake anymore.

Sunset Circle Road curved between the woodlands that hugged the lake on one side of the road, and farm fields on the other. Midway up the east shore, Andy slowed for a set of brick pillars supporting cast iron gates. The gates hung open. At the end of an asphalt driveway, the lights of the late Senator Bob Stone's lake home, a Cape Cod-style near-mansion set among tall hardwood trees, cast a warm glow across a broad lawn.

A car parked at the top of the driveway loop in front of the house, lights on. Exhaust puffed from the tailpipe.

"Do you think I should do *the other thing*?" I asked Andy.

She shook her head. "Keller sounded like she was alone."

We pulled up behind the car, a nearly new Cadillac. As we did, the motor stopped. The driver stepped into our headlights. An attractive woman between thirty and sixty, hair colored blonde, slender, dressed in what were probably designer labels, walked toward us.

"Sergeant Stewart?" She shielded her eyes from our headlights.

"Yes, ma'am," Andy answered. "This is my husband, Will." Under other circumstances, approaching a house at night, Andy would have operated differently. Headlights off. Interior car lights off. Not closing the car door to avoid making noise.

If anyone waited for us in the house, our arrival had been well telegraphed. Lights burned inside, but they had the look of lights on timers. At this hour, any legitimate occupants would have been in dark upstairs bedrooms sleeping.

"I'm Lorna Keller, Senator Stone's chief of staff—well, former chief of staff." She shook hands with Andy and paid no attention to me.

"I'm so sorry for your loss," Andy said.

"Why don't we go inside'" Andy hesitated. "It's alright. I have a key. I just didn't want to wait inside alone. Come."

A woman accustomed to giving orders. We followed her.

Keller's key opened entry to a light and airy home, trimmed with white woodwork and decorated in a nautical theme throughout. She turned on lights like someone who felt at home. She led us through a large foyer to a great room at the back of the house. A bank of black windows spread across the outer wall, no doubt yielding a splendid view of the lake in daylight. White wicker furniture with plush blue and teal cushions offered seating, separated by coffee and end tables, some with lamps, some exhibiting nautical instruments that lured my pilot's eye.

Andy searched the room and its connecting doorways.

"There's no one here," Keller said. "Sandra was supposed to be here."

Andy opened her coat for access to her weapon.

"I'd like to look around," Andy said, "Will can stay here with you. It'll only take a minute." Andy moved off on her own.

"Would you like coffee?" Keller offered.

"I'm kinda swimming in it," I said. I pointed. "Is that a bathroom?"

"Yes. I'm going to make a pot."

Andy returned by the time I finished, satisfied that the house was empty. I joined her in the great room. Keller returned moments later from the direction of what I assumed to be a kitchen.

"You said you think something has happened to Sandy?" Andy asked.

"She's supposed to be here. I've been trying to reach her." Keller substituted anger for panic in her tone. "Sandra told me to meet her here."

"When?"

"When did she tell me? This morning, at the hospital."

"When were you supposed to meet here?"

"It wasn't firm. She told me to call, and we would work it out. We were going to make the arrangements—for the funeral. I helped her with the transport details."

Andy gestured for Keller to sit in one of the chairs with a view of the lake. Andy took a seat facing her.

"Sandra said she was going with Todd, to meet the governor, to make the announcement about Bob's passing. But then I saw it on television, and she wasn't there—and that business about Todd!" Keller waved one hand in the air dismissively. "That was all wrong. So, I called her, and she didn't answer, and I called the hotel, and she had checked out. And then I called Todd."

"What did the grieving son-in-law have to say?" I asked.

Keller huffed a single-note opinion. "He told me my services were no longer needed. I asked to speak to Sandra. The little snot hung up on me! Sergeant, that's not how this was supposed to go."

"Todd fired you?"

"If he assumes he has the authority. And I know what you're thinking. That I'm upset, disgruntled. That's not it. Let me—let me back up, so you understand. Things have been—well, more than a little difficult this week. I've been with Bob a long time, and as you can imagine—this has not been easy."

"I'm sure it hasn't," Andy said.

"We all knew, almost from the start, that Bob was gone. The damage was severe. He had no brain activity, nothing to give us hope. The plan was to let him go today. Sandra and I discussed it at length."

"Was Todd involved in the discussion?"

"Todd involves himself in everything. Could I say he drove the decision? No. But there was no need. Bob's condition was obvious. Todd had no need to tip his hand."

"Tip his hand?"

"Todd Jameson had it in his head he would become a state senator before his wife washed her father's blood off her hands last Saturday. I'm certain of that."

"Ma'am, I don't really know if I'm the one to talk to about the politics of all this. I'm here because you said you thought something happened to Sandy. Why?"

"I told you. She's not here!"

"Why would she be here? Don't they have a home of their own, she and her husband?"

"He has his place in Madison. She has hers in Essex."

"So, wouldn't they go to one or the other?"

"Sandra was firm about meeting me here."

"With—or without Todd?"

"I suppose with." Keller spoke the words as if they tasted bad. She leaned forward to make her point. "I helped Sandra arrange with the hospital to have her father come home, here, to Essex County where he grew up. She had no reason to go anywhere else. She told me she was coming back here, *specifically here*, to the lake house and that I should join her here. That she and I would organize her father's affairs and deal with the funeral from here. She said Todd told her he had arranged for his friend to fly them home, here, after the announcement."

I started to ask the aviation question, but Andy cut me off.

"Walk me through this part. When they left the hospital."

"When it was—over—for the senator—when he passed—we were all very upset—Sandra was upset—and Todd said they should go straight to the hotel and check out before the press got wind of everything—and Sandra went along with it. He said he had spoken to the governor, and the governor offered to make the public death announcement. Todd made it sound like he had taken care of everything. That's when she told me she would call me, after the announcement, and we would meet here."

"You were there for all of this? At the hospital?"

"Yes."

"Did Sandy know that the governor would appoint Todd to fill out the senator's term?"

"Absolutely not! Neither Sandra nor I knew that the governor's announcement included Todd taking over his term. In fact, Sandra told me she had already spoken to the governor about serving out her father's term. An absolutely horrible idea, by the way. Second only to Todd, that is."

"She told me the same thing, this morning," Andy said, "except the part about the governor."

"Thank heavens! At least someone else knows! She told me she would see the funeral through, *and then* address the question of succeeding her father. I planned to talk her down, of course. Neither Sandra nor I had no idea that Todd and the governor would do what they did."

"Why did you call me?" Andy asked.

Keller stood and walked to the kitchen. As she returned with her purse in hand, she pulled out a curled piece of paper. She handed it to Andy.

"That's your card, with your number. You gave it to Sandra."

"Yes. How did you get it?"

"I think Sandra thought something might go wrong. Right as she was leaving, we hugged. You know—I practically raised that girl. After her mother passed." Keller's crisp façade fractured. She pushed back tears and adjusted her affect the way a woman adjusts a skirt. "Anyway, we hugged—and she pressed this card into my hand. And then Todd hustled her away."

I went back to the question that struck me earlier. "Who's Todd's friend? The one with the airplane? Was it Parks?" I asked.

"Yes. Pearce Parks. He has his own jet. Do you know him?"

"No."

"I still do not see how any of this suggests something has happened to Sandy, Ms. Keller."

"I am *very* concerned that I cannot reach her. That *never* happens. I've been calling her cell. I tried the hotel—her house—Todd's condo, his cell. I tried all day. This evening I started calling here, to the house, the land line. I got no answer. There's always staff here when the house is open. There's a cook and usually a maid. I spoke to both and they said they heard nothing from Sandra. I tried all the lines. I know them all. So, after a few hours, I drove up here. And…" Keller waved her arms at the emptiness around us.

"Maybe they went to Sandy's house. Or decided to check into a hotel. Maybe all this—" Andy mimicked Keller's gesture at the house "—was too much—reminded her too much of her father."

"You don't understand. That's *why* she wanted to be here. To be closer to him. That girl grew up in this house."

Andy frowned.

"Parks has that Falcon 20 that Dave flies," I offered to Andy. "It wasn't at the airport when we got back, but that doesn't mean they didn't drop Sandy and Todd off and fly right out again."

"Sergeant…"

"Andrea, please," my wife said.

"Andrea, this is going to sound—well, I guess I should just say it—I have been thinking about this a lot since the wedding. I think that man meant to shoot Bob."

Andy didn't speak. I followed her lead.

"I know how that sounds, and to be honest, if Sandra were here, and if—if everything had just gone the way she and I discussed—well, I probably would be the first to dismiss the idea as crazy. It's just—the way things are happening—the way Todd has been, and with Pearce Parks in the picture…"

"Who's Litton?" I asked.

Keller looked at me, surprised. "Bargo Litton?"

"Sounds like a movie villain. Who is he?"

Keller broke a thin, rueful smile. "He certainly is a villain, if you want me to be honest. He's an energy billionaire, a kingmaker. He's the biggest money behind Republican national politics and policies. But don't let that fool you. His only party affiliation is himself. Last presidential election, you probably saw the story of how all the candidates went to his home in California for a—" she raised both hands and made quotation marks with her fingers "—meeting. The truth is, they all went to suck his dick and be anointed, excuse my language."

"Why would he write a check for a hundred million?"

"To whom?"

"I don't know," I lied, partially. "Something I heard."

She studied me with sharp, smart eyes. "You're running in very special circles, Will, if you heard something about money like that."

I shrugged.

"Litton can buy a lot of state senate seats with that kind of money, but state politics is small change for him. He trades in power on the national stage. A hundred million gets him a Senate race, maybe a president. You're sure about this?"

"Another question. What's seventy-six-oh-eight?"

Her expression grew sharper, wary. "Where did you hear that?"

"Maybe you should tell us," Andy said in her cop voice. "You're the one who called us." Andy's terse tone didn't affect Keller. She maintained her posture as someone accustomed to being in charge. I think Andy wanted her to know she wasn't.

"It's a bill, a dead bill, or would be as long as Bob was alive," Keller said slowly, thoughtfully. Her eyes focused on a distant thought. "It's a bill to allow construction of private prisons in Wisconsin."

Andy and I must have adopted the same blank expression.

"In Wisconsin, private prisons are illegal, did you know that?"

"I wasn't aware," Andy said.

"Well, they are, but our governor, back when he was a state assemblyman, pushed through a little piece of legislation that allows Wisconsin to ship prisoners out of state to serve their time, with the loophole being that there are no restrictions on putting the prisoners in private prisons in other states."

"Until a week ago, I didn't even know there was such a thing," I said.

"It's a billion-dollar industry. And Pearce Parks is the CEO of Evergreen Reform. Clever name, don't you think? Evergreen is not the largest private prison player, but one of the larger second-tier players. Thanks to our governor's little piece of loophole legislation, the state spends around fifty million a year with private companies, housing around nine percent of our prison population out of state in private prisons. Evergreen Reform prisons. And guess who is one of the biggest contributors to the governor's campaigns?"

"I'd rather not," I said. "Not on an empty stomach. So, Senator Stone, although he was a Republican, stood in the way of some big money to be made by introducing private prisons in Wisconsin."

"It was never going to happen while Bob held a seat in the state senate. Private prisons have a bad record for security, for the health of their prisoners, for being short-staffed and low-paying—all the things that add up to making a profit, but which make them wrong for a man like Bob Stone. Only now …"

Keller suddenly stood up and paced, one hand waving like someone plucking shapeless pieces out of thin air and arranging them.

"Parks needed the legislation passed. He has the governor in his pocket, but the governor can only push it so far. They could not get seventy-six-oh-eight off the ground, not with Bob in the way. But now—"

She put her hand to her forehead, seeing something we could not, astonished by it.

"Todd!" she exclaimed. "He's the golden boy! He's been anointed."

"What do you mean?"

"Litton! The hundred million! He's giving the hundred million to Todd!"

Andy and I traded looks. I wasn't about to reveal how my eavesdropping at the capitol confirmed Keller's deduction.

"He's giving Todd one hundred million? Dollars?" Andy asked.

Keller shook her head emphatically and waved at us. "No! Not directly. Litton doesn't do anything that directly. He's twelve moves ahead of everyone else on the board. He doesn't buy sitting senators. He buys two elections down the road. Same with presidents. If he's putting out a hundred million, it's going into a PAC—like Citizens for Freedom, or Prosperity America or some bullshit name—a PAC that's being built around Todd's future." Keller stopped. "*That son of a bitch!*"

"What?"

"Todd's on a trajectory for much bigger things. Todd, the governor, and Parks had to prove themselves to Litton to convince him to make the investment, so they did. *They took Bob out of the picture!*" She said the last with venom in her voice.

"Do you seriously think the governor is part of an assassination plot?" Andy asked.

Keller scoffed. "Of course not! He's too fucking stupid. They would never include him in something like that because he'd get caught and sell them all out to save his own hide. But Parks, he's a snake. And Todd is a snake, too. And the governor likes having snakes around him. People who can do things he can deny."

Keller folded her arms across her bosom and stared at the floor in front of her, eyes blazing.

"And Sandra...Sandra was going to mess up everything...the announcement today. That's why she wasn't there. They needed to announce that Todd will finish Bob's term. That's Todd's point of entry on the political stage. Sandra would have blocked it. One word of her plans to the press and they would have been helpless to stop her. Even the Madison liberals loved Bob Stone. Can you imagine if his daughter stepped up to finish his term? A political virgin?"

Andy stood up and paced toward the windows. She fixed her gaze on something distant, something hidden in the black. Her reverie held us in silence until Andy said, "Ma'am, I get that there are high-level politics here, but you're talking about two people who just got married. And as you said, Sandy is a kindergarten teacher, not a politician. Her husband may be a politician and he may know the governor—but assassination? Conspiracy theories sound great in the middle of the night, but they break down in the light of day. Maybe Sandy and Todd worked it out. Maybe tonight they're staying at Todd's place, or her place. Maybe it was nothing but a robbery with tragic, collateral damage. Maybe Sandy will call you in the morning."

Andy's down-to-earth tack surprised me. An hour ago, she had been making plans to look at a suspect who could not possibly be involved.

Keller turned to Andy. "Sergeant, do you want to know the real reason I called you? The reason I trust you?"

Andy looked at Keller guardedly.

"Because you looked like you didn't know what the fuck they were talking about at that press conference today."

40

Keller walked with us to the car.

"Ms. Keller, I have no choice. I have to start with the theory that Sandy simply decided to go home tonight. We'll have officers check both residences. We'll also check hotels. If they stayed at Todd Jameson's place, maybe they never left Madison."

"She won't be there."

"We'll see. I just need you to understand that my priority at this point is to find Sandy."

"Mine, too."

"I don't know how much I believe that, but rest assured, if it comes down to a choice between helping Sandy or exposing a political plot, for me, there's no contest."

"Andrea, I may come across as a cold political hack, the win-at-all-costs operator I had to be to do my job, but Bob Stone was an honorable man, a man who served. You can't work for a man like that and not have a moral compass. He wouldn't allow it. Ask *his* boss." She pointed at me. "Oh yes, I know who you are, Mr. Stewart. And I know your boss. Earl Jackson is the same kind of man. Bob and Earl were more alike than different. You go find Sandy, make sure she's okay, and if you can, get her free of her husband so that I can talk to her. Whatever else comes to pass will be for the historians or the special prosecutors to sort out."

Andy shook Keller's hand and we departed, leaving her standing alone in front of a huge, empty house.

ANDY CALLED Mike Mackiejewski on patrol. She asked him to drive to Sandy Stone's home in Essex and knock on the door. If she's not there, she told Mike, check the better hotels in town. As an afterthought, he told Mike to add several of the better B&Bs to the list. It would mean waking people, but it covered the possibility that the newlyweds may be genuinely trying to hide from the media.

After her call to Mike, we rode in heavy silence, simmering dark thoughts, until her phone chirped. The call from Mike lasted only a few seconds.

"She's not at home," Andy said, stowing the phone.

"Transition," I said. "Parks and Jameson. They called it 'transition.'" I explained again what I had heard in the hallway outside the Governor's office.

The word hung between us, collecting weight.

"Dee, I think Sandy's in real trouble."

Andy didn't take her eyes from the road, or the strand of hair from across her forehead where it had fallen.

A flag, declaring war.

"I think you're right."

PART II

41

We broke through the cloud tops at nine thousand feet, climbing to ten thousand in smooth air. Behind us, thin light marked dawn's imminent arrival on the eastern horizon. The Navajo's twin engines hummed at climb power, which I held for a moment after reaching ten thousand. I touched the autopilot and gave it command of the aircraft while I tinkered with the power setting and cowl flaps. Stabilized at cruise power, the airspeed indicator showed close to two hundred knots. I checked the GPS and read a ground speed of just over one seventy. Bit of headwind. The Foreflight app on the iPad showed an estimated time of arrival at Aberdeen, South Dakota in just over two hours.

Sioux Valley, Montana, our ultimate destination, lay at the precise range limit of the Navajo, which mandated the Aberdeen fuel stop. Even with good weather ahead, I never cut it close on fuel.

Andy occupied the co-pilot's seat, hair tied in functional ponytail, headphones on. She paid no attention to the panel full of instruments lit in subtle night vision red. Instead, she gazed out at the skyscape, black above and studded with stars. The clouds below took on a glow in advance of the dawn. She seemed to appreciate the mystery and magic in this world I love so much. At least I hoped so.

Pidge sprawled under a light blanket on two of the club seats in the back. If she wasn't sound asleep, she did a creditable imitation. She had changed out of the little yellow dress and into black slacks and her white uniform shirt topped with a light leather flying jacket.

In addition to putting on the uniform, by the time Andy and I arrived at the field, Pidge had the plane fueled and a flight plan filed under her name. On the way to the airport, Andy diverted for a stop at home. She dismissed the idea that we could fly to Montana, conduct our business, and fly home in the same day. She insisted we pack overnight bags. I didn't argue. The flight tallied to a five-hour trip, allowing for the fuel stop. Not having slept, I knew I would be in no shape to pilot us home at the end of a long day, even with Pidge along. We would be returning Earl's airplane tomorrow, Sunday.

"One Nine Alpha, ten thousand," I reported to ATC.

"One Nine Alpha, proceed on course."

"One Nine Alpha."

Pidge stocked the cockpit with a thermos full of coffee, but I left it alone. The nearest restroom lay four hundred miles ahead. Plus, her coffee isn't the equal of coffee made by Rosemary II. I have no idea how Pidge manages to screw it up. They use the same ingredients and the same brewing machinery.

Andy and I didn't speak much between the Stone lake house and the airport. Mike Mackiejewski called again after he struck out at the Ramada and the Holiday Inn. He asked if he should keep checking hotels. Andy told him yes and reminded him about the B&Bs. Check them all, she told him, then go back to the station and get the Madison police to check Todd Jameson's home. She added instructions to call Lorna Keller and get Todd Jameson's cell number—and start calling it. Mike wanted to know if we were investigating a missing person, an abduction, a person in imminent danger, or what? Andy didn't answer for a moment. At length, she said we just want to confirm Sandy's location. That we may need to speak to her. She told Mike she would be out of touch for a few hours, but would check in. She didn't tell him where she was going.

Fifteen minutes into the first navigation leg, I intruded on Andy's thoughts.

"What if he's there?" I asked via intercom. "Your guy. Foyle."

"I don't know," Andy replied. My Bose headset delivered her voice to the center of my skull, lending intimacy to the conversation. "It's the perfect alibi. It makes him the ideal tool for the job. In a way, if he's there, sitting in his cell, it proves the theory as much as if he were missing."

"How much of Keller's conspiracy theory do you buy?"

She laughed lightly. "Too much. I should have started formulating the same theory while I stood like a fool on the steps of the capitol rotunda yesterday."

"I wanted to make you disappear."

"You and me both."

"I'm going to call you 'Deputy Detective' from now on."

She smiled at me. "Really? I had no idea you had embraced a life of celibacy."

"Good point, Sergeant," I corrected myself.

She reached over and squeezed my forearm.

"Seriously, do you really think Jameson and Parks engineered an assassination—of Bob Stone? I mean…"

"That's the thing about theories," she said. "You're all in one minute, then ridiculing yourself for thinking something so crazy thing the next."

After a few minutes she said, "More than anything else, I just want to look at him."

She lost me. "Who?"

"Foyle. I don't need to talk to him. He wouldn't respond to me, anyway. It's not about talking to him," she said. "I just need to see him in person. Then I'll know."

Her gaze settled on the sea of clouds below us, but her eyes were fixed on a man wearing heavy makeup.

42

Dawn chased us into South Dakota. I tapped the coffee thermos sixty minutes out from landing. It was either too soon or the coffee flowed straight to my bladder, because after landing and parking the Navajo at the gas pumps I had to beat a hasty path across the ramp to the fixed base operations office. Pidge and Andy followed suit.

After emptying my tank, I filled the Navajo's tanks using an Essex County Air Service credit card. There would be a reckoning with Earl. Pidge belatedly confessed that although the airplane wasn't booked for today, the Navajo had a charter scheduled tomorrow, and we had nothing available as backup.

"You're telling me this now?"

She gave me an impish smile. "If I told you before, we wouldn't have taken it. See how it all works out?"

"Works out? Now I have to call Rosemary II after we land in Montana and confess to the theft of Earl's airplane and beg her to see what she could do with the schedule."

"That's what I mean," Pidge curled up again in her seat, "you'll work it out."

We broke the bond with Aberdeen runway 31 a little before seven a.m., as the sun did the same with the eastern horizon.

Two hours later we landed at Sioux Valley Municipal Airport.

Andy got the answer to one question as we taxied to a tiedown spot on the ramp.

"Is that…?"

"It is," I said.

We both stared at the gleaming Falcon 20 jet sitting on the ramp.

"MORNIN'!" the ramp rat behind the counter greeted us as we stepped into the FBO office. He looked fresh out of high school, wore coveralls, and gawked at the two women who had just walked through the door, both of them striking on their worst days. I doubt he noticed me at all.

"Hi," Andy said warmly.

"What's your name?" Pidge zeroed in on him.

"I'm Mark," he managed to say.

"Well, Mark," Pidge said, "we're going to need a car. Do you have a crew car?"

A look of genuine pain crossed Mark's face. "We got one, but it's already gone."

"Did the crew of that jet take it?" Andy asked.

"I guess so. That's the only other transient we have right now."

"What kind of car is it? The one the jet crew took?"

"Buick LeSabre. Kinda old, but it's what we got." Almost all crew cars are old. They sit unlocked at small airports all over the country, often with the keys hanging in an unattended office. Pilots simply sign them out, take the keys, and fill the gas tank as a courtesy for the next pilot.

"What about the passengers? Did you see them arrive?"

"I just got here. They must'a come in yesterday," Mark said. "I wasn't here yesterday. Bobby might know."

"Could we talk to Bobby?" Andy asked.

"He ain't here today, 'cept he might be later," Mark said definitively.

Pidge put her forearms on the counter and pressed her breasts into them, causing enhanced cleavage to rise where the top of her shirt had somehow come unbuttoned.

"So, no car, Mark? Are you sure?" Pidge asked, leaning closer. "We won't be long. Just want to get into town, maybe get to know the local area better."

Mark's eyes all but vibrated as he worked to keep them above Pidge's shirt collar.

"Well, um—there's only the one," he said. "Of course, there's Mr. Donnelly's car. He keeps it here for when he comes up from Denver to go hunting. He lets us use it, so I suppose it would be okay for us to let you use it. Season doesn't start for another couple of weeks."

"You're so sweet!" Pidge put her hand on Mark's arm. "Where are the keys?"

MR. DONNELLY from Denver owned a green four-door Jeep Wrangler. Pidge liberated the keys from poor Mark and let him guide her to the vehicle. It sat under an open-sided carport at the back of the FBO office. She made a point of walking down the hallway to the back door ahead of Mark so that he wouldn't have a chance to collect his wits and change his mind. Once behind the wheel, she rocketed around the building and across the open ramp to the Navajo. I finished tying the aircraft down while Andy and Pidge loaded our overnight bags into the Jeep.

Andy rode shotgun. I climbed into the tiny back seat.

"My new boyfriend says the best diner is on Main Street, and the best hotel is the motor court on the other end of town," Pidge announced, wheeling us off the ramp and onto a service road.

"Breakfast first, then I want to check you two into the motel," Andy announced.

"What do you mean, 'you two'?" I asked.

"I'm going out to the prison alone."

"Uh, no, that's a bad idea."

"Will, I did not call ahead. I do not have a court order. I have no local law enforcement contacts and no authority. I plan to just show up and see if I can badge my way in, which—given the circumstances—is unlikely. But I certainly can't do that with my civilian husband *appearing alongside me.*" She looked over her shoulder at me.

"Oh," I said, getting the message. "Okay."

"Wow," Pidge said, looking at me in the rearview mirror, "Cave in much?"

"She carries a gun." I settled back to watch the Montana scenery.

"And wears the pants," Pidge muttered loudly under her breath.

Andy threw me a conciliatory smile.

I LIKE SMALL TOWN DINERS. Some Saturday mornings I let Andy sleep in while I slip away to the Silver Spoon for breakfast with Earl and most of the retirees in Essex County. I'm more interested in the scrambled eggs than the solutions to all the world's problems, which are passed around the table along with the salt and pepper. But with the food and conversation comes a sense of belonging. You'll find one in almost any small town if you look past the franchise food.

A teenaged waitress guided us to a booth in the Prairie Diner, which we found on Main Street exactly as Mark described. Andy and I realized as we were ordering that our all-nighter and too much coffee left us ravenous. For an infusion of protein, salt, butter, and carbs, we had come to the right place.

"Did you notice?" Andy asked after the plates arrived and the waitress departed. She tipped her head in the direction of the counter.

There were no empty seats at the counter, and no women among those holding down a stool. Of the dozen or so men, five wore tan uniforms. Prison guards.

"Must be a big employer in town," I said. "We'd best tread lightly."

Andy flashed her green eyes in agreement.

"You guys going to tell me what we're on the hunt for?" Pidge asked.

"No!" we said in unison.

"C'mon! Is it that guy you showed me? It is, isn't it! Is he around here somewhere?"

"Pidge," Andy spoke in cop voice, "I promise to share with you what I can, but most certainly not here, not now, not in a public place."

"Oooooh…I get it." Pidge tapped her finger to her lips.

"Exactly."

We finished the meal and just one cup of coffee, perhaps the worst I've ever tasted, then made our way to the counter with the check in hand. I fished for my wallet and cash. Andy hung back a few steps, pausing where the corrections officers finished their after-shift breakfast.

"Excuse me, gentlemen," she touched one of the younger ones on the shoulder and flashed a smile, then just as quickly flashed her badge, "are you fellas from Great Western?"

"Yes, Ma'am!" the young guard brought himself upright on the counter stool. His eyes ran down, and back up, my wife quickly, and he gave back his best smile.

"I'm on my way out to the facility to drop off court transfers. I wonder if you could tell me who the duty officer is this morning?"

"Captain Leeson," the next guard over said quickly, looking to peel off some attention from the pretty woman. Both guards shot a glance over at me, assessing.

I threw my arm around Pidge, changing the dynamic in Andy's favor.

"C'mon, honey, let's get this show on the road," I said.

"Can I get a pack of gum, snuggle-bear?" Pidge beamed up at me.

"Captain Leeson?" Andy feigned a look of confusion. "Huh."

"Problem?" the guard asked, turning on his stool. "Something maybe I can help with?"

"That's so kind of you!" Andy touched his shoulder again. "It's just —I thought they gave me someone else's name, but I can't for the life of me—"

"Burton," the leaning-back guard said. "Captain Burton was supposed to be on this weekend but his wife's due any minute. He took her up to Billings for the delivery. He switched out with Leeson."

"Burton! Yes!" Andy gave the second guard a sparking smile. "That's it. Gentlemen, thank you so much!" She swept away toward the door, trailing their lingering eyes.

"Marshmallow, you know gum makes you car sick," I said to Pidge and pulled her away from the counter. We followed Andy out into the sunlight.

"Wow," Pidge said after climbing into the driver's seat, "way to pimp out your wife, Stewart!"

Andy laughed.

I didn't. "You two shouldn't be allowed out in public without supervision."

43

The Sioux Valley Motor Court nestled beside Montana State Highway 59, just shy of the sign that said the City of Sioux Valley Appreciates Your Visit, and Please Come Again. Cut from the classic motel cloth of the 1950s and 1960s, it looked like a row of shoe boxes, glued together side by side, extending for several hundred feet. Doors, painted red with brass numbers running from 1 to 14, marked off the rooms under the flat roof. Cars sat in front of a few but not all the room doors, giving truth to the word Vacancy written in neon at the bottom of a sign near the edge of the highway. We booked two rooms from the retiree-clerk, number 2 and number 7. Pidge claimed room 2 and declared that we should wake her if we planned to do anything for dinner or anything exciting, otherwise knock on her door only at risk of life and limb.

Andy and I dropped our bags in room 7. The room showed wear, but seemed clean, with fresh sheets, clean towels, and no sign of bed bugs. I had taken Ramp Rat Mark's designation of "Best Hotel" as being earned by default but gave credit where it was due. It was nice.

Andy phoned home.

"Hi, Chief. Did we get anything from Madison PD?"

I could not hear the other end of the conversation.

"Uh-huh."

"What? When?"

"You did? Can you send it to my phone?"

"No, not yet. I'm about to head out there now."

"Right. I will. Send me that video."

She ended the call and turned to me.

"They found Sandy," she said, but her distant, distracted expression made it more question than statement.

"Is she okay?"

Andy put up a finger, telling me to stand by. Cell towers between Essex and Sioux Valley did their jobs and a minute later Andy's phone chirped. She tapped the screen and slid in beside me so we could both watch.

The video was handheld, a shot of a television set I recognized. It hung on the wall in Chief Ceeves' office at Essex PD. Moiré patterns wiggled back and forth across the image. Tom had the Green Bay affiliate tuned. A news crawl ran across the bottom. The caption said, "State Senator's Daughter Distraught." Below that, a sub-caption said, "Family Video."

On the television screen, amateur video showed Todd Jameson walking with his arm around his wife, embracing and supporting her. Sandy moved in step with him along a wall. She wore dark glasses and didn't turn to the camera. The shot of the couple ended quickly, changing to a shot of Todd Jameson, standing in front of framed photos, speaking to the camera.

"…a terrible, terrible trauma, very devastating to my wife, who has lost so much this week. We want to thank everyone who has wished us well, and ask you to respect our privacy, particularly that of the senator's daughter, who is extremely distraught. Thank you."

The image jumped back to a television news anchor team before the cell phone video stopped.

"Tom got this off the news this morning. He got a call from someone at DCI telling him the newlyweds have retreated to an undisclosed family home and suggesting we stop chasing our tails. My guess, Madison PD tipped DCI that we were looking."

"Well," I said, because I could not think of anything else to say. Something bothered me about the video. "Can I see that again?"

She played it again. I shook my head, unable to scratch the itch.

"I have three missed calls from Ms. Keller," Andy said after taking back her phone. She touched the screen and raised the device to her ear. The call connected.

"Ms. Keller, this is Sergeant Stewart."

"Yes, I saw it."

"No, we have no idea where they are, but it's evident they are together."

"Right, but you must understand, to put out something like this actually protects Sandy. The whole world knows she and Todd are together now."

Which the whole world had assumed anyway, I thought.

"I understand your feelings, but—"

"Yes, but—"

The call ended. Andy lowered the phone, staring at it for a moment.

"I don't like that woman," she said.

"On that we can agree. Does she still think Sandy is in danger?"

"Most definitely."

"And do you?"

My wife slipped her phone in her pocket and looked up at me.

"Most definitely," she said. "Let's go to prison."

"Hang on," I said. I pulled my fishing vest out from my overnight bag. "Not without my ZIPPY units."

Eyes rolled. Andy planted her hands on her hips.

"Seriously? ZIPPY units?"

"Zoom Implementing Personal Propulsion in the Yard."

"No."

44

"That does not look like a prison," I said.

Several miles out of town, following a state highway that roughly traced the flow of a small river before curving on a wide arc through low, brown hills, we found what we were looking for.

The sign said, Great Western Correctional, and below that, An Evergreen Reform Facility, and below that "Tomorrow's Correctional Concepts Today."

"It looks like an office park," Andy said. "Nice slogan. Um, you better…"

Fwooomp! I vanished. I had seen the camera mounted above the sign, too.

The building, or buildings, formed a three-story block, set in Montana's uneven sweep of smooth brown hills. Except for decorative trees planted along a large parking lot, the landscape lacked trees or shrubs for half a mile in any direction, which is approximately how far from the road the building had been built. No other structures lay in sight.

"I don't see any walls, or guard towers," I said.

"Look at the first floor."

The building appeared to be constructed of prefabricated concrete. The first floor, at a distance, appeared to have long spans of windows, but on closer inspection, the "windows" were darkened panels with a reflective sheen. The same panels spanned the second and third floors, but in smaller rectangles, separated by small slots, actual windows that were too narrow for human passage.

"So, the first floor is a wall," I said.

"The whole thing is the wall," Andy said. "It's built like a fort, with a central yard. When the government builds a prison, they don't care if it looks like a prison. When you sell a private prison to a community, you have to *sell* it. People are less likely to object if they don't have to look at walls, barbed wire, and guard towers."

"This looks like anybody can just drive up to the place."

Which is exactly what we did. We found parking in an expansive lot. Signs segregated Visitors from Employees.

"Okay," Andy said after finding a spot in the nearly empty Visitor lot. "Wish me luck."

"Whoa! I'm tagging along. Like we did at the bar."

"No, you're not. I've got this." She reached in her pocket and dropped her phone in a console cubby. "They use cell phone disruptors, so it's useless anyway."

"Dee, I can't just sit here."

"That's exactly what you're going to do. Give me two hours." She looked at her watch. "If I'm not out by twelve-thirty, well…I guess come and get me." She looked at the building, massive and foreboding up close. "To be honest, I don't expect them to give me the time of day."

I gave out a loud sigh in protest, leaned over quickly and kissed her cheek.

"Okay," she jumped, "that's still weird."

"Love you."

"Love you, too!"

She opened the door, stepped out, and left me stewing as she walked authoritatively toward a set of heavy-looking doors beneath a sign that said Administration.

"WE'RE GETTING NOWHERE FASTER than usual, Pilot," my wife said, sliding back into the driver seat of the Jeep an hour and forty-five minutes later. I knew the time because I checked Andy's phone approximately every five minutes.

She slammed the car door.

"Did you see Foyle?"

"Of course not." She started the Jeep and threw it in gear. The tires squeaked out her anger. We shot out of the parking lot.

"What happened?"

She covered the half mile of service road in a hurry and wheeled sharply onto the highway.

"First, they had me wait half an hour. I expected that. Then this Captain Leeson came along. I told him I was investigating a connection to the Cinnamon Hills robbery, which he says he never heard of—which felt like a lie to me. So, I explained the whole thing to him, with emphasis on the neo-Nazi angle." Andy accelerated the Jeep down the highway. Not the most airtight of vehicles, the seventy-five mile-per-hour wind roared around us. She glanced over at me. "Are you going to rejoin me here?"

"Oh, sorry." *Fwooomp!* I settled into the seat and cinched the belt tighter as she followed curves where the highway mimicked the path of the river.

"I told him we're looking at connections to white supremacists, and links to other potential or past crimes, and blah, blah, blah. He got all pissy that nobody called ahead or made an appointment, and he made a point of telling me they have better things to do all day than have people drop in out of the blue, so I told him I had spoken to a Captain Burton, and I told him to please call the guy."

"That's taking a chance."

"Not really if his wife is in labor. So our new friend Captain Leeson says, 'Burt! That S.O.B. always does this sort of thing and leaves me holding the bag.' And he goes on a rant about Burton. This Leeson, he's one of those little fiefdom builders, you know?"

A strand of hair fell across her eye. She left it there, perhaps thinking that driving with one eye at—we were up to eighty-five—would make it half as scary when we flew off the winding road into the river.

"He probably wasted twenty minutes going on and on about how Burton always leaves a mess for him to clean up, and how he can't be reached now because his wife has chosen this inconvenient moment to go up to Billings to give birth and—"

"But, is he there? Foyle? Do they have him in custody?"

"I'm getting to that!" Andy said. "So, I asked him again, politely, if he could just get me a short interview with Foyle, because I've come all this way—and now he starts down an all new path, about how I need to obtain authorization from the state attorney general's office, being an out-of-state and out-of-jurisdiction law enforcement officer, and I need some Form Number Eighty-Six-Thirty-Eight that needs to be sent over to him by the AG's office, before they can authorize that kind of interview, because of some truth-in-sentencing law, and how me showing up without Form Number Eighty-Six-Thirty-Eight means that his pudgy little hands are tied. And I'm apologizing all up and down and lying to him about how I knew that we had the Form Number Eighty-Six-Thirty-Eight all filled out by our AG's office, and they promised me they would fax it over yesterday, and how there's nobody there today, and how screwed I am because I came all the way out here on a Saturday so I can get back home because my daughter has a pageant on Monday night and she's supposed to be the Harvest Queen so I have to sew her dress for her, and I just can't wait until Monday when the AG's office opens so some dumb S.O.B.—which is this Leeson's favorite term for anyone who isn't Prince Leeson—can fax over what they were supposed to send yesterday."

"We can't miss our daughter's pageant!" I cried.

"*I know!* So, at that point he gives me that I-am-so-powerful 'Let me see what I can do, missy' bull crap, and he pats me on the knee and goes off and leaves me sitting there for forty-five minutes! Forty-five *fucking* minutes!"

Andy never uses the f-word. Suddenly our speed, edging up to ninety, was no longer the scariest thing in the Jeep with me.

"Finally, this fat shithead comes back and tells me the problem is that the inmate is in solitary confinement, and even if I had Form Number Eighty-Six-Thirty-Eight, there is no way we can do an interview because that would reset the clock on his solitary confinement, which is a rule they have, and he's in the middle of a one-year protocol—I kid you not! —he called it a 'Protocol!' And it would all have to reset if he's given any contact, because of the definition of Solitary—oh, yes! He did explain the definition of *Solitary* to me. What an officious moron! So, I asked him, all wide-eyed and terrified of this bad, bad man, what he did to be put in Solitary Confinement for a full year, and Leeson tells me he stabbed another inmate to death."

She dropped it like a bomb.

"When?"

"One hundred-and-seven days ago," she said. "Walked up to the guy, Anthony Beauregard Tyrell and stabbed him nineteen times, right in front of three guards. Left the shiv in the guy's liver and surrendered to the guards with no quarrel."

I gave a low whistle. "Holy shit."

"Straight to solitary, he went. Do you think this idiot could have led with that? The guy is in solitary and has been for one-hundred-and-seven days."

"I'm guessing that means he wasn't sipping bottled water at Sandy Stone's wedding a week ago."

Andy didn't answer. Her eyes had gone into a shallow squint, looking at the road ahead, only the road in her sights wasn't necessarily the pavement in front of the jeep.

"So, he's not the guy," I offered.

Andy's lower lip extended, ever so slightly.

"And we'll be back in time for our daughter's pageant? Little Ethel will be so pleased."

She glanced at me. "You're not calling our daughter Ethel, and I'm not calling your propeller thingy a ZIPPY Unit."

She drove for a moment, thinking. It had the beneficial effect of getting her to ease off the accelerator.

"Solitary…" she said.

"That's a pretty solid alibi."

"A very good alibi," she said, distantly. "Where no one has seen or spoken to him for the past one-hundred-and-seven days."

She turned her head and looked pointedly at me.

"No one sees or speaks to him," I repeated.

"Right. Like he's not even there."

45

Andy parked the jeep in front of door number 7. We had both been contemplating the next step. Fatigue ruled out flying back to Essex today, even though it would have eased the pain I expected Earl to inflict when we returned his airplane. I stretched my arms, legs and back as I slid out of the Jeep seat.

Andy's phone rang. She took the call.

I strolled to the back of the Jeep and studied the landscape. The motel occupied a lonely lot on the fringe of town at the beginning of the nowhere that lay between Sioux Valley and the next town, a metropolis probably sixty miles down the road. I thought about how it might be nice to plan a road trip with Andy through this country. Eastern Montana had the rugged edge I expected to find. If you ignore the billboards advertising breakfast burritos, the landscape looked untamed in sharp contrast to the domesticated farmlands of Wisconsin.

As if to emphasize the point, a jacked-up pickup rolled past the motel, sporting aftermarket brush guards, a light bar on a bed rack, and a see-through stencil of a Confederate flag in the rear window. I could not tell if the pickup had a gun rack, but I imagined one. I also imagined another neo-Nazi.

Or maybe the driver was just the local Methodist minister. Out here, the community librarian probably drove a four-by-four. No sense in letting my imagination run wild.

The truck rolled down the road into town, probably on the way to pick up rugged, untamed frontier supplies, like a gallon of milk and some toilet paper.

"No, sir, that's no trouble at all." Andy stepped around the back of the Jeep and giving me a thumbs-up. "Nine o'clock sharp. I'll be there."

She ended the call and looked at me in wonder.

"That was the benevolent dictator himself, Captain Leeson."

"How did he get your number?"

"I left my card. He took pity on poor little Ethel and spoke to the administrator—I guess they don't call him a warden. They're making a special exception and letting me interview Foyle tomorrow morning."

"Okay," I said slowly, "which now proves and disproves the theory that Foyle is here and isn't here. This is kinda like that scientist's dead cat in a box."

"An interview won't prove he's being allowed in and out. But if I see him, face to face," she said, "I'll know if he was at Cinnamon Hills. C'mon, let's go inside. I need to get on my laptop, and you look like you could use a nap."

I slipped my hand into hers. "You know what would help me sleep?"

"No," she declared. She tossed me a sly glance through the lock of hair still slung low over one eye. "Maybe later."

My heart soared.

COFFEE, good and bad, notwithstanding, I slept like the dead for the better part of the afternoon. Andy set up her laptop at a small desk in the room, taking advantage of the free Wi-Fi advertised on a desktop card. She lost herself in her work and I lost myself somewhere inside my eyelids.

Andy's laptop screen glowed—the only light in the room—when I resurfaced from a dream about flying the RNAV 31 approach into Essex County Airport. I'd had the dream several times before. In the dream, a smooth, steady approach to the runway ends with something looming ahead, something I can't see. The dream is me about to crash Six Nine Tango and the looming object is my lost memory of the accident. In the dream it hangs in the air like a black hole, then floats into the path of my aircraft. I wake, or the dream simply evaporates, before we collide.

"Jesus, how late is it?" I propped myself on one elbow.

"Hey, there!" Andy said it a little too brightly.

She popped up from the small desk and went to the window at the front of the room. She peeled back the curtain. Harsh slanted sunlight lit up the tan landscape, casting sharp pre-twilight shadows. "Not that late. Seems like it gets dark a little earlier here, and the days *are* getting shorter. It's only quarter to five. You hungry?"

"Yup. Did you get any rest?" Andy had accumulated less sleep than me in the week since Cinnamon Hills.

"I did," she said. "About fifteen minutes after you conked out, I could not keep my eyes open, so I caught a nap, too. Almost an hour. We need to talk."

"Let me visit our old friend, John, and I'll be all ears."

I hit the bathroom, took care of business, and splashed some water on my face to chase away the thick mix of fresh sleep and lingering fatigue. Andy could hardly wait for me. I hadn't even stepped through the bathroom door when she asked, "Did you know the State of Oklahoma was considering a measure to ban private prisons?"

I propped up pillows and sat against the head of the bed. She hopped on the end of the bed and sat with her legs folded beneath her. She looked like a college girl digging some poetry on the quad. She dropped her laptop on the mattress and flipped it open, fingering the touchpad.

"Pretty sure I knew that or read it on a Trivial Pursuit card."

"The measure was floated by a democratic state senator last year. It didn't fly, but then the press ran a string of negative news stories about how private prisons operate, about inmate abuse, and poor training for supervisors and guards. The same things Keller mentioned. Things picked up steam. It looked like legislation would be introduced this fall."

"There's a 'but' coming along here."

"But…the daughter of the aforementioned state senator was raped and murdered in April. They caught the guy. A parolee from California. An early release. Someone who got let out because of overcrowding. And suddenly the narrative changed. Tougher sentencing. More three-strikes laws. No early release programs. And instead of banning private prisons, the state renewed their contracts for ten more years and authorized new construction to meet the demand for increased capacity."

"I'm guessing the senator in question lost both his support and the heart for his cause."

"He resigned to be with his family. The governor appointed a former prosecutor, someone much 'tougher on crime.' Sound familiar?"

"I think I've seen this movie."

"Now look at this guy," Andy spun the laptop to face me.

A mug shot filled the screen, portrait and profile. Mid-fifties. Weathered. Shaved head. The familiar pattern of glyphs and symbols etched his skin in dull blue ink, much of it faded and old. There was no mistaking the swastika, the initials, the numerals.

"Is that the guy who did it? The guy from California?"

"No," Andy said. "The guy from California was an addict, and they got him in a drug raid. He had some of the girl's clothing in his possession. History of sex crimes. Convicted of rape in California. Set free to prey on the innocent again, was the way it played. Guy practically had a 'Convict Me' sign taped to his back."

I knew this game well. I gave Andy a few seconds to set the trap, then said, "So they got the guy."

"Wrong!" she wagged a finger at me. "In my opinion, anyway. I called the Oklahoma City PD and talked to one of the investigating officers about the case. He said they were headed down a completely different path, looking at someone else, because they got a DNA sample from the girl's body. But the DNA sample had problems, and ultimately, they decided it had been contaminated, and shelved it because they didn't want to give a defense lawyer a platform for reasonable doubt. Guess who the DNA sample led to?"

I pointed at the screen, at our latest visitor from Nazis-R-Us.

"Give the man a teddy bear!" Andy said. "And guess who this cherub is."

"I have a feeling he's the very same Anthony Beauregard Tyrell you learned about from our benevolent dictator."

She touched her nose.

"Countless arrests, convictions for sexual assault, ultimately serving two consecutive life sentences for rape and murder. Life without parole on both."

"Another satisfied guest of Evergreen Reform, A New Concept in Corrections."

"Yes. And what a coincidence. He was a guest of an Evergreen Reform facility in Tulsa, Oklahoma at the same time his DNA made him a person of interest in the rape-murder case. But he was ruled out—"

"—because he had the perfect alibi."

Andy cocked her head at me, eyes intense. "Then somehow—and I have no idea how—Mr. Tyrell gets gutted in the yard of *this* Evergreen Reform facility by one Garrett Foyle."

I pulled a long, deep breath and weighed what she was telling me.

"You understand what you're suggesting here, Dee."

She nodded gravely.

"The junkie was set up—easy enough to do. Evergreen let Tyrell out and he did the crime, but he screwed up. He left DNA. Anybody watching police procedurals on TV knows better than that. Maybe it was just supposed to be a murder, but he could not help himself and did the rape. Or it was supposed to be a brutal rape, but he wasn't supposed to leave DNA. In any case, he screwed up and became a liability. I mean—seriously, if somebody like the Innocence Project starts poking around and looking at the DNA again, there could be trouble."

"Evergreen moved him up here and used Foyle to get rid of him."

Andy gave me a long, right-on-point look.

"Tyrell. Foyle. Evergreen is recruiting hit men from the perfect labor pool. And providing them with the perfect alibi."

I suddenly felt something cold climbing up the center of my chest. Looking at my wife, posed on the bed proposing criminal conspiracy ideas like a co-ed debating Chaucer, I felt fear. That's not the deal. She's the cop. She's tough. I watched her blow the top of a man's head off and have since heard her tell me she's glad she did it. But at that moment, she was just Dee, a young, beautiful woman I loved to a degree I would need a lifetime to measure. And this scared me. Deeply.

She read my face. "What?"

"Dee, you can't go out there tomorrow."

She blinked at me.

"What are you talking about? As soon as I see the guy, I will know."

"No," I scooted forward on the bed. "Listen to me, do you fully understand what you just told me?"

"Clearly," she said. "Tomorrow I will personally ID this Foyle character as the man I saw at the wedding."

"And by extension?"

"And by extension have the grounds to bring a full investigation down on Evergreen, and Parks, and maybe even Todd Jameson. Will, without *something* I won't get the time of day from DCI, or the FBI, or even Tom. I'll just be some patrol sergeant with an over-active imagination. A perfect alibi is precisely that. Perfect."

"Dee, think about what you just said. It *is* the perfect alibi. Guys in prison—better yet—in solitary confinement, recruited like this. Recruited and let out to commit perfect crimes. Think about it. Who's behind it?"

"Parks. You saw his jet out at the airport."

"Okay, and who makes it happen?"

"What do you mean? Parks does."

"No, he doesn't. Who opens the cell door? Who walks Foyle down the hall? Who opens the front door and sends him out into the night? Who makes sure none of the other prisoners see him come and go? Who delivers on whatever it was Parks promised him as payment?"

She stared at me.

"Dee, I'm not saying you're wrong about any of this. I'm saying the opposite. You're right. But going out there tomorrow means you walk into Evergreen Reform, where someone—Leeson, or Burton, or half a dozen underpaid guards getting envelopes full of cash in their mailboxes—or maybe all of them—are doing *all this* to keep the place open, operating and making millions. And there you are, poking around, alone."

"Will, nothing—"

"Really? Somebody turns their back for a minute. There's a tragic incident. Some triple-lifer with nothing to lose goes crazy. Attacks a law enforcement officer. You certainly can't go in armed. They can easily say you provoked the attack. They can write it up any way they want."

She said nothing.

"Why do you think you suddenly got invited back? It's not as if the Wisconsin AG's office woke up and faxed over a form eighty-six-whatever-the-fuck. I bet there is no such form. Have you asked yourself why they went from stonewalling you to issuing a gracious invitation? They want you to come back alone. *Dee, you can't!*"

She stared at me.

"You've built a case. Call in the cavalry and go back there and storm the place with half a dozen FBI agents and start interviewing everyone. Ask the cook if they deliver meals to solitary confinement every day for Foyle. Ask who else is in the solitary block and talk to them. They'll know who's coming and going." I reached for both hands. Took them. Held them tightly. "*You can't go out there again!*"

She lowered her eyes. This had to feel like I was asking her to retreat on the cusp of victory.

I waited. Held my breath. Then I felt her hands squeeze mine. Her head bobbed, fractionally.

"You're right." She spoke in a voice that came from the far-away place where logic had taken ambition for a quick heart-to-heart talk. I blew out a sigh of relief, thinking about how close we had come to unthinkable things.

"Williams," I said. "The DCI guy—he invited you to go straight to him and write your own ticket. Take this to him."

She shook her head. "He's a political appointee. The governor's appointee. I can't say for certain, but on the wild chance that Keller's crazy ideas are valid, he won't let this go anywhere."

"He may be an appointee, but he's a cop. And if he is just a political animal, who better to see the writing on the wall and rush to get on the right side of it? Maybe the governor's gravy train with Parks will come to an end, but even our dumbass governor is smart enough to abandon one donor over going down with Parks. In a heartbeat."

"Maybe."

"Besides, you now have foundation for the entire theory. Tyrell." I pressed on, sensing victory. "We need to get out of here in the morning, first thing. We'll fly directly to Madison. You ride in like Paul Revere and lay it all out. And then we'll find Sandy. Because I think Todd's plan is to minimize her first, then—then, God forbid, take her out of the picture."

Andy nodded slowly. I began to breathe again.

"Foyle," I said, "Maybe he'll be there tomorrow. Maybe they're putting him back in his cell right now. Maybe you'd get your interview. But I doubt it. I think you're not meant to walk out of there alive."

"Okay." She closed the browser on her laptop and folded the screen onto the keyboard. "Okay, we'll do it that way. It will be a tough sell, but I think Williams might be the way to go."

"Thank you!" I leaned in and kissed her.

She cracked a small smile. "I'm not that intractable, am I?"

"Did I mention I love you?"

"Cute. I'm sorry about the wild goose chase. Coming all this way."

"Don't be silly! Without this trip, you wouldn't have made the connection to Tyrell. Think of this as a scouting mission."

"Scouting…" She shifted her gaze to a vague middle distance.

I waited.

"That was the other problem." She pushed both hands into her dark hair and glared into that distance. "That was the other problem I had. Remember?"

I had no idea and she read the ignorance in my face.

"Foyle! I told you I had two problems with him. Prison, being the major one. But the other problem was the makeup. Why show up in the tent before the robbery? Now I know. Now I know why he had the makeup on!"

"I give up. Why?"

Andy waved her hands in a gesture that cleared the chalkboard so that she could map it out for me.

"Foyle went in to scout it out, to find out where Bob Stone was sitting. He starts walking out, firing in a slow pattern, everybody is face down, and he follows a path that takes him right past the table where Stone is, which is as close to the head table as possible. Two shots with a handgun—in semi-dark, on the move—that's not easy. He needed time to aim and fire. The slow shot cadence gave him that. Two shots into Stone, then two more shots at random."

"That's why they waited until the dinner was served. It put Stone in a fixed position. Son of a bitch."

"Yeah, speaking of bitches, Keller may be one, but she got it right. Stone was targeted."

Andy hopped off the bed and shoved her folded laptop into her carry-on bag.

"Okay, Pilot," she said. "Let's get Pidge, get some dinner, get some sleep and get out of here at first light, before they know we're gone."

46

"Well, if it isn't Marshmallow and Snuggle-Bear!"

I turned around. The voice rose above the Saturday night crowd gathering in the restaurant-bar-dance-hall of the Sioux Valley Hotel where we occupied a booth. Tall and muscular, the young prison guard from the diner strolled up with a bottle of Budweiser in hand and a broad grin on his face. He wore Saturday-night-out civilian clothing, but the corrections officer demeanor bled through.

"Now, I'm a little confused," he looked at Andy and me, sitting side-by-side. He pointed at Pidge and then me. "I thought you two were a couple."

Pidge broke out a come-hither smile and prepared to slide over, but I cut off her plans for conquest quickly.

"That's our daughter," I pointed at Pidge. "Our seventeen-year-old daughter."

Pidge glared at me. The young guard's smile dimmed. "Well, you two must'a got married in grade school! You sure she should be drinking beer?"

"Perfectly legal if she's with her parents," Andy chimed in. "And do I need to remind you I'm a cop?"

I watched him adjust course, now that his plans to hit on my wife lay in flames.

"How did it go for you out at the prison today?" he asked Andy. "Did old Captain Lee-Ass take care of you?"

"As a matter of fact, he did. We had a little paperwork snafu initially, but it's all worked out. I'll be there tomorrow morning at nine to complete my business."

"Surprised that son-of-a-bitch helped you at all," the guard said, glancing over his shoulder. "Must be a full moon. Turns him into a decent human being once a month."

"What part of the facility do you work in, officer…?"

"Ray Sidousky," he put out a meaty hand for Andy to shake. "I do third shift on surveillance. It's mostly video monitors throughout. I watch TV for a living."

"Do you mind me asking a question?"

"Shoot!"

"I'm interviewing a prisoner who's doing a protocol in solitary. Do you typically do the interview in the confinement area? Or do you move the prisoner to another location?"

"I never heard of an interview with anyone on a protocol. I guess they'd take you down there. Can't imagine they'd move the prisoner out to a general cell or the visitation area," he said. "Don't want to remind the mole people what sunlight looks like during a solitary protocol."

"I've only been to the Evergreen facility in Tulsa," Andy said. "Never to solitary. Where is it?"

"Oh," he said, "it's down below. As close to Hell as they could build it, I guess. I only been down there once. Gave me the creeps. On top of being two stories underground, they used all kinda sound-deadening materials. It's so quiet down there you think you've gone deaf. A man can scream at the top of his lungs in one of those cells and the guy next door wouldn't know it. Which is probably another reason they'll take you down there for the interview."

Nobody's taking you anywhere, I thought. I squeezed Andy's knee under the table.

"It must put the fear of God in the other prisoners to see someone being taken down to Solitary."

"Prob'ly would, but nobody sees a man come or go. Solitary's got its own access. Might be a good thing for you, ma'am, that you don't have to traverse past any of the gen pop residents, being a woman and all. You'd create quite a stir, and we try to avoid stimulating the guests."

"That is a relief."

"You folks staying here, at the hotel?"

"Yes," Andy lied. "Seems like a nice place."

Sidousky flipped a flat hand back and forth, equivocating. "Nice enough on a weekday, but you're not going to get much sleep tonight. This is the only real watering hole in town, and it gets pretty darn rowdy on a Saturday night. The band strikes up in the big room around nine, and I guaran-damn-tee you, there's no soundproofing in this place. Same goes for the rooms, if you get my drift. A few of them are rented by the hour on a Saturday night," he said it surreptitiously in front of Pidge, who rolled her eyes. I had to suppress a smirk. He said to Andy and me, "Just fair warning."

"Appreciate the warning, officer," I said.

"Well, then," he raised his Bud in salute, "you all have a pleasant evening. Good luck with your interview in the morning, ma'am."

He strolled into the gathering bar crowd, glancing back once with a look of mild confusion over our changing family dynamic.

"Are you fucking kidding me!" Pidge protested. "Gee, thanks, *Dad!*"

I laughed.

"We don't want to keep you up past your bedtime, Marshmallow."

"Well, I am sure as fuck going to bed alone tonight, now that Officer Do-Right over there is telling everyone in the bar I'm underage!"

"It wasn't an option, Pidge," Andy said. "We're leaving before dawn."

She gaped at us. "When did that shitty idea come up?"

"Around the time we decided it was the best way to get out of town alive," I said.

"Oh."

47

Andy latched the motel room door. I sat on the end of the bed.

"So that's how they get him in and out with nobody seeing him," I said. "I wonder if they designed it with this whole scheme in mind."

"Maybe. I was wondering something else. What do you suppose they offer an inmate like Foyle?"

"Death."

Andy considered it.

"And I don't mean the kind they gave Tyrell."

"Work for us. Do a couple jobs. Then we'll write you up as a death in custody," Andy mused.

"They cremate the 'remains' and a lifer with no option for parole gets a midnight pass out the back gate. Maybe even a new identity. It could work."

"Or they double-cross the guy each time. Who's going to complain? It's not as if the next candidate to come along can read his predecessor's Yelp reviews about the job."

Andy slipped out of her jacket and removed her weapon, which she put on the nightstand beside the bed.

"Foyle knows what happened to Tyrell," I said. "Wouldn't he assume he's going to get the same treatment?"

Andy reached behind her head and shook her hair free of the ponytail she'd been wearing all day. "I don't think so. Foyle got offered the deal. But they wanted to move him to solitary for the *perfect* perfect alibi. So, what gets a lifer to solitary? They point out a newbie to kill. He doesn't ask and they don't tell. Foyle might never have known that Tyrell was a colleague in the same scheme. He did it right in front of the guards and gave up without a struggle. Everybody knew what role to play, except Tyrell, who got the short end of the shiv."

"With a couple corrections officers as witnesses?"

"Who cares about witnesses? It's highly unlikely that the attorney general is going to waste time and resources prosecuting a three-time lifer, especially when the victim is another lifer. Not after the good people of Evergreen inform the AG's office that they've taken administrative action and issued a one-year-in-solitary protocol. At the very least, it gives the AG a year to sit on his hands and do nothing. By that time, as part of the plan, Foyle will have died in custody. Perfectly plausible. Forty percent of all prison suicides occur in solitary."

I kicked off my boots. Andy came around the bed and stood directly in front of me. I put my hands on her hips. She ran her fingers through my hair.

"You're sexy when you talk statistics, you know that?"

She bit her lower lip and wiggled her hips. I reached up and pulled her blouse out of her waistband.

"Four percent of all lost television remotes are found in the refrigerator or freezer," she said in a low, smooth voice.

I worked free the button on her slacks.

"You're more likely to be attacked by a shark than you are to win the Powerball lottery," she whispered.

I eased her slacks to the floor, sliding my hands down the smooth skin of her thighs as they went. She stepped out of them and kicked them aside. I slid my hands up under the back of her panties, closing a grip on each cheek and pulling her closer. She worked her fingernails on my scalp, sending electric shivers down my spine.

She leaned over and licked my earlobe, then said, "Eight thousand stars are visible from the earth."

I began working the buttons on her blouse, releasing them from bottom to top. Once done, my hands slid down the slope of her breasts, then I pushed the two blouse panels apart like a curtain. The blouse slid down her arms to hang from her elbows.

"Eighty-six percent of all statistics are made up on the spot."

She released my hair and dropped her arms to her sides. The blouse fell. Andy being Andy, she bent over, picked it up along with her slacks, took both to the closet and put each on a hangar. She took her time, allowing me to study her. When she finished, she slowly moved across the room and flicked the main light switch off, leaving the small lamp beside the bed as the sole source of illumination in the room. The single-source light lent intoxicating contrast to her curves.

My breathing went shallow. My heart hammered.

She stepped back across the floor and stood in front of me. Her smile reflected my feelings as I let my eyes roam. She reached behind her back with one hand and released her bra. This she let fall.

"One hundred percent of the men in this room are overdressed," she said, now kneeling in front of me, tugging my belt free.

"Not for long," I said, reaching for her.

48

We lay in the dark, cooling off, trading long, slow breaths and running our hands over each other's skin. I traced patterns on her back with my fingernails. She hummed appreciatively.

At some point sleep intruded, not altogether welcome.

THE DOOR SLAMMED OPEN. The sound of it striking the wall catapulted us out of sleep.

Andy tried to tear herself from my arms. I fought back, using everything I had to hold her. I saw what she could not.

The man filled the doorway, backlit by the parking lot lights. His silhouette stood fully formed. I saw him swing a black rifle against his shoulder. In the time it took to get there, four things happened.

I realized Andy's weapon lay out of reach.

Andy fought to escape—I fought to hold her.

FWOOOMP! I pushed everything I had into the levers in my head.

A single thought filled my consciousness.

UP!

Not as a word. Not as language. Not as an image. But as pure thought.

I had no way to push off the mattress. My arms were rigid around Andy. We had no time to escape. The rifle reached the man's shoulder.

For the second time since *the other thing* became part of me, I felt a pull—I felt motion. A form of inertia. Geometry and perspective shifted. The room dropped abruptly.

Light and sound exploded from the rifle. On full automatic, the gunfire ripped the room down the middle. The rifle reports slammed my eardrums and sucked the air from my lungs.

We hit the ceiling and stayed there. I saw a steady stream of fire tear into the mattress. Andy stopped fighting. She locked her arms around me.

Against the brilliance of the muzzle flashes, the man standing in the doorway had gone black and disappeared. My eyes could not adjust, even when, after an eternity, the gunfire stopped.

He moved forward.

He pivoted and fired into the space on the floor beside the bed where he assumed that we had fallen. The blast tore through the small room.

He stopped.

He turned and kicked open the bathroom door and fired into the shower stall.

He stopped.

Shell casings clattered to the floor. Tiles fell and shattered.

He searched. First the bathroom. Then the closet. Then the room again. Frustrated, he swung the rifle from side to side never taking his eyes from the optical sight, like a trained soldier moving through a jungle.

Nothing.

He returned to the door and turned. He flicked on the main light, a dome-like lamp set in the middle of the ceiling, just inches from my head. The light assaulted my eyes.

He wore black tactical clothing and a black balaclava. His pale, hooded eyes scanned the room. I felt Andy squirm, twisting to see. My ears throbbed.

The empty bed smoldered where the rounds had torn through the sheets and the wall behind it. I feared for anyone in the next room.

He surveyed the damage for one more moment, then turned and left. We heard a vehicle door slam and an engine start.

"Let me go!" Andy cried. She pushed, hard, and caught me by surprise. I could not hold her. The electric cool sensation flickered as we separated.

She appeared suddenly and dropped to the mattress. In one motion, she closed her hand on her weapon, peeled it from the holster, and rolled away in the opposite direction. In two steps she was out the door. I saw her long legs disappear toward the parking lot.

I heard her fire. Rapid fire. Faster than I ever could have managed. She emptied the magazine.

Tires squealed on pavement and an engine roared away.

I pushed against the ceiling and shot to the door. I almost missed a grip on the jamb but managed a one-handed stop.

Andy stood naked in the parking lot, arms extended, the smoke from her gunfire swirling away in a cold cloud. Far up the highway, a square pickup cab with a light bar on top raced away, silhouetted against the spray of the pickup's headlights. One taillight winked an insulant goodbye.

49

Andy and I dressed quickly. We knew anyone within half a mile was awake and would be poking their heads up from whatever cover they had found. Calls to 9-1-1 were already being dialed. We didn't bother.

Andy went into command mode. "Run down to Pidge's room and tell her to stay put, keep out of sight, and not come near us until we come and get her," Andy ordered me as I pulled my boots on. "Go!"

I jogged down to room 2 and pounded on the door, which burst open before I rapped three times.

"MOTHERFUCK!" Pidge cried out. "Did you fucking hear that? What the shit was that?!" In bra and panties, she tried to push past me to look out in the parking lot. I caught her arm and pushed her back.

"That was meant for me and Andy, mostly Andy," I said quickly, quietly.

"FUCK! WHAT?"

"*Shhhhh!* Don't ask. Stay out of sight. Keep your door locked. We'll come and get you."

I slammed the door in her face before she could utter another sound.

A siren sang in the distance, closing in fast. I ran back to our room. A few doors opened. Without turning on lights, heads peered out. I hurried back to where our room door hung open. The door jamb had been torn to pieces. Parts of the door lock lay on the floor. One good kick. Perhaps a battering ram, but that would have required two men. I saw only one and he entered with the semi-automatic rifle at the ready. It had to have been a kick.

Andy shoved my overnight bag into my hands.

"Put this in the car. Quick." She turned and scooped up hers. From the key fob in her hand, she transmitted an unlock command to the Jeep doors. I threw my bag in the back seat, took hers, and repeated the action.

The siren stopped about a block away, but the sheriff's car shot toward us under its blue and red strobe lights.

"Are we making a run for it?" I asked.

"No. I just don't want anything of ours in the room." Andy reached in one pocket for her badge and palmed it. As the squad car skidded onto the gravel parking lot, she stepped past the rear fender of the Jeep with her badge held out, and her left hand extended at her side, well clear of any weapon.

"Put your hands where he can see them, Will. Do it!"

I did, emphatically, when the deputy emerged from his cruiser behind his drawn weapon.

"Police!" Andy called out. "I'm Sergeant Andrea Stewart, City of Essex Police Department!"

50

An hour later we sat in front of a second-hand desk in the Sioux Valley Sheriff's Substation. Three unoccupied desks were randomly arranged in a room that ran long and narrow back from glass storefront windows. Except for a few posters on the walls, the law enforcement presence seemed temporary. I wondered what the space had originally been. Yarn store? Gift shop?

"God!" Andy said again. "How could I be so *stupid*?"

I knew better than to protest her assumption.

Sioux Valley had no municipal police. The county sheriff's department maintained a substation in a storefront office at the center of town, one block over from the hotel where the bar remained open and music still throbbed. I looked at my watch. Three-oh-five.

Andy repeated her self-deprecating mantra under her breath, out of earshot of the deputy who didn't seem to know what to do with us. He spoke into a phone at the other end of the room.

"How could I have been so stupid?" She turned to me. "That bullshit about coming back out to interview Foyle in the morning was just to keep us here, fat dumb and happy. They knew where we were and how to get to us. *God!*"

Each desk had a lamp from a different rummage sale, all lighted with low-wattage incandescent bulbs. The effect was warm and easier on the eyes than I expected of law enforcement decor.

The deputy—Larson, the tag above his shirt pocket said—still holding the desk phone to his ear, turned around and looked at us as he talked. He seemed like a decent guy, bright and alert. At the scene, he was quick and efficient, checking each adjoining room for collateral damage. By a stroke of luck, the room backing up the head of our bed was vacant, because the .223 rounds went effortlessly through the wall and into the floor beyond. The rounds tearing up our shower stall also went through the wall, but the bathroom buttressed the back wall of the motel, and nothing but scrub brush and low hills extended beyond the property. Andy treated him respectfully, handed over her weapon without protest and followed his instructions. He quickly taped off the room and moved us downtown.

He nodded a few times, then pointed at Andy and waved her to come to the phone.

"Your chief wants a word," he said. He stepped away like someone moving away from a couple about to launch an argument in a restaurant.

Andy assumed a pose with one hand buried in her thick hair and the phone in the other, tucked against her ear. She faced away from the deputy, speaking in low tones. After a few minutes, she handed the phone back to the deputy. He dropped it onto a cradle on a desk.

"Okay," Deputy Larson said, "Your chief vouches for you. I don't know what else we need from you. Unless you can think of something. You're absolutely sure you got no idea what that was about?"

In the few seconds we had before the deputy approached us, Andy had given me one clipped command. *Say nothing about Foyle!*

"I've been thinking about it," Andy said. Larson perked up. "There is one. You might want to check with the people at the airport." I looked at her, clueless.

"The folks at the airport?"

"Yes. They have a crew car, but it was already taken when we arrived. We needed a car, so they gave us a Jeep belonging to a Mr. Donnelly from Denver. He keeps it at the airport. The only thing I can think of is that someone might have an issue with that gentleman, saw the Jeep parked in front of the motel, and thought we were him."

Larson nodded thoughtfully. "Wouldn't be the first time someone from outta town who hunts up here caused some ill will. We had a guy, couple years ago, got frisky with the wife of one of his guides. She certainly contributed to the problem, I'll say. Found his remains up near the Yellowstone."

"Just a thought," Andy said.

"I'll look into it."

"Alright, then." Andy rose. She extended a hand. Larson placed her weapon in her palm. He cast a wary eye in her direction.

"And you're sure your business out at Evergreen mightn't have sparked any of this?"

"I can't be sure of anything, Deputy," Andy said. "I just came to interview an inmate, looking to build some background information on some neo-Nazis. Turns out the guy is doing a year in solitary, and they won't let me see him, so I go home empty-handed. That doesn't seem like something to shoot up my room over."

"Well," he measured the story in his head, "those Nazi dumb shits can be vicious. We have a few around here."

"Seems like they'd be drawing an awful lot of unnecessary attention to themselves with something like this," Andy said. "I guess I wouldn't rule it out, but…"

"'Specially if it's tied into that robbery you told me about." Andy had been truthful in ninety percent of what she told the deputy, which was backed up by Tom Ceeves on the phone. She made no mention of Parks or Foyle or Tyrell.

"Maybe," she allowed, "but that case is all wrapped up. I'm just here following up on ancillary connections. Busywork, really."

"Well, I'll see if anybody around here has a bone to pick with Mr. Donnelly. Lemme get my hat and I'll drive you back out to the motel."

"Don't forget to tell your investigators that the nine-millimeter casings in the parking lot are from my weapon. I can send you a match for ballistic testing if you need it."

Larson laughed. "Ma'am, unless you pegged the guy on his way outta town, I don't think we'll be doing much forensic work on this. By God's grace, despite all the fireworks, it looks like nobody got hurt. Damn lucky you were over by the ice machine when they lit up the place. If you'd'a been in that bed … well, we would have a whole 'nuther case on our hands."

Larson let Andy ride shotgun in the cruiser. I got the cage in the back. He let us off in the quiet-once-again parking lot outside our taped-off room.

"Best if you don't disturb anything in there," he said through the open window of his cruiser. "I'll have people in there in the morning. This might be a grudge against that Donnelly character, but that don't mean we won't be going after whoever thinks they can shoot up a place like this."

"We won't touch anything. We're checking out and heading for the airport." She handed him a card. "Call me if you need anything, Deputy Larson. That's my cell."

"Will do."

He dropped the car in gear and drove into the night, leaving me mildly amazed that the episode appeared to be concluded.

Andy waited until he was out of sight, then spun and started marching toward the far end of the parking lot.

"Hey! Where're you going?" I hurried after her.

Andy said nothing. She worked a long-stride walk to the last door in the motel, room number 14.

"This wasn't here when Deputy Larson drove us to his office."

"What?"

She pointed at an old Buick LeSabre nosed up to room number 14. She looked at me, expecting me to understand. I gave her a blank shrug. I had no idea what had wound her up, except perhaps the same two-ton jolt of adrenaline that was still doing NASCAR sprints in my veins.

She flipped me a frustrated glance and marched up to the door to room 14 and started pounding on it.

"What are you doing?" I jogged up behind her.

She ignored me and continued pounding. A light flicked on behind the thick curtains. The door latches rattled and the door swung open.

"What the hell—Andy?"

Dave Peterson stood in the doorway in his boxers.

Andy turned to me and pointed at the Buick.

"Crew car," she said. She turned around and pushed past Dave.

"Dave, we need to talk." She didn't sound friendly.

51

"Lemme get some pants on fer Chrissakes!" Dave hopped on one leg, pulling his pants up the other. "You want to know what?"

"I want a detailed list of every flight your company jet has made in the last two weeks. And all the passengers you had on board." Andy planted herself in the center of the room, arms folded, feet planted.

"Andy, that's—" Dave hesitated "—I mean, I can get in a lot of trouble giving out that kind of information."

"Dave," I said, "we're way past trouble here. Did you not hear what happened tonight?"

He gave us a blank look.

"What time did you get back to the room tonight?" Andy asked.

"About fifteen minutes ago. We were at that dive in town, listening to those Creedence cover guys. Why?"

"So were we," I said. "We had dinner there, in the front bar, but left when the band fired up."

"We were in the big room, with the band. I wish I'd known," Dave finished with his pants and found a shirt. "Not that crazy, I guess. It's the only place in town. Why does it matter when I got back here?"

"Because," Andy said, "about two hours ago someone working for your boss shot up the bed we were sleeping in with a machine gun."

Dave's jaw dropped.

"Yeah," Andy said. "They just missed us."

"Jesus Christ!"

"So, I have to tell you, Dave, that the concept of 'a lot of trouble' has an entirely different meaning to me right now. And I'm going to give you a heads-up—when the shit really hits the fan, I think there's a good chance your boss will be in custody."

And there goes your job, I thought. *Sorry, buddy.*

"Really?" Dave looked stricken. "You're serious?"

"As machine gun fire," Andy said.

Dave looked at me for an out, which I could not give. He looked back at Andy, who held him in a cold stare.

"What the hell is going on?"

"A police investigation," Andy said. "So, I'll ask the questions. I need flight schedules and passenger manifests. Last two weeks for starters. Now, please."

He heaved a sigh and sat down at the small desk, a twin to the one Andy had used in our room. His flight bag sat on the floor. He reached in and pulled out an iPad.

52

Dave produced everything Andy wanted. The Evergreen Reform corporate flight department kept online records, so that crews could update those records on layovers or while killing time in crew lounges. Dave tracked the movements of the Falcon 20 jet going back two weeks, providing routes, stops, arrival and departure times, and when he could, passenger manifests. Andy took detailed notes. As Dave spoke of certain flights, she and I exchanged confirming glances. The flights matched our guesses about the sixth man's movements. Andy stared at her notes, absorbing the connections.

"These 'Uber' flights you talked about," she said. "What's to stop you from just looking out the side window at who's coming and going?"

"Oh, no," Dave said. "They're serious about their security. They rigged shades on the side windows. They tell us when to go black."

"Ever hear anyone mention the name, Foyle?" Andy asked.

"Negative," Dave said.

"What about the flight from Madison to here?" Andy asked. "You've said Parks was on the manifest, but that he still treated it as an Uber."

"He does that sometimes. Word is, he brings women up to the ranch, women who don't want their husbands to know they're spending a weekend at a ranch in Montana."

"Where's this ranch?"

"About forty miles up the highway, along the Yellowstone River."

"Parks is there now?"

"Until someone tells me otherwise. We were told to be ready for a Sunday evening departure, but they didn't give us the destination yet. Probably back to HQ in Chicago. Jesus, Andy, you really think Parks is responsible for whoever shot up your room?"

"Dave, our personal history aside, right now I'm treating you as a witness who works for a prime suspect. I'm sorry, but I can't be sure you won't be on the phone with your boss the minute we go out the door. So, don't ask me questions."

"C'mon, Andy! This is me! We were friends long before I took this job. I just told you enough to get myself fired."

Andy let go of a long sigh. "When this is over, Dave, we'll talk, okay? If you want to show some loyalty, then promise me something."

"Anything!"

"Promise me you won't pick up the phone to tell anyone we had this conversation."

"Done. I swear." Dave crossed his heart, emphatically. "I've got no reason to say a word. Until twenty minutes ago, I didn't even know you were here."

"Even if someone asks. Not a word."

"Not a word."

"One more thing," she softened her tone. "When you get the call, as soon as you know where you're going and who's on board, will you text me the information?"

"Yes, absolutely!"

Andy waved her notebook at me and said, "We need to get this back to Madison, to Williams like you said. This should do it."

I nodded. I turned to Dave and stuck out my hand.

"Sorry about all this, buddy." We shook. "Come by the farm in a couple weeks for a beer and we'll tell you what you've been up to these past few weeks. Unless it's all over the news by then."

Dave looked drained. I felt bad, laying this on him.

"I don't know what to say, guys."

Andy opened the room door and checked the parking lot.

"Say nothing."

53

"Pidge, it's me," I tapped on her door. "We're leaving."

"What the fuck?!" She jerked the door open. Fully dressed, flight jacket on, she had her bag in hand and almost bowled me over coming out the door. "Are you going to fucking tell me who declared World War Three last night? Where's Andy?"

"Later. She's in the car. Let's go."

"What about checking out?" She held up her room key. I took it and tossed it back into the room.

"Better if someone thinks we're still here." We hustled to where the Jeep sat running. As we passed the open door to room 7, Pidge stopped in her tracks.

"Motherfuck!"

"Yup." I took her bag and pulled her toward the Jeep. We loaded up and wheeled out of the gravel parking lot as a red dawn broke across the eastern Montana sky.

Pidge didn't stop asking questions all the way to the airport. Andy and I inserted a "Yup" or "Nope" but not much else. The "Nope" answer came largely in response to demands to know what the hell was going on.

Andy drove carefully, religiously holding the Jeep to the speed limit.

She flexed both hands on the wheel, constantly searched her mirrors, and occasionally dropped her right hand to touch her pistol grip.

From the moment she dropped onto the bed, there had been no letup. I feared touching her, for the electric charge she might give off.

When we pulled onto the airport service drive, Andy wheeled the Jeep to a stop in a half-U-turn. She let it idle, poised across the drive, ready to go either way. She scanned the long highway running into town, then the opposite direction, then studied the low buildings and hangars at the airport.

Sioux Valley Municipal Airport shares characteristics with Essex County Airport and thousands of other general aviation fields across the country. A main hangar attached itself to a low office building housing the fixed base operation. Sets of t-hangars, probably built in the fifties, stretched away on one side of the main hangar. A pair of newer, larger corporate hangars sat on the opposite side of the broad ramp.

Two cars and a pickup truck nosed up to the front of the FBO. The pickup was an old two-tone Chevy with no light bar; not a match for the model with the big cab Andy had fired on during the night.

"If they're waiting for us, I'm not seeing it." She turned the wheel and rolled forward.

Remembering the rip of gunfire in our room, I thought that if someone waited for us, it would be over before we knew it. A shooter rounding a building corner with an automatic weapon could easily fill the Jeep cabin with rounds that would go through the sheet metal like paper. There would be no chance to vanish and float out of the line of fire.

Andy must have thought the same thing. She suddenly floored it. We shot forward, followed the road to the parking lot, and wheeled sharply away from the FBO office. She launched left, onto the airport ramp, toward the corporate hangars. After following an arc across the front of the two hangars, she stopped suddenly, pointed toward the expansive ramp.

The Evergreen Reform Falcon 20 wore foam engine covers, a sign of inactivity. Our Piper Navajo occupied a tiedown two spaces away. Nothing moved on the ramp or near any of the buildings.

We waited. I noticed that Andy kept the Jeep in reverse. Empty space beside the second corporate hangar lay directly behind us. I followed her thinking. At the first sign of trouble, she could rocket backward, using the building as cover.

Nothing happened.

"Okay, Pidge, we'll drop you at the plane. You load up. Will and I will get rid of this vehicle and be right out."

"Untie it," I said, "and be ready to fire up as soon as we close the door. If anything happens, or anybody rolls up on us, go. I don't care what runway, or taxiway, or if you use the damned ramp. Just go. Got it?"

"Got it," Pidge said.

Andy threw the car into gear and shot forward. She pulled up to the Navajo and stopped with the anti-lock brakes chattering. I jumped out and helped carry the bags to the airplane, then left Pidge to load the plane and release the tiedowns.

Andy, searching every building, every window, every possible ambush option, waited for me to board again. Then she drove the Jeep around the main hangar and parked under the open carport. We hurried through a long hallway into the FBO where Mark stood by the window, watching the girl on the ramp.

"Oh, hey!" he greeted us as we walked in. Andy laid the keys on the counter. I pulled a ten from my wallet.

"For the gas," I said. "We didn't have time to fill it."

"Folks need anything? Top off the tanks?"

"Nope, we're fine," I said. The airplane had less than half-filled fuel tanks, but I didn't care. All I wanted to do was get in the air. We could land at the first airport in any direction and refuel. "Thanks for the crew car!"

Andy said nothing. She remained on full alert, searching the dimensions of the small office, the adjoining hallway, the doors and windows, and the view outside the windows. I glanced around at all the same things, but realized she saw them entirely differently from what I was seeing. To me it was like any other aviation office. Maps and pictures on the walls. Old *Flying* magazines on a second-hand coffee table in front of the rummage sale sofa. I've been in scores of offices like this one. They all feel the same. They all feel like home.

Andy studied the scene with her coat open and her hand on her service weapon. The frequent glances she sent to me said we needed to go.

"Okay," Mark said, sensing the tension, trailing us toward the ramp door, "You folks have a great flight!" The door closed behind us.

Halfway across the open ramp it hit me.

"Stop!" I cried. Andy took two steps, turned, and tensed, expecting trouble.

"What?"

"Give me your phone, quick!"

She didn't question. She handed it over. I turned and jogged back to the office.

"Will, where are you going?"

I pulled open the doors to the office. Mark stood at the window again, watching the women. He looked sheepish when I entered, like he'd been caught peeking. I ignored him.

Andy jerked open the doors behind me and followed me toward the hallway that led to the other side of the building, to the parking lot. The usual office doors lined the hall. Pilot briefing. Maintenance. Office manager.

Just yesterday, Pidge had walked down this hallway, letting Mark walk behind her, hypnotizing him with her backside. Andy and I had returned to the plane, but I remembered seeing Pidge lead the poor kid away. I remembered the hallway.

I stopped and saw it.

"Sikorsky flying boat," I said. I pointed at one of the pictures on the wall.

Andy looked at me blankly.

"And a P-40 Warhawk. Not the Kittyhawk you normally see," I said, pointing at the next framed photo.

Before she could unleash her frustration on me, I jabbed through several screens on her phone, brought up a video and held it up for her to see.

Todd Jameson, making his plea for privacy.

Standing in front of framed photos of a Sikorsky flying boat and P-40 Warhawk—in the Sioux Valley Municipal Airport fixed base operations office hallway.

"She's here. They brought Sandy here."

54

"Pidge, I want you to reposition, over there, on the corner of the ramp, facing across the ramp," I pointed. "Be ready. That puts you out of sight from the road, and it's a quick right turn, onto the taxiway and onto the runway. When we get back, we'll pull right up to the door."

We stood beside the Navajo's left engine. She studied the location and acknowledged the instructions with a nod.

"Stay in the cockpit, out of sight."

"Fucking cold out here, Will. How long do you think you'll be?"

"No idea." Andy had returned to the office to get the location of Parks' ranch from the kid. "Just stay out of sight but keep watch. Can you do both?"

"Fuckin' A."

Donnelly's Jeep roared around the corner of the office and raced across the ramp with Andy at the wheel again. She pulled up with the window open.

"Got it. Let's go," she said.

I turned to Pidge. "If you see a black pickup truck, jacked up, with light bars on top and a Confederate flag stencil in the rear window, don't hesitate. Just go."

"What?" Andy squinted at me. "Where's that from?"

"I didn't put it together until we got here," I said. "When we were looking to see if anybody was waiting for us, I saw that old truck out front, and I realized it wasn't a match to the one driving away last night —but I also realized I saw a truck go by yesterday, right after we pulled into the motel. I think they followed us from the prison. That's how they knew where to find us. And the Jeep sitting outside our door put a lock on the target."

"I should have seen it," Andy berated herself.

"I didn't—until now." I turned to Pidge. "You see a truck like that, fire it up and get out of here, got it?"

"Shit hot," she said. "Where are you headed?"

"There's a ranch about forty miles up this highway," Andy said. "We're going up there to pick up a Sandra Stone, turn around, and come right back."

Pidge's eyes widened at mention of the name, but she said nothing.

I hurried around the front of the Jeep. "Hey!" I called to Pidge. "You call us if you see anything, too. Put the headset on Bluetooth and have your phone ready."

"Roger that."

"Now get this thing over there and hide!"

"And be careful!" Andy added.

Pidge gave us a thumbs-up. I strapped in. Andy floored it.

55

Andy shot up to over one hundred miles per hour as soon as she hit the highway. She drove at full speed for several minutes, silent, staring ahead with both hands gripping the wheel, the knuckles of her elegant fingers white. Blessedly, the highway ran straight, wide, and dry, and Sunday morning traffic was nonexistent.

She startled me when she backed off suddenly, stomped on the brakes. I grabbed the dash. She brought the Jeep to a tail-wagging halt on the gravel shoulder. She threw open the door and jumped out.

"What?" I scrambled out the door on my side. She darted around the square signature hood and grill and plowed into me at the right front fender. Her arms went around my chest and pulled the air out of me.

"*Oh-my-God-oh-my-God-oh-my-God!*" She whispered in my ear. She shivered, and I caught it from her. I pulled her tight. My knees nearly buckled. We gripped each other, both needing the same thing, both releasing the tension that held us together for the last few hours. For a moment, I knew we both felt the shockwaves of gunfire in our souls and saw blinding muzzle flashes inside our closed eyes.

"Half a second, Will." She breathed the words in my ear. "Half a second!"

I knew what she meant. She reached up and took my face in both hands and we kissed, each of us trying to hang on to the other forever.

When she pulled away, her eyes and cheeks were wet.

"I love you so much." I touched her face, knowing that I could not get my voice to work just at that moment. I thumbed a tear from her cheek. She said, "Can we please not do that again?"

I laughed, and it broke something loose. I took her in my arms again.

"Big, tough, cop," I whispered, holding her. "I love you more today, Dee, than I did yesterday."

We took us a few minutes to reassemble ourselves. The wind whispered around us, respecting our privacy.

Half a second, I thought. She was right. We had come that close.

"Yeah," she said, looking away, "big, tough cop. Almost got us both killed."

"No," I took her chin and brought her face back to mine, "some asshole named Parks used some asshole named Foyle to almost get us killed. And they killed two little girls and a good man. So, I'd like to see a big, tough cop kick their fucking asses. Okay?"

"Oh, believe me," she said, now brushing the last of the moisture off her cheeks and letting the dry wind finish the job, "that's on the agenda."

With one more embrace, we parted and jumped back into the Jeep. Less than a minute later the speed needle said one hundred and ten. Andy had relaxed. I tightened my seat belt.

"I need to know," she said. "In the room…*what was that?*"

I hesitated.

"I went for my gun," she said. "You stopped me. You fought me. And then… I don't know how to ask this. *What was that?*"

"Which part?"

"Up."

I shot her a look. "*Up?*"

"I knew what you did—as soon as you did it. I got it. *Up!* Like a radio transmission. Right through me. I could not see him, and I'm sorry I fought you on it. You saw the rifle, didn't you?"

"Yeah."

"We wouldn't have had a chance. Half a second and it would have been over. I get that. But what you did. That was different. I felt it." She struggled for the words. "And—it wasn't like in the barn—I heard it —*Up*—like it was inside my head. That was you, wasn't it."

"Yeah."

"But it wasn't a word. I can't express it." She paused. "You didn't push us off the bed, did you."

"No."

"Did you know you could do that?"

Now it was my turn to hesitate. To think.

"Not really," I said, not having a better answer. "Remember what I told you about finding Lane? The fire?"

She knew the story. How I found Lane with a steel collar around her neck, chained to a wall with the building on fire. Andy knew from the recording made by emergency services through an open 9-1-1 connection that Lane cried out for me to leave her and go, because I could not break the chain and free her. Andy knew—because I told her—that I wrapped my body around Lane's and made us both vanish, and because the border between what's visible and what isn't seems to weaken metal, I had been able to break the chain and get Lane out of the room.

What Andy didn't know was how. Because I didn't know how.

I didn't take Lane in my arms to help her escape, I did it because I could not let her die alone. The room we were in had filled with toxic smoke and lung-destroying heat, and we were finished, so I gave the child the only thing I had to offer. I held her. I didn't know that a part of my mind had fixed on the window, on *life* beyond the window. I didn't know that *the other thing* which leaves me floating helpless without a handheld power unit, moved us across the floor, through the smoke, and out a window neither of us could see, and in doing so, snapped the steel chain.

And now it happened again.

UP! Raw thought in my head.

"You heard it? In your head?" I asked.

"Up. Yes."

"And you felt it? Something yank us up to the ceiling?"

"I thought you pushed us, but it wasn't like when you push us—you know, around in the barn? It wasn't like that. It was like—"

"Like it came from inside—from our *center*."

"Yes!"

"Dee … I have no idea what that is. Or how to do it."

"So, it's happened twice now? With Lane? With me last night?"

"I think it's happened three times," I said. "I think it happened the night of the crash. I think it pulled me out the side of the airplane."

We flew over a hill and confronted the back end of an eighteen-wheeler. Andy flicked the wheel left. We shot past it.

I said nothing. She made no move to let up on the gas. Montana scenery streaked past us, but I could not take my eyes off the pavement ahead.

I felt her hand take mine.

"I love you, too, Dee, now get your hands back on the wheel!"

After a few minutes, I asked, "Are you sure we shouldn't call Larson? Have him meet us there?"

"I thought about that," she said. "I don't have jurisdiction here."

"So?"

"We're not going up there to make an arrest. We're going to get Sandy. Do you see how it would play out if we took along local law enforcement?"

"He could help us," I said.

Andy shook her head. "Who are we to interfere with a private, married couple? There's been no complaint. No domestic disturbance called in. She might not want anything to do with us. Or she might be restrained. For all we know, we'll be met at the door by the company lawyer, threatened with lawsuits if we don't vacate."

"So why not take Larson?"

"He would be forced to protect Parks from us."

"You're not making this sound like a great idea."

"It's a terrible idea."

"So…what is the plan?"

"I'm going to go in there, put my gun in Todd's face and kidnap his wife," Andy said. "And if Parks gets in the way, I'm going to shoot him in the stomach and leave him to die in the name of Christine and Paulette Paulesky. That's the plan."

I gave it some thought.

"Okay, then. It's good to have a plan."

Andy's phone rang.

"Keep your hands on the wheel," I ordered her. I groped her clothing, found the phone in a pocket, and extracted it. The caller ID said Pidge. I put it on speaker.

"The fucker is here!"

"Pidge, I have you on speaker. Where is he?"

"That fucking truck! Drove right onto the ramp and parked on the taxiway. He's blocking it. I can't get to the runway."

"What's he doing?" Andy asked.

"Sitting in that fucking black pickup truck. It has the Confederate flag on the back window, just like you said. So, now what?"

"Pidge, are you on the headset?"

"Yeah," she replied.

"Are you in the pilot's seat? Can he see you?"

"I'm in the pilot's seat and it's set all the way back like you left it. Fuck, I can barely reach the pedals when you goddamned giants fly these things. No, he can't see me. He's just sitting there. Oh, and did I mention, he's got a fucking AR leaning up against the dash? Probably that illegal full-auto shit he used to decorate your room last night."

"Hang on." I touched the Mute button. "We have to get her out of there. If he finds out she's inside, he'll kill her."

Andy nodded. I took a breath and released the Mute function.

"Pidge, you're going to get out of there."

"What, run for it? Fucker will shoot me before I get ten feet!"

"No, fly out."

"Will, did you not read me? He's got the taxiway blocked."

"And that ramp in front of you is a good five hundred feet. Maybe six hundred. You should be nose into the wind, too."

"Are you shitting me? Take off across this ramp?"

"Pidge, you're light on fuel, you got no passengers, the pilot is practically a tiny little pixie. Plus, you're a shit-hot-motherfucking kick-ass pilot. If anybody can do it, you can."

The line remained silent for a moment.

"Well, you got the pilot part right. The rest of it sucks."

"You gotta do this right. Can you reach everything without him seeing you move in the cockpit?"

"It's a little like screwing in the back seat of a Fiat, so yeah."

"Okay. First, make sure all the lights are off. Beacon. Strobes. Everything off."

"Everything off."

"Turn the Master On and drop five degrees of flaps."

I held my breath. The electric flaps would lower slightly. Someone concentrating might see the movement, but only if they were looking directly at the back of the wing. "Did he see you do it?"

"I don't think so. Flaps five."

"Okay, now run the startup checklist and do it for both engines, but don't prime them yet. Got it?"

"Got it."

I heard Pidge muttering checklist items.

"Let me know when you're ready to start the left engine."

"I'm there."

"Okay, here we go. Get your seat ready but stay down!"

"Ready."

"Alright. Prime *both* engines. Both of them."

"Done."

"Here's what you're going to do. Hit both starters simultaneously. Even if you hear one fire, hold 'em both down. You know that right engine always needs a few extra cranks. When you're sure, absolutely sure, that both engines have fired up, you firewall the throttles. All the way, no warmup. No hesitation. The second they're running, slam them. Got it?"

"Got it."

"Just before you run out of pavement, lift the nose. If the mains run through some brush, it's no big deal. Get it up in ground effect, but don't go any higher. And hey! If you can angle left, and put those hangars between you and him, all the better. That AR can shoot a thousand yards."

"Thanks. I know what an AR can shoot. I have two of them."

"Why am I not surprised?"

"Engines are primed. Here goes."

I crossed my fingers. Over the thin phone speaker, I heard the familiar sound of aviation engines cranking over. I prayed the battery could handle both engines being started at the same time, and that she hadn't over-primed, or under-primed, and that the plugs were strong and clean—and please, God, don't let anything screw this up. Because it would take Foyle only a second or two to realize what was happening.

One engine popped and for a split second I heard a starter continue to crank.

The second engine popped, fired, ran.

Pidge firewalled the throttles and both engines roared. I closed my eyes. The roar overwhelmed the small phone speaker. I strained, listening, praying not to hear anything but the engines. Not to hear a break in their powerful run. Not to hear a scream.

I heard no change until a thudding sound joined the engine chorus. It stopped my heart. The ramp hadn't been enough. She'd gone off the asphalt into—

"TAKE THAT SHIT YOU MOTHERFUCKER!" Pidge screamed.

"Pidge!" Andy cried out. The aircraft roar continued, but the note changed.

"I'm up! Ground effect. Earl's gonna have to clean the weeds outta the wheel wells! *Whoooohooooo*!"

I sank back in the Jeep seat. In my mind's eye, the Navajo broke ground, dragging itself tail low into the air, then leveling off in Ground Effect, the cushion of air that wings form when close to the earth. I saw Pidge push the nose over, level off and let the aircraft accelerate rapidly to over a hundred miles per hour. I saw her bank slightly left, putting the hangars between her and Foyle. I saw Foyle caught off guard, jumping from the pickup, raising the rifle too late as Pidge disappeared behind the hangar at weed-top height, now accelerating to one hundred thirty—one hundred fifty—one hundred eighty. Disappearing behind low hills until, more than a mile away, she could climb at a point where all Foyle could see was the glint of white wings in the sunshine.

"Pidge, you okay?"

"Fuck, yes! Climbing now."

Andy and I traded thankful glances.

"Hey, Will?" Pidge called out.

"I'm here."

"Which way did you guys go? On the highway, which way?"

"North," Andy said.

"Roger that. Headed north."

56

Mark the ramp rat said the Parks ranch property sat on a bluff overlooking the Yellowstone River, about forty miles up highway 59, he guessed. Did he know the address? No. Did he know what it looked like? No. Are there any other properties up there? No. Maybe. He "dunno." He heard that the company that built the prison bought the ranch from some Detroit auto executive who had daughters that liked horses, until they went to college and liked boys better.

Andy and I both forgot to check the mileage on the Jeep when we tore out of the airport, so the forty-mile figure became a guess. I pulled up the map feature on my phone, and after the service had time to get a cup of coffee and wake itself up, the blue dot landed on the highway we were tearing up. I scrolled ahead and found a place where the highway veered close to the Yellowstone river.

"This could be it," I said. "About four more miles."

Andy eased back to ninety-five. "I don't suppose you can get a satellite image, can you?"

I tried. The phone went back to sleep.

On either side of the road, empty Montana terrain rose and fell, as if the land were once an ocean, and the swells had frozen during a storm. A few properties passed us. I studied them, to see if they might be attractive to a private prison multimillionaire. None came close. Not unless Parks liked old houses, decaying machinery, and livestock. None matched his private jet lifestyle.

"It'll have a horse barn, and probably a training corral," I said.

"Like that?" Andy pointed as we crested a hill.

The road dipped into a long, flat valley, at least three, maybe four miles long, then rose again to climb a low bluff. To our right, a shimmer revealed the Yellowstone River.

On top of the bluff, overlooking the path of the river, a white structure nestled in a grove of the only trees in sight. Even from miles away, the property sprawled.

"Like that," I said.

Andy pushed us up over a hundred again. I glanced over to see if the Jeep engine had registered any protests with warning lights. I thought about the tires. They weren't made for this kind of speed.

I pulled up Andy's phone and called Pidge.

"Fucking Awesome Airways," Pidge answered.

"Where are you?"

"How the hell should I know? This whole state looks the same. About ten miles up the road, I guess. Or twenty."

"Okay," I said. "We're almost there. How do you feel about landing on a road?"

In the middle of trying to describe our location to Pidge, Andy's phone beeped to announce an incoming call.

"You got all that?"

"Affirmative," Pidge acknowledged.

"Gotta go," I told Pidge. I fumbled with what I hoped were the right buttons. The caller ID showed a Montana area code, so I held the phone closer to Andy.

"Andrea Stewart."

"Sergeant Stewart, hello!" Andy and I traded quick looks, recognizing the voice. "Deputy Larson here."

"Good morning, Deputy, what can I do for you?"

"I wasn't sure I'd reach you. I see your airplane is gone and thought you might have left. Where are you?"

Andy made a face at the phone. "Something I can do for you, Deputy?"

"Well, I just wondered if we might talk again. Got a couple new developments here."

"Deputy, this isn't amateur hour. Remember who you're talking to here."

"Do you mind telling me where you are?"

"About forty miles north of you on state 59. On our way to see Pearce Parks. Your turn. What's going on?"

Larson didn't speak for a moment.

"Deputy, I know you're calling the highway patrol to intercept us. That's fine. Tell them to meet us at Parks' ranch. We could use the help. We believe Parks has abducted the daughter of a recently murdered state senator from Wisconsin, and that her life is in imminent danger. We're on our way to retrieve her and I don't expect it to go well."

"Ma'am, why don't you wait—"

"Deputy Larson, I think you better tell me why you're calling or we're just going to put any further conversation on hold."

He let silence hold the line for a moment. Then he said, "We're at the airport, Sergeant. I came out here to talk to them, like you said, about Donnelly. Do you know a Mark Johannsen?"

"Is that the kid in the office?" she asked.

"Yes, ma'am."

Larson let it hang.

"What about him?" Andy asked.

"He's been shot. Do you know anything about that?"

Shit! I punched the door panel.

"Is he okay?" Andy demanded.

"No, ma'am, he is deceased. He was shot numerous times—like somebody wanted to ask him some questions and didn't want him to die right away. Now, I think you need to tell me what you know about this."

"Listen carefully, Deputy," Andy said. "I would bet my badge he was shot by a man named Garrett Foyle. Foyle is currently serving three consecutive life terms at Evergreen. And if you call over there, they're going to tell you he's tucked in nice and cozy on a solitary confinement protocol. But he's not. He's driving a late model black pickup truck with a light bar and a confederate flag stencil in the back window. Got that? I also suspect he's northbound on 59, coming our way. He is heavily armed and extremely dangerous, do you copy?"

"Okay," Larson said, "Garrett Foyle. Do you mind telling me how you know all this?"

"I sure as hell mind! I don't have time. You need to get on this in a big way. Foyle is carrying an AR with full auto capability. The one he used on us last night. He's already serving three terms with no parole, so don't expect him to surrender if you offer to put in a good word for him."

"And you didn't think any of this was important last night?"

"I wasn't sure you weren't on the payroll, Deputy. Still not sure."

Larson gave that a moment's thought.

"Ma'am, I'm going to have to check all this out. I really need you to head back down here—"

"No. If you're really not working for Parks, then you need to send officers out to Evergreen, and don't take any shit from them about protocol—you need to get into their solitary and see for yourself that Foyle is gone. Parks has been using him as a killer with a perfect alibi. Parks engineered Cinnamon Hills to kill a state senator. Foyle killed five adults and two children a week ago in Wisconsin—just to cover his tracks. And now that poor kid. If you want verification, go out to Evergreen."

"Ma'am, that's going to take some time."

"Do you have an FBI office around here?"

"In Billings."

"Call them—but don't wait for them."

"I will do that, ma'am, but I want you to turn around and come in."

"And run right into Foyle? He's coming this way, Deputy, and we are seriously outgunned. Who do you think he was looking for at the airport? I have only one interest, and that's retrieving Sandra Stone who I believe is in peril at Parks' ranch. After that, you can deal with Foyle. I am not sticking around here to trade nine mil shots with an AR on full auto. I intend to be long gone before he gets here. You tell your people what he's carrying. You can't traffic-stop him. Tell them to bring a goddamned tank!"

Andy punched the phone with her finger and cut off the call.

"Well," I said, "I guess that cat's out of the bag and out of solitary confinement. Why on earth did he kill that poor kid?"

"To find out where we went," Andy said. "Which means we only have about fifteen minutes, tops."

I thought about the kid, and the girls in the woods. I felt it again, cold and black. Murder in my heart.

"Do you think Larson gets it?"

"Maybe. You know what I hate about that guy?" She threw the question at me. "He's doing everything exactly the way I would."

57

Andy took the turn onto the gravel driveway a little fast and the Jeep fishtailed wildly for a few seconds. She didn't blink. She calmly goosed the accelerator halfway through the slide. We shot toward a broad white structure, graced with green trim, green shutters, and a gabled roof. A western-style porch spanned the entire front of the home, which had to be close to two hundred feet wide. Off to the left, a neatly painted and trimmed horse barn took shade from old hardwood trees. A complex of white board fences enclosed what looked to my eye like horse play-ground equipment in a series of pens. Sprinklers worked to keep a lush green lawn alive, even though the landscape in all directions lay brown and dry. Rose gardens fronted the house, rich with blooms defying a fall chill in the air. White arched trellises, symmetrical on either side of the front walkway, stood over a path winding through the gardens.

We parked on a circle driveway in front of the house and dismounted the Jeep. Heat poured off the engine as I stepped around it.

A man in cowboy boots, jeans and a flannel shirt stepped onto the porch to meet us. Every inch the ranch foreman, he cradled a rifle in his arms and wore a forbidding face. A little under six feet, he looked sun-dried and hard-bitten, with not an ounce of excess weight—somewhere between forty and sixty.

"Private property," he said coldly. "Get the fuck out of here."

Andy paid no attention. She unleashed a big smile and strolled up the walk, adding a little extra swing to her hips. I hung back and put my right hand on my hip. I watched him narrow his gaze on me and the move I made, choosing me as the greater threat. Mistake.

"Hi," Andy said sweetly. She stepped onto the porch. "I just stopped by to say hello to my friend, Sandy. Could you kindly let her—"

In one swift move, Andy lifted the rifle out of the man's cradled grasp and slammed it into his forehead. One hand came lose or was torn lose. Andy inverted the wrist, forcing him to twist away from her. She brought her right foot up and stomped his right knee just as he turned it to a perfect ninety-degree angle to her. I heard something crack. The knee folded in a way it was never meant to fold.

He dropped to the wooden porch floor, his forehead dripping blood. The rifle clattered away. Andy still owned his right hand and wrist. She brought it up to an unnatural angle behind his back. He cried out. She planted a knee in the center of his spine.

"Where—is—she?"

I fetched the rifle and pointed it at the man's grimace. Andy gently pushed it aside with her free hand.

"Who?" he squeezed the question out with what little air Andy allowed him.

"Sandra Stone. Pretty blonde. In the company of an asshole," Andy flexed the wrist and I heard something snap. The man shrieked.

"You're going to need knee surgery, and this wrist will be in a cast for a month. I'm going to ask you one more time, and then my husband is going to shoot you in the elbow, the other one. Do you have someone who can feed you for a couple months?"

"She's inside!"

"I am a police officer. Do you understand? Right now, you're looking at charges for menacing a police officer with a deadly weapon. If you get any more involved, you'll be looking at accessory to multiple murders. Are you going to be a problem for us?"

"No ma'am!"

Andy let him go and stepped away quickly. He stayed prone, easing his right arm back to a normal angle, moaning as he moved. Andy took the rifle from me and went back down the steps toward the Jeep, ejecting rounds. When she got far enough out, she turned and hurled the empty weapon onto the roof.

"That might have come in handy," I protested.

"Or it might have complicated things in a very bad way."

She went for the front door. She threw it open and stepped to one side, gesturing me to stay away from the opening. Darting glances told her the path was clear. She stepped through. I followed.

Inside the ranch house, I closed a hand around Andy's arm.

"Hey," I said softly, "that was a bit … strong. Are you sure about this?"

She let go of a tense breath. "I wasn't. Until Foyle showed up at the airport. And then—that poor kid."

I studied her face for hesitation. She showed none. "I don't think we have time to second-guess."

We moved forward.

The interior of the house took Old West décor well beyond a point any local resident would have considered acceptable. Indian blankets and buffalo skins and totems and rifles seemed to hang from wood beams and paneling everywhere. Remington sculptures sat on heavy wooden mantles. Animal skin rugs, I guessed bear, lay on the wooden floor under hanging lamps made of wagon wheels. A row of cowboy hats hung from pegs near the door. Glass cabinets displayed Indian artifacts with little apparent order or organization or respect for their meaning. This was the Old West according to a Hollywood set decorator. The only thing missing was a velvet painting of John Wayne.

The dimensions of the interior mimicked the dimensions of the territory, wide and high. A dining room contained a table that could easily seat twenty. Beyond that, a sitting room the size of a hotel lobby offered a view out the back of the house, capitalizing on the small bluff overlooking the Yellowstone River below.

"You have no business here."

Pearce Parks stood in the center of the sitting room. He held a phone in one hand. Tall and white-haired, with narrow features and a runner's body, he wore crisp new jeans and a white shirt that had western-style pockets. He accessorized the costume with brightly polished cowboy boots and a belt sporting a huge buckle. I would have hated to be seen in public with him.

He worked his face into a portrait of fierce domination, but a trace of panic slithered beneath his tanned skin.

"Your job is already history, Deputy Stewart, and I plan to file—"

"Oh, shut—up!" Andy marched impatiently into the room. "Why do you guys always roll out the employment threats? And it's Sergeant Stewart, not Deputy! Now, where is Sandra Stone?"

Andy searched the room.

"How dare you come into my home like this!" Parks barked at her. "Mr. and Mrs. Jameson are my guests, here to recuperate from the terrible events of last week. I'm putting my lawyer on speaker phone so that he can bear witness to your reckless behavior!"

Parks held up his phone and poked the screen. Andy took one step and slapped the phone from his hand. It clattered to the polished, hardwood floor, shedding plastic pieces.

"Destruction of property. Assault." Parks ticked the threats off on his fingers.

Andy drew her weapon, turned, and fired. The phone exploded. The shatteringly loud report filled every corner of the huge room. Parks jumped backward, collided with a fat leather sofa, and flopped onto the cushions. His jaw dangled and the color drained from his skin.

"Where—is—Sandra—Stone?" Andy asked in a low, deadly voice.

Parks worked his mouth, but nothing came out. Andy leaned forward, and with her free left hand grabbed his right ear and pulled him to his feet. She pushed the hot muzzle of her weapon up under his jaw.

"Lead us to her. Now."

She nudged. He staggered forward with his head canted to one side where her fingernails dug into his ear. Looking less like a boardroom warrior, and more like a guilty five-year-old, he marched across the open room to a wooden staircase. Andy let his ear go. He rubbed it to relieve the pain. He said nothing. She gestured with her weapon. He trudged up the stairs. A man accustomed to command, to knowing the scheme ahead of everyone else, he now moved in a mild state of shock as events he did not foresee unfolded around him.

The stairway led to an upstairs hall, with bedroom doors spaced evenly on either side. From one of the rooms, Todd Jameson spoke.

"Pearce, for God's sake! What the hell was that? I told you I need it quiet!"

Todd Jameson stepped halfway out one of the bedroom doors, holding a plastic turkey baster in one hand. Surprise and shock at the sight of Andy stopped him cold. His eyes grew into panicked twin moons when he recognized her.

A choking noise came from his throat. He cleared it. "Ah—Deputy Stew—"

"SERGEANT!" Andy yelled. "God, you people are morons. It's Sergeant Stewart. Back up, Todd."

Jameson backed into the room. Andy pushed Parks through the bedroom door after him. We followed.

The sunlit bedroom rioted in frills and flowery colors. The same Hollywood set decorator must have been told to make this a frontier woman's bedroom, and don't spare the lace. A four-poster bed sat against the wall to our right, layered in thick comforters made of a fabric inspired by a prairie flower garden. Antique dolls sat on sconces between the windows, looking down on the scene with porcelain eyes.

In stark contrast to the color and light flooding the room, the odor of vomit hung thick in the atmosphere.

Sandy Stone lay in a tangle of damp blonde hair on the bed, eyes half lidded, face expressionless. One hand, her left, extended above her head where it had been bound to one of the bed's four posts with what looked like a torn pillowcase. A collection of pill bottles littered the nightstand, watched over by a dusky bottle of expensive Tequila.

Todd backed away into a corner of the room. He dropped the turkey baster. Liquid speckled with white fragments dribbled out onto the wooden floor. I picked it up and touched a drop to my tongue.

"What, no salt on the rim for her?"

"We were just—she—she needs rest!" Todd stammered. "We were just trying to help her." Sweat beaded on his forehead. "Pearce, what the hell is this?"

"Shut up, both of you," Andy said coldly. "Will, get her loose and make sure her airway is clear."

I set to work on the bindings, noting that one ankle was also ensnared.

Andy picked up the pill bottles, one by one, never moving the muzzle of her weapon from the two men standing in the corner of the room.

Parks rubbed his ear and glowered. Jameson's mouth tried to form words but could not come up with sound.

"Valium. Xanax. Oxycodone. With a tequila chaser," she said. "Christ."

I freed Sandy's wrist and ankle. She looked up at me from a deep, distant place. Her blue eyes lacked comprehension.

"How much have you put into her?" Andy demanded.

"We didn't—"

"DON'T FUCKING LIE TO ME! HOW MUCH?!"

"Two Valiums and two Xanax, but she kept vomiting it up. That's all! That's all!" Todd cried out.

"What's in that thing?" I gestured at the turkey baster.

"Um—I guess a couple more of each," he said.

"Well, Todd," Andy said through gritted teeth, "I *guess* I'm going to start shooting you. Ankles first. Then knees. Not sure how many shots it will take to kill you. I'll just *guess*, if that's what we're doing here. Unless you want to get real precise, real quick!"

"Six more!" he cried out. "Of each!"

"Holy shit!" I said. "How much did you get in her?"

"I didn't! I swear! I heard the shot, and she woke up and I could not get it in her mouth! I swear!"

Todd stared directly into the muzzle of Andy's Glock. The whites of his eyes formed terrified pale rings around his irises. Focused on the black hole, he did not see Andy's face over the gun sights.

I did.

"Dee," I said softly, trying to pull her attention away from the gunsight and the weight I was certain she applied to the trigger. "What do I do? Should I make her vomit?"

Andy didn't answer. Todd quivered, far closer to death than he had taken his new wife.

"Dee?"

She released a breath. Without taking her eyes from the gunsight, she said to me, "How's her breathing?"

"Shallow but steady."

"Check her lips. Fingertips. Are they blue?"

"Lips seem a little purple, but not blue. Can't tell the fingernails. They're painted. Fingertips look okay." I noticed dried vomit between her fingers. She must have known and fought back by inducing herself to retch. "Sandy! Sandy, are you with me?" I called down to her, down to a deep, deep place. I prayed she could still hear me.

"Roll your knuckles across her breastbone," Andy said. "Hard."

I eased her onto her back, keeping her head turned. She wore a flannel night gown, meant for comfortable sleep. The front was stained and smelled bad. I made a fist and rolled the knuckles down her sternum.

She flinched and moaned.

"Sandy!" I called to her. "Wake up! Time to go!"

The eyelids fluttered. Her hand moved and closed on my arm. She squeezed weakly.

"She's responding," I said to Andy.

"Can you carry her?"

I scooped her up. She felt hot. The back of the nightgown was saturated in sweat. Her head fell against my shoulder, her hair hung in strings across her face.

"Andy, this isn't what it seems like," Todd pleaded. "You can't just take her out of here. She—she's depressed—she needs care. She…" He trailed off, realizing the play had ended, and much more with it. Blood drained from his face and neck.

Parks glowered at us silently, a feral dog backed into a corner, waiting.

"You two stay right here. Will's going to take her outside. State patrol is minutes away. Don't either of you move. I'll be in the hallway. First one to step through this door gets shot in the groin. Understand? I don't want you dead. But I don't care much beyond that."

Neither man, now ashen, spoke. Todd muttered.

"We didn't mean … we were just …"

I swung Sandy's bare legs to fit through the door and hurried out. A part of me prayed to hear two quick gunshots. A greater part asked God to prevent Andy from executing them both. I heard her slam the door shut behind us.

"We need to get out of here before Foyle gets here," Andy darted past me in the hallway, leading with her weapon, clearing the space ahead as we went.

58

We broke into the sunshine. I hurried to the back seat of the Jeep. Something didn't look right.

"Shit!" I cried out. "That goddamned cowboy slashed the tires!"

Andy swung her gun around, three hundred sixty degrees, searching. I had the feeling that if the ranch foreman planned to ambush us, he would have already fired.

"Get in!"

I slid onto the back seat with Sandy in my arms, working her feet onto the seat beside me and cradling her body against mine. I leaned down to listen to her breathing. Slow but steady.

Any one of the three drugs could kill her by slowing her heart rate and breathing until she simply winked out like a candle. If she had enough of the pills in her system, I could not imagine what good I might do, or how to stop the process.

I gave her a firm squeeze. She moaned in response.

She's just a kindergarten teacher, I thought. I pressed my lips to her ear.

"Don't you leave us, Sandy. Your kids need you. They want you back."

Andy climbed behind the wheel.

"How far do you think we can get on the rims?" she asked.

"Far enough," I said. "That valley is the only straight stretch for ten miles. The only place Pidge can pick us up. We sure as hell aren't going to outrun Foyle now."

"I don't know, Will, it's going to be close."

"Are you thinking we should hunker down here?"

Andy gave it a moment's consideration, then shook her head. "Too many variables here. And Foyle still outguns us."

She fired up the Jeep. She threw it in gear. We lurched forward, thumping on the flat tires. We wheeled around the driveway circle, then kicked up gravel as she shot toward the highway. Wrapped in noise and vibration, our speed seemed higher than it was.

I rolled down the window to draw cold air across Sandy's face.

Andy made the turn out of the driveway. On pavement, the din rose to a metallic roar. Andy floored it. I glanced back to see rooster tails of sparks rising from both sides of the vehicle. We began the run down the slope toward the long straight stretch in the valley.

"There she is!" Andy ducked down and pointed up through the windshield. I could not see, but a moment later I heard the twin-engine song of the Piper Navajo passing low overhead.

Andy started to slow down.

"No! Keep going. Get to the center of the valley and then get this thing as far off the road as it will go. She needs room to land, and then room to take off without turning around."

We rolled forward. Chunks of torn tires flew off the rims and slammed into the wheel wells. I smelled burning rubber. Wisps of smoke entered the cabin. Looking forward and behind us, I saw no traffic and crossed my fingers that it would stay that way. Andy pushed the Jeep harder and harder as the friction from the steel rims slowed us. Thunderous shaking invaded the passenger compartment. We screamed down the road. I glanced over Andy's shoulder. Our speed hovered just over forty miles per hour.

I leaned to the right to look through the passenger-side window at the sky. High over the dry rolling landscape, I spotted the Navajo, now paralleling us. Pidge had the airplane on a downwind leg, preparing to land. I saw the wheels drop, looking awkward as they fell into place and locked. The noise from the screaming steel beneath us drowned out all other sounds, but I imagined Pidge throttling back, lowering the flaps, preparing a left turn to the base leg of the pattern, then a left turn onto her final approach to this highway-turned-runway.

When we had driven halfway across the valley, I shouted over the din, "Good enough! Turn off here!"

Andy slowed and cranked the wheel left. We crossed the oncoming lane, rolled over the gravel shoulder and down a small embankment onto a flat, grassy area that sloped away from the road. The Jeep bounced and ground to a rough halt in a cloud of smoke and dust. Andy jumped out and opened the door for me. I eased out of the car keeping a grip on Sandy, unable to see in the smoke. Andy grabbed my arm and led me away from the car.

We stumbled up the embankment to the road.

High to my left, about a mile and a half away, Pidge rolled out of a shallow bank onto her final approach, aligned with the road. The Navajo dipped lower and lower, until it eased below the crest of the small bluff that formed the southern border of the valley.

"Oh, no." My heart went cold. "No!"

"What?" Andy asked, but I didn't need to answer. She saw it, too.

We were too late.

Black and racing toward us, a pickup truck crested the bluff and began its own descent into the valley.

Foyle.

"Call Pidge, now!" I cried.

Andy pulled her phone and pressed the screen. She held it in her hand and begged, "Pick up pick up pick up!"

The Navajo settled below the bluff line. It descended to meet its own shadow, which raced across the dry hills beside the road. Pidge had no idea. She could not see behind her as the pickup dropped down the slope and onto the flat that formed her runway.

"A little busy here!" Pidge's voice came across the line.

"ABORT! GO AROUND!" I shouted. "Pidge, he's coming up behind you! Go around!"

She was committed, in the flare, nose high and settling onto the mains—the worst possible time to try and convert an aircraft from diminishing energy and lift to full power and flight.

I saw it before I heard it. The Navajo swung, yawing nose left, then right as Pidge heaved power to the engines by shoving the throttles forward. Never fully in synch, one engine came up before the other, and she fought the yaw, trying to hold a line on the road. The main landing gear touched the pavement. White smoke puffed from the tires, then she bounced back into the air, accelerating.

"Yes!" I cried. "Go! Go! Go!"

She held it. She smoothed out the yaw and pitched the nose down to build speed. She came on fast now, fully in control. The wheels folded up. The silhouette of the wing thinned as the flaps retracted.

She shot over us. The prop wash stirred the smoke cloud. The wing tips generated vortexes that curled smoke into small horizontal tornados.

"WHAT THE FUCK?" Pidge called out through the phone speaker. "I had that!"

"Foyle!" I said. "He's going to be on us in thirty seconds!" Pidge might not have understood, but I knew that all Foyle needed to do was drive up behind the airplane as we tried to board and fill it and us full of holes.

"We need to get to cover," Andy cut the connection and left Pidge on her own. I heard the Navajo climbing behind me as Andy pulled me back down the embankment behind the Jeep. Still carrying Sandy, the muscles in my arms began to burn.

"What about here?" I asked. "Use the Jeep."

Andy shook her head. "Cars are only bulletproof on TV. We gotta find a hole. C'mon! Keep the Jeep between us and him!"

The smoke worked in our favor, providing cover. A gray cloud flowed in the direction of Foyle and the highway. The red-hot steel of the wheels had set fire to the grass under the Jeep. In short order, the whole vehicle would be burning.

We jogged through the dry grass. The terrain could not have been less in our favor. After an initial drop, the ground sloped upward, rising away from the road, exposing us. We could not outrun Foyle's automatic rifle. Our only hope lay in finding a depression and diving into it, forcing him to come closer. Rifle against pistol; a contest, it was not. Beyond fifty yards, Andy's best shot would have to be a miracle. Whatever he had for optics on the rifle would make him lethal at five times that distance.

"Here!" Andy cried. She pulled me to one side. A slight depression rolled away beneath us. I doubted we could get ourselves flat enough to be out of Foyle's line of sight. He could just stand at the road and pick us off. Nevertheless, I followed Andy several steps and dropped to my knees where she indicated. "Get her down, flat."

I laid Sandy out. She blinked and moved languidly. "Lie down! Stay flat!" I ordered her, and she gave me a vague nod.

"Stay here!" Andy ordered. She dropped the magazine out of her pistol to count the rounds remaining. The look on her face told me more than I wanted to know. She slapped the magazine home.

I heard the black pickup truck roaring across the flat valley highway, less than a quarter mile away. The grass fire encircling the Jeep crackled and popped. Andy started to rise, looking away to our left. She made a move. I reached out and caught a fist full of her jacket and pulled her back down.

"What!" she snapped at me. "I think I can get in position over there!"

"There's nothing over there, and you know it! This is it. This is all we got. Now get down. You're not doing this."

She glared at me.

"Dee," I said quietly, "that's a futile gesture. You can't trade shots with him. Look." I pointed at the highway.

One hundred yards beyond the Jeep, Foyle slowed to a roll, then swung the wheel and brought the truck to a stop across both lanes, eliminating any hope of Pidge landing on this valley highway. The truck door opened. Foyle stepped out, holding his rifle high in one hand. With his other hand to his ear, he spoke into a phone.

Parks, I thought.

"I should have shot them both," Andy said, making the same assumption.

Foyle stood motionless, a black figure with a bald head that shone in the sunlight. He finished the call, secured the phone, and aimed the rifle, searching for us through the weapon's powerful optics. We ducked.

Our refuge was nothing more than a shallow depression in the earth. As if to make the point, Foyle fired a three-shot burst. Dirt kicked up on the slope beyond us. He knew roughly where we were.

Andy hugged the earth on her belly. I lay on my back. I grabbed a handful of grass, then another. Slowly, I moved the bouquet of dry grass into position above my head. Next, I rolled my head to one side, putting my left eye as close to the top of our cover as possible. I edged up, peering through the grass.

Foyle walked slowly down the center line of the highway. He held the rifle in firing position, patiently waiting for his quarry to panic.

I slid back down again and took a deep breath. Overhead, Pidge swung a wide arc in the Navajo, holding a steep bank. She had a perfect vantage point to see it all play out.

"Do you think Larson sent the highway patrol?"

"Yes. And it's highly unlikely they'll be here in the next three minutes," Andy squirmed around, rolling onto her back, switching her head and legs so that she lay in the depression facing Foyle. She held her weapon in both hands on her belly.

"Give me the gun," I said.

Another burst of three shots broke against the muttering sound of the flames consuming the grass around the Jeep. Dirt kicked up on the slope, this time a little farther away. I took heart in the belief that Foyle didn't have a precise bead on us.

"What are you talking about?"

"I'm going to go over there and shoot that bastard in the head," I said. "Give me the gun."

She looked at me as if I had asked her to saw off her right arm and hand it over.

"You know it's the only option."

"How? Your propeller thingies are in your bag, up there." She gestured toward Pidge, high above. "How are you going to get there without getting blown all over this valley?"

"The wind is in my favor. I just need to position a little more upwind, push off on a decent angle, and let the wind carry me."

"No."

"It's the only way to get close. He can stand off all day and hit us from long range. Eventually, he's going to figure out where we are, and then it's just a matter of getting into position to see over this lousy little hump."

"Maybe that puts him close enough for me."

"Firing what? How many rounds? Against automatic fire?" I held out my hand. She gripped her weapon tightly.

"Maybe the state patrol gets here."

I held out my hand.

Another burst of three chewed into the slope, closer now.

Andy made a pained face and slid closer. She pressed the Glock into my hand. I closed my other hand on hers.

"Will you *please* be careful?"

"What day is this?"

She blinked. "Sunday. Why?"

"I'd have to check my calendar, but I think Sunday is a 'be careful' day."

Three more shots sent soil into the air, now farther away from us. A good sign.

"After I go, hang on to her," I gestured at Sandy. "If she gets up at the wrong moment…"

"I got it!" Andy snapped, frustrated. Then, a little softer, "I got it."

I slid the Glock into my belt and pulled my shirt down over it.

Fwooomp! I disappeared. Not wanting to catch a bullet, I raised my head only slightly. Foyle continued stalking us from the centerline of the highway. The Jeep transformed into a jolly bonfire between us, slightly right of my sight line to Foyle. The wind drove the smoke away from us, on an angle across the pavement, and not one that favored me.

"Dee," I said. "This is going to get weird."

I leaned down and kissed my wife, full on the lips. She issued a brief moan and then press her lips to mine.

"Be right back."

I didn't tell her about the geometry problem. Instead, I gripped her belt and passed myself over her. I gripped tufts of grass and crabbed up out of the shallow depression. I moved to the right, away from his line of fire.

I saw Foyle easily now. He ambled slowly toward us, holding the rifle up in firing position, sighting through a telescopic scope. I saw him move the rifle back and forth, searching. He knew we were using the contour of the terrain for cover. He didn't have far to walk before he would see over the shallow hump that hid Andy and Sandy.

I had only a minute, maybe two. I needed to get this right the first time.

I wasn't completely honest with Andy. The angle of the wind didn't favor me. Getting to a position where the flow of the wind could carry me directly to him meant traversing the ground he was chewing up with his short bursts of fire. Vanishing didn't protect me from harm.

Bullets would pass through my flesh whether Foyle could see me or not.

It left me no choice. I went right, which took the use of the wind out of the equation. On the plus side, by going right, I moved to a position that put the burning Jeep between us.

I gripped the grass and pulled myself over the ground, practically slithering. Going any higher would cost me a grip and leave me floating. The only out from that would be to reappear in full view of Foyle.

I worked my way forward until the Jeep obscured Foyle.

Fwooomp! I reappeared and pancaked to the ground. I jumped to my feet and jogged as close to the burning Jeep as possible, mindful that the fuel tank had yet to make its opinion of the fire known. The jog closed ground with Foyle. Stealing a quick glance around the right side of the burning vehicle, I estimated that I was now less than fifty yards from him. I saw the glyphs and lines tattooed into the skin of his head.

He scanned and fired. Three-shot bursts. He walked inexorably forward. Pidge circled less than a thousand feet overhead. The Navajo's engines throbbed.

I crouched and gripped the dry grass.

Fwooomp! I vanished again. I crabbed around the Jeep, toward the embankment that sloped up to the pavement. As I drew closer, the grass thinned, and my grip on it became tenuous. I worked my way forward, parallel to the highway, sometimes pinching roots with my fingertips to stay anchored.

Thirty yards now.

Another burst. I didn't have time to see where the rounds landed.

As I skimmed closer, my confidence grew. I calculated a path to a point almost directly between Foyle and Andy, less than ten yards from him. At that distance my chances of hitting him substantially increased.

I decided to raise the odds by going back to Plan A and using the wind.

I slithered forward beneath the smoke drifting across the road. Roaring flames covered the crackle of the dry grass when I gripped it. I could not hide the strange movement the blades of grass made as unseen hands gathered it. I prayed that Foyle's concentration remained fixed on his gunsights and the shallow terrain beyond the Jeep.

At a point dangerously close to his line of fire, I stopped. I raised myself to a crouch. He walked slowly forward less than thirty feet away, keeping to the highway centerline, as if he saw himself in a movie. The smug confidence on his face cemented my determination to shoot the ink out of his Nazi head tattoos.

Slowly, struggling not to push off, I brought myself fully erect.

He fired again. The rifle shots assaulted my unprotected ears. I sensed the rounds cutting the air.

I curled my legs upward, releasing my feet from contact with the earth without pushing off. The breeze coming from behind me immediately pushed me in Foyle's direction.

The embankment sloped up to meet the highway shoulder. From my launch point, the pavement lay level with my knees. Floating toward that higher plane meant having to lightly tap my trajectory higher. But once on an up-angle, I could not stop it. I no longer floated horizontally, but at a slight angle, climbing.

Twenty feet. I reached the edge of the shoulder, then the edge of the pavement.

I pulled up my shirt and felt for the Glock. It filled my hand with reassurance of the murder I now wanted so badly to commit. I pulled it free of my belt and held it in both hands, bringing it into firing position.

With no idea how to aim it.

The weapon, tucked away, had vanished just as I had. I expected that. But now I drifted twenty feet from Foyle, moving on a track that angled across the road in front of him—and I could not see the gun or gunsight.

In a few seconds, the geometry of my path would increase my distance from him. Worse, I was rising.

I glanced back at Andy. From my vantage point, now slightly higher than Foyle, I saw the crown of Andy's head and gold strands of Sandy's hair.

Foyle was seconds away from seeing the same thing.

This was the best shot I would get.

I pointed the weapon blindly and made one of the worst mistakes of my life.

I fired.

My entire body jolted, seared by an electric explosion. My teeth slammed together. My muscles constricted and turned to stone. Something punched me in the center of my being. I jerked away from Foyle. I would have seen him receding if my vision hadn't gone white.

Fwooo—CRACK! I reappeared. Gravity pulled me down. My feet hit first, sending me tumbling backward. My head hit the pavement. A second flash of white burst across my vision. I felt pain *everywhere*.

A moment later I lay on the pavement trying to pull my eyes open. When I did, I saw only blue, and the flash of the Navajo's white wings high overhead. I lay flat on my back. My hands and feet shivered uncontrollably. All ten fingers were splayed open.

Andy's Glock was gone.

"What the fuck?" I heard Foyle's voice.

I saw him, roughly twenty-five feet away, frozen in the road. He held his rifle on me.

"How the fuck did you do that?"

My vision slowly cleared. His features sharpened. He looked at me over the rifle, not through the sights. Genuine wonder blazed in his hooded eyes.

"Answer me!" I recognized the voice, giving commands, just as he had in Sandy Stone's wedding tent.

Foyle had seen me. He had seen it happen—the impossible moment when I appeared out of the empty air above the highway in front of him. Something had gone terribly wrong when I pulled the trigger on Andy's gun.

He fired, and I expected to die, but the three-shot burst chipped pavement beyond me. My ears rang.

"How the fuck did you do that? Answer me!"

Not *Who are you?* or *Where did you come from?* He had no doubt of what he'd seen. Nothing in his mind second-guessed his eyes.

I looked up at the man who shot two children running for their lives because their mommy told them to *Run!* A man who shot big sister first because he knew baby sister would stop. A man who believed in Nazi ideology seventy years after the world saw for itself the full depth of depravity and soul-blackening corruption of that ideology—and he held his belief so fervently that he marred himself for life with its symbols and slogans.

Staring at him, and the blue sky beyond him, I tried forming words.

"Uh—"

The air suddenly fell quiet. Something changed—something went missing. For a second, I thought I lost my hearing, but I heard the fire muttering, popping, and sparking.

Foyle approached.

"You just fucking appeared outta thin air!" He looked down. I followed his eyes to the Glock on the pavement. "Thought you were going to kill my ass, did you?" He fired again. Three shots chewed into pavement near my feet. Gravel shrapnel hit and stung my legs. "How the hell did you do that?"

My eyes flicked past his bald, tattooed head. In the blue sky, I saw hope.

Distract him!

I raised my left arm and pointed at it with my right index finger.

Foyle creased his forehead, not comprehending. I held my breath. My senses sharpened, and the deep pain receded. My muscles, so rigid a few moments ago, now felt weak and watery. I knew I would hurt for days. It didn't matter. I needed to speak. Speaking suddenly became terribly important.

"Cloaking device," I said thickly, pointing at the metal wristband on my watch. "U.S. Government—Department of Defense—top secret." I pointed emphatically. He squinted at the wristwatch. I looked past him, at the high blue sky.

"You better not be shitting me, you son of a bitch. What else you got on you? You got weapons? Other than that plastic piece of shit Glock? You got any other weapons?"

I shook my head and held my breath.

Just stay right where you are, you stupid Nazi shithead.

Hope. Coming fast and silent.

"Take that off and gimme it! Now!"

"If I take it off without entering a code—it self-destructs. Will kill us both."

He took a step back. Such utter bullshit, but bullshit made entirely plausible because he had seen me do the impossible.

"Then enter the fucking code!" He made a prodding gesture with his rifle. "Now!"

"Okay! Okay!" I waved a *wait a minute* gesture at him. "Something went wrong with it—"

"Sure as fuck did. You were trying to kill me, and you flew right outta fuckin' thin air. You looked like you had a 'lectric cable up your ass."

"Okay, just give me a second. Don't kill me. It's wired to me. You kill me, and it self-destructs. Give me a second, will you?" I pretended to work the dial on my watch with fingers I barely controlled. While I worked, I said three words.

"Christine and Paulette."

His face went blank.

"What did you say?"

I looked him in the eye. I said slowly, "Christine and Paulette."

Recognition flashed in his dead eyes—he knew the names. Doubt wormed under the skin of his face, like the fading blue lines of his prison tattoos. He opened his mouth to ask.

Too late.

Silence—it had replaced the steady drone of the Navajo's powerful twin engines when Pidge, circling a thousand feet overhead, suddenly chopped the throttles. That's what went missing. That's why the world went still. And while I bullshitted this Nazi fool, I watched her.

In the sky behind Foyle, she rolled the big cabin-class twin-engine airplane into an aerobatic bank, showing me the full span of the aircraft's wings. At the same time, she pulled into a tight spiral curve toward the earth. Gravity replaced engine power and silently accelerated the plane well beyond normal cruise speed. She had to be doing over two hundred fifty miles per hour when she leveled off just feet above the rolling domes of grass.

Behind Foyle. Unseen. Unheard.

At full speed she covered more than three hundred fifty feet per second.

A little over three hundred feet from the road, she slammed the throttles full forward and for one last shaved second, Foyle heard her coming.

He had time to turn. He had no time to run. No time to duck. But in that last second, he knew the names of the children he had murdered.

Pidge hit him with the full disk of the right engine's three-bladed propeller spinning at max power.

Foyle exploded into a cloud of red nothing over two legs left standing in the road.

Pidge tore across the road hauling a thunderclap that shook me where I lay. The slipstream or maybe the sheer terror of it all sucked the air from my lungs. I rolled to one side on instinct. The Navajo's right wingtip passed over me. Had I been upright, the wing would have taken my head. I've never been so close to anything so fast.

The red cloud that had been Foyle swept after her.

Doppler effect changed the scream of the engines as they passed. I heard explosive, metallic bangs. I continued to roll until I saw her roaring away, covering more than three hundred fifty feet of ground for every two heartbeats pounding in my chest. Black smoke erupted from the right engine, an engine destroying itself from within. Something white—cowling—flew off and tumbled through the air behind her.

The airplane yawed wildly right, and I saw the rudder swing to counter it. In the cockpit, Pidge would have her left foot stomped to the floor on that rudder pedal. Dead foot, dead engine. Her right leg would be idle, and her left leg would be fully extended, fighting the to conquer the powerful adverse yaw of a twin-engine airplane with one engine out.

She tried to climb.

"Feather it!" I shouted at her. "C'mon, Pidge! You got this! Feather it!"

She's light! She can do this!

She fought the plane with rudder and a shallow left bank, into the live engine, the engine that would overpower all the controls and flip her over, sending her to her death if she allowed the aircraft to decelerate below its single-engine minimum controllable airspeed.

"C'mon, Pidge! I trained you!" I screamed after her.

The Navajo scribed a line across the valley floor, losing speed, clawing for altitude. Bluffs rose in the distance. She needed to clear them, but if she pulled too hard, the speed would fall, and she would face a choice—cut the power to the good engine and crash—or leave the power on and crash out of control.

"C'mon! C'mon! C'mon!" I urged her. Smaller and smaller, the plane fought through the air into the distance.

Tethered to a sooty trail of oil smoke, Pidge and the Navajo dropped out of sight.

59

"Lie still!" Andy cried. She dropped to her knees and began tearing at my clothes. "Where are you hit? *Where are you hit?*"

"Stop!" Horrified, I saw that she was bleeding. "Are you shot? Andy, are you okay?"

"What? Yes!"

"Blood! You've got blood on your hands!"

She shook her head. "It's yours, Will, you've been shot! Where are you hit?" She probed my torso and pulled at my shirt.

"I'm not shot!" I grabbed her hands. She froze. "I'm not shot."

"You're bleeding!"

I looked down at my clothes. At the pavement.

"That's not mine. I'm okay." It was overstating the case. Every inch of my skin hurt. The back of my head hurt. My muscles burned. My joints felt sore and stiff. My hands would have shaken if I didn't have them clamped on Andy's wrists. "That's Foyle's."

Andy, kneeling beside me where I lay across the highway centerline, turned her head. She looked at the legs that had fallen over, at the arc of red glistening across two lanes of highway. She looked at the trail of smoke breaking up and floating away, pointing at the bluffs to the west.

"Pidge hit him," I said. She blinked.

"What?"

"Pidge took the son of a bitch out with One Nine Alpha."

Andy gaped at me.

She said, "I heard her—but I didn't dare look up. I heard him shooting—and I thought he was still firing at us. I never heard your shot. Did you—?"

"Yeah … no. That didn't work."

She pulled her hands free and continued to touch me, searching. "Are you sure? Are you sure you're okay?"

"I don't know about okay, but I'm not shot." I pointed at the legs. "I got some blood on me, I guess. Help me up."

I started to see what had Andy so upset. Most of my right side was damp with fresh blood. I wiped it from my face and felt it in my hair. She helped me to my feet.

"Where is she? Where's Pidge?"

I pointed. "I don't know. Hitting Foyle took out the right engine. I don't know."

As if to suggest the worst, at that moment the Jeep's gas tank blew with a bone-jarring *Whomp!*

60

"Deputy Larson, it's Sergeant Stewart." Andy held her phone in one hand and used the other to hug Sandy Stone. Sandy shivered in Andy's coat. We stood as close to the burning Jeep as we dared. The fire spread to the dry grass and worked its way downwind.

After the gas tank blew, Andy hurried back to Sandy, got her to her feet and took her to the warmth of Mr. Donnelly's bonfire. Now she held the phone between us. "Where are your HP units?"

"On the way. It's a big state, Sergeant," Larson said. "Where are you?"

"On the highway, just south of the Parks ranch. Long stretch of valley. We're sending up smoke signals."

"I know the valley. I'll be there in about five minutes."

I waved urgently at Andy. She held up a finger.

"We need transport to a hospital. We have Sandra Stone with us. She needs medical attention," Andy said. "Also, if you really do have highway patrol headed this way, get some units to come from the north and stop a bronze-colored Range Rover and detain Pearce Parks and Todd Jameson. A couple minutes ago they came our way, but something persuaded them to turn around and go north."

Something, hell. It had been me, scooping up Andy's Glock and running toward them the instant I saw who was behind the wheel of the approaching vehicle. Parks nearly rolled his expensive brush cruiser, wheeling through a high-speed U-turn before I could fire. Andy shouted at me to *Put that thing down!*—after which, she took the gun away from me and muttered something about not needing more paperwork.

Andy dictated to Larson, "Hold them on murder, attempted murder and anything else that comes to mind."

"Used to giving orders, Sergeant?" Larson asked. I pictured him grinning.

"Please," she said nicely.

"Deputy, this is Will Stewart," I leaned toward the phone. "Our pilot may have gone down. Do you have any reports of a plane making a forced landing west of this valley—or maybe between here and Sioux Valley Airport?"

"Not that I've heard," he said. "Not many people out that way to report something like that."

"Can you initiate a search? She had one engine out, possible airframe damage. She went out of sight due west of our position."

"I'll call Billings and get a search going."

It hardly seemed enough, but I bit my tongue against saying so. "Appreciate it."

"What about Foyle? Did he show up there?"

"Yes."

Larson waited. Then said, "And is he there now?"

Andy looked at the legs laying on the highway.

"He was," she said somberly. "He had a plane to catch."

LARSON ARRIVED TRAILING a second sheriff's car just as he predicted, about five minutes later. I could not hold back. I met him at the door to his cruiser.

"Lord Jesus, are you okay?" he stared at me, wide eyed.

"Anything on our plane?"

He shook his head. "I called dispatch. They're putting a call in to Civil Air Patrol. Nobody's phoned anything in yet, which is good news, I guess. Seriously, are you okay? You've got blood …"

"It's not mine."

He looked past me at the mess on the highway. A few Sunday

morning cars rolled by. "Jesus, Joseph and Mary," he said. He crossed himself.

Andy came toward us with Sandy, who walked haltingly on bare feet, shivering, her eyes glazed and distant.

"I need a blanket, Deputy. And we need to get her to a hospital." Andy added, "Please."

Larson darted to his trunk and produced a rescue blanket. He tossed it to Andy and issued orders to the second deputy to do something about the legs in the road. He threw a second blanket at me. "You're not getting in my car like that."

"Whaddya want me to do with them?" the other deputy asked, pointing at Foyle's legs.

"Drag 'em off the road and cover 'em up!" Larson snapped. "And get that pickup truck outta the highway. Put some flares out. See if we can get people to slow down and use the far shoulder. Christ, they're driving through the blood!"

Larson turned to Andy.

"Are you gonna tell me what the hell that's all about?" he asked. "Where's the rest of … him?"

"We'll tell you on the way."

Larson called to the other deputy, "I'm taking these people back to Sioux. HP should be here in a few minutes." He looked at the Jeep, fully engulfed, and the spreading grass fire. "I'll call the fire department."

Andy opened the back door of Larson's cruiser and helped Sandy inside. She tucked the blanket around her, closed the door and jogged around to the other side and hopped in. I called shotgun.

"WHY DIDN'T you tell me all this last night?" Larson asked after we spelled out the string of events leading up to the moment.

"Deputy, I wear your hat in my hometown," Andy spoke up from the back seat, where she kept her arms around Sandy. Even though Larson turned up the heat in the car, Sandy shivered. Nevertheless, she looked stronger by the minute. I caught her eye and she blinked at me.

Andy broke it down for him. "A couple strangers come from three states away and start making wild accusations about one of the town's largest employers. You give them the benefit of the doubt and drive out to Evergreen and poke your head into the solitary cells to find—guess who—sleeping like a baby. But you're a thorough guy, and you take it seriously when there's a possibility of abduction, so you check out the Parks ranch and find the woman safe, with her husband. The husband tells you she's suffering from depression, from the trauma of losing her father and having her wedding day ruined. She wishes to be left alone. Does that sound about right?"

Larson shrugged and said, "I might've made a few calls."

"As would I," Andy said. "Maybe even paid a second, surprise visit to the ranch. But by then, it would have been too late. A tragic overdose. So many of those, these days."

Larson's radio interrupted. "Two fourteen, dispatch."

"Go ahead, dispatch."

"HP says they have the Range Rover and both occupants. The occupants are claiming someone attacked the ranch, assaulted one of their employees, and the one says a man and a woman kidnapped his wife."

From the back seat, Sandy coughed and cried out in a broken, hoarse voice, "Tell him to go fuck himself!"

Andy, startled, laughed, and pulled her friend into a tight embrace. Tremors in Sandy's shoulders told me she began to weep. Another good sign.

"Dispatch, the wife is with me, and she politely requested we detain them. Have HP bring them both down to Sioux. Don't mention anything about the wife."

"Okay."

"And hey! Anything on that airplane going down?"

"No reports yet."

"Thanks," Larson said, glancing at me. "Oh and tell somebody out at the airport to put some chains on the landing gear of that Evergreen jet."

"Or just park a truck in front of it," I said.

"Or park a truck in front of it. Okay?"

"Okay."

I looked out the window at the Montana scenery under the Montana sky. Both were big, as advertised, which did nothing to ease my spiraling worry. I told myself Pidge would know what to do. She would maintain control. She would put it down in one piece. But where?

I glanced back at Andy, who read my expression. She pulled out her phone, looked at it, and shook her head. "Probably no cell service," she said.

"Or she's really, really busy," I muttered to myself.

Larson's foot wasn't quite as heavy as Andy's and he spared the siren but played the light bar all the way back down the highway to Sioux Valley. We covered the forty-mile distance in a little under half an hour.

Larson eased off as the city limits approached. I saw the airport, spread out on the west side of the highway.

"Turn in! Turn in, here!" I waved my arms and pointed. "The airport! Turn in here!" I spun around in the seat as Larson worked the brakes. I looked at Andy, who saw it, too. Her eyes lit up and she ignited a huge smile.

Larson drove us directly onto the ramp. An ambulance and several squad cars sat grimly nosed up to the FBO office. I knew they were attending to the murder of the kid, Mark Johannsen. I tried not to let my joy feel like disrespect—but it was hard. I pointed across the ramp and Larson followed my lead.

One Nine Alpha sat in the sun with the right engine missing half the cowling. She bled oil under bent prop blades—the wing and right side of the fuselage was streaked and dripped rusty red.

A blonde pixie in a leather flying jacket sat on the left wing just outboard of the good engine, dangling her feet.

Larson stopped. I jumped out and opened the back door for Andy.

Pidge grinned at us.

"I am the greatest motherfucking pilot *EVER*!" she announced.

She hopped off the wing and strutted toward us, but we ruined her moment of triumph by sweeping her into our arms like a child.

61

"You did *not* really say, 'He had a plane to catch'!" Pidge aimed open wonder at Andy. My wife smiled at Pidge, then at me.

"Told you that you weren't the biggest smart-ass in the family."

I picked up the iced Corona and clinked it against Andy's.

The cold beer felt like good medicine going down, a salve on so many levels. We gathered in the Sioux Valley Hotel bar, at a table not far from the booth we had occupied less than twenty-four hours ago.

"When I saw you diving on him, I figured you were just going to scare him. Distract him. Maybe give me a chance to do something," I said to Pidge.

"You pretty much looked like you were lying around on your ass. And the guy was popping off rounds at you. I figured it was better to fuck him over."

"Wait!" Andy turned on me. "He was shooting at you?"

"Did I forget to mention…?"

My wife punched me in the shoulder. "You did *not* mention!"

"Well," I raised my beer again, "here's to some shit-hot flying."

"Fuckin'-A!" Pidge clicked my glass.

"And thank you," Andy joined the toast.

The Sunday night bar was empty except for the three of us. Pidge seemed mildly disappointed.

Most of the day had been spent at the sheriff's substation. Deputy Larson graciously provided me with a set of orange coveralls to replace my blood-soaked clothes. While I washed blood out of my hair and changed, Andy gave a detailed report on everything we'd done since he dropped us at the motel early in the morning.

The highway patrol arrived with Parks and Jameson in handcuffs. Parks took one look at me, dressed in orange coveralls, and shouted, "That's him! Excellent work, officers! Her, too! Arrest her, too!"

Larson waved the highway patrol officers onward, saying nothing as both men were taken to temporary holding cell in the back of the storefront office. Parks proclaimed outrage at his treatment. Jameson yammered incoherently.

"Andrea, make Sandy understand—the medicine—it was to help her —I'm sure we can clear up—this is all a…a…" He plodded forward with his hands cuffed behind his back. His pallid skin set off his bulging eyes —the look of a man gone over the edge.

After they moved out of sight, Andy turned to me and said for the third or fourth time, "I really need to get a picture of you in that outfit."

Larson put a call in to the proprietor of a sporting goods store down the street. He asked if they would open the store long enough on this Sunday morning to sell me some clothes. Right after church, the owner promised. Not soon enough for me. I was still in orange when the state department of corrections team arrived to interview us. I was still in orange when the FBI team from Billings arrived to interview us. And I was still in orange when a team from the Montana division of criminal investigation arrived to interview us. For the owner of the store, "after church" turned out to be after church, after Sunday noon dinner, and after the Denver Broncos took a beating from the New England Patriots. By that time, most of the suits crowding into the substation had gone to Great Western Correctional.

While waiting for my clothing rescue, we spoke to Lorna Keller, sharing the news that Sandra Stone was alive, well and on her way by helicopter to Billings Clinic Hospital. I could not tell what made the woman happier. Knowing her late boss's daughter hadn't been murdered or anticipating the field day she was about to have at the governor's expense. Ending the call, Andy and I agreed once again that despite her maternal instincts toward Sandy and the help she provided, we didn't like that woman.

Pidge and I ganged up on Andy and made her call Earl. Andy looked at us like a pair of misbehaving siblings, which I reinforced by calling out, "Pidge did it!" preemptively into the speaker phone as soon as Earl picked up.

"I don't give a crap who did what—you're both fired!" Earl snapped at us through the phone. He might have been eight hundred miles away, but I still eased away from the phone, ready to dive for cover.

"Hi, Earl, this is Andy," my wife said sweetly.

"Oh, hi Andy! Tell your worthless husband and his co-conspirator they're both fired."

"Pidge did it," I said again. Andy waved me off and Pidge poked me in the ribs.

"Earl, I'm afraid I put them up to this." And like a shaman charming a cobra with her voice, my beautiful wife soothed Earl with the story of how we came to borrow his airplane to travel to Montana to prove that the sixth man was Garrett Foyle, the man who murdered Bob Stone.

"Did you arrest the fucker?" Earl asked.

"Well," Andy said, "no. Um, this might be the part you don't like so much." She explained to Earl how Pidge ended Foyle, causing considerable damage to his airplane.

Earl let silence fall on the line. Enough so that Andy had to ask:

"Earl, are you still there?"

Earl said nothing.

"It was one hell of a piece of flying, boss," I said, sincerely.

"Fuckin' A!" Pidge said.

We waited.

Finally, Earl spoke. "Andy, you tell those two that if they ever break another airplane of mine, they'll wish *all they was*—was fired."

"I will," Andy said.

"You take care now, honey," Earl said. I thought I heard his voice crack, although it may have been the connection. He let another long pause linger, then said, "And thank you. What you did. For Bob."

He ended the call.

"God, he loves you," I said in awe.

"Not as much as he loves you two," Andy replied.

Pidge didn't understand, and I didn't necessarily agree, but Andy is rarely wrong about things like that.

Eventually, a woman wearing a Sunday-go-to-meetin' dress under a long coat appeared in the sheriff's office. She looked like Deputy Larson's mother, or first grade teacher, and she greeted him accordingly.

"Good afternoon, Douglas," she said. She spotted me in orange. "I take it this is the gentleman in need?" Introductions were made all around. Like most people, Mrs. Randall took an immediate shine to Andy, and seemed impressed when Deputy Larson called her Sergeant Stewart. To me, she said, "Well, let's get you into something a little less criminal, shall we?"

I never felt more self-conscious than I did on the short walk down the street from the sheriff's substation to Randall's Sporting Goods and Guns. Mrs. Randall unlocked the store and turned me loose. I picked out a fresh pair of jeans, a denim work shirt, and a t-shirt. I paid cash, and she thanked me for not having to fire up the credit card scanner. She rounded off the tally in my favor to avoid making change, so I tried to offer her something extra for her trouble. She stoutly refused. I thanked her sincerely for taking time from her Sunday afternoon.

Eventually, people ran out of questions for us. Larson cleared Andy, Pidge and me to leave. He offered to drive us to the motel, but we opted for the Sioux Valley Hotel, which had vacancies. Andy told Larson she would check with him in the morning.

After a I took a quick shower to feel more assured that none of Garrett Foyle's blood or brains lingered in my hair, I joined Andy and Pidge in the bar.

"So," Pidge said after I toasted her piloting skill, "what's the plan?"

"Sleep," I said. Andy concurred. I tried to think ahead. "Tomorrow we'll see about securing One Nine Alpha. Maybe they have hangar space. Then, I don't know, maybe our new friend, Deputy Larson, can get us up to Billings and we can book a flight home."

"Sounds good—but don't knock on my fucking door until noon," she looked in the direction of the bar. The corrections officer, Ray Sidousky, had arrived. He pulled up to the rail with a pair of companions. He saw us and tipped a friendly wave. I speculated that he had the weekend off and was not yet aware of the federal and state invasion of the Evergreen facility. Andy picked up on Pidge's intentions.

"Pidge," she warned, "he might be a person of interest in a far-ranging criminal investigation."

"Well then," she appraised the situation, "I guess I better make his last night of freedom a fucking night to remember." She took aim and launched in Sidousky's direction, pulling her wallet and ID from her jacket pocket.

"Ah," I said. "They grow up so fast."

Andy turned to me and took my hand.

"Are you okay?"

I tried to look surprised by the question. It didn't fly.

"You've been moving a little …" she hunted for the word "… gingerly. What gives?"

This was the first chance I had to tell her all of what happened on the highway with Foyle. She had been head-down the whole time, hanging on to Sandy. I told her I was glad she did not see Foyle firing three-round bursts at me as I lay on the pavement. If she had, she may have done something that would have cost us both. The story left her staring, at war with her emotions. I braced myself for anger.

What I got was wonder.

"A top-secret government cloaking device?" She sat back in her chair, then picked up her Corona and lifted it in my direction. "I take it back. You're the reigning smart-ass in the family."

"Recognition! At last!" I clinked bottles with her.

"So … *the other thing* … what happened?"

"My guess? When I fired at Foyle, *the other thing* trapped the energy from the discharge. Or it backfired. Or something. Beats me. But it was like stepping on a live power line. Hurt like hell."

"Do you think it—um—damaged it?"

I shrugged. "I haven't tried it since." I looked around the bar. Pidge enthralled Sidousky and his companions. The bartender, who doubled as our server and didn't seem in a hurry to take our order, had disappeared. We were the only patrons occupying a table.

"Will, no, not here!"

Fwooomp! The cool sensation spread and consumed my body. Not a chill, but a comfortable, refreshing sensation. The aches in my muscles eased. It felt good. I held on to the chair to avoid floating.

"God! I can't get used to that!" Andy complained. "Come back!

Before somebody—oh, what am I saying."

Fwooomp! I reappeared.

"Sees me?"

"Well, I guess it still works."

I slipped my arm around Andy's shoulder, and with my other, reached for her chin and brought her face to mine for a long kiss.

"What was that for?" Her smile added icing to the kiss.

"Well, we've only been married—what, a week or so? I was thinking maybe we get a room. They rent by the hour here, you know."

"Only an hour? You must be tired."

"Hey, I seem to recall making love to you once when I had a broken pelvis."

"I seem to recall doing most of the work."

"Well … last time I took you to bed, I had to dodge machine gun fire."

She took on a serious look. She lowered her head a little and let a lock of hair, one of her war flags, slip down over one eye.

"Parks is in deep trouble. Along with Evergreen. The whole house of cards," she said, thinking out loud with a jarring change of subject.

"Good," I said. "I hope he fries. For the little girls."

Andy tipped her head back and forth, looking uncertain.

"What? You think he won't?" I asked. We'd both seen the squad of Parks' lawyers that arrived at the sheriff's substation late in the afternoon. Parks wasn't going anywhere, but it wasn't hard to imagine him working the system for every advantage that money could buy.

"Oh, no," Andy said firmly. "He's toast. Both sides need a public execution on this one. To us, he's guilty of multiple murders for hire and countless other crimes. To his cronies, he's guilty of getting caught, and worse, putting their private prison enterprises in the spotlight. A cardinal sin. The same goes for Todd. Either way, he's finished. Our governor will get a stitch in his side from running as fast as he can away from those two. No, that's not it."

She adopted a faraway look. A look that I'd seen before. When she returned, she cast her eyes toward me, toward the one place where she knew she had complete trust—the one place where she could say something no one else would believe.

"I don't think we got the man responsible," she said. "Yet."

EPILOGUE

October slipped into November before I was ready to abuse Andy's trust. Thanks to the sunny, windless days that led up to Halloween, the leaves tumbled silently from the farmyard maple trees, forming colored tree skirts on the lawn, I resisted the temptation to rake or mow them. Sooner or later, a low-pressure system would sweep out of the northwest, kicking the wind speed up into the thirties and removing the leaves for me.

I had better things to do as the days shortened.

62

Earl bought the King Air, the one I was supposed to examine in Tulsa. I didn't make the trip. Our hopes of quietly leaving Sioux Valley collided with the Montana attorney general's realization that exposing murder and corruption in the private prison system put him squarely in the spotlight one month ahead of mid-term elections. He arrived in Sioux Valley early Monday morning in a motorcade that took up most of the parking on Main Street.

Andy and I watched the circus unfold as we ate breakfast at the Prairie Diner. We foolishly commented that we were glad to be in the diner, not the sheriff's substation, when Deputy Douglas Larson jogged across the street.

"You need to come with me," he said to Andy. "The attorney general is here with the head of DCI and they want a word." He stood over us, literally with hat in hand. Andy gave him a warm smile.

"Give orders much, Deputy?"

He rolled his eyes.

"Please."

She laughed and followed him out the door, leaving me to finish breakfast and my coffee as slowly as possible while our chances of a low-profile escape evaporated.

The Montana AG pulled Andy into a lengthy rehashing of the entire story, starting with Cinnamon Hills, all the way through the tale of how Pidge finished off Foyle not a moment too soon. Next, the AG's entourage swept Andy up on an expedition to Evergreen Reform, where she toured the cellar housing solitary confinement, and where guards and staff insisted that Foyle served his time quietly. No one present could explain the empty cell. She told me later that the little dictator, Captain Leeson, failed to report for duty Monday morning.

After my third cup of coffee, watching my wife being escorted off to prison by half a dozen state troopers and deputy sheriffs, I reached a decision about the trip to Tulsa.

"C'mon, pick up," I said to my phone.

"This is Dave."

"Well, buddy, it's the first day of your new job," I said.

"What? Where are you? Are you back in Essex?"

"Still in Sioux Valley."

"Where?"

"I'm sitting in the Prairie Diner, having breakfast."

"I'm sitting in this stupid motel room and nobody's telling us anything! Lemme put on some pants and join you."

"I got a better idea. Since your boss is headed to prison, your company is headed into the shitter, your airplane is chained to a truck—and you're out of a job—how would you like to go to Tulsa and look over a King Air for Earl? And then maybe fly it for him?"

"What the hell?"

I explained what I could. When I finished, he said, "Well that's probably why nobody's picking up at HQ. We've been trying for the last couple hours."

"Yeah, a lot of shit is headed for a very large fan," I said. "You might want to lay off calling. Chances are good, the FBI will soon be answering the phones at Evergreen."

I knew, based on the information Dave laid out for Andy, it might be better for him if he quietly slipped out of the picture. I wondered how zealous prosecutors might get—possibly implicating the pilots who shuttled Foyle around the country to commit murder. Dave didn't deserve that.

I strongly recommended Dave call Earl and offer to sub for me, and then pack his bags. Quickly. After a short discussion, he agreed.

63

They fired Sandy Stone.

The superintendent of the Essex Unified School district fired Sandy on Tuesday, around the time she stepped out of the hospital in Billings, escorted by Lorna Keller. Hundreds of e-mails from concerned parents containing social media evidence of Miss Stone's drug use and alluding to mental instability bombarded members of the school board. One board member, the deeply religious and easily outraged Armand Collingsworth, immediately launched a crusade for Sandy's summary dismissal.

Collingsworth considered the evidence damning. The superintendent quickly caved to demands that Sandy be fired.

As soon as Keller heard the news, she called Andy, still in Sioux Valley. Keller made a guess. Andy asked the Montana AG's office to interview Todd Jameson, who admitted that he and Pearce Parks had hired hackers to create the phony e-mails and a trumped-up social media blitz, which was to follow Sandy's death by overdose in the throes of depression. Already bought and paid for, the propaganda campaign launched on schedule, oblivious of the fact that Parks sat in jail. Somebody in Slovenia didn't get the memo.

Earl Jackson flew into a rage. He took out a full-page ad in the Thursday edition of the Essex Courier. The ad announced a special school board meeting on Friday at 4 p.m. at the high school. It was news to the school board.

Friday afternoon, fifteen minutes before the afternoon bell rang at James Madison Elementary School, Lisa Washington, Sandy Stone's flower girl, announced to her substitute teacher that she was leaving to "go get Miss Stone back." Half of the other children in her class stood up, gathered their coats and backpacks, and followed Lisa out the door. Word of this kindergarten revolt spread to the next classroom, where a colleague of Sandy's told her entire class to put their coats on because they were going on a field trip. Soon all of the James Madison Elementary teachers followed suit. A stream of teachers and children flowed out of the school and across the playground toward the high school next door. Helpless to counter the flood, the administrative staff and principal followed. Parents arriving to pick their kids up were redirected to the high school gym. Busses sat empty in front of the elementary school.

Around the same time, Andy put word out to her fellow officers to pick up the members of the school board and deliver them to the high school.

Just before four o'clock, Andy called me at the airport and told me to join her at the high school, pronto. I arrived in time to see Earl Jackson thundering toward the superintendent, the image of malice afoot. Moments later, Andy rolled up, delivering two of the six school board members.

Basketball practice in the high school field house came to a halt as children, parents, cops, and school board members poured in. Somebody produced a microphone and handed it to the scary-looking man. Earl told everyone, "Sit down and shut the hell up!"

It took another twenty minutes before the full school board could be rounded up and seated on folding chairs at half court. Some of them entered utterly bewildered, others beaming with pride, having somehow learned of the plot. Once they were all seated, Earl spoke.

"This week, Superintendent Glower announced the firing of Miss Sandy Stone."

The crowd roared at Glower.

"Shut up and let me finish!" Earl snapped. "Miss Stone was fired because of what some jackass is calling a 'flood' of e-mails from concerned parents. Well, you internet trolls wanted to have your say, so now's your chance! Stand up and be counted if you were one of those 'concerned parents' sending e-mails! Stand up!"

Earl marched the line in front of the bleachers. Not a soul moved.

"If you're brave enough to post rumors and lies—be brave enough to stand up now and be counted!" Earl demanded.

No one stirred. Earl turned on the superintendent.

"Mr. Glower, this is BULLSHIT!"

The crowd cheered. Little children giggled and covered their ears. Older kids laughed. I stood with Andy near the door, grinning.

"The same people who destroyed that fine young woman's wedding, killed her father, then nearly killed her, are responsible for this internet e-mail BULLSHIT!"

A woman I didn't recognize hurried forward, taking her life in her hands. She pried the microphone out of Earl's fingers. Andy leaned over and told me she was Leah Harrison, the school board president.

"Thank you, Mr. Jackson," she said.

"BULLSHIT!" Earl shouted at Glower one more time, to the delight of everyone under the age of ten.

"I think we can all agree that events have shown that a grievous injustice has been committed," the woman said, attempting to restore order. She waited for the crowd to settle down, then said, "Members of the school board, I call for a vote. All in favor of reinstating Miss Stone, signify by saying, 'Aye'."

Five of the six school board members stood up and shouted, "Aye!"

Armand Collingsworth, a large man with a meaty face that grew redder by the moment, remained fixed in his seat.

As the cheers died away, the woman said, "Those opposed?"

Collingsworth began to rise, but before he could speak, a man in the bleachers jumped to his feet and shouted, "I'm Richard Sorensen and I'm announcing my candidacy for HIS school board seat!"

The crowd erupted.

Andy leaned close to me and said, "I may need to escort Collingsworth out of here."

The woman with the microphone raised and lowered her arms, begging for quiet so that this *ad hoc* meeting could conclude its business.

Someone tapped Andy on the shoulder.

"Are we too late?" Lorna Keller, looking perfect and dangerous, stepped up behind us, firmly holding Sandy Stone by the arm. Sandy looked tired and worn, but vastly better than the last time I'd seen her. She also looked more than a little afraid—and entirely reluctant to be standing at the fringe of this event.

"She didn't want to come. Nonsense!" Keller scolded Sandy.

"I think you just got your job back," Andy said.

Sandy's eyes watered. "I don't know what to say."

"Please!" the woman using the PA system urged, "everyone please, can we have it quiet!"

The crowd hushed as best they could, given the charge running through it.

The woman turned to her colleagues and said, "The vote is five to one in favor of—"

"MISS STONE!" A single small voice cried out.

Lisa Washington spotted Sandy and broke from the front row of the bleachers, a flying cloud of puffy pink jacket, knees, and elbows under bouncing waves of black hair. Her new glasses bobbed on her nose as she raced across the floor.

Sandy rushed forward and dropped to her knees in time to wrap her arms around her flower girl. Then another child piled on. Then another. The circle around Sandy became impenetrable.

"Looks like you just lost your state senator," I said to Keller.

She laughed. "Oh, heavens! I've already had a very *direct* conversation with the governor about who will be taking that dirty job!" She grinned, then pointed at Sandy. "She has far more important work to do."

64

I went to California.

On my third day there, I floated thirty feet up beside a desert palm, listening to Andy's voice in my head.

I don't think we got the man responsible. Yet.

The warm sun had set. In purple twilight, the air cooled quickly.

Not yet, I thought.

The artificial desert community sprawled behind me.

I didn't like the desert. Dry, dusty, brown, and endless, I could not find the beauty in it that some claim to see. Rocks and dirt. Wisconsin, now in the first days of early November, can be brown and barren once the leaves have fallen and the farm fields have been harvested. But even in the silhouettes of black, dead-looking trees set against iron skies, I still sense life. Or the promise of life. Not so in the desert.

Pumping millions of gallons of water onto lawns and gardens only made it worse. Green lawns and gardens snipped and manicured around multi-million-dollar homes felt to me like putting a pretty dress on a corpse.

This would be my last night here. Tomorrow, I would catch a flight home to Andy. And then she would kill me.

The journey to this hot, dry place started at Cinnamon Hills, of course. But this part of the journey followed a trail marked by Andy's words.

I don't think we got the man responsible. Yet.

She was right, as always. But she knew, if not logically, then instinctively, that she could follow the path no farther. She found Foyle. She exposed Parks. She destroyed Todd Jameson, along with his political career and his political marriage—and pending the opinion of a jury of his peers, his freedom. But one perpetrator remained untouched. Andy's power ended where the justice system draws its lines.

Mine didn't.

You asked, Dee. What do you want to do with it?

The day after the great Kindergarten Revolt I gave Earl my notice. I even handed him a letter of resignation. He tore it up and told me to get the fuck out of his office. But he could not hide from the truth forever. With Dave back on staff and the King Air expected to be on the charter line in a few weeks, Essex County Air Service limped forward without me. The loss of the Navajo I crashed, and the loss of the bird Pidge had destroyed (the insurance company refused to repair it) certainly hurt, but it wasn't terminal. Earl almost immediately sent Pidge off to Flight Safety International for simulator training for the King Air. He claimed he did it to get rid of her—so he wouldn't have to listen, one more time, to her damned story about being the greatest pilot who ever lived. I knew better. He did it because the part of her story about being a great pilot is true.

As ordered, I got the fuck out of Earl's office. I gave an unsuspecting Rosemary II a cheery goodnight wave, and I walked out of Essex Air Service for what I expected to be the last time.

That was eight days ago.

Andy reverted to a reasonably normal schedule, although the trip to Montana had its consequences and they were swift. On the Monday after our return, she walked in the house at close to midnight after her shift, deep in thought.

"How do you feel about pizza?" she asked, drifting through the house, unbuckling her belt, her mind elsewhere. Pizza signals *I need to talk something through* so I said "Yes" and started the oven.

In the cold weather months, our budget can't handle pumping a lot of heat into the old farmhouse. Andy returned wearing a heavy robe over a flannel nightgown. She slid onto the sofa and pulled a satin blanket up to her chin. Warm or cold, we still take our Corona iced with a slice of lime. I handed her one.

"Tom got a call from someone at DCI today," she said.

I thought of Bryon Williams, and of his offer to Andy.

"And?" I asked.

"They strongly suggested to Tom that he terminate my employment," she said matter-of-factly. She looked at me blankly. I returned the stare, expecting her to burst into a grin and tell me about some fantastic offer from DCI.

She didn't.

"What are you talking about?"

"They suggested to Tom that he terminate my employment. That my unauthorized investigation, both here, and out of state, showed a lack of discipline and reflected badly on his department, on law enforcement in Wisconsin, and—on—" She ran out of words.

"What the hell?!"

"They said the Montana attorney general had an angry conversation with our attorney general, who had an angry conversation with Administrator Williams. My activities in Montana, they told Tom, were not appreciated."

She tipped back the Corona and slugged away a quarter of the bottle.

"Where the hell did that come from? That Montana AG practically asked you out on a date—right in front of me! You probably got him re-elected. They wanted to give you a medal!"

Now she spared me a pitying look. "Oh, Will, don't you see? This didn't come from Montana. This came from Madison—from the very top."

"Williams?"

"The governor, through Williams, to some lackey, who called Tom Ceeves. Tom said the guy wasn't even a cop, just some pencil pusher."

"He's not going to do it, is he?"

"Tom? Fire me?"

"Yeah."

Andy laughed. "Have you met my boss? Hell, no! He promoted me to Detective. Waived the test. Issued the rank and gave me a raise." She lifted her bottle.

"Holy shit!" Mildly stunned, I touched my bottle to hers. "Here's to Detective Stewart! Long may she sleuth!"

Andy toasted with me, but it felt half-hearted. I knew why. She had worked hard toward achieving the rank of Detective. To have it come to her like this took a little of the shine off.

She said, "This whole Parks-Jameson thing threw a lot of dirt on the governor. Did you know that right now he's on an unscheduled trade mission? A suddenly important trip to Scotland—although, I doubt they know what to do with him. Came up at the last minute, his office said. That's how far he's going to distance himself from the excrement hitting the HVAC system. Not to mention that losing Parks as a donor is going to cost him a ton of PAC money."

"Jeff okay with this?" I asked about Essex PD's only other detective.

"He suggested it. Tom talked to him before telling me. Jeff's not what you call a go-getter. He likes the idea of another detective in the case rotation. My workload, however—that's a different story. We're suddenly short a patrol sergeant, so I get to keep some of those duties for a while."

She gave me a long, wistful look, and as so often happens when I stop to appreciate her, I struggled to grasp how lucky I am.

Which made me feel that much worse about leaving her.

I worked on the propulsion units for a few days, then did some shopping, loading up the credit card again. Tactical clothing. Batteries. A box of frangible nine-millimeter ammunition—for which I paid cash. Good, stealthy, crepe-soled boots. With what remained on the credit limit, I bought a ticket to LA and lined up a rental car. I figured I would find a hotel when I got where I was going, which turned out to be short-sighted. Had I done the research I would have learned that the community to which I was headed did not have hotels in my limited price range.

I booked an evening flight, so that Andy would be at work when I left.

I wrote her a note, folded it, and placed it on the kitchen table where she always checks for the mail when she walks in the door.

Dee, I will be gone for five days. I need this. It's about the other thing *and NOT about us. You are the brightest, most important thing in my life. I love you more today than I did yesterday. Will.*

I left my phone on the note, making the point that she shouldn't call me.

Before leaving for the airport in Milwaukee, I went to her gun safe. She keeps a Beretta M.92a among other weapons. She also has a government-sanctioned suppressor for the weapon, which can make the discharge so quiet you hear little more than the snap of the slide ejecting the spent round and seating the next round. I took the gun and suppressor and packed it with the box of frangible ammunition.

I parked in the airport parking garage at General Mitchell International. Leaving my bag with the weapon in the trunk, I went into the terminal and through security, obtaining the marker stroke of approval on my boarding pass from the TSA agent at the podium. Once through security, I did a U-turn and walked back through the terminal to my car and retrieved my backpack containing the weapon and ammunition.

Returning to the terminal, I stopped at a rest room and—

Fwooomp! I vanished along with the backpack. The noise in the terminal covered the low hum of the propulsion unit I used to glide over the security station and down the long terminal hallway. Finding a restroom at the concourse mid-point empty, I reappeared and went on my way carrying a loaded weapon on a U.S. domestic flight.

That was two days ago.

After flying through the night, I rented a car and drove to this desert community, where the average home price hovers a little over seven million and the typical car is a six-figure luxury sedan or SUV. Ferraris and Aston Martins scoot around like Hondas on any other city street in America. Money oozes from the pores of this community, but even here there exists a hierarchy. Homes on planned streets with surreal green-grass lawns are for the common wealthy. Homes on the fringe, sprinkled among golf resorts, are for the celebrity wealthy. And finally, homes in the foothills of a low, brown mountain range, are for the American kings. Nearly every residential area is gated, but the latter have their own gates, their own walls, their own strolling, armed security guards.

Like the estate I studied from my palm tree perch.

A twelve-foot faux adobe wall surrounded the entire estate. Then, within that wall, inside a perimeter of perfectly planned natural gardens, another wall protected the house, which surrounded itself with expanses of constantly-watered lush green lawn.

Yesterday, a simple contingent of one or two security guards strolled the outer garden zone and manned a post at the main gate.

All of that changed overnight.

On my first excursion, just before dusk yesterday, I floated over the outer wall, over the inner wall, into the inner perimeter, over the lawns, and onto a patio outside a second story wall of French doors and floor-to-ceiling windows. The desert evening kissed me with a warm breeze, simplifying my task. The broad patio doors stood open to stimulate fresh air within the living spaces.

I floated inside, found an anchor point on a highbacked chair, and stowed the propulsion unit. The interior of the house felt surprisingly comfortable and low key. Simple marble, light wood, and conservative furnishings. Art hung from the walls, probably worth more than every penny I ever earned.

I immediately found what I wanted. The room that overlooked the patio had a sitting area with several comfortable-looking sofas. In the center of the sofa array, a broad, low coffee table anchored the furniture.

I used the backs of chairs and sofas as grip points and pushed myself to the table where I stopped. Wearing gloves, I reached into one of my web vest pockets and extracted a plastic bag containing two things—a card and a bullet. I placed the card on the table, and the bullet on the card. A light electrical sensation danced through my fingertips as each item reappeared.

Done.

TOMORROW NIGHT I WILL RETURN TO KILL YOU.

Simple. Direct. Handwritten in block letters. The shiny brass bullet sat on the card, emphasizing the point like deadly jewelry.

Satisfied with my delivery, I worked my way around the room and turned on every lamp within reach. The lamps would draw attention to the card.

I left the way I came.

After launching from the patio and letting the wind carry me off the estate, I fired up a propulsion unit and flew across a span of golf courses to where I had parked at a resort with public access. After reappearing in the parking lot, I drove out of the oasis of wealth, almost forty miles across far less attractive desert before finding a motel in my price range. The credit card was dying a slow death, but I booked two nights on the last of it.

I RETURNED to the estate early the next afternoon with fresh batteries in the single propulsion unit I had used, and three units in reserve. Once more I parked at a golf resort that allowed public access. Once more I found a spot to disappear unnoticed. From there, I launched, catching a desert tail wind for most of the trip across fairways, across the pools and patios of the celebrity rich, to the estate set in the foothills. The sensation of flight washed my soul and lifted my spirits. I did not belong in this gaudy community, but they did not belong in my sky.

I pulled up next to my favorite desert palm, hooked an arm around it and floated in place, despite a dry breeze that tried to pull me away. Dramatic changes to the estate were immediately evident. Several tinted-glass SUVs parked near the main gate. I counted four security guards at the gate. Two more patrolled the outer perimeter, with another two patrolling the inner perimeter. I anticipated more in the house. All the security guards wore body armor and carried semi-automatic rifles with red-dot tactical sights. Serious fellows.

My objective had been to spook the owner with the bullet-pointed message, but I had no wish to scare him into leaving—not with the opening salvo. As I hoped, the owner stayed in his fortress to solve the problem with money and manpower.

Perfect.

I spent the remainder of the afternoon in the shade of the high palm tree overlooking the estate, watching, attempting to read the patterns of the security staff, but largely bored out of my mind. Twice, I patrolled the estate, flying about twenty feet up, careful not to use the humming propulsion unit near any of the security men strolling below on foot.

As the sun began a final approach toward the horizon, I finally saw him. I remembered him from the wedding. If I had been asked to describe what a billionaire wears around the house, I could not have come up with more of a cliché. White slacks. White polo shirt. White deck shoes.

A bullet would make an ungodly mess of all that white.

He emerged from the house through the same doors I used for entry when I left the calling card. He crossed the deck and took a seat at a table under a trellis designed with motor-driven slats intended to perfectly block the evening sun. He used his phone and worked at a laptop, sipping tall glasses of what looked like ice water. A security guard walked the open deck forty or fifty discreet feet away.

Bargo Litton.

Mid-seventies. A full head of hair, or a billionaire's perfect implants. Fit, not fat. Worth more than forty billion, some said. A little shorter than I remembered, but I'd only seen him once, and that was with the governor, who only looks tall on television.

I released my hold on the palm tree. To avoid the noise of the propulsion unit, I let the soft breeze carry me over the massive house to the edge of the outer perimeter. From there, I circled around to a position directly upwind of Litton. I set myself up on a glide, letting the breeze carry me back to the second-story patio. I pulsed the propulsion unit to add a downward vector and floated silently until my feet touched the marble just outside the open patio doors, less than thirty feet from Litton.

Inside, seated on a sofa, wearing a shoulder holster with a weapon tucked under one armpit, a second security officer read a magazine, occasionally looking up to observe his charge outside. My note did the job. The strength of their security had been largely invested in the wall and the perimeter guards, but clearly, they weren't taking chances near their principle.

I fixed a grip on the patio door frame. From there, I redirected myself inside, away from the seated guard, first to a bar, then to the railing of a central stairway.

I used the stairway railing as an anchor, floating high in the room on the outside of the railing, keeping watch on Litton. I had no way of knowing if he had an evening commitment, or date, or event to attend. I gambled that his security detail would insist he spend the night at home —that they would argue that the estate constituted safe, defensible ground behind a strong perimeter. Yes, it had been breached—but I pictured Litton's security people making the case that the bullet and card message had been intended to get him away from the secure ground of the estate. Better that he should remain here, protected.

Their quadrupled efforts meant nothing to me.

Litton took a late dinner in a dining room large enough to feed a battalion. The aroma of a seafood stew reminded me I hadn't eaten. Hovering near the ceiling by the door, I schemed different ways to steal bites from his meal. None of the schemes formed into a viable plan.

After dinner, Litton spent time with his laptop in a smallish study. I waited for him outside. Shortly after ten, he secured his laptop in a small safe and walked to the large room off the patio where he had a conference with key members of his security team—the in-house guard, the patio guard, a supervisor, and another guard from the main gate.

"Donaldson, what do you have for me?" Litton addressed the supervisor, who carried himself like a cop, or an ex-cop. Probably ex-military. The man looked tough and strong. He looked familiar. I conjured an image of him stomping on a cell phone.

"Mr. Litton, we've got all the cameras up and running," Donaldson, the supervisor, reported with a crisp martial cadence. "All feeds checked, all stations live and manned. Motion detectors are active on both walls. Four men on the outer perimeter, four on the inner, and you'll have three in the house, with one outside your bedroom door all night and one on the deck. Nobody gets through. We'll be on a rotation, just to keep everyone alert. We've got plenty of coffee."

"Very well," Litton accepted the report. "I am in good hands." The eighth richest man on the planet walked and talked like a demure college professor, but I could not help but sense something more dangerous beneath the calm coating.

"That you are, sir! Have a good evening!" Donaldson, the supervisor, nodded in salute. I wondered how much heat Donaldson had taken for the bullet and card message—a serious breach.

Litton climbed the stairs with the outside-the-bedroom-door guard immediately behind. When they reached the upstairs hallway, the security guard asked Litton to stop and step aside. The guard made an elaborate show of opening the dual doors to the master bedroom and entering first to sweep the bedroom and master bathroom for threats. I thought it funny—the threat being me—that I floated serenely through the open door while the guard searched and Litton waited in the hall.

"It's all clear, sir," the guard announced. "Sir, I prefer you not lock these doors. I will be right outside and will want to have rapid access if you need me."

"Very well," Litton said to the guard, closing the doors.

Litton's bedroom had more square footage than most homes I've seen. Rosemary II and Lane lived in a house that would fit twice in Litton's bedroom. A huge bed occupied one end of the space, and a sitting room, bar and small office occupied the other end. Floor-to-ceiling windows filled most of one wall. In the center of all the windows, a set of doors opened onto another broad patio, this one overlooking the larger patio below. I floated to the doors and checked the view. A security guard with a rifle strolled the lower patio. An alarm wire ran to the top of the doors.

I found a comfortable corner and concentrated on not watching the man undress. He dropped his clothing on the floor for a servant to pick up in the morning, then disappeared into a master bathroom. I had no interest in his bathroom routine.

After a shower, some senseless pottering around the room, and a trip to the in-room bar for a bottle of water, Litton turned in. He touched a control panel on the nightstand and the room went dark. He did not close the curtains on the wall of windows. Soon desert starlight defined shadows on the floor and walls of the bedroom. Lights throughout this artificial desert community were shielded—undoubtedly controlled by light pollution laws so that the rich could enjoy the stars they thought they owned.

I waited. I heard him breathing, then snoring. My wristwatch disappears with me, but Litton's bedside clock and another on the wall near an entertainment center revealed that time crawled, painfully.

I resisted impatience and waited for the small hours.

When the digital clock on his nightstand read 2:01, I pushed off the ceiling until my toes touched the floor.

Fwooomp!

I stood in the full grip of gravity and gave myself a moment to stabilize. I'd been in a weightless state since early afternoon.

Once oriented, I reached into my backpack and extracted a black balaclava. I slipped it over my head and adjusted it until only my eyes were visible. From the backpack, I removed the Beretta with the suppressor. A round lay snug in the chamber, waiting.

I thumbed off the safety.

I pulled back the hammer which issed s soft *click.*

I walked to the bedside where Litton slept. He favored the right side of the mattress, viewed from his perspective. I wondered if he and his wife, long divorced, had established the preference, she on the left, he on the right.

Like Andy and me, I thought, with a pang of longing.

Her words came to me again.

I don't think we got the man responsible. Yet.

I reached down and pushed the tip of the suppressor into the thin flesh on his forehead, where I held it until his eyes flashed open.

He jolted.

I pressed harder, which persuaded him to freeze. He stared, wide-eyed, up at me.

"I want to make sure you understand," I said softly.

He tried to nod, to show that he did—most certainly—understand whatever the man with the gun wanted him to understand.

I pushed harder and said, "Don't move."

Even in the dim starlight, I saw the blood drain from his skin. He began to shiver, like someone with a fever. The fear and the shock on his face aged him. Lines he kept at bay with money emerged around his eyes. His lips went thin and pale.

"I want you to understand," I said again, slowly, "that I can come to you like this, anytime, anywhere. Do you understand?"

His shivering worked in a vertical axis—movement of the head that said once again he absolutely did understand.

"I don't think you do," I said. "I think the moment this gun is no longer aimed at your head you will decide that your money and your security guards can protect you. They can't."

He didn't respond.

"Think carefully, Mr. Litton. Here I am, inside your perimeter, inside your inner wall, inside your home, inside your bedroom. There is no video of me entering. There will be no video of me leaving. None of your motion detectors or security people will sense my coming and going. Your man Donaldson will not have a clue. I want you to understand that I can do this whenever I want—and nothing you can do will stop me. Do you fully grasp what that means? Say 'Yes' if you do."

"Yes," he whispered, dry and toneless.

I didn't think he truly understood.

"Do you have the bullet?" I asked. "The one I left here last night?"

He swallowed, worked his dry mouth, and spoke.

"I gave it to the police," he said, and I detected a note of satisfaction, a note in his voice that told me the police around here jumped when Bargo Litton snapped his fingers. I also caught his subtext—the one that smugly said that by his action, I was well on my way to being caught.

"Of course, you did," I said. "Did they tell you it's a Home Defense round."

He wiggled his head, no.

"It's called that because it's a frangible bullet. It shatters on impact. When you're blasting away at an intruder in your home, you don't want over-penetration. You don't want the bullets to go through the drywall, through the next room, out the side of your house and into the neighbor's house to kill their children while they sleep. That would be bad."

I leaned closer and said, "Killing children is a bad thing, wouldn't you agree?"

He agreed, silently.

I thought for a long moment about puffy jackets lying in a bed of leaves. My finger tightened on the trigger.

"A frangible round shatters on impact when it hits drywall," I said. "Or flesh. Or bone. Which makes it far, far worse for the intruder, because almost any hit is going to tear a huge hole in the body. Do you understand?"

He moved his head in tiny increments to show me that he did understand.

"This weapon is loaded with Home Defense rounds. If you make me come back here—or wherever you think you can hide from me—I will fire one of these Home Defense rounds into your right ankle. They'll have to amputate. No amount of reconstructive surgery will repair the damage. Then I will fire another into your left ankle, and you will never walk again. After that, I will fire one into your right elbow, and one into your left elbow, and you will never wash yourself again, never feed yourself again, never wipe your own ass again. Do you understand?"

His head bobbed urgently up and down.

"Why don't you say it for me, quietly," I said.

"I understand."

"Okay."

I sat on the bed, like someone attending the sick.

"Let's talk." I pulled the pistol away from his forehead, leaving a red crescent indentation in his parchment skin. He wiggled away from me.

"Who are you? What do you want?"

I ignored his questions.

"You promised to give Todd Jameson—or some PAC in his name—one hundred million dollars. Lie to me, Mr. Litton, and I will start shooting off your fingers. And the hulk outside your door won't hear a thing."

Litton worked up some saliva, so he could speak. "I support many with political aspirations. Jameson had the potential to be one of them, but I never—"

"No, you didn't get around to writing the check. But the deal was done. Jameson was your golden boy, or maybe one of many. I suppose you hedge your bets, don't you? Jameson in Wisconsin. Joe Albert in Arizona. That Baptist shriek in Alabama. Who else? Doesn't matter. Jameson was your boy in Wisconsin. Eight years, tops, and he's a young, dynamic U.S. Senator announcing a run for The White House. Your hundred million puts him on the path, right? Sooner or later, one of those bets pays off. Senate races. The White House. Right?"

Litton's face grew less stunned, more contemptuous.

"The Supreme Court upheld the right to contrib—"

"Yes, yes. Citizens United. I love the cute names. Citizens United, like there were any actual citizens behind it. Americans for Prosperity. Liberty Foundation. Let me stop you right here. I didn't bring the law with me tonight. There are no cops here. There are no cameras to lie to. There are no lawyers here to hide behind. I am not subject to the rulings of the Supreme Court. If I decide this conversation is tiresome and you're beyond hope, I will step back far enough to make sure you don't splatter me, and I will end the discussion. This is not a debate. This is a hostile takeover."

We stared at each other for a moment. Arrogance and domination struggled to well up inside him, but he began to grasp that this was a playing field on which he had never played. He kept his mouth shut.

"You dangled your backing and one hundred million dollars in front of Todd Jameson—but with conditions. He had to put himself in Bob Stone's shoes. So, he enlisted his friend Pearce Parks to help him remove

Senator Stone, to help him measure up for Bargo Litton. Nod if I am right. Lie to me if you don't need your right thumb."

He nodded, but said, "I had nothing to do with Parks and what he did!"

"Of course, you did. That's the magic of one hundred million dollars. Lay it in the road and see who will lie, steal, cheat, kill, rape, plunder—just to be in the game. Just to get a piece. You sat back and watched it all happen."

"They acted on their own!"

"They acted the way they needed to act to get your backing, your money. Parks set Foyle loose to kill Stone. With Stone dead, Parks gets his private prison deal in Wisconsin, the governor—a governor you bought and paid for—gets a new shot of money and another term, and Jameson can start down the path you designed. And just to keep things tidy, Foyle kills his five fellow thieves, and a woman, and her two children and a poor kid who showed up for work on a Sunday morning at the Sioux Valley Airport. Children, Mr. Litton. I believe we agreed killing children is a bad thing."

Litton didn't move, didn't change expression. A man accustomed to mine fields, he knew when the safest move was not to move.

"And when she got in the way, Parks and Jameson tried to kill Sandy Stone. *She's a kindergarten teacher, you dumb son of a bitch.*"

Litton worked his head back and forth. Like a driver trying to convince himself he didn't just hit a child.

"They took it too far!" he said desperately. "I would never—I have never—"

"Stop. Please," I said. "You and I both know none of it surprised you. They were pawns. Foyle and his gang at the wedding, just six pawns on your political chessboard. You watched Parks and Jameson dance for the money. Without your money laying in the road, none of it happens. You knew exactly what you were doing—and what they would do."

In the shadows, in the thin starlight, something glimmered in Litton's eye. I suddenly saw him in a fresh light.

Thoughts formed and dissipated in my mind like images from a dream. I moved them around, looking for the question I needed to ask.

In a moment, I had it.

"Tell me something," I said. "Why were you at the wedding?"

"I was invited!" he snapped, mustering indignance.

"Bargo Litton, a man sitting on top of billions, a man who owns half a dozen senators, governors, congressmen—shows up at the wedding of a someday-maybe political tool and a kindergarten teacher? In Wisconsin? No," I said, thinking. "That's not it."

I saw it again. That glimmer, the look of a man who knows someone is sneaking up behind you and enjoys–

It hit me.

"*You went to watch*! You went to watch them kill Bob Stone!"

His expression confessed a split second before he denied it.

"Ridiculous!"

"You knew exactly what was happening. You wanted to see it, up close, for real. Why? To get your dry old heart pumping? To smell the gun smoke and taste the blood in the air?"

"Absurd! Ridiculous theories!"

"You hated Bob Stone *that much.* You wanted to be there to see him die." I remembered Earl's words. "He blocked you on two big votes. He didn't need your money and he stood in your way—on the prisons, and what else? Mining? Pipelines?"

Litton pressed his teeth together.

"You knew they were going to kill him, *and you went to watch!*"

"You can't possibly prove—"

I laughed. "That's funny. Proof. Are you under the mistaken impression there's some sort of due process at work here? I'm all the jury you're ever going to get—and I just saw you plead guilty." I raised the pistol again and pointed it at his face.

"Wait!" He threw his hands up. "You said you wanted me to understand. Fine! I do understand! What do you want from me?!"

I shook my head. "I came here with a list," I said. "But now … now I just want you to die."

A long breath cleansed my lungs. A relaxed sensation ran down the back of my neck. I wiggled my fingers, like I do when lining up for an instrument approach or a challenging landing. I felt tension slip away, replaced by a calm that brought clarity and slowed time.

"Please! I'll do anything! I can make it better! I have mon—"

I fired.

Even without a muzzle flash, Litton's features froze in a starlit mask of terror.

I could have lived with that image, even cherished it.

If I had killed him.

The Beretta clicked and snapped a fresh round into the chamber. The fat, padded headboard sprouted a white blossom of downy filling where the Home Defense round hit and shattered, inches from the side of his head.

Litton ducked forward, throwing his hands around his head. A strangled mewling sound came from his throat. I smelled urine and saw the stain spreading on his sheets.

"*Please please please please please,*" he chanted, head down, hands imploring. "*Anything you want! Anything you want!*"

I glanced back at the double doors, ready to see them burst open, ready to vanish. They remained closed. I stood up and walked around the large bed. I bent to the floor and picked up the hot casing and pocketed it.

I studied Litton, cowering in a puddle of his own piss.

Killing him would be easy. No regret.

Murder. Black and cold. In my heart.

But murdering Litton would only pass his billions on to the next Litton. Nothing would change. No payment would be made for two little girls and their mother, or for the kid at the airport, or for Bob Stone.

"*Anything! Please!*" he begged, his hands outstretched.

"Do you understand now?"

"*Yes! Yes, I do understand!*" he snapped at me, showing anger, showing true contempt—the kind that comes with the cold recognition of defeat.

65

I swiped the key card and pulled open the motel room door. Musty, stuffy air greeted me. Cheap motel smell. It didn't matter. Exhaustion dug into my bones. I would sleep soundly on the reasonably clean sheets. Behind me, the desert held its breath for the moment when dawn would ignite the eastern sky. I might hate the desert, but I give it credit for the sunrises and sunsets.

As I stepped in, patting the wall for the light switch, I caught another scent. Almost imperceptible. Fresh fruit in summer. I found the light switch and flicked it up.

She sat in the only chair, wearing a business suit with a skirt, long legs crossed, rich hair spilled onto her shoulders, one strand across one eye. War flag.

"Did you kill him?" she asked coldly.

Andy drilled me with her eyes. In that instant, my last, lingering regret that I hadn't killed Litton evaporated. She would never have forgiven me. Ever. No other form of punishment could come close or cost as much.

"We made a deal," I said. I closed the door and slipped the backpack off my shoulder and dropped it on the bed. She didn't move.

"A note? You leave a note, Will?"

She held her stare, letting the silence hang between us like a blank canvas on which I was supposed to paint my excuses, my explanations, my apologies.

"How did you find me?"

"They made me a Detective, remember?" She delivered it with a note of scorn that drove right through me.

Neither of us spoke for a moment.

"So that's it? You don't talk to me? You don't trust me? *You left me a goddamned note!*"

"Litton—"

"I don't care about Litton!" she cried, launching to her feet. "I don't care about *any of it!*" Her hand shot out like she wanted to pull something from the air. "Don't you understand? None of it matters—if *we* don't matter."

Her eyes blazed. I took a step toward her. She backed away and it drove a knife into my heart. I stopped.

"Litton. We made a deal," I repeated.

"Which probably destroys any chance of prosecution!"

"Prosecution?" I wanted to laugh. "You're kidding, right?"

"Will, we talked about this. In Montana. We agreed it all came back to Litton, and if we could trace the money—"

"Dee, you know as well as I do there's no chance of prosecution."

"You can't know that!"

I love her for many things, and her unflinching, if unrealistic, belief that law and true justice could overpower billions of dollars ranks high on the list.

I shook my head.

"There's no money trail. You'll never get close to him. If you do, he'll bury you in lawyers and court orders. He'll buy the judge. He already owns the governor and if, by some miracle, you win a conviction, he'll get a pardon. Nothing you can say or do will persuade a prosecutor to even try. Dee, they already tried to fire you. One day they pronounce you the hero—and the next they try to fire you. Why? Because you separated the governor from just one of his bush league donors. Imagine what they would do if you tried to go after the real gravy train."

She could not argue the point, but at the same time would never fully agree with me. She avoided the question altogether. "So, what deal?"

I gestured at the chair. At least sitting, we weren't posturing for battle. She made a face that protested, but sat down, crossing her legs again.

I sat on the bed.

"He has twenty-four hours. I gave him an invoice for seven hundred and fifty thousand dollars from Essex County Air Service. He's buying One Nine Alpha from Earl, as is. He has twenty-four hours to pay."

She shook her head, disapproving.

"I gave him the name of Mark Johannsen's mother in Sioux Valley. The kid had two younger sisters. No father. He was working at the airport to help support the family. Litton writes the mother a check for ten million."

She didn't move or change her rigid expression.

"I gave him an account number. It's for the Christine and Paulette Paulesky Education Foundation, a trust with Sandy named as administrator. I had James Rankin's attorney set it up." Our farmer landlord had been only too happy to help Sandy, after hearing that one of his least favorite people, Armand Collingsworth, got shot down during the Kindergarten Revolt. "Litton is to take the hundred million he planned to give to Todd's PAC and transfer it to the trust."

The hard glare in her green and gold-flecked eyes softened.

"And he has twenty-four hours to appear in person on Fox News and announce that Litton Industries, and the Litton family, will no longer participate financially in the American political process. All contributions to PACs, campaigns, candidates, and other means of influencing the process ends. Today."

She shook her head, doubting.

"Why would he agree to any of this?"

"I kinda shot a hole in the head of his bed. And told him that if this wasn't completed to my satisfaction in twenty-four hours, I would be back to shoot off his arms and feet," I said. "That was actually your idea."

She looked at me like I'd spoken Chinese.

"Dee, this is the reason I could not let you in. This is not your game. You're the law. You're law enforcement. You believe in probable cause and warrants and money trails. But that's all a silly game to Litton and he doesn't play because he doesn't *need* to play. I played by *his* rules—

which is no rules. I showed him a game with absolutely no regard for due process or his money—"

"Or the law! Will, you committed a home invasion, threatened a man with a deadly weapon, extorted money!"

"Yes! All things you could not be a part of—but the only way to show him a game he can't win."

"What makes you think he'll see it that way?"

I thought about Litton, shaking under his urine-soaked silk sheet, staring into the black barrel of a gun while his expensive security guards patrolled, and his cameras and motion detectors proved useless. Terror didn't make him understand. Defeat did.

"I made it pretty clear that I can get to him, anywhere, anytime. If he doesn't make things right, I'll visit him again."

I saw her struggle with the anger she felt. She could not find the words. Nor could she risk opening a floodgate that might release an admission that I was right, that my tactics were the only tactics that would close the last question in this entire chain—the question she herself had posed.

I don't think we got the man responsible. Yet.

After a moment, her voice went soft.

"You told Earl you quit."

And didn't tell you, I finished the sentence in my head.

"Why?"

Okay, now the hard part.

My eyes began to sting. A knot jammed my throat.

"Talk to me, Will. What happened? What changed?"

I can't lie to Andy. Not to her face. I can come close with omission. Or stalling the truth. But when she looks directly at me, into me, there's nowhere to hide.

"When we got back, from Sioux Valley, I—um—I went down to Madison. Stephenson left me a message. He said he had my report, and I should come by and pick it up."

"You didn't tell me."

Omission.

"Pidge flew me down and back. Quick trip."

"Well, that's good news," she offered cautiously. "You can send it to the FAA now."

"Yeah … no. Stephenson showed me some of the images. There's —um—"

Oh, my god! I rehearsed this! And yet I choked on the words.

"What?"

"The scans—they had something on them. That's why Stephenson didn't just send the package to me. He wanted to discuss it."

Andy's fast. Too fast for her own good. The spreading look of horror on her face said she knew where this was going.

"Something showed up. Stephenson didn't want to call it a brain tumor—"

Her hands flew to her face. The whites of her eyes grew. I heard the breath escape her lungs.

I reached out for her. I slid closer to her and put my hands on her knees.

"Listen to me, Dee! It's not what you think it is."

"*Will–!*"

"No, listen, Dee! He refused to describe it as a brain tumor. He honestly didn't recognize it as anything he's seen before."

The swelling horror on her face told me she didn't understand.

"Dee, I think it's *the other thing*!"

"*What*?"

"He said it looked like nothing he'd ever seen. Organized. Like wiring."

"Can he do something? Can he treat it? Operate?"

I shook my head. "He doesn't know what it is. He doesn't know if it's too deep, too entangled."

"No, no no no no…" she begged softly, tears welling in her eyes.

"You're not listening. I believe, completely, with all my heart that it's *the other thing*. I mean it. I believe whatever happened to me last summer put it in my head. It's a thing. It's a mechanism. It's what makes *the other thing* happen."

"Did Stephenson tell you that?" she demanded.

"No, but I certainly wasn't going to tell him about—you know."

"Then how can you be sure?"

I stalled with a deep breath.

"It's the only thing that makes sense."

"No, it isn't! It could be—" she could not say it.

"No."

"But how can you know?"

"Because I know! Dee, it saved my life three times already. It's not going to kill me!"

She pushed her hands into her hair, staring sharply at the space between us, standing her ground.

"God damn it, *it better not*!" she cried. "Or I'm going to be really, really pissed!"

"Good to know."

I put my hand out and after a moment, she slid onto the bed beside me. She let me put my arm around her.

"Will, why? Why didn't you tell me? This—this thing with Litton. It's meaningless. It's nothing. Why didn't you tell me any of this?"

I thought about it for a moment. "Because this changes everything."

"With us?"

"No! No, not with us. Never with us."

She watched my face and the internal struggle that played out there. I tried to find a way to tell her.

"Dee, I can't show the scans to the feds. And they won't give back my medical without a set of scans."

I saw realization blossom in her eyes.

"It means … I can't fly anymore." I started to add *ever* but my throat had pinched into a tight knot, denying the word.

She looked at me. In her eyes, I saw exactly what I had run away from.

I saw pain—the reflection of my own.

Flight.

Until I met Andrea Katherine Taylor, flight was the only thing I ever *truly* wanted. In the last ten days, after meeting with Stephenson, I dealt with losing it. Logic and argument and concession swirled around in my head. I worked every one of them like clay, shoving them into the shapes I needed—first to deny the truth—then to accept the loss—then to move on. To soothe the loss, I traveled to California to deal with Bargo Litton.

And it worked. Except for one thing.

I could not handle seeing my loss in her eyes. In her eyes, it became real.

"That's what changed," I whispered.

"Oh, Will…"

I pulled her close to avoid the look on her face.

She put her arms around me. She pulled me into her, and I pulled her into me, and we held on, as if holding on would do the trick when all else failed.

After a long moment and a deep breath, I said, "You asked me what I planned to do with it—with *the other thing*."

She waited.

"This. Litton. People like Litton. This is what I plan to do with it."

66

We held each other for a long time. Silent at first. Then we talked. We talked about Litton and justice and *the other thing.* We talked about flying, and what my life might be without it. We talked about why I believed that the tiny, wire-like things Stephenson found in my head were not there to kill me. We talked about her fear that they were. I told her I loved her for coming all the way to this God-awful desert for me. She told me she liked the desert. I told her I would never raise little Ethel in the desert, what with all the rocks and dirt and scorpions. She told me we were never having a child named Ethel. I asked her to take all her clothes off and have pity sex with me, because, you know, I have a brain tumor and all. She told me never to joke about that and refused. I asked her if she would have cheap motel sex with me instead, and she took her clothes off, and after a while we both slept, and when we woke we wrapped our arms around each other and held on tight, because sometimes holding on tight *does* do the trick when all else fails. Eventually I turned on the television and we watched Fox News break the story of one of America's richest men pulling his money out of politics.

DIVISIBLE MAN
THE SIXTH PAWN

Sunday, September 24, 2017—Sunday, December 3, 2017

ABOUT THE AUTHOR

HOWARD SEABORNE is the author of the DIVISIBLE MAN™ series of novels as well as a collection of short stories featuring the same cast of characters. He began writing novels in spiral notebooks at age ten. He began flying airplanes at age sixteen. He is a former flight instructor and commercial charter pilot licensed in single- and multi-engine airplanes as well as helicopters. Today he flies a twin-engine Beechcraft Baron, a single-engine Beechcraft Bonanza, and a Rotorway A-600 Talon experimental helicopter he built from a kit in his garage. He lives with his wife and writes and flies during all four seasons in Wisconsin, never far from Essex County Airport.

Visit www.HowardSeaborne.com to join the Email List and get a FREE DOWNLOAD.

PREVIEW

DIVISIBLE MAN: THE SECOND GHOST

Tormented by a cyber stalker, Lane Franklin's best friend turns to suicide. Lane's frantic call to Will and Andy Stewart launches them on a desperate rescue. When it all goes bad, Will must adapt his extraordinary ability to survive the dangerous high steel and glass of Chicago as Andy and Pidge encounter the edge of disaster. **Includes the short story, "Angel Flight,"a bridge to the fourth DIVISIBLE MAN novel that follows.**

Available in print, digital and audio.

Visit us at **HowardSeaborne.com**

DIVISIBLE MAN - THE SECOND GHOST

CHAPTER 1

The four worst words in any relationship.

"We need to talk."

Andy lowered the martini glass to the checkered tablecloth and issued a serious look shaded by her long lashes. She's not a heavy makeup user, but for our date night she had applied something extra, to breath-taking effect.

"God, no," I said, "you're finally dumping me. Was it the toilet seat? Because I can work on that, I promise."

She flashed one of her smiles; the small, private one. The one that creases the corners of her lips and forces dimples to peek from her skin like shy spirits.

Her hand slipped across the table between the two long-stemmed glasses. She closed her fingers around the third finger on my left hand and slowly rotated my wedding ring.

"Pilot, if that day ever comes, it will be because you throw your socks in the laundry inside-out. My lawyer tells me that's a slam dunk in divorce court."

"Dammit! Tripped up by my own feet!"

We took a moment and like two dumb kids swallowed by first love, we stared across the table, across the martinis, across the flickering candle meant to bring romance to a cozy venue already awash in it.

I love this woman beyond any ability to measure.

Andy sat with me in the candlelight of Los Lobos, a small Mexican restaurant attached to the other bowling alley in Essex, a goddess in a blue velvet holiday dress. She'd done her hair up for our date night, wrapping her wavy auburn locks in a sculpted work of art that offered the added benefit of showing off her slender neck. Like a beacon drawing me into rising seas, a single tiny diamond mounted on a slim chain hung from her neck, dipping to a place I wanted to go. Her dress had a blessedly low-cut line on top and high hemline below.

We chose Los Lobos because we had a coupon and because the drinks are two-for-one during Happy Hour. Andy and I are on a tight budget. Los Lobos won't make anybody's list of Most Romantic Getaways, but tonight New York or Paris had nothing on it. A light snow descended outside the window. Holiday pepper lights hung from rafters. Mexican music warmed the ambiance.

"I'm serious," she insisted. "We've been putting this off since California."

She did not exaggerate. It had been a month. I can't say I'd intentionally avoided the subject, but I had readily accepted the way her busy schedule delayed confronting it. Andy had been promoted to Detective, however staffing in the City of Essex Police Department required her to carry on many of her patrol sergeant duties. November pulled a disappearing act on us. We found ourselves atop the first weekend in December, a scant twenty-four days from Christmas.

"Maybe we could save this discussion for a night when you're not seducing me with that dress," I suggested. A bald attempt at procrastination.

"Maybe I should put on my coat," she countered.

My hands went up in surrender.

"Fine, but after we talk, I get equal time to stare at you." I tried to pout. I'm not good at that.

"Love, at some point I'll give you this dress and you can stare all you want." It was a bribe because she went right to the matter at hand. "I want you to see Dr. Stephenson."

This again.

"I really don't see the point."

"How about to confirm that it's *not* a brain tumor! You insist it isn't. Why not make sure?"

I sat back and considered the question.

November marked five calendar months since I fell out of a disintegrating airplane on a landing approach to Essex County Airport. Five months later I'm no closer to understanding the cause of the accident, or the origin of the gift I took from it.

The investigator from the National Transportation Safety Board believes I hit something. Whatever I hit left no evidence. No paint scrapings on my airplane. No debris. The federal government doesn't like a void, and while the investigators at the NTSB don't judge, one individual from the Federal Aviation Administration decided that—absent a better conclusion—the blank space under Cause of Accident should be filled in with "Pilot Incapacitation." My pilot's license and medical certificate were suspended, pending a full medical evaluation. Pure bullshit, but bullshit with a Grade A government stamp on it. Which meant I had to leap through hoops, bend over and cough, and get re-certified. I went through all of it, including examination by a neurologist.

That's when things went south.

A few weeks ago, I sat in Dr. Doug Stephenson's office while he showed me images of my brain. He pointed at something that didn't belong. He ventured to say it didn't look like any brain tumor he had ever seen. It looked to me like wiring for a car stereo, but since I can't blast tunes out my ears, I leaped to the explanation that made the most sense to me.

I think the car stereo wiring in my head is what makes me vanish.

"I'm telling you, it's *the other thing,*"

My stance frustrated Andy. She prefers conclusions supported by evidence.

"All I'm asking is that we make sure," she said. "And confirm that it's not growing."

"That's not all you're asking. You're asking me to explain *the other thing* to Stephenson."

"You know, we really do need a better name for it."

"I'll get to work on that." I sensed an opening to change the subject.

"That can wait. And—yes."

"Yes, what?"

"Yes, we should tell Stephenson."

That took me aback.

"Seriously?"

Andy let the underbite to her otherwise perfect teeth jut slightly. The effect was both alluring and a warning. She leaned closer.

"I'm not the only one worried. Earl is concerned. He doesn't know about the scans and the—you know."

"It's not a tumor." I filled in the word she could not bring herself to use twice in a conversation.

"He wants you back, Will."

Nice try, I thought.

Earl Jackson owns Essex County Air Services. It was his airplane I wrecked. Since the crash, during my recovery and while the government demanded proof of competency, Earl kept me on the payroll as a ramp rat, parking and gassing airplanes, and a grease-monkey in the shop. A menagerie of useful. Earl's loyalty to me had the dual benefit of a steady paycheck and keeping me around airplanes. After talking with Stephenson about the new wiring in my head, everything changed.

The FAA will never remove a suspension once they get wind of a brain tumor.

Shortly after Stephenson did his show-and-tell, I walked into Earl's office and handed him my resignation. He tore it up, threw the pieces at me and told me to get the fuck out of his office. Since then, I've tried to make the point by not showing up for work. My paycheck direct-deposits as usual.

"Earl wants to talk to Stephenson," Andy told me.

"Stephenson won't tell him the problem. I don't care how close they are."

Earl Jackson knew Stephenson during the Vietnam War. No matter what their back story, Stephenson would never betray my patient confidentiality to Earl. I was about to point that out when I realized patient confidentiality worked in favor of Andy's argument.

"Earl's no dummy, Will. He knows something is wrong."

"You shouldn't involve him."

"I didn't involve him. He called me. He's been calling me."

Her eyes, subtle green flecked with gold, fixed on me and held a mildly angry stare as Julio, our server, deposited a fresh basket of chips and new bowl of salsa between us. Julio must have felt some heat on his hands because he slipped away quickly.

"Dee, flying is risk management. Being a cop is risk management. We both know how that works. We don't know the risks of someone—someone outside of our little circle of trust—finding out about *the other thing.* For starters, there are all the clichés. Winding up in a secret government lab. Having to wear tights and a cape. Becoming the boy toy of a female super villain."

She stabbed a chip into the salsa, suppressing a smile.

"The point is, *not* telling Stephenson why there are little wire-looking things on my brain scan is a means of managing risk."

"Knowing that the *thing* in your head isn't growing, isn't a tumor, isn't going to hurt you—that's also risk management." She pointed the salsa-painted chip at me. "You're the one who insists it isn't a—a *problem*. Prove it."

As so often happens in a debate with my wife, I felt the earth slipping away under my feet.

"I'll think about it."

"Well, think about it all you want, but Earl set up an appointment with Stephenson for Tuesday morning."

"We can't go Tuesday. We've got that thing with Sandy." Sandy Stone, a close friend who teaches kindergarten in Essex, also suddenly found herself the administrator of a one-hundred-million-dollar education trust fund—because I recently extorted one hundred million dollars from a corrupt old bastard and set it up in a trust. No good deed goes unpunished. Both Andy and I got roped into serving on a board to help Sandy manage and disperse the fund, even though I protested vigorously, citing the fact that I know nothing about such things.

"That's Thursday. Evening. Tuesday is all set. Earl wants you to fly down to Madison. Says you're going to get rusty sitting around on your ass." She smiled triumphantly at me.

To administer the *coup de grace*, she tugged the low neckline of her dress down slightly and said, "You may now stare."

CHAPTER 2

"It's Lane."

We had just ordered dinner and the free Happy Hour second round when the phone in Andy's purse chirped. I gave her a reproachful look for picking it up.

"Wishing us a pleasant and un-interrupted date night?"

Andy read the incoming text. Her face said not.

"She needs us. Both of us. It sounds serious. See if you can get the check. I'm going to the Ladies and then to get my coat."

With no small regret, I watched Andy's short dress and long legs weave their way out of the room toward the hall with the restrooms. So much for our romantic dinner. I clung to hope for the remainder of our evening plans.

At the same time, I felt a low-wattage alarm at Andy's rapid assessment. Lane Franklin, the fourteen-year-old daughter of the office manager at Essex County Air Services, possesses an exceptional intellect and advanced maturity. She wouldn't send up a flare unless it was serious.

I found the waiter, explained we had an emergency, and asked for the check. He offered to ask the kitchen staff if the entrees had already been made. The news wasn't good when he returned. I handed him the coupon and enough cash to cover the bill plus a decent tip. Andy reappeared, slipping her arms into her winter coat. She hurried out the door.

"Hey!" I caught the waiter's attention. "Give our entrees to these folks." I pointed at a couple stepping into the restaurant and shaking flakes of snow off their shoulders. To the startled pair, I said, "Don't know if you want 'em or not, but we have a couple meals ordered and paid for, and we have to run. Babysitter problem. Merry Christmas!"

I hustled out, leaving surprise and hasty gratitude in our wake.

"What, exactly, did she say?" I asked as Andy wheeled out of the parking lot. Andy's car has a better heater, and one of her cop habits is to insist on driving. She has a heavy foot, but tonight she gave ample respect to the snow that had been falling all afternoon, our first of the year. The temperature hovered just above twenty, which made the snow stick. Roads not treated posed a slick hazard. I wondered if Bob Thanning, who plows our driveway, might have the job done by the time we got home.

Probably not. He tends to show up at four in the morning and wake us with his rattling diesel pickup.

Andy handed me the phone. I read the text.

"*Emergency. Need help. Serious. Bring Will.*" The address that followed wasn't Lane's home.

Andy's reply read, "*Coming.*"

"She might be at a party," Andy offered. "I had a talk with her. A couple months ago. You know, if you're ever in a circumstance you don't like, or you do something stupid and need an out, call me. No questions asked. It could be a situation like that."

"Lane's fourteen. Her wildest activity is Philosophy Club."

"Lane's a living, breathing, growing adolescent girl. An attractive one, to boot. With a mature mind and body. Don't think for a minute that boys aren't interested in her."

"Sounds like you two have talked about more than designated drivers."

"We have." Andy let it go at that. Lane, an only child, had found a big sister in Andy. According to Andy, Lane nurtured a bit of a crush on me.

The address took us to an unfinished subdivision on the west side of Essex. Andy followed a winding street to one of only four homes that had been completed before the housing market collapsed in '08, and the builder went bankrupt. The saltbox-style house stood beside an attached two-car garage on a landscaped lot. The property wore the appearance of stability and success. Fresh snow covered the driveway, which displayed no recent tire tracks. Christmas lights lined the eaves. Lane's bicycle lay on the lawn, becoming a snow sculpture as flakes gathered on the frame and tires.

"She rode her bike? At night, in the snow?"

"Dangerous," Andy said, scanning the house, the yard, and the street. She parked in the driveway and killed the lights. We stepped out of the car, closing the doors without attempting stealth.

A yard light came on as we stepped to the front door. The door opened before we could knock. Lane Franklin appeared. Her long black hair hung damp on her shoulders. She wore sweats, and the knees and thighs of her pants were wet. Despite her milk chocolate complexion, she looked flushed, like someone warming up after a serious chill.

"Andy, Will, thank you *so much* for coming!" Lane spoke at barely a whisper. She hurried us in the door. As soon as we were inside, she closed the door and turned to me. "Will, you need to disappear!"

"What's going—"

"Quick! You have to be here, but you can't be here!" Lane gestured with her hands, making an urgent winding motion. I glanced at Andy, who gave a play-along nod.

Fwooomp! I vanished. I relished the comfortable cool sensation enveloping my body. It chased away the winter chill. I immediately began to float, weightless. I clamped a hand around the belt on Andy's coat.

"Do I have snow melt on me?"

Lane did a quick survey. "Can't see any."

I had not yet experimented with disappearing in a snowfall. I wondered if I would show up as an outline of accumulating snow on my head and shoulders.

"Lane, what's going on?" Andy asked, her tone laced with concern.

"It's my friend Sarah. Hurry! And whatever you do, Will, don't show yourself!"

We moved into the house. Weightless and without my battery-powered propulsion units, I can only move by gripping objects and structure or by hanging on to my wife's coat. Andy towed me forward.

A dozen different scenarios involving kids, drugs, partying, drinking, sex, and other teen mischief ran through my head. I had no idea what to expect as we passed through a comfortable, tidy kitchen into an open-concept family room.

A girl, fair-skinned and blonde, the same age and size as Lane, sat cross-legged on the floor in front of an unlit fireplace. Like Lane, she wore comfortable sweats. A phone lay on the carpet at her knee. In her lap she held a large-caliber revolver. She sat with her small hand wrapped around the grip and index finger inside the trigger guard.

Andy stopped cold when she saw the weapon. I released my grip on Andy's coat and pushed against the floor with my toes. I immediately rose to the ceiling. I touched the ceiling with my fingertips, stopped, stretched my legs horizontally, then used the kitchen door frame to propel myself into the family room above the girl.

"Sarah?" Lane started forward, but Andy threw an arm out and stopped her. "Sarah, this is my friend Andy."

The girl had been looking down at her lap. At the sound of Lane's voice, she raised her head, showing us a petite and pretty face with long black lines of melted mascara on her cheeks. Wet smears ran to her chin. Her nose and eyes were red from crying. Her blue eyes were alert but fixed on a distance. I looked around the room for drug paraphernalia, empty bottles, anything that might complicate matters. Nothing revealed itself.

"Hi, Sarah," Andy said softly. "May we come in?"

Sarah didn't answer. She shook her head minutely, a gesture that said it didn't matter one way or the other.

Keeping Lane behind her, Andy moved into the room, slowly. She slipped her coat off and draped it over a chair. From the same chair, Andy pulled an ottoman toward Sarah, careful not draw too close. Andy sat on the ottoman with her hands folded on her knees.

My mission appeared clear.

Andy spoke gently. "Sarah, no one is going to do anything. We just want to make sure you're safe. Okay?"

Again, Sarah's head shook, side to side. Like it didn't matter.

I didn't have much to work with. The smooth ceiling lacked light fixtures or beams to grip. I fixed a course toward the space on the floor beside the girl and pushed off carefully. In mid-flight, I curled my legs up into a cannonball position. I arrived a few feet from the girl, adjacent to the fireplace hearth. The hearth had a slate stone surface with just enough overhang to grab. It anchored me within reach of the gun.

"Sarah is anyone else home?" Andy asked.

"My parents are at the movies," she replied in a small but clear voice.

"So, it's just you and Lane?"

"Just me and Lane. I told her to go home because she shouldn't be here when I kill myself."

Andy glanced at Lane, who nodded.

"But you know Lane. She's—she's—" Sarah began to cry. "She's a *really good person.*"

"She is. Lane is a really good person," Andy said. "She's my best friend. I tell her everything."

"Me, too," Sarah said, high, thin, weeping.

"Did you tell Lane about this? About what's going on?"

"Uh-huh."

"That's good. Maybe, since Lane is your friend, and Lane is my friend, maybe we could all be friends. Together. Just us girls."

"That would be nice. But I need to be dead soon. I'm sorry."

"The thing is, Sarah, I don't get to see Lane very much, and I miss her. And it would really be nice to have another friend to talk to sometimes. Is Lane your best friend?"

"Lane is *the* best friend. OMG, she rode her bike all the way out here tonight, in like this snowstorm. That's like two miles."

"She cares about you."

"I really, really do, Sarah!"

"Sarah let's talk about it. Okay? Just us girls. Let's talk about why you think you need to be dead. Because that's kinda forever, and it would be so hard on Lane."

Sarah squeezed out the words, high and thin. "I need to be dead because I don't want to be a whore."

"Nobody can make you be a whore," Andy said. "Nobody."

Sarah huffed out a breath. She leaned forward and pushed her phone toward Andy.

"That's not true! See what he sends me? If I won't be his whore, he's going to put it everywhere. My parents will see it. My boyfriend will see it. Everybody will see it!"

Andy picked up the phone and opened the screen to a photo. Lane leaned over, but from her expression I knew she'd seen the photo. Andy's face remained neutral, despite the image she confronted.

"Everybody is going to see me naked," Sarah declared with helpless resignation.

"Who's doing this? Is it your boyfriend?"

"No! I don't know! Some guy. He just texted it to me. Then he started texting me and telling me what I had to do to keep him from sharing it with the whole world. He told me *exactly* what I had to do. Like, in really gross detail. And if I didn't…"

"Do you have any idea how this picture was taken?"

"No."

"Okay." Andy backed off the subject. "Your boyfriend—is he a good guy?"

"Yes."

"Would he have taken this picture? And maybe shared it with someone?"

"Ohmigod, no. He never…we never...did it. We don't do it. God. I only let him touch my boobs once!" Sarah suddenly burst into loud sobs. Through the sobs, she cried out, "I'm going to kill myself and I never even got to *do it* once!"

She pulled the revolver out of her lap and swung it toward her head.

I leaned forward and clamped my hand down on the cylinder and hammer. My grip prevented her from bringing the pistol to bear on her head. Sarah startled. Her finger convulsed on the trigger, pulling it all the way through. The hammer snapped back, then forward, pinching the flesh of my palm. I tightened my hold, preventing the action from dropping the hammer and firing. I jerked the pistol upward, breaking Sarah's grip. To Andy and Lane, the weapon shot up a foot or two on its own, then floated away from Sarah's reach.

Sarah didn't pay any attention. She bent double and wailed. Andy flashed Lane a signal and Lane dove to the floor, pulling her friend into a tight embrace.

I eased the hammer down into a safe position and handed the revolver to Andy. With practiced fingers, she removed the ammunition and carried the weapon into the kitchen. She laid the revolver on top of the refrigerator and dropped the cartridges into a drawer. She spent a moment there, thumbing the phone. I pushed off the hearth in her direction. Lane and Sarah held each other, both crying.

"What the hell?" I floated to a position beside Andy and spoke softly.

"I don't know, how does someone get a picture like this?"

She showed me. It was Sarah, nude, standing full frontal to the camera. The picture had been retouched so that everything around Sarah was blurred. Her body glittered, wet. Water glistened at her feet.

"She must have let someone take it."

"Maybe," Andy didn't commit. "Keep out of sight. Look around, okay?"

"Got it."

Andy found a glass and filled it with water. She took a box of tissues from the kitchen counter and walked back to the girls on the floor. She dropped down beside Sarah and drew both her and Lane into a comforting hug. It renewed Sarah's capacity for crying.

CHAPTER 3

I cruised through the house. Had Sarah managed to kill herself, the newspaper article would have commented on what a happy, healthy home she came from. Appearances can certainly deceive, but the house had all the trappings of being comfortable, full of life and belonging to a close family. Photos told a story of mother, father and daughter loving and enjoying each other. Not just posed portraits, but candid shots that showed impromptu smiles, warm embraces, and caught-off-guard looks of love and admiration. A china cabinet displayed soccer trophies. Perfect-grade report cards hung on the refrigerator door. A piano sat in the living room, not as a dusty decoration, but with sheet music tipped against the front panel, including paper lined with stanzas full of hand-scribbled musical notes. Sarah composed, old school.

I cruised upstairs. Her bedroom looked practical. School books from Essex High School lay on a desk beside a laptop. Clothes lay on the floor. The bed was made but bore the impression of someone lying on it, along with more books and a bag of Cheetos. She had her own television and cable box. Clothing nicer than Lane's mostly second-hand collection filled a closet and overflowed onto a dresser. An electronic keyboard sat in one corner. MIDI cables ran from mysterious boxes into her laptop.

If there were signs of something amiss in the house, I didn't see them. In the photos, her father appeared young and well-groomed. Nothing I saw suggested his occupation. Her mother took pretty pictures that captured warm, friendly eyes. The house was tidy, but not obsessive-neat-freak clean, if the master bedroom and her mother's cluttered closet were any indication.

Conversation in the family room continued at a low murmur as I glided back through the kitchen. I floated into a hover over the kitchen island.

Andy, Lane, and Sarah had moved to a U-shaped sofa, with Sarah in the middle. The two girls sat like sisters, hugging. Andy sat with her legs folded under her, facing Sarah. Andy spoke softly, steadily, looking like a big sister telling bedtime stories to the siblings.

"Well, he's tall, handsome, smart," Andy said, ticking each item off on her fingers. "I met him when I arrested him—well, not really arrested him. I stopped him—like a traffic stop—but really, and don't tell anyone I told you this, I did it to ask him out."

"That's so cool. What else?" Sarah asked. Her voice carried weakness and strain, the traces of crying, but her question had the energy of genuine interest. I got the impression that this girl talk was about love, and about caring for and connecting with someone.

"He makes me laugh."

"My parents are like that, too." Sarah told a halting story of a couple that met over a steaming sink in a campus kitchen; two college freshmen serving time in a work study program.

"You're lucky to have them." Andy put a hand on Sarah's leg. "When are they supposed to be home?"

"They went to a four o'clock show. Mom always makes dad take us to the matinee-priced shows. They like to go to Los Lobos after."

Andy didn't mention the coincidence. She took a serious tack.

"Honey, you know I have to stay here and tell them."

"*No!*" Sarah's composure collapsed. "*No, please don't tell them!*"

"Sweetie, can you even for a second imagine that they love you less or care for you less than Lane and I do? Even for a second?"

"You can't show them that picture! You can't show my dad!"

Andy gave it a moment of serious thought.

"I don't think I will have to. Do you trust me?"

Sarah's head bobbed.

"I need to keep your phone. For police business. Okay?"

Another head-bob.

"Good. And I promise you, while I have your phone, no one will see this picture except me. No one."

I thought it a tough promise to make, but Andy seemed determined.

"Andy's a kick-ass cop," Lane said. "She shot a guy." Lane didn't elaborate on her role in that tale. I wondered if she ever told the story of her abduction.

"He was a very bad man who attacked me," Andy said. "As a rule, I don't go around shooting people."

"You can shoot this guy," Sarah said.

ALSO BY HOWARD SEABORNE

DIVISIBLE MAN

The media calls it a "miracle" when air charter pilot Will Stewart survives an aircraft in-flight breakup, but Will's miracle pales beside the stunning after-effect of the crash. Barely on his feet again, Will and his police sergeant wife Andy race to rescue an innocent child from a heinous abduction—*if Will's new ability doesn't kill him first.*

Available in print, digital and audio.

Learn more at **HowardSeaborne.com**

ALSO BY HOWARD SEABORNE

DIVISIBLE MAN: THE SIXTH PAWN

When the Essex County "Wedding of the Century" erupts in gunfire, Will and Andy Stewart confront a criminal element no one could have foreseen. Will tests the extraordinary after-effect of surviving a devastating airplane crash while Andy works a case obstructed by powerful people wielding the sinister influence of unlimited money in politics.

Available in print, digital and audio.

Learn more at **HowardSeaborne.com**

ALSO BY HOWARD SEABORNE

DIVISIBLE MAN: THE SECOND GHOST

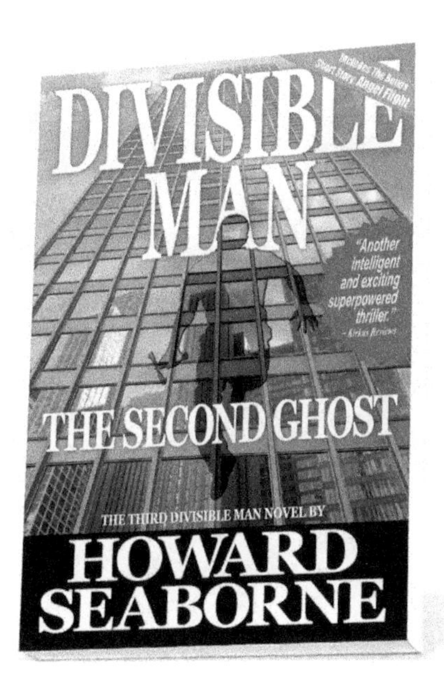

Tormented by a cyber stalker, Lane Franklin's best friend turns to suicide. Lane's frantic call to Will and Andy Stewart launches them on a desperate rescue. When it all goes bad, Will must adapt his extraordinary ability to survive the dangerous high steel and glass of Chicago as Andy and Pidge encounter the edge of disaster. **Includes the short story, "Angel Flight,"a bridge to the fourth DIVISIBLE MAN novel that follows.**

Available in print, digital and audio.

Learn more at **HowardSeaborne.com**

ALSO BY HOWARD SEABORNE

DIVISIBLE MAN: THE SEVENTH STAR

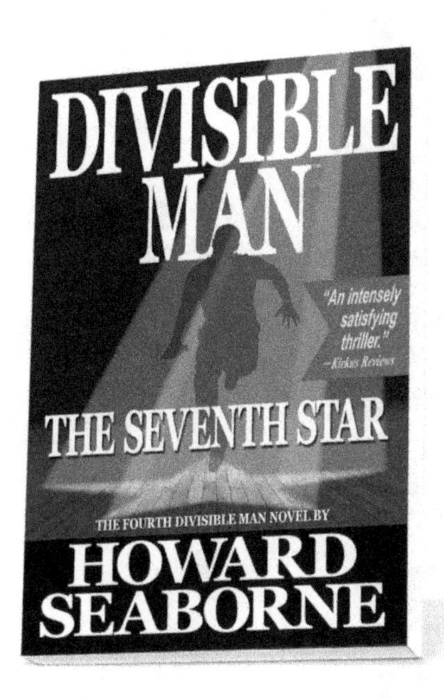

A horrifying message turns a holiday gathering tragic. An unsolved murder hangs a death threat over Detective Andy Stewart's head. And internet-fueled hatred targets Will and Andy's friend Lane. Will and Andy struggle to keep the ones they love safe, while hunting a dead murderer before he can kill again. As the tension tightens, Will confronts a troubling revelation about the extraordinary after-effect of his midair collision.

Available in print, digital and audio.

Learn more at **HowardSeaborne.com**

ALSO BY HOWARD SEABORNE

DIVISIBLE MAN: TEN MAN CREW

An unexpected visit from the FBI threatens Will Stewart's secret and sends Detective Andy Stewart on a collision course with her darkest impulses. A twisted road reveals how a long-buried Cold War secret has been weaponized. And Pidge shows a daring side of herself that could cost her dearly.

Available in print, digital and audio.

Learn more at **HowardSeaborne.com**

ALSO BY HOWARD SEABORNE

DIVISIBLE MAN: THE THIRD LIE

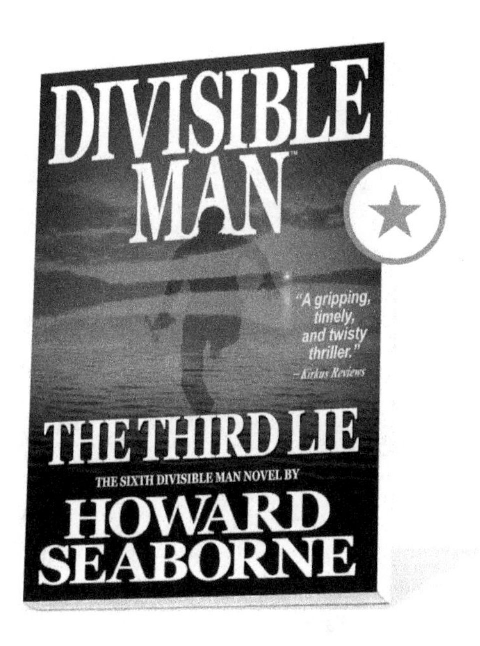

Caught up in a series of hideous crimes that generate national headlines, Will faces the critical question of whether to reveal himself or allow innocent lives to be lost. The stakes go higher than ever when Andy uncovers the real reason behind a celebrity athlete's assault on an underaged girl. And Will discovers that the limits of his ability can lead to disaster.

A Kirkus Starred Review.

A Kirkus Star is awarded to "books of exceptional merit."

Available in print, digital and audio.

Learn more at **HowardSeaborne.com**

ALSO BY HOWARD SEABORNE

DIVISIBLE MAN: THREE NINES FINE

A mysterious mission request from Earl Jackson sends Will into the sphere of a troubled celebrity. A meeting with the Deputy Director of the FBI that goes terribly wrong. Will and Andy find themselves on the run from Federal authorities, infiltrating a notorious cartel, and racing to prevent what might prove to be the crime of the century.

Available in print, digital and audio.

Learn more at **HowardSeaborne.com**

ALSO BY HOWARD SEABORNE

DIVISIBLE MAN: EIGHT BALL

Will's encounter with a deadly sniper on a serial killing rampage sends him deeper into the FBI's hands with costly consequences for Andy. And when billionaire Spiro Lewko returns to the picture, Will and Andy's future takes a dark turn. The stakes could not be higher when the sniper's true target is revealed.

Available in print, digital and audio.

Learn more at **HowardSeaborne.com**

ALSO BY HOWARD SEABORNE

DIVISIBLE MAN:

ENGINE OUT AND OTHER SHORT FLIGHTS

AVAILABLE: JUNE 2022

Things just have a way of happening around Will and Andy Stewart. In this collection of eleven tales from Essex County, boy meets girl, a mercy flight goes badly wrong, and Will crashes and burns when he tries dating again. Engines fail. Shots are fired. A rash of the unexpected breaks loose—from bank jobs to zombies.

Available in print, digital and audio.

Learn more at **HowardSeaborne.com**

ALSO BY HOWARD SEABORNE

DIVISIBLE MAN: NINE LIVES LOST

AVAILABLE: JUNE 2022

A simple request from Earl Jackson sends Will on a desperate cross-country chase ultimately looking for answers to a mystery that literally landed at Will and Andy's mailbox. At the same time, a threat to Andy's career takes a deadly turn. Before it all ends, Will confronts answers in a deep, dark place he never imagined.

Available in print, digital and audio.

Learn more at **HowardSeaborne.com**

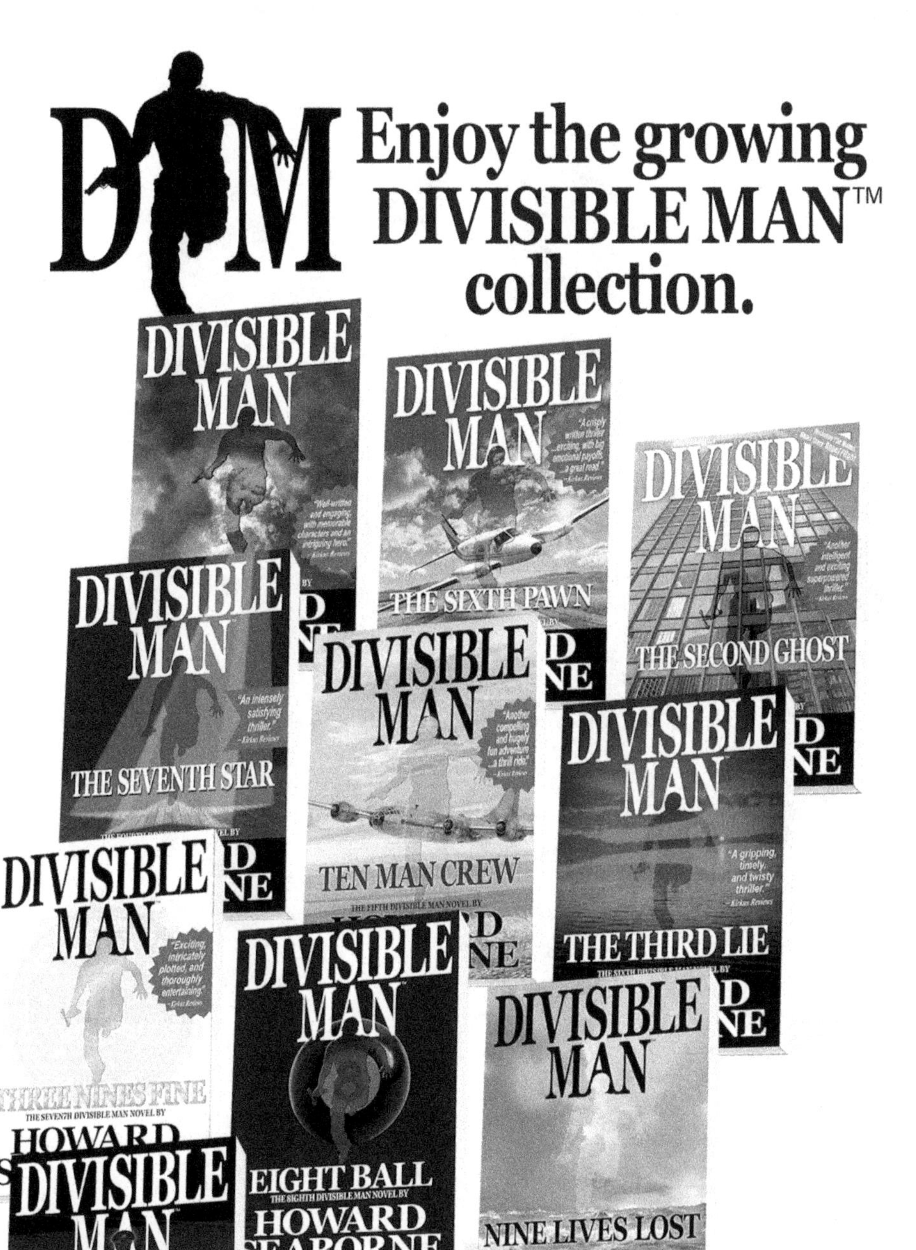

In Print, Digital and Audio

CPSIA information can be obtained
at www.ICGtesting.com
Printed in the USA
JSHW031504050722
27623JS00002B/9